HIDE THE CHILD

JANICE KAY JOHNSON

WYOMING COWBOY PROTECTION

NICOLE HELM

MILLS & BOON

First Published in Great Britain 2018
by Mills & Boon, an imprint of HarperCollins*Publishers*
1 London Bridge Street, London, SE1 9GF

Hide the Child © 2018 Janice Kay Johnson
Wyoming Cowboy Protection © 2018 Nicole Helm

ISBN: 978-0-263-26603-0

1118

MIX
Paper from
responsible sources
FSC™ C007454

This book is produced from independently certified FSC™ paper to ensure responsible forest management.

For more information visit: www.harpercollins.co.uk/green

Printed and bound in Spain
by CPI, Barcelona

HIDE THE CHILD

JANICE KAY JOHNSON

For Jeff Hill, consummate woodsman,
reader and generous friend.

Prologue

Squeezed into the tiniest space, Chloe tried not to look through the narrow crack where the cupboard door hadn't completely closed, but sometimes she couldn't help herself. Daddy was lying there right in front of her. All she had to do was crawl out and— No, no! Mommy said she had to stay here and not make a sound. Not even a teensy sound. Mommy said to wait, no matter what she heard or saw.

But she could see Daddy's face, and the face of the man who bent over him, too. Except… No! Mommy *said*.

Hugging her knees to squeeze herself into the smallest ball possible, Chloe closed her eyes. Tears wet her cheeks and she could taste them. She shuddered, trying to hold back a sob.

"Shh. Stay right there," Mommy had whispered. "Don't move a finger or make a sound. No matter what. Do you understand?"

She didn't understand at all, but she was scared, and she was *almost* doing what Mommy said, even when tears dripped off her chin onto her bare arms. Chloe peeked. Daddy's eyes were open, but she could tell he didn't see her. Or anything.

Now she couldn't see anybody else, but she heard the

man talking. There weren't any other voices, but she didn't move. She didn't whimper, even when the house became quiet and stayed quiet for a long time. She had to wait until Mommy came or Daddy woke up.

She didn't move, didn't make a sound, even when different people came. They all had the same color of blue pants. Now she saw a man crouching beside Daddy, and even though she didn't move, she didn't, he lifted his head and saw her.

Her teeth chattered and she shook all over, but he stepped right over Daddy and opened the cupboard door all the way. He bent low, his face nice, and held out a hand.

"You're safe now, honey. I promise."

As he reached for her, the sob burst out, but not another sound.

Mommy said.

Chapter One

"Shall we leave the frosting white?" Trina Marr had already mixed up a cream cheese icing to go on the cupcakes cooling on a rack. "I might have some sprinkles. Or let's see." Being obsessive-compulsive neat, she knew right where she kept the small bottles of food coloring. "Green? Red? Or if we use just a tiny bit, pink?"

The little girl looking up at her nodded vigorously. The pigtails she'd started the day with sagged crookedly.

"Pink?"

Another nod.

Trina had become accustomed to the lack of verbal response. As Dr. Katrina Marr, she specialized in working with traumatized children. Three-year-old Chloe Keif had started as a patient but was now her foster daughter. Chloe still wouldn't talk, but she relaxed with Trina as she didn't with anyone else. She'd remained stiff and unresponsive in the receiving home where she was first placed. An aunt and grandparents both were hesitant to take Chloe when she had such problems. Offering to foster had seemed a natural step for Trina, if a first for her.

"Ooh," she said now. "You know what we could put on top?"

Chloe waited, bright-eyed and expectant.

Trina rose onto tiptoes to reach a jar in a high cupboard. "Maraschino cherries. Have you ever had one?"

A suspicious shake of the head.

"They're super sweet, like candy. The flavor just bursts in your mouth when you bite into one." Trina wrinkled her nose. "Don't tell anybody, but every once in a while when I'm feeling mad or sad, I open a jar and eat every single cherry." She winked. "Which makes me sick to my stomach, but I don't care."

Chloe laughed, then clapped her hand over her mouth, eyes wide with astonishment and...fear? Yes.

It was the first sound to come out of her mouth in the two weeks Trina had known her. She crouched and tickled Chloe's tummy. "It's okay, cupcake."

That almost earned her another smile.

"It was really smart of you to stay quiet when the bad men were in your house, but you're safe now. Anytime you're ready, you can start talking. You can make all kinds of noises." She blew a noisy raspberry. Neighed, like a horse. Revved, like a motorcycle engine.

And Chloe giggled again.

Heart feeling as light as a helium balloon, Trina swung Chloe up to sit on the kitchen counter. "Here, try your first maraschino cherry." She opened the jar, stuck a fork in and popped one into her own mouth. "Yum." She offered the next one to the little girl, who sniffed it cautiously, then touched the tip of her tongue to the cherry.

Chloe's face worked as she savored the taste before she opened her mouth and snatched the cherry off the fork.

Trina waited for the verdict.

"Yum!"

Trina grinned and said, "Then let's make our frosting pink." Her mouth fell open. "Wait. You talked."

Chloe's freckled nose crinkled mischievously.

Laughing exultantly, Trina swung her to the stool she'd pulled up to the counter. "Now you're just teasing me."

The little girl nodded. It was all Trina could do to concentrate on how many drops of red food coloring she ought to add to the bowl of icing to turn it a pretty pink.

Her delight was quickly dampened by the sobering knowledge that once Chloe really began to talk the police would be ready to pounce.

If investigators had a clue who'd murdered her mother, father and older brother in their home, they hadn't confided as much in Trina or even hinted when pressed by reporters. Admittedly, the crime was not only horrific, it was puzzling. Chloe's mother hadn't been raped. Expensive electronics weren't stolen. Neither was the nearly thousand dollars in Michael Keif's wallet that had been left on the counter of the island in the kitchen. His Piaget watch, which according to the detective sold for over ten thousand dollars, remained on his wrist. If Michael, a wealthy businessman, had been the target, why had the rest of his family been killed, too?

Chloe wouldn't have been mute and terrified when she was found if she hadn't seen her father murdered within feet of her hiding place. With the investigation seemingly going cold, the detectives had latched on to the hope that this preschool girl could crack the case. It was making them nuts that so far, Chloe hadn't been able to answer a single question.

Trina worried about what the weight of their expectations might do to Chloe. What if she was never able to tell them anything, and had to live with that failure for the rest of her life?

But there was another really scary possibility. Somehow reporters had learned that the three-year-old survivor of the massacre couldn't say a word. On the local TV news, they'd even flashed a photo of Chloe as the anchor talked solemnly about the mystery and the devastating impact witnessing the horror had had on a little girl. Chloe had said her first word today, and Trina didn't want anyone else to know. Because…what if this incredibly vulnerable child became a threat a killer couldn't ignore?

Trina shivered. *Pay attention*, she told herself. She had to be careful not to turn this frosting bloodred.

GABRIEL DECKER SWUNG his rope with practiced ease. The loop settled on the ground just in front of a calf's hind legs, tricky to do in such tight quarters in the temporary corral. The second the calf stepped into the loop, Gabe pulled in the slack, wrapped the rope around the saddle horn and drew the calf toward the fire. Once a pair of wrestlers tossed the struggling calf to his side and pulled off the rope, Gabe would coil it up and go back for another one. Today, four ropers and four teams on the ground were moving things along well. They aimed by the end of the week to have every spring calf branded, dehorned, castrated and vaccinated.

His eyes stung from the dust cloud raised by bawling calves penned in the corral and their mothers milling outside it. Unpleasantly reminded of a dust storm in Afghanistan, Gabe had to keep pushing the memory back. The work demanded focus. At least he felt useful, which he hadn't much lately. He was irked that he couldn't be one of the men tossing the calf and holding it down, a task he'd performed by the time he went to live on a Texas ranch when he was fourteen. Size and muscle were appreciated for that job, since even two-to-three-month-old calves could weigh up to two hundred pounds.

Now he was lucky to be able to sit astride for hours at a time, although he'd suffer for it later. Actually, he was already suffering but refused to let anyone else suspect. He'd been wounded before but never taken so long to heal.

This had been a bad one, though. An IED had thrown him into the air and he'd landed poorly, breaking his femur on top of the damage done to his pelvis by the explosion. The doctor had suggested age might be an issue. A twenty-two-year old healed faster than a man closing in on forty, he'd said with a shrug. Gabe knew that, at thirty-six, he was close to aging out of active duty with his Army Ranger unit. But damn it, he wasn't ready to hang it up yet!

He'd tightened his legs in a signal to his gelding and gripped the rope in a gloved hand to start swinging it, when his partner waved him over to the side of the temporary corral.

Boyd Chaney rested one booted foot on a lower bar and his forearms on the top one. "If you're hurting, take a break."

Gabe stared expressionlessly at his friend. "What makes you think I hurt?"

"I know you," Boyd said with a shrug.

He did. They'd served together for a decade and become best friends. On recent deployments, Gabe had missed Boyd, who had been shot and crushed beneath his jeep when it rolled two years ago. He'd spent the next year in rehab and conditioning, trying to achieve the state of fitness required for their elite ranger unit, but had finally accepted that he'd never pass the physical. Unwilling to accept a desk or teaching job, he'd retired to the Oregon cattle and cutting horse ranch the two men had bought together with an eye to the future.

"I can manage," Gabe said now, tersely, and reined his horse back into the melee. Even over the bellowing cattle, he heard Chaney call after him.

"Stubborn bastard."

Yeah, so? Since that was the working definition of a man tough enough to make it as a spec-ops soldier, Gabe didn't bother responding. He'd make it back. He told himself that every day. Two, three more months, tops. But right now he could contribute here on the ranch. A little pain had never stopped him before, and it wouldn't now.

"I'LL BE THERE in ten minutes," Detective Risvold said.

"No!" Trina was in her office, seizing the chance to make the call between patients. In the past week, Chloe had made enough progress that Trina felt obligated to report that there was hope she'd soon be able to talk about what she'd seen.

Trina was thankful she'd been careful not to tell either of the investigators who called her on a regular basis where she "stashed" Chloe during working hours. That had been Detective Deperro's word. When he used it, Trina had almost said, *Oh, when I'm not home, I keep her in the third drawer to the right of the sink* but had managed to refrain. If either of the men possessed a sense of humor, she had yet to see it.

"What do you mean, *no*?" Risvold snapped. "She's

talking, and you know how much is riding on what she can tell us."

"I wanted you to know she's begun speaking." Already regretting she'd made this call, Trina leaned on the word *begun*. "She's not back to natural chattering, and if I even tiptoe toward asking about that morning, she goes silent again for hours. Anyway, how is a three-year-old's description going to clinch anything for you? If I asked her to draw her father, it would be a stick figure. You do know that, don't you? What little she can tell you would be useless." She paused. "Unless you have a suspect?"

The answer was slow coming. "We're looking at a possibility," he said grudgingly. "Several 911 calls had come in from that neighborhood in the week before the attack on the Keifs. Someone may have been casing houses."

"But you told me nothing was taken."

"The guy may not have had robbery on his mind. He might have been a nutcase looking for the right opportunity."

Making it a random crime. It happened, of course, but rarely. So rarely she had trouble buying it now. "Do you even have a good description of him?"

"One of the homes he wandered around had security cameras. We have footage. If we have confirmation from the girl about what he looks like…"

Her eyes narrowed. The girl? What was with these guys? Were they deliberately trying not to see Chloe as a real person? Maybe cops had to do that, because keeping an emotional distance was healthy for them, but she didn't like it. "So you'd arrest him if she says the man had brown hair and brown eyes, and that matches the camera footage. Even though half the men in Sadler meet that description."

More silence. There were undoubtedly things he wasn't telling her, but...

"From what I understand, you didn't recover any weapons or meaningful trace evidence."

"No weapons, but we have a wealth of fingerprints and hairs we can match to the killer once we have him."

Usually he said "or killers." Had he become enamored of the idea of the wandering nutjob? And unless, say, they'd found a hair in the blood, she wasn't convinced. The Keifs probably entertained. Chloe's six-year-old brother had undoubtedly had friends in and out, the friends' parents there to pick them up and drop them off. Maybe in the kitchen to have a cup of coffee. However tidy the house, there were bound to be hairs or fingerprints or whatever that didn't belong to family members.

But investigating was up to the two detectives. Her obligation was to protect Chloe.

"I'm sorry," she said firmly. "She's not ready. I wanted you aware that she has begun to speak, that's all. When I'm sure she can handle it, I'll let you know."

They sparred some more, with her the winner—although she wasn't so sure she would have been if either investigator knew how to lay his hands on Chloe while Trina was tied up with her patients.

TRINA AWAKENED WITH a start. Her phone must be ringing, she thought blearily as she reached out to grope for it on the bedside table. If that annoying Detective Risvold was calling again—

Except...did she smell smoke? With returning consciousness, she realized the shrill scream wasn't the phone. A fire alarm downstairs had been set off, and suddenly the one in the hall up here began to squeal, too.

Trina shot up to a sitting position, fear punching her in the belly. Her eyes watered, and when she inhaled again, she bent forward coughing. There was a sharp undertone to the smell that she knew she ought to recognize.

Chloe!

Trina grabbed her phone and dropped to the floor. She crawled faster than she'd known she could to the door and into the hall. Even in the dark, she could tell the smoke was thicker here, and she heard the roar of fire. Heat radiated from the staircase, and when she turned her head, she saw flame burning up the wall.

No escape that way.

She crawled into Chloe's room and kicked the door shut behind her. *Block the crack at the bottom.* She'd read that advice before. A door could slow the flames.

Nothing she could use lay in easy reach. Like Trina, Chloe seemed to be obsessively tidy by nature, which meant no dirty clothes strewed the floor. Trina gave it up temporarily and pushed herself up. Heart beating wildly, she hit the light switch, but nothing happened. Then she ran to the bed and shook the small figure that formed a lump beneath the covers.

"Chloe! Wake up!"

A snuffling sound was her only answer—and if anything Chloe drew herself into a tighter ball.

Trina yanked back the bedcovers. "The house is on fire." Somehow she kept her voice calm. "We have to get out."

The three-year-old sat up. "I don't know *how* to get out," she whispered, and then jerked. "Look!"

Trina turned to see the orange glow already beneath

the door. How could the fire move so fast? She yanked the comforter off Chloe's bed and hurried to cram it against the base of the door. Then she said, "We have to go out the window."

Nothing to it, she thought semihysterically. She unlocked and lifted the sash window, peering down at lawn that in early April was still winter brown and probably rock hard. She could scream for help…but what if men who had set the fire came instead of neighbors?

Gasoline, that's what she smelled. This fire hadn't started with a spark in the wiring or a frayed electrical cord.

After shoving the window screen until it popped out and fell, she said, "Come here, sweetie."

Chloe obeyed, thank goodness. Trina rushed to the bed for the two pillows and, leaning out the window, dropped them to the ground. They looked puny below. What were the odds they'd help break a fall? But she couldn't think what else to do. Remembering her phone, she picked it up and dropped it, too. It bounced off one of the pillows onto the dark ground.

A sheet. She snatched it from the bed, horrified to see that the door glowed fiery orange and was dissolving before her eyes.

Twisting the sheet into an impromptu rope, she tied one end around Chloe's waist. Then she cupped the child's face with her hands. "I'm going to dangle you as far as I can with the sheet, but then I'll have to drop you. Just let yourself roll, okay?"

"No!" Chloe flung her arms around one of Trina's legs and held on frantically. "I don't wanna! Please! Don't make me!"

Throat tight, chest hurting, Trina said, "We don't have

any choice." She wrenched a squirming, fighting Chloe away. Maneuvering her out the window was a nightmare, with the sobbing child flailing and trying to grab hold of her again. Finally, she was able to start lowering her.

The sheet ran out sooner than she'd hoped. Heat seared her back. She was out of time. *I have to drop her.*

But somebody ran across her yard and positioned himself below the window. "Let her go. I've got her."

Trina recognized the voice of a brawny young guy who still lived with his parents on the block. With a whimper, she released the sheet and saw him catch Chloe.

The fire behind her had become so intense she didn't hesitate. She climbed out, turned and grasped the edge of the window frame…and let go.

ACHING, STILL FILTHY, grateful for the pain meds that kept her from fully feeling the burns and bruises, Trina sat holding an armful of little girl. Her position was awkward, rocked to one side so that most of her weight was almost on her hip. Her back and butt had been slathered with ointment and covered with gauze before nurses helped her put on scrubs to replace her ruined T-shirt and flannel pajama bottoms.

"There's some blistering," the doctor had told her. "Minimal, but you had a close call."

No kidding.

"It's going to hurt," he'd continued, "but if you have someone who can reapply the ointment, and if you take the pain medication as prescribed instead of trying to tough it out, I won't insist you be admitted."

He hadn't asked if she had anywhere to go to, given that her house had just burned to the ground, but she'd called one of the two partners in her counseling practice. Josh Doughten and his wife, Vicky, had become good friends. Good enough to be a logical choice for her to call in the middle of the night. Plus, their two daughters were both away at college, so Trina knew they had empty bedrooms. Josh hadn't even hesitated; he said he would get dressed and come immediately for her and Chloe.

But they wouldn't be able to stay with the Doughtens long. She couldn't endanger Josh and Vicky. What Trina wanted to do was jump—okay, climb slowly and carefully—into her car and drive away. Far away.

Two problems with that. Her car had been in the attached garage and was presumably part of the "total loss" the fire captain had described. Problem two? So was everything in the house, from her clothes to her purse, wallet and credit cards. The only thing she'd salvaged was her cell phone. Until she visited the Department of Motor Vehicles and the bank, she couldn't even pay for a motel. Assuming anyone would rent a room to a crazy-looking woman with bare feet, wearing scrubs and carrying a kid who didn't look any better than she did.

The police would probably offer her and Chloe protection, but it would come at a price. After all her effort to hold them off, they'd have the access to Chloe they'd been so desperate to get. In phone messages left in the last day and a half, initial begging had progressed to pestering and finally threatening. They didn't understand the damage they could do to a fragile young child by trying to dig out answers too soon. And yes, Trina sympathized, but the murder victims were dead. Arresting the killers wouldn't bring Chloe's family back. But she was alive, and protecting and healing her had become Trina's mission.

As if she'd conjured them, the two men entered the cubicle where she waited. Risvold was middle-aged and softening around the middle, his blond hair graying. His partner, in contrast, had to be over six feet and was strongly built. His skin was bronzed, whether from sun or genetics, and he had black hair and dark eyes.

His eyes as well as Risvold's latched on to Chloe with an intensity that made Trina want to shrink back. Her arms tightened protectively.

"I already talked to the arson investigator," she said. "I'm sure he'll give you his report."

Detective Risvold slid one of the plastic chairs to face hers, and sat down with a sigh. Deperro hung back. Good cop, bad cop?

"I'm sure he will, but his job has a different focus than ours," Risvold said. "So I'd like you to tell us what you saw and heard."

"Just a minute." She stood up with Chloe in her arms and left the cubicle. Several people glanced up from where they sat at the nurses' station. "Excuse me. The police are here to talk to me. Is there any chance someone could hold Chloe for a few minutes so she doesn't have to be there?"

A motherly looking nurse leaped up and volunteered.

"You won't take your eyes off her for a second?"

"Promise."

Fortunately, the little girl was still asleep, a deadweight when Trina transferred her to the other woman's arms.

Then she returned to the cubicle, where she repeated her story briefly.

"You hadn't seen anyone hanging around?" Risvold

asked. "No car parked on your block that didn't look familiar? Think hard, Ms. Marr."

She was really tempted to remind him that she was actually Dr. Marr. Not something she usually insisted on, but this man's condescension raised her hackles. "The answer is no. I didn't see anything out of the ordinary."

"The faster we're able to hear what, er, Chloe saw, the sooner you'll both be safe."

Hurting, scared and mad, Trina said, "If I were you, I wouldn't make her your focus right now. For one thing, it's obvious your wandering crazy is off the table as a suspect."

"What do you mean?" Gee, Detective Deperro spoke.

"I mean, would he have it together enough to understand that a small child might be able to identify him? And know where she was staying? Oh, and set the fire without a soul seeing him?"

Deperro's jaw tightened.

She leaned toward them. "Try looking at your own department, why don't you? It's been nearly a month since the murders. Chloe and I have been fine. The day before yesterday, I told you she'd begun to speak, that I thought it wouldn't be long before we could try asking her questions. Then tonight someone set my house on fire when the two of us were asleep inside. How many people knew what I told you? Who did *they* talk to?"

"Miss Marr… Katrina." To his credit, Detective Deperro looked worried. "What about her day care? Is there anyone there who would have talked?"

"No," she said flatly. "And since even you don't know where she is, how would the killer have known who to cozy up to for news about Chloe?"

"I'm authorized to give you twenty-four-hour protection," Risvold offered.

Even without a plan, Trina said, "Thank you, but no."

He frowned. "But where will you go?"

Long-term? The correct answer was *I have no idea.* But she only shook her head.

Chapter Two

Not two minutes after the cops had left her alone, Trina knew what she to do.

Call her brother. Three years older than her, Joseph had never let her down, any more than she would him if he ever needed her. He'd be mad if she didn't turn to him.

Unfortunately, he'd take at least a day to reach her, but she and Chloe could surely stay with the Doughtens that long. Trina went out to check on Chloe, but the nurse smiled and rocked gently. "If you need to do anything else, she's fine," she whispered.

"Then I'll make a call," she said gratefully, and returned to her cubicle.

Her brother's phone rang once, twice, three times. It wouldn't be the middle of the night for him, or even the crack of dawn. Georgia was three hours ahead, which made it…eight o'clock there.

"Trina?" he said sharply.

She started to cry. She hadn't yet but couldn't seem to help herself now. Lifting the hem of the faded blue scrub top to wipe damp cheeks, she said, "Joseph? My house burned down."

"What? How?"

"It was—" She had to breathe deeply to be able to finish. "Arson. It was arson."

He swore. "Do the cops think it's random? There's no reason you'd be a target, is there?"

She took a deep breath. "It's a long story."

"Tell me," Joseph demanded.

The story didn't take all that long, after all. He had already known that she was now a foster mom, although she hadn't explained the background. Now she did.

At the end, she said tentatively, "I don't know what to do. I was hoping…" She hesitated.

"I'd come?"

The tension she heard told her the answer would be no.

"You know I want to be on the next flight to the West Coast. But I don't see how I can. We're wheels up tonight, Trina."

He was the one who'd shortened her name, to their parents' frustration. They'd been determined she would be Katrina, but ultimately even they had started dropping the first syllable.

She could call them…but she couldn't put them in danger, either. Joseph… Joseph was different. He could handle any threat.

"I'll wire you some money," her brother said.

"Thanks, but… I have money. I just have to get some ID so I can claim it."

"Okay." He was silent long enough that she was about to open her mouth when he said in a distracted way, "I'm thinking. I can ask for an emergency leave."

"You'd have said that in the first place if it was so easy."

"Yeah, it's not. We've been training and studying intel on this op for the last month. The major won't be happy."

He wasn't supposed to have told her as much as he had. Her heart sank, but she knew what she had to say. "Then…then I'll think of something else. I could hire a bodyguard." From Bodyguards 'R Us? Feeling semihysterical, she wondered whether that was a subject heading in the Yellow Pages. Craigslist? The bulletin board at the hardware store that was covered with business cards? How was someone as inexperienced as she supposed to judge the competency of some beefy guy who claimed he could protect her?

That's why she'd turned to her brother. She *knew* he could.

"Wait," he said, relief in his voice. "I'm not using my head. One of my buddies is half an hour or less from you. I'd have tried to hook you two up, except…we're not good marriage prospects."

Despite the fact that she was desperate and in pain, Trina rolled her eyes. "I can find my own dates, thank you." Bodyguards, not so much. "Why is this guy in rural Oregon instead of at Fort Benning?" Or in some war-torn part of the world?

"IED." So casual. "Had his stays in the hospital and rehab, but he still needs some time to come back all the way. He and another friend of mine bought a ranch out there in Oregon. I think Boyd was from the area."

"They bought a ranch."

"Yeah, thinking of the future. You know? At best, we'll all age out."

She shuddered. Usually, she didn't know when Joseph dropped from the radar, which was fortunate. She worried enough as it was. He'd had regular deployments, but more often conducted raids in hostile territory, the kind of place where Americans were not welcome. She knew he'd been involved in international hostage rescues.

Perfect training for protecting her and Chloe, Trina couldn't help thinking. "So, do you have this Boyd's phone number?"

"No, this guy's name is Gabe. Gabe Decker. Boyd retired a couple of years ago. He might be getting soft. Gabe is deadly."

"But if he's injured…"

"He's on his feet. Even riding, he said last time we talked. Listen, I'll call him. Where are you?"

She explained that she was still at the hospital, but her practice partner was taking her home temporarily. She told him the address.

"I want you in hiding now," Joseph said, with the cold certainty of a man to whom her current troubles were everyday. "Keep your phone on, but don't be surprised if he just shows up. Be ready to go."

Okay. But wasn't that what she wanted? Well, yes, but this Gabe Decker was a stranger. Was she willing to trust him? Follow his orders, if he was anywhere near as dictatorial as Joseph could be?

Her inner debate lasted about ten seconds. Because, really, what other option did she have?

The police.

All she had to do was picture Chloe's sweet face, her freckled nose natural with her red-gold hair. No, Trina didn't trust the detectives, one of whom must have a big mouth or been careless in some other way with dangerous information.

"I'll be expecting him," she said, and offered the Doughtens' address. Only after she'd let him go did she wish she'd thought to ask what this Gabe Decker looked like.

GABE'S PLEASURE AT seeing his friend's number on the screen of his phone took a nosedive as soon as he heard what Joseph wanted. Sticking him in close quarters with a clingy woman and whiny kid, right when he felt especially unsociable. Even so, he didn't hesitate.

"Anything," he said, which was the only possible answer. "Tell me what you know."

Listening, he remained lying on his back on the weight bench where he'd been working out.

Hearing that the sister was a psychologist didn't make him want to break out in song and dance. He'd had his fill of social workers and counselors both at the hospital and rehab facility. They were positive he had to be suffering from PTSD. Guilt because a teammate had died in the same explosion. Talking about it was the answer. Reliving the horrific moments over and over being so helpful to his mental health. When he balked, that had to mean he was refusing to acknowledge his emotional response to his own traumatic injury as well as Raul's spectacular death. No chance he just didn't need to talk about it, because this wasn't the first time he'd been injured and he'd seen so much death in the past decade he was numb to it.

If this woman thought she'd fix him out of gratitude for his help, he'd make sure she thought again.

His protective instincts did fire up when he heard what had happened to the kid, followed by the cold-blooded attempt to make sure that little girl couldn't tell anybody what she'd seen that day.

"Why don't the cops have them in a safe house?" He finally sat up and reached for a towel to wipe his face and bare chest. His workout was over.

"I didn't ask for details. She sounds wary where they're concerned, at least about the primary investigator."

"Okay." There'd be time for him to ask her about her issues with the police. City, he presumed, rather than the Granger County Sheriff's Department. For her sake, he hoped the murder had happened within the Sadler city limits. The current county sheriff was a fool, the deputies, whether competent or not, spread too thin over long stretches of little-traveled rural roads. Boyd had nothing good to say about the sheriff's department.

"I'll go get her," he said, to end the call. "You watch your back."

"Goes without saying." Which of course was a lie; Joseph would be watching his teammates' backs instead, trusting them to be doing the same for him.

Still straddling the bench, Gabe ended the call. A quick shower was in order. And then, huh, he'd better think about whether there were any clean sheets for the bed in the guest room. If the kid needed a crib…no, she had to be older than that to be verbal. Formerly verbal. Whatever.

Yeah, and what about food?

As he was going upstairs for that shower, it occurred to him that he'd better let Boyd know what was up, too. He was unlikely to need backup…but thinking about the bastard who wouldn't stop at anything to save his own skin, Gabe changed his mind.

Having backup would be smart.

SOMEHOW, SOMEWHERE, TRINA found a smile for Vicky, who had been fussing over her ever since Josh left the two women and Chloe at the house while he went to work.

"I'll have Caroline cancel all your appointments for today and tomorrow," he'd assured her. "With the weekend, that gives you four days to figure out what you're going to do."

Trina hated the necessity. It was bad enough when your patients were adults, but when they were frightened, withdrawn children? They wouldn't understand.

Now she said to Vicky, "Thanks, but I'm fine." More fine if she could take the prescribed pain pills, but she didn't dare, not if she were to stay alert. If somebody had been watching the small hospital, he wouldn't have missed seeing her and Chloe leaving with Josh. Following them would have been a breeze. She'd asked Vicky to pull the drapes on the front window immediately, even though she was uneasy not being able to see the street and driveway.

"You look like you might be feverish," Vicky said doubtfully.

Trina felt feverish. But she couldn't relax and let herself be miserable until the promised Army Ranger appeared to keep Chloe safe. Really, it hadn't been much over an hour since she talked to Joseph. Expecting instant service was a bit much. Joseph might not have been able to reach this Decker guy immediately. Or Decker might have been in the middle of something he couldn't drop just like that.

Tap, tap, tap.

Vicky and Trina both jumped. That knock hadn't been

on the front door. They looked simultaneously toward the kitchen.

"It might be a neighbor," Vicky said after a moment, almost whispering. Trina could tell she didn't believe it. The elegant homes in this neighborhood were all on lots of a half acre to an acre or larger. Most of the wives were probably professional women themselves, not housewives who casually dropped by for a cup of coffee.

Trina would have gone along with Vicky to see who was knocking, except Chloe lay curled on the sofa. Not asleep, but pretending to be, she thought. And the tap on back door could be a diversion meant to draw the two women away long enough for someone to come in the front and snatch Chloe.

Trina heard voices, one slow and deep. Vicky reappeared, right behind her a massive, unsmiling man who took Chloe and Trina in with one penetrating glance. Her first stupid thought was, how had anyone managed to hurt this man, given his height and breadth, never mind all those muscles?

So she wasn't at her sharpest.

"Mr. Decker?" she asked.

He nodded. "Gabe."

"I'm Trina. And this is Chloe." Who had stiffened, even though her eyes remained closed.

"Okay." His voice made her think of the purr of a big cat, assuming they purred. Velvety, deep and not as reassuring as she'd like it to be. "You have anything to bring?"

"A duffel." Vicky had scrounged some clothes from her daughter's drawers, the one who'd left most recently for college, that would probably come close to fitting Trina. Better yet, she'd produced several outfits of little girl clothing from wherever she'd packed them away with granddaughters in mind. Otherwise…otherwise they wouldn't have had a thing.

"Oh!" Vicky said suddenly. "I have extra toothbrushes. And surely I can find a hairbrush for you."

Bless her heart, she came back with both, plus a handful of hair elastics. Something Gabe Decker, with dark hair barely long enough to be disheveled, would not have.

With damp eyes, Trina hugged Vicky. She was grateful the other woman remembered not to hug her back. "I don't know what I'd have done without you and Josh."

"We'd have been glad to have you stay, you know," she said, her eyes wet, too.

"I know, but—"

Vicky nodded. She poked the brush and other things into the duffel and said, "I can carry this out."

Gabe stepped forward. "No, I don't want you outside. I'll take that." When he saw Trina reaching for Chloe, he shook his head. "And her. Joseph said you'd been hurt."

She had no doubt his blue eyes saw right through her pretenses. "I have burns on my back." With sudden alarm, she remembered that he'd have to renew the ointment and bandages for her. A stranger, and male. Very male. With enormous hands that would come close to spanning her back.

That tingle couldn't be what it felt like, not under the circumstances. Especially since she knew perfectly well that no touch would feel good. Despite the gauze, she'd swear the thin cotton of the scrub top was scraping her burns every time she moved. "Can you carry…?"

His lifted eyebrow mocked her question. Yes, he could carry both, and probably pile on a whole lot more. He undoubtedly did on a regular basis, come to think of it.

She'd read that soldiers often packed over a hundred pounds even in the desert heat of the Middle East.

"You're not parked out in front, I take it," she said.

"No. I drove through the neighborhood to see if I could spot any obvious surveillance. Even though I didn't, I left my truck in a neighbor's driveway. Didn't look like anyone was home. We'll cut through the trees out back." He hesitated. "You need to leave your phone behind. Better if it's at your office than with you. Or here."

Trina felt a spurt of panic. Her phone was the only possession she had left. And without it…she'd be even more isolated. But she didn't argue, knowing how easily smartphones could be traced.

"Josh will be home for lunch," Vicky said. "I can have him take it."

Gabe said simply, "Good." Trina hadn't said a word, but he seemed to take her compliance for granted.

She lowered herself gingerly onto the edge of the sofa. Standing had had her light-headed, but putting pressure on her burns was worse. "Chloe, this is Gabe. He's a friend of my brother's. He's going to carry you, since you don't have any shoes." She now did, but they were in the duffel, and they hadn't had a chance for her to try them on. Since she knew Gabe wanted to move fast, it was a good excuse.

"Hey, little one," he said, sounding extraordinarily gentle as he bent over her.

With him so close, Trina could see the dark shadow of what would be stubble by evening, the slight curve of a perfectly shaped mouth…and a white scar that angled from one clean-cut cheekbone to his temple, just missing his eye. That was an old one, she felt sure, not the wound

that had him on leave. Her teeth closed on her lower lip.
If he turned his head at all, they could almost—

No, no, no! Don't even go there.

The muscle in his jaw spasmed, and she held herself
very, very still. Lowering her gaze didn't help, not with
impressive muscles bared by a gray T-shirt. And then
there was his thigh, encased in worn denim.

Maybe he'd turn out to have a girlfriend living with
him. Joseph wouldn't necessarily know.

"Here we go," he said calmly, and scooped up Chloe,
tucking her against his broad chest and rising to his feet.
A moment later he'd slung the duffel over his opposite
shoulder, and looked at Trina with raised brows as if
he'd been twiddling his thumbs waiting for ten minutes.
"Can you walk?"

"Yes." She jumped up too fast. His hand clamped
around her upper arm, making her suspect her eyes had
done whirligigs. She blinked a couple of times and repeated, "Yes. I'm fine." Slight exaggeration, but she
could do this.

He studied her for longer than she liked before releas-
ing her. "Okay."

Vicky trailed them to the back door and locked it behind them. Gabe paused only for a moment to scan the
landscape, then strode toward the trees. With so little un-
dergrowth on this dry side of Oregon, the lodgepole and
ponderosa pines didn't offer much cover, nothing like
a fir and cedar forest would have on the east side of the
Cascades where Trina had grown up. Gabe paused now
and again and looked around, but mostly kept moving.
At first, she was disconcertingly aware of how silently
he moved, while she seemed to find every stick or cone
to stomp on. Crackle, pop… A jingle teased her memory.

She couldn't hold on to such a frivolous thought. She felt his gaze on her a few times, too, but didn't dare let herself meet his eyes. The pain increased with each step until Trina felt as if fire were licking at her back again. Sheer willpower kept her putting one foot in front of the other. She stumbled once and would have gone down, but he caught her arm again.

"Almost there," he murmured. "See that black truck ahead?"

She didn't even lift her head. He nudged her slightly to adjust her course, but without touching her back. Trina didn't remember how much she'd told her brother about her injuries.

She almost walked into the dusty side of a black, crew-cab pickup. He unlocked the door, tossed the duffel on the back seat and placed Chloe there, too. She looked tiny on the vast bench seat.

"I don't have a car seat for her anymore," Trina heard herself say. Right this second, that seemed like an insurmountable problem.

"I'll drive carefully." He buckled a lap belt around Chloe, who stared suspiciously up at him. Then he closed her door and opened the front passenger door. "In you go," he said quietly, that powerful hand engulfing Trina's elbow. "Big step up."

He didn't quite say "upsy-daisy" but coaxed her and hoisted until she was somehow in. He closed this door with a soft thud, too, rather than slamming it, and was behind the wheel in the blink of an eye, firing up a powerful engine. When she made no move to put on the seat belt, he did it for her, not commenting on her grip on the armrest or the way she rolled her weight to the side.

He backed out and accelerated so gradually she was never thrust against the seatback.

"How long?" she asked, from between gritted teeth.

"About half an hour. Do you have pain pills?"

"Yes, but…"

"Take them. Are they in the duffel?"

She nodded.

Gabe reached a long arm back, his eyes still on the road, and tugged the duffel until it was between the seats. The bottle of water he handed her was warm, but it washed down two pills.

"You okay, Chloe?" she asked.

No answer, but Gabe's gaze flicked to the rearview mirror. "She's nodding," he said quietly.

"Oh, good." She thought that's what she'd said. The words seemed to slur. Leaning her cheek against the window, she closed her eyes.

SHE DROPPED OFF to sleep like a baby, Gabe saw. That's what she needed. He was sorry he'd have to wake her up when they got to the cabin.

The little girl was not asleep. She sat with her feet sticking straight out in front of her, her arms crossed and her lower lip pouting. Eyes as blue as his watched him in the rearview mirror. Clearly, she expected the worst. He kind of liked her attitude. He tended to expect the worst, too. That way you were prepared. Optimists could be taken by surprise so easily.

Once he made it onto the highway, he could relax a little. The couple of vehicles he could see in the rearview mirror hadn't followed them from town. At this time of morning, most traffic was headed south into town, not north out of it.

He checked on the kid, to see her eyelids starting to droop, too.

Another sidelong glance made him wince. Trina's contorted position had to be miserably uncomfortable. Burns, Joseph had said, without being specific. Gabe would have known they were on her back even if she hadn't told him, since she'd done a face-plant on the window to avoid making any more contact than she could help with the seat. Twisted as she was, he saw a thickness that could only be bandages. Or, hey, Kevlar, but that wasn't likely.

Since Joseph talked often about his sister, Gabe had known they were close. Funny his friend had never mentioned that she was a beauty, or a shrink of some kind. The stories had all been from their childhood, or repeating some amusing or pointed observation she'd made about life in general, politics and shifting international alliances more specifically. She probably followed the world news with more interest than most people did because she knew her brother was bound to get involved in a lot of the messes.

Gabe wondered in a general way what it would feel like to have parents or someone like her worrying about him. Would he be as anxious to get back in the action if his death would devastate someone else?

Impatiently, he shook off the descent into sentimentality. No family, no reason to think about it.

Instead, he circled back to the beginning. Katrina Marr would be spectacular with makeup, a snug-fitting dress and heels. Face showing strain and streaked with char, hair a tangled mess and wearing sacky, faded blue scrubs and thin rubber flip-flops, she was merely beautiful. With expressive green-gold eyes and hair the color of melted caramel, she was tallish for a woman, slender rather than model-skinny, and still possessing some nice curves.

One corner of Gabe's mouth lifted. Could be this was why Joseph never mentioned his sister's appearance. He might give one or more of the guys the idea of looking her up someday while on leave.

Fully amused now, Gabe thought that was just insulting.

But his amusement didn't last long. To stay vigilant, he couldn't afford any distraction. Somebody was gunning for the cute kid who'd now slumped sideways in sound sleep—and Gabe had no doubt Joseph's sister would jump in front of the bullet to save that kid.

His job was to make sure that never happened. Plan A, he calculated: hide them. Plan B: make sure he fought any battles that did erupt. Plan C: take the bullet himself.

Chapter Three

Trina opened her eyes to a dim room. The window was in the wrong place, she saw first. Light sneaking between the slats of the blinds told her it was daytime.

Her bedroom didn't have rough-plastered walls, either. Awakening awareness of pain discouraged her from rolling onto her back. Instead, she pushed aside a comforter in a denim duvet cover and gingerly sat up.

It all rushed back. The fire, dropping from a second-story window, the hospital. Complete loss. Wasn't that what the fire chief had said? Joseph.

Gabe Decker.

This must be his home, or at least his ranch hideout. The wide-plank floor looked like what she'd expect of a log house. A closer look at the window told her it was set in a wall thicker than usual.

And then her eyes widened. Chloe!

Still wearing the scrubs, she didn't take time to use the bathroom or find her flip-flops. She rushed out into a hall and toward the staircase at the end.

Halfway down, she heard that deep, smooth voice. He was talking to someone, pausing for unheard answers. Telephone?

The vast living room was empty. She followed the

voice to the kitchen, where she saw Chloe, perched on a tall stool, watching as the big, powerful man flipped a hamburger in a pan on the stove.

"Is that a yes or no to cheese?" he asked, glancing over his shoulder.

He took in Chloe's nod, then saw Trina hovering. He didn't smile; the way he looked her over was more assessment than anything. "You're just in time for dinner."

"Dinner." She was dazed enough to feel out of sync.

Chloe swung around, scrambled off the stool and raced to Trina. She threw her arms around Trina's legs and hugged, hard. That she'd regressed to being nonverbal felt like yet another deep bruise in the region of Trina's chest.

"I'm glad to see you, too, pumpkin." Trina found a smile for the little girl, who tipped back her head to look up at her. "Why don't you start on your cheeseburger while I go back upstairs and, um, at least brush my hair?" And pee. She really needed that bathroom.

"Did you see your duffel at the foot of the bed?" Gabe asked.

"No, I suddenly panicked—" She broke off. "You know how confusing it is to wake in a strange place."

His expression of mild surprise said he didn't know. As often as he—and her brother—woke in strange and dangerous places, they probably knew where they were and why instantly, before they opened their eyes. They probably held on to the where and why *while* they slept.

"Never mind," she mumbled, and took herself back upstairs to start over again. The woman she saw in the mirror horrified her. Her face was filthy, her eyes bloodshot and her hair a tangled mess. Lovely.

Washing her face helped only a little. She dug the

bottle of pills out of the duffel and took one, hoping that would be enough to dull the pain without knocking her out again. Then she tackled her hair as well as she could when raising her arms stretched the skin on her shoulders and back. Her left shoulder ached fiercely, too, as did her left hip. No, those two pillows hadn't softened her landing on the hard ground much, if at all. The doctor had warned her to expect swelling and colorful bruises.

A ponytail proved to be beyond her. Changing clothes…not yet, she decided. She craved a shower but shuddered at the idea of hot water on her back. Spot-cleaning was as good as it would get.

And once she had something to eat, she'd have to break it to the Army Ranger downstairs that he now had medic duties as well as KP.

He studied her again when she reappeared, small lines appearing on his forehead. Apparently, she hadn't accomplished miracles.

"Cheese?" he asked.

"Please."

She leaned against a sort of breakfast bar rather than trying to sit on a stool. She studied Chloe, who had made surprising inroads on her burger, which from experience Trina knew was completely plain. She wouldn't have touched the sliced tomatoes, onions or lettuce Gabe had set out, or the ketchup or mustard, either. What surprised Trina was that the three-year-old didn't seem wary of Gabe. She shied from most people, especially men, yet was happily eating food he'd put in front of her, her bare feet swinging.

"Did you nap?" Trina asked.

Chloe nodded.

"She was up for a couple of hours in the middle of

the day," Gabe said, "napped again and got up about an hour ago."

Intrigued, Trina wondered how he'd entertained Chloe for those two hours. The little girl appeared surprisingly comfortable with him. "How long did I sleep?"

He glanced at the microwave. "Nine hours."

"Really?" She'd have had to be deeply asleep for Chloe to have slipped out of bed without her noticing. "I never conk out like that."

"I don't suppose you had a very good night's sleep," he said dryly.

"Well, no, but…" Her stomach growled and she pressed a hand against it. "I'm starved. I haven't had anything to eat since last night."

"I guessed. Here." He handed her a plate with baked beans, corn and a cheeseburger on a fat bun. "Chloe declined the beans."

The little girl wrinkled her nose.

Trina kissed the top of her head. "She's at an age to be picky."

"Figured." He produced silverware, then brought his own plate over to the bar and sat on Chloe's other side, hooking the heels of his boots on a rung as if it were a fence rail.

After gobbling half her meal, Trina said, "It's been peaceful?"

He glanced at her sidelong. "Yep. We made a clean getaway."

"Yes, but… I can't be completely out of touch."

"We'll talk about it later."

Something about his tone made her wonder how two-way he intended that talk to be. Did he really think Joseph's sister would be meek and docile? Dealing with him would be easier if she could read him better, but he was so guarded she wondered what it would take to shatter his control. Something told her pain hadn't done it. In fact, he might have shored up his walls during his lengthy recuperation.

Chloe dropped her cheeseburger without finishing it. She immediately crawled over onto Trina's lap. Trina held her with her left arm and kept eating.

"I don't suppose you have any toys around?" she asked after a minute.

Gabe snorted.

"Didn't think so."

"Actually... Well, I'll look around. I said it was okay for Boyd to loan this place out to a friend of his. Ski vacation. He had a family. Don't know how old the kids were. They might have left something behind."

Chloe's head came up. She'd been following the conversation.

Unable to quite clean her plate, Trina finished eating first. "Do you have a satellite dish?"

"Yeah. Hey. Channel three has the lineup."

She'd seen the living room but not taken it in. She couldn't describe it as homey, exactly; Gabe had furnished it with the basics but not bothered with artwork or homey touches like table runners or rugs. The sofa and a big recliner were brown leather that made her think of saddles. The clean lines of the oak coffee table and single end table might be Mission style. Built-in bookcases lined one wall and held an impressive stereo system as well as quite a library. A big-screen TV hung above a cabinet that had drawers. Trina went to investigate those.

Among a good-size collection of movies for grownups, she found three DVDs aimed at kids: *Finding Nemo*,

A Bug's Life and *Arthur's Perfect Christmas*. Chloe decided on *Arthur's Perfect Christmas*. Trina succeeded in getting it started and Chloe climbed onto the sofa and settled happily to watch.

Returning to the kitchen, Trina reported, "Your renters apparently went home without a few of their movies."

He was loading the dishwasher and glanced up. "Ones she'll watch?"

How a man could look so sexy doing such a mundane task, she didn't know, but he succeeded.

"Yep."

"Then this is probably a good time for us to talk."

"Yes, except…" She nibbled on her lower lip. "I have a problem." Actually, she had so many problems they'd add up to a lengthy list, but one thing at a time, Trina decided. "I'm afraid I have to ask you to change the dressings on my back and apply more ointment. Unless you have a mother or girlfriend nearby who could be persuaded to volunteer."

"Neither."

WELL, HELL. SHE was going to half strip so he could stroke ointment over her skin with his bare hands? Might as well ask him to run his hand along a strand of barbed wire. Dangerous. He wasn't the only one conscious of the risks, either; the pink in her cheeks was from a different kind of heat.

Think of this as a medical problem, he told himself. "How badly are you burned?"

"Not that terrible. According to the doctor, mostly first-degree, spots of second-degree. No worse than a really bad sunburn. The fire didn't touch me, but while I was lowering Chloe out the window and waiting until

I could follow her, flames burst through the door behind me and—" She visibly shied from the memory. "I was just…too close to it."

"Okay." He tried to sound gentle, which had the effect of roughening his voice. "How often do we do it?"

"Twice a day until it's obviously healing. Which shouldn't be more than two or three days."

Gabe thought it over. "I don't want to leave Chloe downstairs by herself. If you'll pause the movie—"

"Why don't we wait until she's gone to bed?"

Yeah, sure. Then they'd be alone, house quiet and dark around them. Her stretched out on *his* bed, since Chloe would be in hers.

He cleared his throat. "If you don't need it done sooner."

"It can wait."

"All right." Needing a distraction, he lifted the carafe from the fancy coffee maker that had been one of his first purchases after he'd had the cabin built. "Would you like a cup?"

"That would be great."

"You okay on the stool, or would a chair be more comfortable?"

"Chair."

"Hey, hold on." He left the room, returning after a minute with a heavy-duty parka. "This should give you a little padding."

He doubled it over, and watched as she sat down gingerly. Looking surprised, she said, "That helps. Thank you. And speaking of… I don't think I've thanked you for rushing to our rescue."

Admit to his initial reluctance? Or that, on second thought, he'd been glad to have the chance to do something really meaningful? Probably not. Gabe settled for an acknowledging nod.

"I should at least call my insurance agent tomorrow."

"It'll have to wait. What phone number would you give him if he has questions?"

"But…"

"A few days is nothing, given the time it'll take to rebuild."

She finally nodded.

"I need you to tell me what's happened so far."

Looking startled, she began, "Didn't Joseph—"

Gabe cut her off. "I want as much detail as you can give me." The cops had one goal; he had another.

She glanced toward the doorway, as if to be sure the little girl hadn't wandered into earshot. "Did you read about the murders?"

Having a whole family killed, and wealthy people at that, didn't happen in these parts. The news had likely riveted just about everyone. "Yes," he agreed, "but I had the impression the cops were holding back."

"They did tell me something two days ago they hadn't admitted up until then, but my impression is that they're stymied."

Gabe waited.

Trina began to talk, starting with the request from a Lieutenant Matson, who oversaw detectives, that she work with a three-year-old girl who was the only survivor after her family had been killed. "Either she'd climbed into one of the lower kitchen cupboards herself, or one of her parents put her there. When the police arrived, the cupboard door was open a crack, and her father's body was right in front of her."

"Once she heard the intruder leave, she might have pushed it open herself to peek out," he suggested.

"Yes, but they didn't think so. She was...frozen, almost catatonic. Stiff, staring, squeezed into the smallest ball she could manage."

He played the devil's advocate. "Seeing her father..."

"The detective said he'd been shot in his back and lay facing her. She couldn't have seen the blood or... damage."

"Unless she crept out, then went back to her hidey-hole."

"I guess that's conceivable, but I think it's likelier that she never moved." Her expression shifted. "You sound like another detective. Were you an MP, or...?"

"No, we do some of the same kind of thing when we've been inserted into a foreign country and discover our intel isn't accurate. It's time you and I start thinking like investigators." He'd realized as much immediately. "If you trust the police, you'd be letting them protect you and Chloe. They offered protection, didn't they?"

"Round the clock."

"But you called your brother instead. Why?"

She made a face. "Two reasons. One is that they're desperate for Chloe to tell them what she saw and heard. They called constantly, dropped by at the office. They were impatient, skeptical. Why wasn't she talking yet? I overheard one of the detectives saying I was being too soft, that they could 'crack her open.' His words. All I could picture was a nutcracker smashing a walnut open."

Gabe winced, sympathizing with her obvious anger. He could empathize with the cops' frustration, too, but nothing justified traumatizing that cute kid any more than she'd already been.

"They didn't like it that I wouldn't tell them where I 'stashed' her during the day, while I worked," Trina continued, with unabated indignation.

"Where did you?" he asked, curious.

"Some of the professionals and staff in the building went in together, rented a small vacant office and started their own preschool, right down the hall from my office. This way, they can have lunch with their kids, pop in when there's a slow moment, be there if something happens." She smiled. "Needless to say, it's not advertised. They were happy to include Chloe."

"Smart." He mulled that over. "Okay, you wanted to keep her away from the cops. What's the other reason you don't trust them?"

"Chloe had been talking for about a week—but timidly, and she'd clam up and stay quiet for hours if I said anything that scared her. Since she was progressing well, though, on Tuesday I called Detective Risvold to let him know we were getting somewhere."

"And Wednesday night, your house was set on fire with you and Chloe inside it, asleep on the second floor," he said slowly. Rage kindled in his chest.

"I thought the timing was suggestive." Anxiety filled her hazel eyes, and her hand resting on the table tightened into a fist. Her fingernails must be biting into her palm. "Do you think I'm being paranoid?"

"No." He started to reach for her hand but checked himself. He wasn't much for casual touching, and didn't even know where the impulse had come from. "You have an enemy. Under the circumstances, it's just common sense to be paranoid."

Her relief was obvious, her hand loosening. "Thank you for saying that. There's a fine line. Until the fire, I figured the detectives were insensitive. Maybe neither of them has children. But thinking they're part of this…"

Gabe pondered that, considering it safer than focusing on his desire to scoop her up in his arms and hold her close. That wasn't like him, either. Yeah, and she wouldn't enjoy close contact right now anyway.

"Odds are against the investigators being culpable," he said after a moment. "Trouble is, unless our guy got lucky and overheard two cops gossiping in a coffee shop, that suggests a killer who has connections in the department."

"Detective Risvold wasn't happy with me when I told him his department must have a leak."

"He was defensive?"

"Maybe?" Her uncertainty came through. "Or worried because the thought had already occurred to him? I couldn't tell."

"I'd like to have a talk with him, except I don't see how I can without giving him an idea where you are."

"Where you stashed me, you mean?"

He gave a grunt of amusement. "Okay, tomorrow, I need to grocery-shop. I'll drive to Bend so nobody I've met is surprised by what I'm buying. I can stop at Target or Walmart and pick up some toys or movies for Chloe and anything else you need."

"Wouldn't it be better if I came? I could definitely use clothes and toiletries."

"No. We can't risk you being recognized." He held up a hand when she opened her mouth to argue. "You can't tell me you don't have clients who live in Deschutes County. You could be recognized."

"The odds of someone I know happening to be in the same store at the right time isn't—"

"Give me sizes." He sounded inflexible for good reason; this wasn't negotiable. He could tell she was irritated, but he couldn't let that bother him. "You hurt besides," he pointed out. "Do you really want to try on jeans?"

She grimaced.

"I'll have Boyd come over while I'm gone."

Her forehead crinkled. "Joseph didn't sound as if he completely trusted this Boyd. He thought he might have gotten soft."

Gabe came close to laughing. "That hasn't happened." Just for fun, he'd tell Boyd what her brother said.

Her eyes searched his. "He won't tell anyone we're here?"

"He already knows. I needed to be sure he was ready to act if I called."

When Trina turned her head, he, too, realized the background voices and music from the TV had stopped in the living room. Before either of them could rise, the kid appeared. So much for everything else they needed to discuss. But maybe one day at a time was good enough, Gabe thought. The last twenty-four hours had upended Trina's life, and Chloe's for a second time.

"Movie over?" Trina asked, holding out her hand.

Nodding, the kid reached Trina and climbed into her lap. The lack of hesitation spoke of her trust.

That got him wondering how Chloe had come to be living with the psychologist who'd been working with her. That had to be unusual. He'd never had the slightest interest in building personal ties with any of the social workers and therapists who'd made him think of mosquitoes, persistent as hell, whining nonstop, determined to suck his memories as if they were blood.

And maybe that was fitting, because his memories *were* of blood, so much he sometimes dreamed he was drowning in it.

Dr. Marr hadn't yet tried to crack *him* open, but give her time.

"Let's go run you a bath," she said to the little girl in her lap. "We'll dig in that bag and see if Vicky sent any pajamas along."

Chloe's eyes widened.

Trina chuckled. "We'll find something. If nothing else, you can sleep in this top and your panties." She nudged Chloe off her lap and rose stiffly to her feet. Looking at him, she said, "I need a mug or something I can use to rinse her hair."

"Sure." He poked in the cupboard until he found a good-size plastic measuring cup with a handle.

"Perfect," she said, taking it from him. She'd reverted to looking a little shy. "Let's march, Chloe-o."

The little girl giggled. His own mouth curved at the sound. Glancing back, Trina caught him smiling, and was obviously startled. He got rid of the smile.

"This bedtime?" he asked, nodding at Chloe.

"Uh-uh!"

It took him a second to realize the protest had been verbal. "She talks," he teased.

Trina shook her head. "Now you've done it, kiddo. You won't be able to fool *him* again."

And damn, he wanted to smile.

SOMEHOW TRINA ALWAYS ended up wet even though it wasn't her taking the bath. Chloe liked waves, and she liked to splash. She did not like having her hair washed or getting water or soap in her eyes.

At home, Trina had had a plastic stool she'd bought for the express purpose of supervising baths and washing Chloe's hair. Today, she'd knelt on the bath mat. Chuckling as she bundled the three-year-old in a towel, Trina said, "As much as you love your bath, I think you're ready for swim lessons."

Chloe went rigid, panic in her eyes.

Going on alert, Trina used a finger to tip up her chin. "Or have you taken them before?"

Lips pinched together, Chloe shook her head.

On instinct, Trina kept talking, if only to fill the silence. "Maybe swim lessons are offered only during the summer." She should know, but she tended to tune out when colleagues and friends who had children started talking about things like that. Had Chloe been disturbed only because she was afraid to put her face in the water? But Trina didn't buy that. Taking a wild guess, she said, "Were you supposed to go to the pool that day? When the bad things happened?"

Suddenly, tears were rolling down the little girl's cheeks. Seeming unaware of them, she nodded.

"Were you going to learn to swim?"

She shook her head.

"Brian?" Chloe's brother had been six, a first grader.

She nodded again, her eyes shimmering with the tears that kept falling.

"Had you just not left yet?"

Another shake of the head. Trina had a helpless moment that gave her new sympathy for Detective Risvold's frustration.

But then Chloe whispered, "Brian pooked."

Pooked. "Puked? He was sick?"

She gave a forlorn sniff. "Uh-huh."

"Did you see who came to your house, pumpkin?"

Chloe buried her face in Trina's scrub top. Her whole body trembled.

Trina wrapped her in her arms and laid her cheek against the little girl's wet head. "I'm sorry, sweetie. I'm so sorry. You don't have to talk about it until you're ready. I promise."

Worried when there was no response, she used a hand towel to dry Chloe's cheeks, had her blow her nose with a wad of toilet paper, then briskly dried her and pulled the My Little Pony nightgown she'd found in the duffel over her head. "Okay, let's brush your hair."

She found no hair dryer in the drawers and thought about asking Gabe if he had one in his bathroom, but then realized how pointless that would be. All he'd have to do was rub a towel over his head. He probably didn't even bother to comb his hair.

Well, it didn't hurt anyone to go to bed with wet hair.

She'd give a lot to have a pile of picture books to read to Chloe to give her something else to think about before she snuggled down to sleep, but she had to find another way.

So she tucked Chloe in, refrained from commenting on the thumb in her mouth, and began singing softly, starting with a lullaby. She knew the words to a couple of country-western songs, a song from *Phantom of the Opera*, and ended up with Christmas carols. After the first verse of "Silent Night," she saw that Chloe's mouth had softened and her thumb had fallen out.

Trina clicked off the lamp and had turned to slip out when she saw the big man lounging in the doorway. When she got closer to him, she couldn't miss the smile in his eyes.

So she couldn't carry a tune. *Chloe* didn't mind.

He murmured, "Grab your duffel if it has what we'll need in it."

What they'd need. Alarmed by her very sexual response to that low, faintly rumbly voice, Trina took a minute to understand. Ointment. Bandages. He wasn't suggesting whatever she'd been thinking.

Trying to regain her dignity, she detoured to pick up the bag and followed him as he backed into the hall. "My room," he said, just as quietly, and indicated an open door.

The idea of taking off her shirt and pulling down her pants for him had seemed mildly embarrassing when they first met. Now her whole body flushed at the idea.

Seeing his big bed—it had to be king-size—didn't help. Faced with that bed, she was only vaguely aware of bare walls, wooden floors and a couple of pieces of plain furniture.

"This going to be messy? Maybe you should lie on a towel," he suggested, more gravel in his voice than usual. When she stayed speechless, he went into his bathroom. By the time he'd reappeared, she had set out a big package of gauze and one of several tubes of ointment a nurse had picked up at the pharmacy for her.

Gabe pulled back the covers, exposing forest green flannel sheets, and spread a huge towel for her to lie on.

She stared at it, all too conscious of him standing less than a foot away. This was the first time since she'd woken up that she'd lost all awareness of the pain.

Feeling silly, she still asked, "Um…would you mind turning your back?"

Without a word, he swung away.

Trina squirmed to get out of her scrub top. She'd been

feeling the discomfort of not wearing a bra, but even if she'd had one, it would be days before she could actually stand to wear it. All but throwing herself down on his bed, she mumbled, "I'm ready." Except for baring her butt. Well, she'd let him start at her shoulders and work his way down.

His weight depressed the mattress when he sat down at her side. While he peeled off the gauze covering, she turned her head to stare at the far wall and tried to bite back groans.

He swore. "This has to hurt like hell."

"It does," she mumbled.

There was a long pause. She heard him take a deep breath…and then he touched her. Stroked her.

Chapter Four

Gabe glanced over his shoulder as he scratched the blood bay gelding's poll. "This is Mack."

Nickering, the horse had trotted over to the paddock fence the minute he saw people approaching. Gabe was hit by a pang of guilt at the thought that the gelding was lonely. Of course he was; horses are herd animals. "Not long until you're back with your buddies," he murmured in one flickering ear.

Carrying Chloe, Trina joined him at the fence. "As in Mack truck?"

He smiled a little. "Yeah. For a quarter horse, he's a giant."

Her sidelong, appraising glance was enough to stir his body in ways that could be embarrassing.

"Kind of fits you," she murmured.

He pulled a cube of sugar from his pocket and held it out. Mack inhaled it, his soft lips barely brushing Gabe's hand. "Put me up on some of the horses here on the ranch, my boots would be dragging on the ground."

Trina's laugh lit her face. Held on her hip, the kid jumped when Mack whiffled.

"Would you like to pet him?" Gabe asked. "Mack likes everyone."

He wasn't sure the horse had ever met a child, but he trusted the good-natured animal not to bite.

The little girl looked doubtful but finally, tentatively, held out a tiny hand. Mack blew on it, making her giggle, then bobbed his head.

Gabe showed her how to offer a sugar cube, wrapping her hand in his so she wasn't in any danger of having a finger mistaken for a treat to be demolished by big yellow teeth. Another giggle, this one delighted, caused a strange sensation somewhere under his breastbone. It wasn't only Trina who awakened unfamiliar feelings. He excused himself on the grounds that he was a natural protector. The little girl's obvious vulnerability—and her surprising strength—spoke to him.

Bad enough letting the kid get to him. Gabe tried not to look at Trina, too sexy even in a pair of jeans from her friend's daughter that she was still wearing instead of the slimmer-fitting ones he'd bought her. Given her burns, the loose fit was more comfortable, she'd admitted.

He hadn't liked leaving the two of them alone yesterday, but he was confident enough that no one could find them to set out on his errands without having alerted Boyd. She'd promised to stay in the cabin and not answer the door while he was gone. Far as he could tell, she'd obeyed. He hadn't had to worry about Chloe; she stuck close to Trina.

Didn't mean Chloe wasn't getting whiny by the time he returned. Three short, animated videos only had so much entertainment value. The toys and games he'd bought had filled the evening, but he'd suggested the walk this morning to head off either Trina or Chloe growing restless.

Gabe's top priority yesterday had been to call Detective Risvold using a cheap phone he charged in his truck.

"Where the hell are they?" the detective had demanded. "Dr. Marr knows better than to disappear with the girl."

Gabe said only, "Safe. Trina asked me to let you know."

"That's unacceptable!" His fury seemed over the top. "This child is a witness to a multiple homicide. Now that she's talking, we need to have access to her. If I have to ask for a subpoena—"

"Do that," Gabe said icily, "and this is the last time I give you an update. And just how do you intend to serve your subpoena, even assuming you can find a judge who thinks it's fine to bully a three-year-old?"

After a significant pause, Risvold snapped, "I haven't heard any update."

"I'm tasked with telling you that Michael Keif was supposed to be alone that morning. The boy had a swim lesson. You can check, but chances were he'd had lessons the previous few Saturdays. That day, the mother intended to take him and Chloe. Brian got sick—puked, according to Chloe, so they made a last-minute decision not to go."

This silence lasted longer and was, Gabe hoped, more thoughtful.

"The killer was surprised by the wife."

"He didn't intend to kill them," Gabe agreed, "may actively not have wanted to, but if the husband was already down when he realized they weren't alone in the house…"

Sounding churlish, the detective grumbled, "If she can tell us that much, she can tell us what she saw."

"No. She broke down after telling Trina that much."

"I have a message for Dr. Marr," Risvold said in a hard voice. "I expect to hear from her daily. If she doesn't show up to work Monday, I'll have to assume she's kidnapped the girl and may even have crossed state lines."

The jackass was trying to intimidate the wrong man. The wrong woman, too, but Trina wasn't here. "You might recall she has legal custody," Gabe said curtly. "Which gives her the right and obligation to keep her foster daughter safe."

"Every day," the detective repeated. "I expect to see her in person, or hear *her* voice on the phone."

Shaking his head, Gabe cut off the connection. Scanning his surroundings in the vast Walmart parking lot, he saw nothing of concern except a marked Bend PD car slowly moving two aisles away from his truck. Probably coincidental, but why take a chance?

He'd backed out, rolled down his window when he saw a trash can, dropped the phone in and peeled off the leather work glove he'd worn to handle it. Still watchful but relaxed, he had continued with his errands, the most painful of which had been choosing toys. New experience, he'd told himself. It didn't take experience to steer him away from anything battery-operated that made noises.

Gabe had been both relieved and damn glad to walk in his door at the ranch, especially since woman and girl both pounced on him with open pleasure. Hair conditioner! Lip gloss! Picture books! He'd felt kinda like Santa Claus.

Now he found a smile for Chloe. "Would you like to ride Mack?"

Her eyes widened. *"Me?"*

"If Trina says it's okay." He shifted his gaze to her fine-boned face and big green-gold eyes.

She bit her lip. "Are you sure…?"

"Mack is gentle as a lamb." He didn't remind her how a well-trained cutting horse could move—sliding stops that would send unprepared riders sailing over his head, turns faster than seemed possible for such a big animal and blazing speed for the short distances needed to run down a breakaway steer. "I'll put her up in front of me."

Amusement in her eyes, she pouted. "You didn't offer me a ride."

The words were no sooner out than fiery color rose in her cheeks. He swallowed and tried not to think about how much he wanted to take her for a ride—preferably in his big bed upstairs. Even so, Gabe had no doubt she saw the glint in his eyes, because she turned her flaming face away to kiss the top of Chloe's head.

"I was being considerate," he said. Hearing the grit in his voice, he cleared his throat. "Don't think you're ready to be up on a horse when he breaks into a trot."

Trina winced. "You're right. I'm definitely not."

Curious, he asked, "Do you know how to ride?"

"Oh, sure." Her cheeks were still pink, but she was regaining her aplomb. "Nothing fancy, just trail riding. I have a friend whose husband has a small ranch south of town. I ride with her regularly."

Good, he thought; in a pinch, he could throw her and Chloe up on Mack and send them cross-country while he held off any threat.

He put a bridle on the gelding to reassure Trina, even though it wasn't necessary. Gabe could control Mack with his legs and subtle shifts of weight. Then he used the fence to mount bareback, and held out his arm. "Ready, little one?"

Chloe was clearly torn between terror and temptation. When Trina lifted her high enough for Gabe to close his hands around her waist, she froze.

"No?" he said.

Mack had been standing as still as a statue, but now he turned his head to look inquiringly. When he blew air out through his lips, Chloe gulped and said a brave, "Yes."

The minute he settled her in front of him, she clutched fistfuls of wiry black mane. She was ridiculously tiny atop the powerfully built horse. Gabe smiled, wrapped his right arm around her and signaled Mack to walk. They circled the paddock a couple of times before he bent toward her ear. "Lope? It's lots faster," he warned.

"Uh-*huh*!"

Mack responded to Gabe's tightened legs; after one bumpy stride the horse reached a canter, the gait slow and easy, his head low. He could have been circling a show ring.

Chloe squeaked and stiffened but quickly relaxed. By the time he slowed Mack to a walk and then to a stop at the fence right beside Trina, the little girl's body was moving with the horse like a pro. She was a natural.

She beamed at Trina. "I *like* fast."

Gabe laughed, drawing a startled look from Trina. Almost...fascinated.

He was working at locking himself down when he heard a sound that instantly sobered him. The steady beat of hooves. Even Trina swung around. If he hadn't suspected who was coming, he'd have reached for the handgun tucked in his waistband at the small of his back, hidden by his denim overshirt.

He recognized the horse before the man. Gabe let go of his battle-readiness. His friend and partner rode toward them on a dappled gray. Gabe preferred quarter horses, but Boyd liked Arabs and Arab–quarter horse crosses. This one had to be a cross, tall and muscled enough to carry a big man, but still possessing the delicate ears and dished face that characterized Arabians.

Boyd's eyebrows rose at the sight of Gabe on horseback holding a little girl in front of him. A girl, he realized uncomfortably, who was wearing pink overalls and a white T-shirt that had a glittery unicorn on the front. He'd bought the damn outfit himself yesterday. Not something he'd admit to Boyd.

His friend reined his horse in and openly studied the threesome before smiling. "Gabe." He nodded. Looked at the girl. "Hi, Chloe. I'm Boyd. A friend of Gabe's." Then he let his smile deepen for Trina. He had a way with women. "And you have to be Joseph's sister."

She smiled back. "I might take insult if you tell me I look like Joseph."

Boyd grinned. "*I'd* take insult if you told me I look like Joseph." Then he considered her, feature by feature, and admitted, "There's something. Your eyes. Hair color. Otherwise…nope."

"You should have told me you were coming," Gabe interjected. He never liked surprises, and especially in the middle of a mission. Which this was, if an off-the-books one.

Boyd shrugged. "Impulse. Thought I should meet your guests."

"We were about to have lunch," Trina said. "You're welcome to join us, if you'd like."

The other man did have the grace to glance at Gabe,

whose instinct was to keep even his best friend far away from Trina, but had to dip his head. They were friends, he reminded himself. There was no reason to feel territorial.

Boyd grinned, seeing right through him, and said, "Sounds good."

While Boyd dismounted and unsaddled his horse, Gabe handed Chloe off to Trina and slid off Mack. By the time he had removed the bridle, Boyd had heaved his saddle from the horse's back to the top rail of the fence and was leading the dappled gray through the gate. After taking off the bridle, too, he whacked his gelding on the butt, sending him into the paddock to join Mack.

The two touched noses, snorted and wandered companionably away to find a fringe of grass they could tear at.

Trina set Chloe down and said, "Lunchtime, sweetie."

"Can I have a cookie?"

"After lunch," Trina agreed, laughing when the kid raced toward the house.

Chloe wasn't the only one who'd been thrilled when Trina started baking last night. Chocolate chip cookies first, followed by cinnamon rolls. Two hefty cinnamon rolls had made a great breakfast this morning. Trina, who had split one with the little girl and still not finished it, had watched him eat in astonishment.

"So, Gabe tells me your brother thinks I've gone soft," Boyd remarked.

She tipped her head to assess a man who was as tall as Gabe, but leaner. "Maybe I should send him a picture so he can see that you don't have a beer belly yet."

He laughed as if that was the funniest thing he'd ever

heard. "Why didn't he ever tell me his sister was right here in Sadler?"

"Maybe because he didn't want you anywhere near her," Gabe suggested.

Boyd thought that was funny, too, possibly because he'd heard the edge in Gabe's voice.

"I'll have to call to give him a hard time," Boyd continued.

"He's away," she said softly. "That's why he asked Gabe to help."

"Yeah, so I hear." He laid a hand on her shoulder and squeezed. "Joseph can take care of himself, you know."

Her smile was obviously forced. "I do know."

Gabe didn't like seeing the shadow darkening her eyes. Yeah, being the one left behind would be a bitch. He should consider himself one of the lucky ones, knowing he wasn't hurting people who loved him, leaving them scared out of their skulls every time he went wheels up. And it would be even tougher for a lover—a wife— than it was for parents or siblings.

He had a feeling Boyd was thinking the same when he changed the subject. "Cute kid."

"Yes." Trina's gaze followed his to the front porch, where Chloe jumped from the top step to the ground, then climbed up and did it again. "She's doing amazingly, considering. Um, Gabe did tell you?"

"Yeah." Boyd's tone was grim. "No place is completely safe, but…damn."

Inside, Gabe heated the soup while Trina put together sandwiches. Two days, and they'd already begun to work around each other in the kitchen as if they'd been doing it for years, he thought, watching as she spun past him to get plates and bowls down from the cupboard. He nodded thanks and caught Boyd's interested gaze. *Like that, is it?*

No. Yes. Even if the conversation had been aloud, he wouldn't have known how to answer. He'd like to get this woman into bed—but he also knew she threatened him on a bone-deep level where he didn't want to go. If he were smart, he'd keep his zipper up and his hands to himself...except he'd be putting those hands all over her long, slim torso and the sweet curve of her ass again this evening. Even purple-and-black bruises, red skin and blisters had failed to shut down his libido.

It was like forcing an alcoholic to guzzle a shot glass full of whiskey twice daily.

During lunch, Gabe discovered something about himself, though. He didn't like the charming smiles Boyd directed at Trina, or their witty byplay. His only salvation was the slightly shy way she kept an eye on him, Gabe. It reminded him of the way Chloe watched her. Trina was the kid's anchor, and he was apparently Trina's. Then there was the fact that she never blushed for Boyd. She was being friendly, no more...which made Gabe realize that he and she never had a conversation that *wasn't* more.

Whatever this was sizzling between them, it was definitely mutual. The understanding was worrisome, even as it allowed him to relax and enjoy seeing Boyd's astonishment because a beautiful woman *didn't* flirt with him.

"YOUR FRIEND'S NICE," Trina observed, as she and Gabe stood on the front porch watching Boyd raise a hand at them and kick his horse into a canter.

"Nice, huh?" An expression that looked a lot like a

smirk crossed his face, although he erased it before she could be sure.

She narrowed her eyes. "Is there something wrong with 'nice'?"

"He wouldn't be flattered. Boyd is no more 'nice' than I am."

"What's that supposed to mean?"

"Men like us…we've seen too much. Done too much."

"You're including Joseph," she said slowly.

He didn't say anything.

"So when you took Chloe for a ride, that was…?"

"Practicality. She can't tell us the scary stuff until she's happy enough to feel safe. Besides, she'll be a pain in the butt if she gets bored."

He was that cold-blooded? Trina's first reaction was shock. But despite his current hard stare, she didn't believe he lacked any softness. He didn't give himself away often, but she'd seen fleeting expressions, the crinkle of skin beside his eyes even when he didn't allow himself a smile, a gentleness in the deep voice.

She snorted, much as horses did. "Don't buy it."

His dark eyebrows climbed. "Why not?"

"First, because I know Joseph. He…talks to me. Being a warrior and nice aren't mutually exclusive." She ignored Gabe's visible disbelief. "And I read people for a living. You know what I do."

What she'd thought was a hard stare became adamantine. Either he didn't like the possibility that she could read *him*—or he detested her profession. Needing to get it out in the open, she said, "You don't like therapists."

"You're right." He leaned toward her, letting her see something close to rage. "We're fine as long as you don't try that shit on me. You got that?"

Shaken, Trina tried to figure out why this had blown up so fast. What was he hiding?

Unwilling to back down, she nonetheless agreed. "I got it."

"Don't forget." Without so much as looking at her again, he walked down the steps and around a corner of the cabin, out of sight.

Mad more than anything, she stomped inside. Chloe sat on the sofa in the living room, clutching her plush purple My Little Pony—a gift from the jerk.

"Can I ride again?"

"Probably. Some other day." Trina found a smile. "Right now it's nap time."

"I don't wanna. I'm not sleepy."

Trina held out her hand and waited.

Chloe let out a giant sigh, slid off the sofa and took Trina's hand. "How come I hafta?"

They had this discussion daily, and Trina produced her rote answers, which Chloe countered. But Trina didn't even make it through one of the books Gabe had bought before the little girl sagged into sleep. Trina kissed her on the cheek, drew the covers up and slipped out of the room, leaving the door ajar. There she hesitated, grumpy enough she'd have joined Chloe for the nap if she'd really thought she could sleep.

Finally, she went downstairs, hoping Gabe hadn't returned. The house was quiet, so she made herself a cup of tea and curled up at one end of the sofa with it and the book she'd picked out yesterday morning.

He eventually did come in the front door, glance at her and nod brusquely, and go to the kitchen. That was the last she saw of him until long after Chloe woke, bumped down the staircase on her bottom and wanted to play a game. Trina gave serious thought to letting him deal with dinner, but she hadn't heard any sounds to suggest he was cooking and she was hungry, so she left Chloe watching a new video and went to the kitchen.

Gabe sat at the table, his laptop open in front of him. Even though she'd swear she hadn't made a sound, his head lifted and those sharp blue eyes focused on her.

"I'm going to start dinner," she said.

"You don't have to. I can—"

"It's fine." If she sounded short, so what? And she wasn't totally playing the martyr—she'd fully planned to make spaghetti this evening. She shouldn't have sulked at all; she and Gabe didn't have to be best friends, or even like each other. He was doing a favor for Joseph, and she had no doubt he was up to keeping her and Chloe safe. Full stop.

After turning on the burner, she dumped the hamburger into the pan and got out a cutting board, knife and onion. "Do you know what happened to the garlic?"

"First shelf, cupboard to your left."

Trina found it, and began chopping. "Joseph said you were still rehabilitating from an injury. I hope having us here hasn't kept you from working out."

"No, I have a gym set up in an outbuilding. That's where I was." After a brief pause, "There's a shower out there, too."

"Oh." Her eyes began watering from the onion, which she hastily scraped into the pan with the hamburger. "You're not limping or anything."

"There's still some discomfort."

And wow, did that sound like a grudging admission telling anyone he had a weakness—*having* a weakness— probably went against his nature. Plus, she felt sure he used the word *discomfort* for what anyone else would call pain—or even agony.

Having dealt with the garlic, she stirred the browning hamburger and then turned to face him for the first time in the conversation. "Joseph said you'd been hit with an IED."

His mouth tightened, and for a moment she thought he didn't intend to respond. "Yes."

"On a trail?"

"Road. Supposedly already cleared. I was in a jeep." It was as if he was trying to reduce any drama by keeping his voice completely flat.

The effect was to distance him from her. She wondered how much of a habit that was. Whether he was truly warm and open with anyone.

"By yourself?" The minute she asked, she knew she shouldn't have. She closed her eyes. "I'm sorry. I'm just being nosy. I'm not trying to get in your head or anything like that." When she let herself look at him again, she saw his spare nod.

"Your walk is looser today." His tone was cool, verging on disinterest. "Is your back feeling better?"

She moved her shoulders experimentally and, surprised, said, "It does. Maybe we can quit with the ointment. I mean, this wasn't much worse than a bad sunburn."

"I'll take a look tonight."

Deciding she'd been as friendly as she dared, Trina stirred again and then opened cans of tomatoes and tomato sauce before starting to dice a bell pepper.

Behind her, he said, "I didn't offer any way for Risvold to get in touch with you. I wonder if we should set up a conduit. Maybe one of your partners."

She shook her head. "I can call when I'm at the office."

"And just when do you plan to be in the office?" The question was lethally soft.

Trina bit her lip and turned slowly. "I've been meaning to talk to you about this."

He rose to his feet. To remind her he was bigger? Or because tension translated into action for him? "You don't want to stay in hiding?"

"No, it's not that." It was hard to argue with someone who appeared so unreceptive. But ultimately, the decisions were hers. He was a bodyguard, not the boss. "I work with traumatized children. Ones who've withdrawn like Chloe did, or are acting out in disturbing ways. These are children who have seen something horrible, or been abandoned over and over. I knew you wouldn't like it, but I can't do the same to them."

He only stared with those vividly blue eyes. "I cannot believe you're even thinking about going to work."

Trina bristled. "Thinking? I *am* going to work Monday morning."

"And if I refuse to take you?" With crossed arms, that big solid body and an implacable expression, he was letting her know the decision *wasn't* hers. "How do you plan to get there?"

Chapter Five

Still pissed Sunday evening, Gabe leaned a shoulder against the wall outside the guest bedroom as he waited for Trina. If he'd tried, he could have heard what she was reading to Chloe, but he let her voice form background music. Funny, he thought, that she had such a beautiful voice, at a lower range than most women, and yet couldn't carry a tune.

He couldn't believe that she'd won the argument. He had crumbled like a soda cracker under minuscule pressure, agreeing to deliver her to work Monday morning and pick her up at the end of the day. They had divided on whether she should take Chloe with her. If that happened any of the days this week, he'd either stay in the building as security or kill the day in town. An extra round-trip would up the risk unacceptably.

One thing he hadn't told her was Risvold's insistence that she show up daily in her office. For one thing, Gabe didn't believe the detective would get anywhere trying to slap her legally. For another…he refused to tip the scales the wrong way on this argument.

The one he'd just lost.

Man, down the line Joseph was sure to hear his good buddy had condoned and participated in this sterling

Hide the Child

plan. Gabe expected a fist in his face at the very least, since he wouldn't be able to duck her brother forever. But damn it, her argument had been persuasive. She worked with a lot of kids like Chloe, and she'd be letting them down if she had to cancel appointments for the foreseeable future. Imagining a dozen scared, mute little kids with maybe some freckles like Chloe's, and he was sunk.

He'd thought of a new argument, though, which he planned to present while he inspected her burns.

Only silence came from the bedroom now. Gabe straightened from the wall. She wouldn't go to bed without talking to him first, would she?

But no, she slipped quietly into the hallway. She jerked at the sight of him only a few feet away. But she lifted a finger to her lips, said, "Shh," and pulled the door almost closed. When she turned back, he gestured toward his bedroom.

After a noticeable hesitation, she entered it. The moment he closed the door, she said, talking a little too fast, "I really don't think you need to do this. I'm thinking I should just peel off the gauze and give my back some air."

Gabe shook his head. "You can't see the damaged skin. I can. You don't want to get an infection, do you?"

She hovered beside his big bed, not wanting to give in, but obviously unable to dispute his logic. At last, she huffed. "Oh, fine."

He couldn't have said whether he was relieved by her surrender, or dismayed. Because he knew—or at least thought he knew—why she was opposed to getting seminaked with him.

This morning, after changing her dressing, he'd been so aroused he'd had to hide out for half an hour before he dared rejoin her and Chloe. Right now…he looked down and grimaced. Sitting wouldn't be comfortable.

He hated thinking she might be uncomfortable not because she shared the intense attraction, but because she'd noticed his body's response to her.

This was probably the last time he'd have to do this, Gabe reminded himself. *Get it done.* He grabbed the towel from the chair where he'd tossed it and spread it out on the bed.

She lifted her T-shirt over her head, exposing the sheets of gauze covering her slim back, then unbuttoned and unzipped her steel blue chinos before lying down on her face.

Wincing, he sat beside her, able to adjust himself because, as usual, she had turned her face away. He peeled off tape, hating to know he was causing her involuntary quivers or see the red marks the blasted tape left behind on her creamy skin.

"Your upper back is still red, but looking good," he reported. "Not peeling yet. I don't know if aloe vera stains, but we could switch to that and skip the bandages here."

"Please."

He wished he couldn't see the plump side of her breast. Or maybe he wished he could really see her breasts, instead of having to resort to his imagination.

Gritting his teeth, he tore off more tape, eased more gauze away from her skin. Kept going until he could see the upper span of her buttocks and the curve of her hip, where the most severe burns had been. Blisters were still visible, some deflated, but a couple had burst.

"We need to keep ointment on here—" he squirted some on, feeling her reaction to the cold. "A couple of these blisters don't look good."

She mumbled something he thought was a swear word.

"Let's see how it looks tomorrow." He gently smoothed the ointment over the whole swath of skin from her lower back to her taut ass, then unrolled gauze to cover the inflamed flesh. More tape—damn, it was irritating her skin as much as the burn had in some places. Finally, he applied aloe vera to her upper back, rubbed it in, and with a supreme effort kept his hand from continuing to stroke upward onto her neck.

"Done," he said hoarsely, capped the bottle of green goop and grabbed the mess of bandages to throw them away in the bathroom. He washed his hands while he was there, too, and shook his head at the face he saw in the mirror.

That was Joseph's sister, out there on Gabe's bed. She depended on him. If he made a move, he'd risk her feeling like he'd put a price on his help.

With a groan he hoped she couldn't hear, he scrubbed his hands over his face and went out to find her sitting on the side of the bed, loose T-shirt hiding her long, slim torso and the breasts he fantasized about.

She eyed him cautiously, making him wonder what he was projecting. "So, tomorrow."

He frowned down at her. "Something else for you to consider. If Risvold can't find you, he has no way to have a subpoena served on you, either. Once he knows you're in your office, that changes. If you're court-ordered to produce Chloe and don't, you could be arrested."

"He won't go that far."

"You so sure?"

Trina pressed her lips together, then said, "What I'd do is let him talk to her. We both know what would happen."

Gabe knew. Chloe would clam up again. "What if he removes her from your care?"

"I'd like to see him try!" she fired back. "I work with the court system on a regular basis. I know judges. I could get him squished like a bug."

Apparently, he'd tossed a spark on dry wood. And damn, Trina Marr's fury and passion fanned the fire of his arousal, too. He forced himself to back away.

"Okay." He cleared his throat. "You win."

Her gaze had dropped to his waist...and below. When her eyes lifted to meet his again, a delicate pink color infused her cheeks. "I...what?"

He did some internal swearing. "I said, you win. I'll take you to work in the morning."

"Um... Chloe?"

There was something about Chloe. Oh, yeah. "Boyd called. He has a woman lined up to watch her. She'll be here in the morning. Boyd will check in with her during the day."

Trina nodded, but he wondered if she'd taken in what he said. "I suppose I should go to bed." But her tone wasn't firm, and she stayed sitting on the edge of his bed.

"That would be a good idea." But he didn't move, either. He couldn't tear his gaze from hers, stupid as it was to keep staring at her. He'd used up his reserves of willpower in that last retreat. What he needed was a cold shower, although he knew any effect it had would be temporary. Finally, he heard himself say her name. "Trina." Nothing more.

She rose to her feet as if he'd tugged at an invisible string. Took a step. Then another. His heart pounded so hard, he heard it. The blood it was pumping was heading south, not to his head.

She whispered, "This isn't…"

"A good idea." He knew that; no longer cared, not with her in touching distance. Without any conscious decision, Gabe lifted his hands, cupped her cheek with one, wrapped the other around the delicate nape of her neck. He took the next step, the one that brought his body close enough to brush hers. The silk of the hair brushing his hand was every bit as thick as he'd imagined, as sensual.

"Gabe."

He couldn't mistake the yearning in her eyes for anything else. That was all he'd needed to know. Even so, he bent his head slowly enough to give her time to retreat, but instead she lifted her own hands to flatten them on his chest as she rose on tiptoe to meet his lips with her own.

TRINA KEPT SNEAKING looks at Gabe during the half-hour drive into town the next morning. He was in soldier mode—his gaze flicking from the side mirror to the rearview mirror to the road ahead. Missing nothing.

They had been businesslike this morning, hustling through breakfast, both pretending the scorching kiss had never happened. She'd dressed as well as she could, given her limited selection, and come downstairs to find him letting in a woman named Diane Jenkins. Diane's husband worked for Boyd. Well, and for Gabe, too, Trina reminded herself. Except she had the impression Gabe hadn't stepped into any role as a boss here at the ranch.

Because he doesn't intend to stick around for long. The reminder left her feeling hollow.

In her early fifties, Diane had seemed nice. "Raised

three girls, one boy," she told them. "You're giving me the chance for a grandmother fix."

Chloe remained suspicious of this new person but took Trina's departure with Gabe well. Her recent day care experience had eased some of her fear of being left behind.

Diane had also delivered an aging, battered pickup truck with Nevada license plates for them to use. Trina was embarrassed not to have realized that anybody watching for her arrival or departure from her office could note the vehicle and license plates. If Gabe had driven his own truck, the cops would have had his name in about a minute. Anyone else watching might have had to jump through more hoops, but she had a feeling it wouldn't take anyone who was really tech-savvy much longer.

"Whose truck is this?" she asked finally, to fill the silence as much as anything.

He barely glanced at her. "Belongs to a young guy who just started working for us. The address on file for these plates is a rental he vacated a couple of months ago. If the cops in Elko, Nevada, are inclined to do some detective work, they could help the local PD track down Antonio, but there's no reason that would be a priority for any of them. Tomorrow, we'll borrow a different vehicle. Maybe switch out plates."

"Isn't that illegal?"

He just looked at her before turning his attention to the highway again.

No, he was probably used to doing whatever he had to to accomplish his purpose.

She went back to gazing out the passenger window to keep herself from staring at his powerful hands wrapped around the steering wheel, or the muscled, sinewy forearms dusted with dark hair, or his thick, taut thighs in cargo pants. All within reach.

Arriving at the office was a relief. Trina immediately reached for her door handle, but his "Wait" had her freezing. He came around, used his body to shelter her and hustled her into the building. He didn't relax even in the elevator, and comprehensively scanned her office once they entered it. Thank goodness, they were early enough that no patients were yet waiting, but behind the counter their receptionist, Sara Houle, stared at Gabe in astonishment and more.

Ignoring her, he said to Trina, "I'll be around. Don't go anywhere without me. Not even downstairs."

"But the coffee shop—"

He tipped one eyebrow up.

Okay, with her usual midmorning latte out, she'd make it through the day on the crap coffee brewed in their break room.

Sara was still gaping. Not until the door swung shut behind him did she blink, give her head a small shake and say, "Um. I have a bunch of messages for you. Two categories."

"Two?" Trina held out her hand for the pink slips.

"Patients, social services, et cetera. The usual." Sara gave her a pile of pink slips.

"What's the other category?"

Sara's lips thinned. "Detective Risvold." This pile seemed an inch thick. "The man is *really* getting on my nerves."

Trina rolled her eyes. "That makes two of us." She glanced at the wall clock. "I should have time to call him right now and get it over with."

"Please. Oh," the receptionist added, "your phone is in your top drawer. I charged it Friday. If it hasn't held the charge, I have my cord here."

"Thanks."

Her phone came to life without hesitation, and, from the number of bars, should hold out for the day. That was good, because she needed to take this opportunity to call her insurance agent and her parents. As she scrolled to the detective's number, Trina added an item to her to-do list: *buy new cord and charger.*

Risvold answered so quickly she couldn't swear she'd heard a ring first. "Dr. Marr?"

"Yes. I understand you've been inundating my receptionist with calls. One message would have done the job."

"Would it? You haven't stayed in contact."

"I had only the one bit of progress," she said with strained patience, "which a friend conveyed to you. We haven't had any further breakthroughs, but I promise I'll let you know the minute we do."

"I want to talk to the girl."

"Your interrogation skills might work for a gang member, but for a three-year-old?"

"You're tiptoeing with her. How do you know she wouldn't respond better to firmness?"

She wanted to say, *Firm? Get real. You're a jackass*, but settled for asking, "Do you have children, Detective?"

There was a pause. "Two. And they listened when I talked."

Gee, she'd bet he and his probably adult children had a warm relationship now. Silly cards in the mail, Facebook friends, laughter around the Christmas tree.

"They didn't see their father slaughtered right in front

of them. Or hear their mother's and brother's alarmed voices, maybe screams, followed by gunshots and then silence. Dead silence."

He made a noise she couldn't interpret. "So you're set on pussyfooting around with this kid?"

"Your lieutenant came to me," she reminded him. "And not for the first time." That's right—go over his head. "There's nobody else on this side of the state with my reputation for working with traumatized children. I do know what I'm doing. Give me some credit."

"Fine," he grumbled after a minute. "You can have a little longer. But *you* need to bear in mind that three people were murdered in cold blood. Kids that age forget things fast. What if what she saw is already fading away?"

"This isn't something she'll ever forget," Trina said flatly. "If it wasn't a deep wound, it wouldn't have terrified her into refusing to speak." She frowned. "Do I gather you have no leads?"

"I'm unable to share the details of an ongoing investigation," he said, clearly having repeated it a million times. Which he probably had. He must have that line on a continuous loop. In this case, she felt confident in translating it to mean no. "It makes me uneasy not knowing where you and the Keif child are staying. We can give you added security if we—"

"I'd tell you if I believed that," she interrupted. "Forgive me, but I don't. I feel safer with no one knowing."

Sara's voice came through the intercom. "Dr. Marr, Mrs. Thatcher and Philip are here."

"I'll be out in just a minute," she replied, then told Risvold she needed to go. She swore she'd call him daily through Friday but wouldn't promise anything about the weekend.

Standing to go out to the waiting room to usher in the seven-year-old boy who woke screaming several times a night, Trina sent out a prayer.

Let Chloe have that breakthrough. Or the investigators find the answer in another way. Trina wanted her normal life back, or at least some semblance of it.

Hand clenching on the doorknob, she closed her eyes. The weirdness of her current life wasn't really the problem. What scared her was that she was in serious danger of falling hard for Gabe Decker, and if that happened, she'd be guaranteed a broken heart.

THE NEXT TWO DAYS, Gabe spent as little time alone with Trina as he could manage without being too obvious. He felt sure she noticed, but he had no idea if she was grateful or insulted.

He'd have been in more trouble if she weren't continuing to insist on going to work. Spending all day with her, no distractions, his bed upstairs in the cabin within easy reach… Yeah, that might've stretched his willpower to breaking. As it was, he just had to deal with the complications of taking her to town and back without being followed.

If this went on, one of these days he'd run out of alternative vehicles and plates. If it hadn't been spring, when Boyd always added some extra ranch hands, Gabe wouldn't have had so many vehicles to choose from. It was lucky that the young cowboys tended to be a transient population, drifting from ranch to ranch, state to state.

Monday afternoon, he'd spotted an unmarked police

car parked half a block away from the professional office building where Trina's practice leased half of a floor. He had detoured by several blocks, approaching from the opposite direction and parking in back. He'd moved her out fast and had her crouch down as he drove away, heading south into town instead of west out to the highway. Only when he was 100 percent sure they didn't have a tail did he take a winding route out to the highway.

Yesterday, he hadn't worried so much dropping her off, but at the end of the day, he had her ride with one of her partners into downtown. The guy had tapped his brakes for a brief stop to let her off in front of a coffee shop. She dashed in, walked right through and went out the back, where Gabe had been waiting.

The minute she'd buckled in, she exclaimed, "This feels ridiculous, like I've wandered into a spy novel. Next thing I know, I'll be poking a packet in a tree boll for my Soviet counterpart to pick up."

Her exasperation triggered his irritation, which he didn't trouble to hide. "The cops are watching your building morning and night. I wouldn't be so worried about them, if not for your house having been set on fire with you in it." Out of the corner of his eye, Gabe saw her chagrin and moderated his tone. "It's harder to pin down whether anyone else is watching, but we have to work on the assumption they are. Thanks to the news coverage, everyone in eastern Oregon who has read a newspaper or turned on the TV knows that a little girl is the only witness to the brutal crime that has them transfixed. You called your brother because he has the same skill set I do. Would you have argued with him, too?"

She'd apologized, and he had felt like a jackass for reminding her that denial was dangerous. He consoled himself that she felt safe with him, which was good. Not so good was that he was only one man. He had backup at the ranch, but not out on the often lonely highway.

Yeah, when Joseph got back and found out what had gone on, it would not be pretty. Gabe felt some chagrin of his own. If her brother learned that Gabe lusted after his sister? Had kissed her until his brain function melted down? Gabe imagined what he'd do to someone in his position, if Trina had been his to protect.

She was, he reminded himself. Not *his*, exactly, but he was all she and Chloe had to keep them safe.

Thursday he drove his own truck, with plates he'd borrowed from an old Blazer rusting behind the tractor barn. According to Boyd, a guy working here last year had intended to rebuild the engine and replace all four tires, but spent his earnings in taverns instead and left the Blazer behind when he moved. Gabe dropped Trina off in back of her building and tried to figure out a strategy for the end of the day.

For the morning, he parked behind a Safeway store among employees' cars, backed up to a painted cinder block wall and with the nose of his truck facing out. Then he eased his seat back and opened his laptop. He'd done some reading about the crime but hadn't really dug into it.

It was past time, he thought. His subterfuges with varying vehicles and license plates might get them through the week, but beyond that? Anyone looking for them would be getting more suspicious, smarter.

Risvold, the lead detective, was leaning too hard on Trina. That bothered Gabe. Maybe it was only that the guy thought his job was on the line, but there was a hint of desperation to his unrelenting pressure. That didn't fill Gabe with confidence. It was time he pursued this as if it was a real mission. He needed to get to know the dead man, and any conceivable players.

Gabe typed *Michael David Keif* and settled back to read.

Chapter Six

Gabe narrowed his eyes at his rearview mirror. They definitely had a tail today. He wanted to think it was a cop, because the police weren't as dangerous as the alternative, but the silver sedan was hanging too far back for him to read the license plate or see the antenna. There was always something that set aside a law enforcement vehicle from everything else on the road. The lack of any of those obvious features set off a flare for him.

He did his swearing internally. Damn it, he'd been almost to the highway, where the direction he turned would be a dead giveaway. Seeing a yellow light ahead, he lifted his foot from the gas and slowed while keeping a sharp eye on the cars waiting on the cross street. If any of them seemed ready to jump the gun… But none were. The second the light flashed red, he punched down on the accelerator and rocketed through the intersection.

Trina clutched her seat belt at her chest. "Oh, my God! What are you *doing*?"

He swung abruptly right at the next intersection, silencing her. In his rearview mirror, he saw the crossover swerve, climb the curb at that corner and turn right, too.

Midblock, Gabe did a U-turn, a fraction of an inch from scraping the fender of a parked car, and sped back the way they'd come. And…yes, he hit the light just before it turned red, making it through.

"Somebody is behind us," Trina said, looking anxiously in the mirror on her side.

"*Was* behind us," he corrected.

Multiple zigzags later, Gabe felt confident he'd lost his pursuit. Just in case, he drove a backcountry route on a narrow road that swung through thinly wooded, flat land before connecting with the highway.

Once there, he took binoculars from beneath the seat and scanned both ways before heading sedately north.

"You could have been ticketed," she said after a minute. "And then they'd have found out the license plates don't go with your truck."

"They had to catch me first."

She'd clasped her hands tightly on her lap. So tightly her fingertips dug into the backs of her hands. Because they'd have been shaking otherwise?

"You okay?" he asked.

"Fine. Just…" She lifted one shoulder. "Having someone actually chasing us kind of makes this real."

"Jumping out a second-story window with fire licking at your back didn't do that?"

Trina frowned at him. "Of course it did! I just thought, I don't know, that they'd wait until Chloe was in reach again."

He shook his head. "That might have been just Risvold or one of his minions, mad that you're hiding the kid." He didn't like the doubt he felt. "If not…whoever was involved in killing her family has to be hot to figure out where you're staying before Chloe blurts out a description of the man she saw holding a gun on her daddy."

"I keep telling Detective Risvold, three-year-olds are lousy witnesses. She might say 'The man had a mean look on his face.' And maybe remember his hair was brown. How is this going to help?"

Gabe glanced at her and decided to tell her what he was thinking. "What if the killer was someone Chloe knows? That would make her a serious threat."

She pressed her lips together. "I…sort of wondered that, too. But all this pressure from above that has Risvold in a stew might only be because Michael Keif is an important man around here."

"I've been doing some research. The guy was seriously wealthy. Open Range Electronics is one of the biggest employers on this side of the state. The manufacturing jobs make a huge difference in the local economy. Plus, did you know he sat on the county council a few years back?"

"I've been doing some reading about him, too," she said. "He chose not to run after one term, you know. He wasn't defeated."

"He resigned so his partner in the company could take his turn on the council," Gabe agreed. "Still, it means the mayor, the police chief, all the movers and shakers knew him."

"Thus Risvold's panic attack."

Gabe wasn't so sure. In fairness to the lead detective, the crime was appalling. A nice mother and child slaughtered? The media had to be pushing hard for answers.

"Do you know anything about this Ronald Pearson?" he asked.

"No more than you'd have found online," Trina said. "I haven't met him or anything. I did wonder…well."

Gabe had wondered, too. If the partners were also

good friends, their families would be well acquainted. You'd think this Pearson and his wife might have wanted to take in Chloe, or at least to visit her, call regularly.

Trina shifted in her seat to look directly at him. "Do you suspect he killed Michael Keif over control of the company?"

"Undecided," he said. "We need to keep him in mind, though. What I'd like to find out is what happens to Open Range Electronics now that one of the two founding partners is dead. Was it set up so that Keif's share goes into a trust for Chloe? You know, it's equally possible that, in the event of a death, the living partner gets the whole shebang."

Trina brooded for a few miles before saying, "If O.R.E. is doing so well, why wouldn't they both have been satisfied? From what I read, Chloe's dad was the engineer who had the original concept for their first product, and supervised engineering and operations, including manufacturing. Pearson is the public face, the one who was always interviewed, who headed distribution, the sales force."

"I saw that. I also saw some indiscreet comments made by a man named Russell Stearns, who seems to have been only a step below Keif. He thought the company could go bigger, that Keif's vision was too limited and he'd been holding them back."

She stared at him. "Where'd you find that? Did this guy really go public with a criticism of the man with the power to fire him?"

"The man who did fire him. I'm guessing Stearns thought Pearson would back him, but he didn't. Doesn't mean Pearson won't immediately offer him the job as chief operating officer. With Stearns, there'd be continuity. No learning curve. And, hey, ambition. So far, they haven't brought anyone new on board. I guess that would look insensitive this quickly."

Trina shook her head. "It's just so hard to imagine a businessman massacring a family. Looking into the eyes of a six-year-old boy and shooting him? Setting the fire to kill Chloe and me?"

"And yet someone did all those things," he reminded her.

He saw her swallow. When she said, "I know," it was softly.

Gentling his voice, he said, "We have the weekend now."

She nodded, but her fingers had locked together again.

"Trina, I think you and I need to get some answers. I don't know about you, but I've lost faith in Risvold. Instead of seriously investigating, he's got himself convinced that Chloe will tell him who to arrest."

"I've noticed."

Her tartness pleased him. He didn't like scaring this woman.

"We can't exactly go canvass neighbors, though." Now she sounded thoughtful. "Or interview coworkers. And then there's the chance the murders were about something else. Say Michael or his wife had been having an affair, maybe broke it off, and the enraged third party flipped out."

"Possible," Gabe conceded, "but remember that Chloe's mother and brother weren't supposed to be there. If this was Michael's lover, would she be up to killing the whole family?"

"Maybe, if she was surprised in the act. Besides, what are you saying? Women aren't as vicious as men?"

He surprised himself with a chuckle. "No, you're right. They can be."

"Anyway, what if the killer was the lover's cuckolded husband?"

Gabe laughed openly. "Didn't know anyone used that word anymore."

She sniffed. "I read a lot. And it's accurate, isn't it?"

"Yes, it is." He was still smiling when he reached the cabin. He braked in front and said, "Go on, I know you're—" he caught himself on the verge of saying *dying* "—itching to see Chloe."

After watching her bound up the steps and go in the front door, he drove around the side of the cabin and maneuvered until he could back into the small barn he used as a garage. Closing the doors but not locking them—there was always the chance they'd need to take off in a hurry—he walked while thinking about what research he and she could, and couldn't, do.

Nobody knew him. Could he get some people who worked at O.R.E. to talk to him? Or any of the Keifs' neighbors? It would be worth asking Trina if she happened to have any acquaintance with another one of the county council members or a spouse thereof, too. Another thought: he knew several Ranger teammates who'd gone into law enforcement after retiring from the military. The option was a common one. The one who was most potentially useful, Chad Bravick, had been a detective with the Portland Police Bureau last Gabe knew. Would he be able to think of an excuse for butting in on this investigation?

Gabe grimaced. If this dragged on, he'd ask.

He said a few words to Diane and watched her drive

away, today in her own sedan. Then he let himself into the cabin, his mood lighter the minute he heard a little girl giggle, and one particular woman laugh.

"AAGH!" TRINA WRITHED, trying to reach the middle of her back and failing. "Crap, crap, crap."

Why hadn't she thought to waylay Diane before she left? Trina really hoped she hadn't been subconsciously setting herself up to have a good excuse to ask Gabe to put his hands on her again. He'd made it plain that he didn't intend to take the kiss anywhere. Fine. She should count her blessings. It wasn't a good idea. *He* wasn't a good idea, not for her—but she wasn't all that sure she had the willpower to be the one to put the brakes on.

Grumbling to herself, she went downstairs with the bottle of aloe vera. She'd been going through the stuff like frat boys did beer. Gabe had had to buy more for her twice this week.

She paused at the foot of the stairs to watch Chloe. A video played—*Finding Nemo*, or maybe it was the sequel. Chloe had her back to the TV. With a frown of concentration, she was putting together a puzzle Gabe had bought for her.

Smiling, Trina went on to the kitchen, where Gabe was hunched over his laptop. However fierce his concentration, he lifted his head immediately. His gaze dropped from her face to the bottle clutched in her hand.

"You need some help?"

"Yes!" *Tone it down*, she ordered herself. "I'm sorry to have to ask, but I itch like crazy, and I can't reach the middle of my back."

"No problem." He rose in that effortless way he had and came toward her.

"You don't move like someone who was injured," she blurted. "Do you mind... I mean, I keep wondering..."

He cocked an eyebrow. "Where I was hurt?"

She bit her lip and nodded. "I know I'm being nosy, but I can't help myself."

He didn't look all that receptive, but he hadn't gone into lockdown, either. After a minute, he said, "I told you it was an IED." When she nodded, he went on. "The bomb blew a little bit behind me. It shattered my pelvis and flung me into the air. I hit part of what was left of the jeep when I came back down. Broke my femur."

She stared at him, aghast. "You can't exactly put a pelvis in a cast."

"No." He visibly debated how much to tell her. "I had internal bleeding," he said finally, "so the docs stabilized me and then shipped me out. I'm being held together by plates, screws, pins." He shrugged. "Not sure how much real bone is left."

"I'm so sorry. Joseph didn't say how bad it was."

"I'm alive," Gabe said curtly. He held out a hand for the aloe vera. Apparently, confidences were done.

She gave it to him, turned around and lifted her shirt. She'd taken off her bra when she got home.

"Huh. You're peeling."

"I *know* I'm peeling. This is the worst part."

"Gotten a bad sunburn before?"

"When I was an idiot teenager. I learned my lesson."

She heard a gurgle, and then the cool relief as he stroked the aloe vera on. She sighed.

"It really helps?" He was carefully lowering her shirt.

"Well, it doesn't entirely get rid of the itching, but it

does make a difference." Trina composed her face before she turned around. "Thank you."

"You're welcome." He nodded toward the bottle he'd handed back to her. "How long does that last?"

"Oh, a few hours, at least."

His eyes had darkened. "So, what happens in the middle of the night?"

"I…don't know. The intense itching started today."

"You can wake me up." His voice had deepened, too, becoming darker, or maybe she was just picturing him sprawled in bed, reaching for her.

It would be so much easier if she was already *in* bed with him.

Bad idea, remember?

"Trina," he said huskily. The heat in his eyes held her in place. "You have to know I'm feeling things for you. That I want you."

Dodging the conversation appealed to the coward in her. Because her alternative was to throw herself into his arms. It was a struggle to find the in-between. "I'm… not very comfortable with short-term."

A nerve twitched on his cheek. "I've never done anything but," he admitted, in the voice that felt so much like the calloused touch of his hands.

Saddened despite her own turmoil, she asked, "Why?"

He kept staring at her, but she felt his retreat well before he rolled his shoulders and stepped back. "That the woman talking? Or the psychologist?"

What amounted to an accusation stung. "The woman. And being an Army Ranger isn't an excuse. Even Joseph has had some relationships that got serious."

Gabe gave a mirthless laugh. "Joseph would kill me if he knew what I'd suggested to you."

"You're *afraid* of my brother?" she said incredulously.

"Not afraid. Respectful."

"Respectful?" Worse and worse.

"There's an unwritten rule. Your friends' sisters are taboo."

The mood had seriously dampened, at least as far as she was concerned. "That is so ridiculous. And you're just dodging my question."

"Your question."

Oh, he knew exactly what she was talking about.

"Why you never actually care about women."

His whole face tightened. "I didn't say that."

"You sleep with them, you walk away. No harm, no foul. That does not suggest an emotional component."

Gabe shook his head in apparent disgust. "You can't help digging, can you? Let's forget about it, okay?"

"Fine!" Her heartburn wasn't from dinner, but if she didn't admit he'd hurt her, it wasn't true. Right? "I need to spend some time with Chloe. Try to get her to open up a little more."

"Have you been trying at all?"

She didn't need criticism from him. "As you pointed out, I'm a psychologist. I *do* know what I'm doing." She stalked out of the kitchen, mad, hurt more than she should have been, frustrated, and suddenly sympathizing with Detective Risvold.

If Chloe would only *tell* them what she saw, this could all be over. Forgotten.

What exactly "all" was, Trina didn't let herself define.

TORN BETWEEN GOING BACK to his online research and eavesdropping, Gabe chose to hover just out of sight of the two in the living room. If Trina caught him, he was damned if he'd apologize.

"Wow!" she exclaimed. "You're a champion with puzzles."

He'd swear the warmth he heard was genuine. Frowning, he shook his head. Of course Trina was genuine. She'd stepped up to foster Chloe when she didn't need to. The trust and affection between the two of them was palpable. Why else did his chest so often feel bruised? The lonely little kid in him, the one he liked to think was no longer there, wanted in on that affection.

Pathetic.

"Do you mind if I turn off the movie? It doesn't look like you're watching it anyway."

Chloe must have nodded, because the background sound abruptly cut off.

"Come and sit with me."

He wasn't the target of that honeyed voice, but he felt the tug. *He'd* go sit with her anytime.

Some rustlings and murmuring ensued.

"I haven't been able to see you in my office in ages, so I thought we should talk now," Trina said.

For the first time, he heard the high voice.

"I don't wanna talk about *that*."

"I know. But there are other things we can talk about, too. What do you think of Gabe's house? Do you like it?"

"Uh-huh. I 'specially like his horse. Do you think he'll let me ride tomorrow?"

Trina laughed. "I think there's a good chance he'll do that."

Gabe smiled. Chloe was a really cute kid who had him wrapped around her little finger. He'd never understood the appeal of having children before, mostly seeing them whining in grocery store aisles, but she'd opened his eyes. She was sweet and gutsy.

"We'll go ask him when we're done talking. How about that?"

"Can we be done talking *now*?"

Gabe's smile widened into a grin.

"Nope," Trina said cheerfully. "Did Diane keep you from being bored today?"

"She's nice. She even watched my movies with me." It was a clear accusation. *If she will, how come* you *don't?*

"Did she tell you she really, really wants grandkids? I'm pretty sure she's practicing. After spending time with you, she'll be ready to be a grandma."

There was a pool of silence, followed by a small "I used to have a grandma."

"You still do, sweetie. She's hurting. Your mother was her daughter, you know. And Brian her grandson. When you wouldn't talk, she thought I could help you better than she could."

"But I talk now."

Trina laughed. "She knows that. I'll tell you what. Once we can quit hiding, we'll go visit her. I'll bet she'd love that."

"Okay."

"Good. So I've been wondering about something. I know you hid in a cupboard in your kitchen."

Silence.

"You remember my kitchen, right? And you know Gabe's kitchen."

He tipped his head. Where was this going?

"And Gabe doesn't even live here most of the time, which means he doesn't have as much stuff as most of us do. So, here's my question. How come there was enough room in there for you to hide? Was that cupboard empty?"

Clever.

"Mommy took the stuff out."

"What kind of stuff?"

"Cookie sheets 'n… I don't know. Flat things."

"Ah. It was that kind of cupboard. I didn't have one of those, but Gabe does. Those are *skinny*. Lucky you are, too."

The giggle told him some squeezing was going on.

"But when did your mommy take the things out? Had she been washing them or something? She didn't leave them just sitting on the counter, did she?"

"Uh-uh. She… I think she put them on top of the pans in the *big* cabinet. It's under the stove."

"Oh, that makes sense. Whew! I kept picturing you sitting in a giant mixing bowl or on top of pans, which wouldn't be very comfy."

"Mommy made room for me."

"Did she tell you to hide in there?" Trina asked gently.

This time the silence went on so long Gabe thought Chloe wouldn't answer.

The voice that did come was Chloe's, but…different. Eerie. "Mommy said to stay and not make a sound, not even a teensy sound. No matter what I heard."

"Oh, honey." Heartbreak weighted Trina's voice. "I'm sorry. So sorry."

"And I didn't make a sound." This was a wail. "I didn't! 'Cept now I am, and Mommy said I shouldn't. Not till she came back. And she's not back! Why didn't she come back?"

The anguish in those sobs had Gabe flattening his hands on the wall and letting his head fall forward. He

98   *Hide the Child*

wanted to wrap his arms around that little girl and tell her that she didn't have to talk about whatever horrible things she'd seen and heard. That she didn't have to be afraid, because he'd stand between her and the rest of the damn world.

If his hands had been pressing wallboard, he might have damaged it. The logs were impervious.

Trina whispered broken reassurances until the sobbing eased, became snuffles and whimpers.

"Did you push open the cupboard door so you could peek out?"

Nothing.

"I think it might help if you could tell me what you saw. Sometimes saying what scared you out loud makes it less scary."

When he didn't hear anything more, Gabe shoved off from the wall and walked into the living room, the hell with staying out of sight. He saw Trina's distraught face first, then, once he rounded the couch, the child clinging to her like a baby monkey—arms and legs both gripping her, head buried against Trina's breasts.

And that's when he heard the soft keening. "No, no, no, no, no."

His horrified eyes met Trina's.

Chapter Seven

Lying in bed that night with his hands clasped behind his head, Gabe stared up at the rafters and soaring, dark ceiling. The faintest hint of light from the hall cast shadows that wouldn't normally be there.

What Chloe had told them today verified the assumption that her mother had had some warning. Had she heard her husband and another man—or maybe more than one person—shouting? If she'd heard a threat, or glimpsed someone pulling a gun, why hadn't she grabbed Chloe and slipped out the back door?

Easy answer: because her son was upstairs in bed, sick. She thought she could get him out, or hide them both. No, probably not hide him—he'd been found dead on the stairs, her at the foot of them, possibly having tumbled a distance. The police would know for sure, from blood on the steps and from her autopsy. Either way, she and Brian had been trying to tiptoe down and slip out of the house, Gabe guessed. One of them had inadvertently made a sound, or the killer had walked out of the kitchen to leave and seen them.

The sad thing was, if they had hidden, they'd probably have survived, given that the killer likely assumed the house was empty but for his target. Rebecca Keif wouldn't have had time to think it through, though. She heard an explosive argument; by the time she got her son out of bed and moving, she might have heard a gunshot. Her only thought would have been of her children, her main goal escaping with them.

After Chloe's breakdown tonight, Trina had sat with her while she took a bath. When Chloe emerged from the bathroom, he'd squatted to give her a big, good-night hug. He'd been newly conscious of the fragility of that small body. He couldn't get his last glimpse of her out of his head. On her too-pale, pinched face, her freckles had stood out like rust-colored paint splatters.

Trina had stayed with her a long time, reading and then singing. He didn't hear a peep from Chloe, who'd lost her voice again after her haunting repetition of "no."

With the night completely quiet, he heard that eerie voice again. *Mommy said to stay and not make a sound, not even a teensy sound. No matter what I heard.*

Gabe mumbled an obscenity under his breath.

He'd spent hours himself crouched in places where he was a breath away from being discovered, and his teammates' lives as well as his had hung in the balance. The creak of a floor, or a faint crunch of rocks underfoot; an involuntary sneeze, or a stomach rumbling, or a small movement that brushed the barrel of his AK-47 against sandstone—any of those would have meant death. And he was an adult, a soldier who'd gone through grueling training and survived countless missions, yet he still remembered the bowel-loosening moments when he thought he'd blown it, or that one of his teammates had. If some of those instances still lurked in uneasy corners of his mind, appeared in dreams, how much worse must it be for a three-year-old child who'd been loved and pampered, probably never knowing any real fear?

And when she emerged from hiding, it was to find she was the only survivor. Career soldiers cracked when that happened. They spent the rest of their lives asking themselves why *me*?

He stiffened at a faint noise from the hall. Bare feet brushing over floorboards. A door closing. Probably Trina using the bathroom, which meant she hadn't dropped off to sleep any better than he had. But there was a small chance it was Chloe who had crept out of bed. While on his shopping spree last weekend, Gabe had bought a plug-in night-light for the bathroom so she'd feel safe getting up in the night.

After he heard the toilet flush and the door open again, the pad of footsteps came back down the hall... and paused in front of his open bedroom door.

"Trina?" he said softly.

"I... Yes," she whispered. "I'm sorry, I didn't mean to wake you."

"You didn't. I was lying here thinking." He rolled onto his side and stretched out to turn on a lamp. "Come on in."

She hovered in the doorway, wearing boxer shorts and a tank top. All that uncovered skin seemed to glow in the diffused light. "I shouldn't. It's just..."

"You itch."

"Yes."

Tending to run hot, he'd pushed all his covers to one

side and had only the sheet pulled up to his waist. She wasn't the only one exposing a fair amount of bare skin.

"Why don't you go get the aloe vera?" he said reasonably.

Her head bobbed. The maple brown hair she so often wore in a ponytail or a twist at the nape of her neck or even French braids hung loose tonight, falling below her shoulders. Once she'd disappeared, his hands tightened into fists. He had to deliberately open and flex his fingers before she came back.

Relaxed, that was him. Not so easy to project, when he was horny as hell. In fact…he glanced down his body, grimaced, and bunched up the sheet. In the nick of time. Given that she'd said a clear "No," seeing his response to her could rightly offend her.

Trina entered into his bedroom, looking shy. "Thank you."

"No problem." He sat up, leaving enough room for her on the edge of the bed beside him. Lucky he'd taken to wearing flannel pajama pants because of his guests.

With another wary glance over her shoulder, she sat where he'd indicated and lifted the tank top, although not pulling it over her head.

Without comment, Gabe took the bottle and began spreading the goop. When he heard a small moan, his hand stilled and he had to swallow hard before continuing.

"What about lower?" he asked after a minute. "Or doesn't it itch?"

"I can reach that."

Well, hell.

"Chloe sleeping okay?"

Trina nodded, easing the tank top down before swiveling a little to look at him. "She conked right out."

"Are we back to square one with her?"

"You mean, will she talk in the morning? I think so. I hope so. Tonight she just…shut down."

"She told you a lot."

"I know. If only her mother had hidden."

"I was thinking the same. But reality is, something horrific blew up really fast and she was in a panic."

A shudder rattled Trina's body. "I know about that."

"Yeah, I guess you do." He didn't like thinking how close she'd come to dying. He knew without asking that, under pressure, saving Chloe had come well ahead of saving herself in Trina's head.

She sighed. "If she'd just tell us."

His "Yeah" came out gruff.

Her eyes searched his. "Do you think we should call Detective Risvold?"

"We just about have to, even though all she did was confirm what I'm sure the police suspected. I need to go out for groceries tomorrow, anyway. You can make me a list after breakfast."

"Yes. Okay." Her muscles tensed. "I should go to bed."

"Don't." Without a conscious decision, his hand closed around her wrist. It was an effort to keep the grip light, so she wouldn't feel trapped.

"But…we agreed."

"Did we?"

"Is this like benefits for the bodyguard gig?"

Stung, he released her hand. "You're right. Get to sleep."

After a hesitation, she stood. "I shouldn't have said that."

"It was as good as a slap in the face." He lay back

against the pillows, hoping he was doing impassive better than he feared. "But I set myself up for it."

"Can't I say I'm sorry?"

Last thing he wanted to hear. "Go to bed."

Something about the quiet talk and the night and the intimacy had apparently blasted his rightful hesitation where she was concerned. He'd really thought, if he put himself out there again... Stupid, and not like him. But whatever seethed in him because of Trina wasn't usual for him, either.

Clasping her hands in front of her, she said with dignity, "I can't have fun and then shrug you off."

She gave him ten or fifteen seconds before she nodded and left.

He turned off the lamp, pounded the mattress with a fist and thought a lot of things he shouldn't be.

FRIDAY, WHILE TRINA WORKED, Gabe continued his so-far unproductive investigation.

Driving a slow path through the Keifs' neighborhood, he scanned the monster of a house owned by their next-door neighbors. Along with the standard attached two-car garage, it also had a separate four-stall garage. His eyebrows lifted at the sight of a red BMW in the driveway. Someone had to be home. On his couple of other forays in the neighborhood, no one had answered the door at this place.

Gabe parked as inconspicuously as possible, tucked up beside an RV beneath a high roof that extended from the detached garage. The Sadler PD might be doing drive-bys, and he didn't want either his truck or the license plate on it to be noticed.

Now came the challenge. He'd found a couple of

neighbors happy to talk about the murdered family, not much caring who he was or what he represented. But he'd had a few doors closed firmly in his face, too, when he couldn't produce any convincing ID.

An attractive blonde he guessed to be around fifty came to the door.

He said apologetically, "I'm sorry to bother you, but I had some questions about the Keifs. I haven't caught anybody home here."

"What a horrible tragedy," she said without hesitation. "But I don't know what I can tell you. Jim and I already spoke to that detective."

"I'm only interested in the Keifs' routines." Gabe aimed for soothing. "People you might have seen in and out of their house."

"Well, no one suspicious! They entertained regularly, you know, and had the two darling children." Thinking about the kids noticeably hit her. "It's so hard to believe…"

When he told her he'd met Chloe and that she was doing well, the neighbor regained her poise and continued to chatter. Yes, she and her husband had gone to parties at the Keifs', and had entertained them here, too. Everybody liked them, she was sure.

Gabe showed her pictures he'd printed of Stearns and Pearson. Pearson, she recognized immediately.

"Well, they were partners, after all." Her forehead wrinkled. "Now that I think about it, I haven't seen them here in a while." But she shook off the thought. "Goodness, Ron and his wife may have been away! The other man…" She couldn't remember ever seeing him.

"The awful thing is," she confided, "I drove by their house that morning. I even glanced at it, I don't know why, you know the way you do if you see movement, but I must have been imagining it."

"Were there any unfamiliar cars in the driveway?"

"I don't know…" Her voice slowed. "I think maybe there was. That could have been what caught my eye." Appalled understanding spread on her face. "Oh, dear Lord. Why didn't it occur to me? That detective never asked."

THE WEEKEND HAD proved to be an oasis in the tension, Trina thought.

Right now, with the exception of the clop of the horses' hooves and the creak of leather, the stillness seemed absolute out here in the lodgepole and ponderosa forest. Sunlight penetrated pine branches in golden streams.

Feeling content for this short interval, Trina rode a dun mare that followed Gabe and Chloe on Mack. Although she felt sure that this mare came to life in a herd of cattle, right now Trina could have been on the kind of plodding horse used in trail rides for urban visitors experiencing the "Wild" West. Reins optional. In fact, she let hers hang loose.

Yesterday, Chloe had been…not mute, but definitely subdued. She'd perked up when Gabe took her for a ride around the paddock again. Today, apparently having judged Trina to be healed enough, he'd ridden to the ranch proper and returned with a saddled horse for her to ride.

She cocked her head when she heard Gabe and Chloe having a low-voiced conversation, but she couldn't make out what they were saying.

The next second, he urged Mack into a lope. The dun

Trina rode leaped to follow suit, startling her. She looked ahead anxiously. Did he know what he was doing? He'd been careful with Chloe so far, but—

Chloe's laugh floated behind her.

Smiling, Trina relaxed.

Gabe eased them to a walk again, and not ten minutes later, the cabin and barns came in sight through the trees.

He abruptly reined in Mack and gestured to Trina to be quiet. What... Then she, too, saw sunlight glint off the roof of a car parked in front of the cabin. One that had a rack of lights on top. A uniformed officer was coming down the steps from the front porch, his head turning as he scanned the outbuildings much as she'd seen Gabe do.

The mare started to shake her head, but Trina laid a hand on her neck to stop her before she blew out air.

After a minute, the man got back into the SUV, swung it around and drove back down the narrow lane.

Still watching it, Gabe asked, "Did you know him?"

"No."

Once the car was out of sight, they rode together to the barn. After dismounting, Trina reached for the mare's girth, but Gabe shook his head. "I'll take care of the horses. You and Chloe need to get inside."

Stress stole the relaxed pleasure of the outing. "But if anybody has been watching, they'll recognize you, too."

"Nobody will see me."

She took him at his word and led Chloe inside. She was sweating, and decided they smelled horsey. They both needed a shower, Trina decided.

Wet hair felt heavenly when she and Chloe went back downstairs to prepare lunch. Trina had cooked an enormous pile of potatoes and eggs earlier, and now she drew a stool up to the counter so Chloe could "help" her make a potato salad.

The back door opened and Gabe came in, hanging his Stetson on a hook just inside the door. His eyes met hers briefly. Then he said, "Let me go wash up," and walked through the kitchen. Footsteps on the stairs came a moment later.

Trina blinked and gazed down uncomprehendingly at the cutting board and her hand holding a paring knife. Sweaty men had never done it for her before, but, well, apparently there was an exception. As short as his hair was, she'd been able to see a line left by the hat. His angular face had gleamed, and she'd focused on droplets of sweat on his brown throat.

Oh, my.

She'd gotten a grip on herself *and* finished the salad by the time he returned, clearly having showered and changed to clean jeans and a T-shirt that fit snugly over powerful biceps and pecs.

She rolled her eyes at herself and starting slapping together sandwiches.

Just as they were sitting down, Gabe's phone rang. He pulled it from a pocket and answered. "Boyd," he said, probably as much for her sake as in greeting. Then he mostly listened, responding with occasional monosyllables.

Once he'd finished the conversation, she lifted her eyebrows inquiringly, but he gave his head a slight shake and asked Chloe how she'd liked the ride.

He was waiting in the kitchen after Trina settled the little girl in bed for her nap, a fan on a low setting stirring the hot bedroom air.

He'd opened his laptop again, but looked up the minute she appeared. "Boyd said he had a visitor. Sadler PD officer, following up on a vehicle he claimed had caused a minor accident and fled the scene."

"What? He lied?" Her surprise felt like naïveté, but as irritating as she found Detective Risvold, she had trouble believing the local police could be corrupt.

"Whoever sent him out here would have had to come up with a story that justified the time and bother."

Trina nodded doubtfully.

"Fortunately, the number he had was from a derelict vehicle abandoned here by a ranch hand moving on. Boyd assured the cop the guy had left last year. He showed him paperwork proving it, and said he'd have sworn that young cowboy had said he was going back to Montana where he'd grown up. He didn't mention that the kid had left his Blazer behind. Not much the cop could do."

"No." They were so lucky the officer hadn't been in pursuit of one of the other sets of license plates Gabe had borrowed.

"Another problem," he said, not giving her a chance to dwell on the last one. "Diane's youngest son was in a car accident last night. She left first thing this morning for Boise. She made Boyd promise to tell us how sorry she was to let us down."

Having really liked the older woman, Trina exclaimed, "Oh, no! Was it bad?"

"The accident? The boy's injuries aren't critical, Boyd says. Broken arm and nose, minor concussion." Gabe shrugged. "Kid's only twenty, though."

"And her baby. Of course she had to go."

"I guess so." He didn't sound convinced. "Boyd's looking for a replacement."

"We could take Chloe," Trina suggested tentatively. "Nobody even knows the day care is there."

"You so sure about that? If a cop came into the building and asked questions?"

That silenced her.

Was her stubborn insistence on going to work endangering the little girl who depended utterly on her? Trina hadn't been able to help asking herself the same thing often last week. But then she'd think about the children she'd be working with the following day, and would come to the same conclusion. Her first appointment tomorrow was with an eight-year-old girl who'd been savaged by a dog and was now facing multiple surgeries and living with scars. Terrified of any and all animals, she didn't want even her friends to see her. The mom had had to take a leave of absence from work because Ashley had screaming fits at the idea of returning to school.

Trina suddenly became aware of Gabe watching her, intensity in his blue eyes. "What are you thinking about?" he asked.

She told him.

He sighed.

GABE GLANCED IN the rearview mirror, seeing Chloe whispering to her stuffed unicorn, and therefore unlikely to pay attention to anything the adults said.

He made sure he had Trina's attention before saying in a low voice, "You know the plan. I want anyone watching to see you go in alone. Chloe and I will be up in a while. Day care is the last door on your hall, right?"

"Right."

He'd argued against bringing Chloe from the beginning. Once—*if*—she was spotted, he knew the killer

would make a move. Probably not armed gunmen as-
saulting the professional building, but he couldn't rule
even that out.

Trina did share his worries. The cop stopping by the
ranch yesterday had made the risks they were running
daily damn real, even to someone who'd been trying to
bury her head in the sand.

The trouble was, Chloe didn't want anything to do
with the replacement Boyd had found for Diane. The
woman—girl—had stopped by the ranch yesterday to
meet them. When Trina explained to Chloe that Diane
wouldn't be able to come the next day to stay with her,
but Kaylee would be here instead, Chloe shrank away.
Kaylee squatted down to her level and coaxed, talking
about how much fun they'd have. Chloe wasn't having
any of it.

She'd latched on to Trina's leg and refused to let go.
She didn't want to watch a movie, or play, or look at her
books. The rest of Sunday, she followed Trina everywhere she went, even waiting outside the bathroom door.

He had a suspicion she hadn't objected to Kaylee,
but rather to one more change. And she wasn't about
to give up.

First thing this morning, she'd started whimpering.
"I wanna go. Why can't I go?"

On about her twentieth teary repeat of "Don't leave
me. Please don't leave me," Gabe had relented, but he
remained on edge.

He'd tried reasoning with himself. If anyone was
watching for Trina, they'd see her go in. Why would
they hang around to notice some man bringing a child
in later? Between the psychologists and doctors with
offices in this building, kids came and went constantly.

Screw reason. If he'd been the hunter, he'd have eyes on this building all day, every day when Trina was at work. Front and back. He wouldn't let denim jeans, plain T-shirt and a kid-sized baseball cap fool him into thinking this particular child was a boy.

Trina had worried about the lack of a car seat, but since Chloe would then sit higher, she'd be a lot more visible using one. They couldn't afford that. In fact, as traffic became heavier, he said, "Okay, kiddo, time to lie down."

Chloe obligingly lay down sideways on the seat. This was a game to her.

Thank God, she didn't throw a fit when Trina got out in the back of her building. Instead, she waved bye-bye without apparent alarm. Gabe had no idea how a kid's mind worked, but he was thankful she considered him to be safe. Her trust actually gave him a little bump in the chest, but he wouldn't have admitted that to anyone.

He drove a winding route through town watching for a tail, but not identifying one. Finally, he parked several blocks from Trina's building, put on a black Stetson and got out. He'd come in disguise today, too: black dress slacks, a crisp white shirt and shiny black cowboy boots. A Western-cut jacket hid his gun. The Stetson would make it more difficult to get a good look at his features. Then, after nixing the purple unicorn, he carried what appeared to be a little boy casually along the sidewalk and walked right in the front door. Father bringing his kid to an appointment.

Well, he got Chloe to her day care safely. He even texted Trina to let her know.

His real fear was how they'd get her *out* unseen at the end of the day.

Good thing he had plans to keep him busy today.

CLOAK-AND-DAGGER STUFF was so not for her, Trina realized, as she clutched Chloe close and squeezed between bodies so that they'd be initially hidden when the elevator opened. She could get a look at anyone in the lobby and, if she saw something worrisome, maybe take some kind of evasive action. She'd made sure to get on an elevator with several other parents who'd also picked their kids up at the day care, plus one unknown woman carrying a baby, probably after a visit to the pediatrician on the same floor.

The elevator lurched and the doors opened. Her pulse raced, but nothing obvious leaped out at her, so she hustled toward the back exit that led into the parking lot.

Of course Gabe had been watching for her, because the black truck roared right up, only feet from the door. Some people looked annoyed, having to circle around it, but she jumped into the back seat with Chloe and said, "Go!" even as she was buckling the seat belt around the little girl.

As planned, she stayed in the back seat, keeping a hand on Chloe, who was once again lying down. Her own gaze roved anxiously, even as she saw that Gabe's flicked unceasingly from the road ahead to each mirror and back again.

He drove a different, meandering route through town each day. Usually, she sensed some relaxation, but today he seemed tense.

"Is everything okay?" she asked.

"I don't know."

That was it. *I don't know.* Her fear ratcheted up.

Eventually, he did turn onto the highway, driving fast. The landscape blurred. It felt as if he was accelerating.

Then, suddenly, he said, "Hell. This is an ambush. They're coming up behind, and someone is waiting up ahead for us."

Her teeth wanted to chatter, but she refused to surrender to that kind of cowardice. "What do we *do*?"

His lack of an immediate answer *was* an answer.

The locks snicked. Their speed climbed.

Chapter Eight

"You and Chloe stay down," Gabe said, keeping his voice level. "Do *not* raise your head for any reason. Do you hear me?"

"Yes."

He opened the glove compartment and removed his SIG Sauer. It fit comfortably in his hand.

Trina must have seen him, because she sounded shaken. "Isn't it likely this is the police?"

"No. If it was, they'd have had no reason not to turn on flashers and pull me over back in town. Aside from refusing to disclose Chloe's whereabouts, you and I have been cooperative. Stayed in touch, passed on what we'd learned."

"Yes. Oh, God. What are you going to do?"

"We'll see."

He couldn't lose focus enough to comfort her. A car had just sailed past going south. In seconds, it would be out of sight. Otherwise, the highway was empty in both directions but for the obviously powerful dark sedan closing the distance on his truck from behind—and the big black SUV that had been waiting on the shoulder ahead, but was now moving. To make a U-turn? No, it had pulled across the highway to form a barricade.

Son of a bitch. He'd almost called Boyd earlier and asked him to make the trip to town so they'd have an escort home. *My mistake*, he thought coldly.

The sedan was close enough that he could see it carried a driver and passenger. He'd count on at least two men in the SUV, too.

He'd begun slowing down, as if he didn't know how to handle this. Braking. The broadside SUV reared ahead.

"All right," he said harshly. "Down. Both of you on the floorboards."

Chloe's squeak of surprise came from behind him, but the click of the seat belt and rustlings let him know Trina was doing as he said. When he took a last, hasty look behind him, he saw that she was lying on top of Chloe. Using her own body to protect a child who didn't deserve any of the crap that was happening to her.

A man had stepped out of the SUV and was waving his arms, signaling Gabe to stop. Looked innocent enough…if the guy hadn't made the mistake of leaving his door open, allowing Gabe to see the rifle aimed right at him.

"Trina, I need you to memorize a license plate number." He didn't wait for any assent, reading off the one displayed on the sedan closing in on them.

He lowered the passenger-side window, waited until the SUV was no more than thirty feet ahead and the sedan was braking—and then slammed his foot down on the gas pedal while yanking the wheel sharply to swerve toward the far shoulder.

The man standing, exposed, leaped back, momentarily blocking any shot from the gunman.

Time slowed, as it always did for Gabe in combat. There was an almost surreal clarity. The tumbleweed and sagebrush land to each side of the highway could almost have been Iraq or Afghanistan.

Judging his moment, he took his first shot out the passenger window. Back tire.

Still coldly, without compunction, he fired at an angle into the windshield. Out of the corner of his eye, he saw a web form in the safety glass…and the gunman slumping to one side.

Then he accelerated, the left wheels off the pavement, tilting the truck. Metal screamed as he scraped the passenger side against the SUV bumper.

Same color paint jobs, he thought, in that strange way one did. In the clear, he braked briefly, long enough to take out another tire—and to ping a bullet off the sedan.

It rocked, swerved, the driver losing control. The left side crumpled as it came into hard contact with the bumper. But—hell!—it was still in pursuit.

Gabe had a head start, though, and he'd halved the enemy. Rocketing down the highway, he set his weapon down on his seat long enough to grab the phone and speed-dial.

"Got a problem," he told Boyd.

MINUTES LATER, THE SEDAN, built for speed in a way the truck wasn't, once again closed in on his bumper.

Two more minutes, he told himself. One…

His back windshield exploded and he heard a thump.

The hair on the back of his neck rising, he swerved, driving in an unpredictable zigzag pattern that would make it hard for a gunman in an also-moving vehicle to make an accurate shot. The big tires squealed. A bullet pinged off metal. Tailgate or fender. Son of a bitch. The Ford F-250 was almost brand-new.

Up ahead, another pickup truck waited on the shoulder. He was almost on top of it before he was able to see the man crouched low in the bed, rifle barrel resting on the tailgate. Just as he flew past, he heard the crack of the rifle. Once, twice, three times.

The sedan spun in the middle of the highway, skidded toward the embankment...and plunged over.

In seconds, Boyd's truck fell in behind Gabe's. The turnoff was several miles beyond. He took it carefully, slowed to a near crawl. A cloud of dust would have been a dead giveaway.

"You okay back there?"

"Yes." Trina was breathless but didn't sound panicky.

"You can get up now. We're almost home."

Home. The word felt like an unexpected speed bump. Despite his investment in the place, he'd never thought of the cabin or ranch as "home." But he didn't let himself dwell.

"Did I squish you?" he heard her ask Chloe. He didn't take in the response, but relaxed when he saw them both pop up and take their seats. Trina didn't even reach for the seat belts, obviously recognizing where they were.

Boyd stuck with him when he veered right at the Y, following him behind the cabin but giving him room to maneuver so he could back into the outbuilding, as always.

Gabe unlocked the doors, using the moment when Trina got out carrying Chloe to slip his gun into his waistband at his back. He tugged the white shirt out to disguise it and followed them.

Boyd was already waiting. Leon Cabrera hopped out of the bed, landing lightly on his feet. No sign of the rifle.

Trina smiled at them. "Thank you for...for coming."

She looked down at Chloe, resting her on one hip. "You remember Mr. Chaney, don't you?"

Chloe buried her face.

"Trina Marr, meet Leon Cabrera. He's another retired Ranger. I'm sure Joseph would remember him. I was lucky enough to talk Leon into coming to work here as our foreman."

Leon happened also to be a trained sniper as well as unflinching in action. Lucky he'd been readily available, although Boyd had tried as much as possible to hire people with a military background. Made the ranch damn near impregnable, although neither he nor Gabe had ever expected to have to defend their property.

"Come on in," Gabe said. "You've got time for a beer, don't you?"

"Sure." Boyd sounded as if this were a casual stop by to say hey.

Inside, Trina got out a tin of the cookies she'd baked and plopped it in the middle of the table, then poured milk for Chloe. The two left the room. The men didn't say much until they heard the TV come on in the living room.

Finally, Boyd said quietly, "Whoever this is has an army."

Trina returned to the kitchen and sank down in the fourth chair at the table. "Tell me what happened."

Realizing how blind and helpless she must have felt, Gabe gave her a quick summation.

She stared at him. "Did you kill anyone?"

"I don't think so." At this point, he wasn't sure he cared if he had, but he didn't say that. "I winged one of them. Shot out a couple of tires."

"That's what I did, too, Ms. Marr," Leon said. He managed to look boyishly guileless rather than deadly.

"Trina, please," she said with a tremulous smile. Then she looked at Gabe. "They shot at us."

"Yes, they did, and they weren't going for the tires." Thank God; it had been a miscalculation on their part. "In fact, I'm pretty sure we'll be able to dig a bullet out of one of the seats. It came through the back window but didn't make it to the windshield."

One of Boyd's eyebrows lifted. The bullet would be of limited value unless and until they had a rifle it could be matched with…but Gabe had become grimly determined to bring these scumbags down.

Trina blinked several times as she took in the hard reality that they'd been ambushed by men ready and willing to commit murder to get their hands on a little girl. She finally said, "They were trying to shoot *you*."

"Yep." Although he doubted they'd have quit shooting if they'd seen her.

"They knew Chloe was with us."

That hardly bore comment, since killing Chloe was the idea. Still, frustrated but not surprised that his efforts hadn't been enough, Gabe said, "They did. What's more, they must have seen me taking her inside this morning, otherwise there wouldn't have been time for them to set up."

"And they'd seen which way we went on the highway."

Also not a surprise.

Her gaze stayed fixed on him, as if she'd forgotten the other two men were there. "Do you think they know we're *here*?"

Gabe shook his head. "I've been damn careful not to turn off the highway when any other vehicle was in sight.

Twice, I've kept going when I saw another vehicle, even if it was barely a pinprick."

She nodded, having asked him about the first time he'd continued past the ranch road without even having slowed. He'd had to backtrack several miles on both occasions.

"If only the press hadn't found out about me."

"The fire drew a lot of attention," Gabe said gently. "Neighbors were eager to talk about how brave you were, how you saved the life of the little girl you were fostering. The Sadler PD may have trouble keeping secrets, but your name getting out there wasn't their fault."

Trina seemed to sag. "No. Of course not."

Boyd pushed back his chair and rose. "Let me get you something to drink. A beer?"

"Oh...no, thank you." She started to rise, too, but Gabe laid a hand over hers, stopping her. Her startled gaze met his again, and she subsided. "A pop would be great. No, wait. Milk. Milk and cookies, right?"

Boyd smiled, found the right cupboard, and soon brought her a glass of milk. "Beer and cookies work, too." He sat back down and studied the tin. "What kind are those, with the Hershey's Kiss on top?"

"Mint flavored. And those are peanut butter, and I guess the molasses are obvious. I think Gabe ate all the chocolate chip."

He smirked.

He was glad to see her nibbling on a cookie and drinking her milk. An adrenaline crash could do a number on a person. A boost to her blood sugar would help. As soon as the guys left, he'd offer to cook dinner tonight.

"The little girl," Boyd said. "Was she scared?"

Trina nodded. "She sort of...shrank. When bullets

started flying, I covered her ears, but...that had to have thrown her back to when her parents and brother were shot, don't you think? She looked glassy-eyed when I put her in front of the movie. I wouldn't have left her, except she did take a bite of her cookie, and I wanted to hear about everything I missed."

"I don't want her to be in the middle of any more violence." The roughness in Gabe's voice had the other three staring at him.

After a minute, Boyd asked matter-of-factly, "What's the plan for tomorrow?"

Gabe's teeth ground together in his effort to give her a chance to make the right decision before he had to force a heated confrontation.

"I can't go to work again." Trina sounded numb. "I shouldn't have insisted."

No, she shouldn't, but... "You had good reason," Gabe said.

"Thank you," she said softly, then jumped up. "I'll start getting dinner on."

He pushed back his chair, too. "Let me do that."

"No, I need to keep busy." She smiled at Boyd and Leon. "You two would be welcome to stay. I'm going to stir-fry, so it won't take long."

Both stood, as well. "Thank you," Boyd said, "but I'm sure Leon's wife expects him. My housekeeper probably already has dinner on, too."

"Oh. Well." This smile appeared brittle. "Another time."

"Sounds good." Boyd gave a slight nod toward the back door.

Gabe moved toward the door, too. "I'll be right back."

He had no trouble interpreting Trina's expression. She knew they wanted to talk out of her hearing.

Outside, dirt kicking up from every step, Boyd said, "Looked like your truck sustained some damage."

Gabe ground his teeth.

"I know someone over in Salem. I bet I can get him to come over and replace that window."

He sure couldn't replace it locally. If Boyd "knew" this guy and trusted him, he was undoubtedly also retired military. The scrapes and dents from bullets would have to stay for now. He counted his blessings that the idiots hadn't taken out a tire.

"They didn't know about me," he said thoughtfully. "If I didn't have plenty of experience with ambushes, their plan would have worked fine. They got flustered when I didn't stop like a good boy."

"None of them had any serious military training," Leon said.

"No," Gabe agreed, "and I doubt any of them were law enforcement, either. They do roadblocks themselves, would think better under pressure."

"Did you expect them to be cops?" Boyd asked, obviously surprised. "That detective is a nuisance, from the sound of it, but why would he go to these lengths when he could get a subpoena?"

"Because he isn't sure he can? Trina has probably appeared in front of most judges in these parts, her opinion respected. What judge is going to say, 'The woman is trying to protect this kid? Ridiculous! We've got to hurry on this. You go ahead and crack her open.'" He added as an aside, "She heard one of the detectives say that about Chloe. Risvold, especially, is trying hard not to see her as an individual. He wanted to know where Trina had 'stashed' Chloe."

Both the other men were shaking their heads. Leon, he knew, had two kids of his own.

Gabe decided not to say anything about what he'd learned from the Keifs' next-door neighbor last week. The information had been frustrating; the woman had almost certainly seen the killer's car but hadn't paid enough attention to give him much to work with.

It was a sedan, she knew that. Maybe a Lexus? Or a Genesis, or an Acura. It could have been a Cadillac, she'd added. He had later checked online, and could have added to that list. The contours of a number of the big luxury cars were similar, as were grills. "Sort of gray or silver" wasn't real helpful, either. What happened to the days when cars came in real colors?

Having reached Boyd's pickup, Gabe dismissed his frustration and contemplated the out-of-state license plate. "Doesn't look like they so much as tapped your truck."

Boyd laughed. "Not a chance." He sobered. "That gun of yours isn't traceable, is it?"

Gabe pretended indignation. "All those crime sprees I go on, how can I be sure? No. It won't be in any databases."

"Good, we're clear, then. You dig that bullet out and tuck it away." He opened his door. "Let's stay in close touch. Do you have Leon's number, in case I'm unavailable?"

Gabe didn't but entered it in his phone, after which he held out a hand to Leon. "Thanks."

"No problem." The two men shook, and Leon grinned. "A little adrenaline now and again is good for the heart."

Gabe laughed, even though he felt more sick than energized. He didn't go back into the cabin immediately, instead inspecting the damage to his truck.

If Trina had still been sitting up, the bullet that came through the back window might well have hit her in the head. Dead-on. He had a hard time tearing his gaze away from the hole in the front seat headrest.

No, he hadn't gotten any charge out of today's live-round exercise. Protecting Trina and Chloe wasn't a job anymore, or a favor to her brother. It was deeply personal.

Which meant that rage simmered—and he was afraid in a way he hadn't been since he was a boy.

TRINA WAITED UNTIL Chloe was asleep that evening to tell Gabe what little she'd learned today and find out what had happened with the surveillance on Russell Stearns, the fired vice president who'd worked under Michael Keif. Gabe was clearly bothered by Stearns, with good reason. Given how limited opportunities for an executive at his level were in the area, why had he stuck around after he got fired? Had he even interviewed elsewhere? What was he *doing* with his days?

They'd agreed, too, that between patients she should make some calls, find out what she could about Keif, his partner, Pearson, and Stearns.

As usual, they sat at the kitchen table, both with cups of coffee.

She went first. "I called the mother of a boy I worked with for almost a year. Vanessa's job is actually at city hall, in planning, but her husband is an engineer at O.R.E. I was pretty up-front with her, told her about Chloe being too freaked to tell us what she saw, and my worry that's because the 'bad man' is someone she knows."

"And?"

"She was more open than she should have been, really. Vanessa admitted her husband liked Chloe's dad but has problems with Ronald Pearson. Apparently, he pushes to get products out on the market before they've been perfected, and Vanessa's husband, Bob, thinks too many of the company's resources go to maintaining a fleet of trucks. He'd argued to Michael Keif that they should outsource shipping, concentrate on development and manufacturing. Oh, and he'd heard some of the gossip about Russell Stearns but didn't really know him."

She went on to tell him the rest of what she'd gleaned: a female county commissioner whose granddaughter was a current patient had hinted at her dislike of Pearson, calling him "bullish." She didn't think he did his research or had any interest in huge swaths of what the commissioners handled. She'd finished by saying, "He's serving on the board—and I use the word *serving* loosely—to protect his interests. And yes, Michael probably was, too, but he at least did his part. He said he was raising kids here, which made Granger County home." Grief tinged her tone. "I'm sorry he wasn't willing to do another term."

Gabe listened intently, his ability to concentrate without so much as fidgeting out of the ordinary and sometimes a little unsettling.

"None of that is very helpful." She made a face.

"I wouldn't say that. I wonder what 'interests' he's protecting. Is the company polluting? Doesn't seem like manufacturing electronic components would lead to that kind of problem, but you never know. Or is he concerned

O.R.E. might be expected to come through for additional traffic mitigation? Taxes? They're mostly state and federal." He seemed to shake himself. "Stearns played a round of golf this morning. I took some photos so I can try to identify the others in the foursome. He had lunch with a woman—" Gabe named the fanciest restaurant in Sadler "—escorted her to her car and then followed her out to O.R.E. She went into the executive offices on her own, never glanced back. Couldn't tell if she was pretending she didn't know him, or whether she hadn't realized he was behind her. He gave her a couple of minutes, then went into the office building, too, stayed for about an hour, strolled out looking unconcerned."

"They're really going to hire him back."

"Probably. But I wonder about the woman. I haven't had a chance to identify her yet, either. Is he seeing her because he thinks she can help his cause?"

"Hmm. I bet Vanessa could find out—"

"You don't have your phone, remember?"

She mumbled a swear word. Except for when she'd been at work, she hadn't had her phone for nearly two weeks, so why did the reminder make her feel so isolated now? So she'd lost some independence. It was temporary, and Joseph would probably be making the same decisions Gabe was.

Suck it up, she told herself.

"Are you going to call Detective Risvold tomorrow?" she asked. Gabe had already asked if they needed any groceries, so she knew he was planning a trip to Bend in the morning.

"I don't like it that Risvold was the one who talked to the Keifs' neighbor and apparently didn't ask if she'd been home, and if so, taken a look in the direction of their house around about the time of the murders. That feels off."

It felt "off" to her, too, but then she'd despised Risvold almost from their first meeting. That didn't mean he'd gone to the dark side.

"His style is brisk," she pointed out. "He might have assumed she'd be eager to tell him if she'd seen anything."

Gabe grimaced. "Yeah, okay. I'll call him."

Trina nodded, realizing that, for the first time in her life, she couldn't begin to identify everything she felt. Terror was easy—all she had to do was remember the fire—or, nice addition, lying nose down on the rubber mat on the floor behind Gabe's seat while the truck rocked violently, the back window dissolved and bullets pinged on metal. Intense gratitude was in the mix, as was resentment because she was having to depend so utterly on another person, when she'd taken care of herself for a long time.

But now, looking across the table at his hard face and the blue eyes that never wavered from her, she untangled another thread of her emotions. Trust. She didn't believe Gabe Decker would ever let her down.

And that made her wonder if what he'd said the one night—*You have to know I'm feeling things for you*—didn't have a lot deeper meaning than she'd read into it. It wasn't as if she'd expected him to tell her he was madly in love with her, not so soon. That awkward admission might have been his equivalent of passionate declaration.

Which meant maybe she ought to trust him in *every* way.

She took a deep breath, saw a flicker in his eyes and nerved herself to ask, "Will you kiss me?"

Chapter Nine

Trina had a bad feeling Gabe would think she was a flake. Yes, no, yes, no. Bungee cord bounces in the messages she had been sending.

But he didn't even hesitate. He exploded into motion, his chair clattering back, and he reached her in two strides. She expected to be grabbed, for him to take powerful, sensual control immediately.

Instead, he cupped her face in his broad palms and bent his head slowly. His gentle kiss came as a surprise. His mouth brushed hers. He nibbled a little. His tongue stroked the seam of her lips.

Through the fog in her head, Trina realized he was giving her time. Waiting for an answer.

What do you really want? Why did you change your mind?

She'd changed it because she didn't want to miss something amazing out of fear.

She pushed herself up on tiptoe, wrapped her arms around his neck and nipped his lower lip sharply.

A groan rumbled out of his chest, and yes, he took charge, because that's who he was. Didn't mean she couldn't kiss him back with everything in her. One of his hands gripped her hip while the other wrapped the back of her head so he could angle her to find the best fit.

And the fit was amazing. Perfect. His neck was thick and strong, his entire body powerful. That body was so close she could feel the vibration of his heartbeat. When he breathed, her nipples tightened.

The kiss went on and on, until the rest of the world might as well not have existed. He was everything. Trina heard odd sounds, and distantly knew they came from her. She wanted to climb his body, and was practically *en pointe* in her effort to get higher. She must have raised one of her legs, because he made a guttural sound, shifted so that he could grip both of her thighs and lifted her. She squeaked, wrapped her legs around his waist and held on.

Somehow he walked and kissed her at the same time. And they said men didn't multitask as well as women. Here was an exception. The way she felt, Trina wasn't sure she'd have cared if he *had* banged her into a wall or the staircase banister, but that never happened. At the foot of the stairs, though, he stopped. When his mouth left hers, she rubbed her cheek against his rough jaw, then did some experimental nibbling.

"Trina." That deep, dark voice felt as good as his hands on her.

She licked his neck, tasting soap and salt.

"Trina." This time he shook her.

Dazed, she tipped her head back to see a look of pure desperation on his face.

"Do you want this?"

Want this? She was on fire. No, bad analogy. Fire *hurt*. This was…hunger. An aching kind of pleasure. She tried to rub herself against him.

"To hell with it," he muttered, and started up the stairs. Once he stopped to kiss her, swore when they swayed and wrenched his mouth away. Reaching the top, he strode down the hall.

Trina felt a momentary jolt at the sight of the guest room door, standing open the requisite four inches. What if Chloe saw…? But Trina didn't hear anything from within. Or without. Gabe had the ability to walk silently, even carrying her. He got her through his bedroom doorway without a single bump. He must have nudged the door with his booted foot, because it closed quietly behind them.

Enough light from the hall reached into his bedroom for her to be able to see fierce need on his face, so far from his usual, carefully assumed lack of expression that her meltdown accelerated.

Beside the bed, he lowered her slowly to her feet. After sliding down his body, she wasn't so sure she could stand, but she managed. Lucky, because he used the opportunity to first rip the bedcoverings back and then strip her with astonishing speed.

"You, too," she whispered, and he paused long enough to let her pull his shirt over his head, baring that broad, muscular chest.

He knelt to take off her shoes and pull her jeans off. Trina braced herself by resting her hands on his shoulders. Except that wasn't enough. She kneaded, felt the ripples of reaction quiver through his strong body. And then he surged up, laid her back on the bed and planted a knee between her thighs.

He reached out a long arm and flicked on the bedside lamp. Trina blinked in the sudden light, not sure she liked being so exposed…except the look in his eyes was reverential.

"You're as beautiful as I thought you'd be," he murmured in the voice that reminded her of her first impression: the rumbling purr of a big cat.

"You are, too." She flattened her hands on his chest, then moved them in circles. The dark hair beneath her palms was surprisingly soft. He jerked when she found his small nipples. Swore when her hands stroked downward, following the line of hair to the waistband of his jeans.

When she lifted a hand to cover the hard ridge beneath the fly, he straightened away from her. "Damn. Give me a minute."

He had to sit on the side of the bed to remove his boots. She happily explored the contours of muscle on his back, flexing with his every movement. Socks went flying. He stood and shed jeans and shorts. And then, finally, he came down on top of her and went for her mouth again.

They discovered each other's tastes and textures. He sucked on her breasts until her hips rose and fell. The frustration of being able to feel him between her thighs drove her crazy.

Trina moaned and dug her fingernails into his sides. "Now. Please, now."

He swore some more, and for the first time displayed clumsiness as he fumbled for the drawer of his bedside stand and found some packets. He tore one with his teeth, covered himself and without an instant of hesitation, pressed into her.

She pushed herself up to meet him. Gabe muttered something under his breath, covered her mouth with his again and set a hard, fast rhythm that was exactly what she needed.

Not until she imploded and cried out did he let himself go.

IN THE AFTERMATH, Gabe didn't want to move. Ever again. But damn, he must be crushing her. Reluctantly, he rolled, taking her with him. She ended up with her head on his chest, her hand splayed over his heart and one leg draped over his.

Holy hell, he thought dazedly. He liked sex, missed it during intervals when it wasn't possible. But what he and Trina had just done? The equivalent of an explosion versus him stubbing his toe.

Of course, he knew why that was. He'd never before felt more than attraction and mild liking for a woman he took to bed. Trina was different. So many unfamiliar emotions churned in his chest, he envisioned those pictures he'd seen of hurricanes taken from the space station. The relentless force spinning, unstoppable by human hands. The layers upon layers that made up the monstrous power unleashed by nature. The still, quiet eye at the center.

He clenched his teeth together. Man, what was getting into him? This was ridiculous. Okay, he felt more for her than he'd ever let himself feel for any woman. After struggling to come up with a label for one component, he finally did. Tenderness. That was something he'd lived his entire life without.

The respect…that was what he had for his teammates. Men who had proved themselves, who had his unshakable trust.

He lifted his head from the mattress so he could see

her face, but he discovered hair that looked more than ever like melted caramel blocked his view.

Trina Marr, he thought, suddenly uneasy, could be trusted. She'd committed herself to Chloe, and would do anything for her. She wasn't the kid's mother, but she acted as if she was.

Except he, of all people, knew mothers weren't always trustworthy.

With no inner debate at all, he realized there wasn't any chance this woman had that flaw.

In fact, she was unnervingly like her brother in some respects. The steady gaze that saw deeper than he liked. The stubbornness, the courage, the determination that kept her going no matter what flew her way.

Damn. He was scaring himself. This thing with her couldn't go anywhere. He'd be back at Fort Benning in no time, training for the next operation in some hell-hole. She'd...fade in his memory. She had to, or he'd be in deep trouble.

She stirred, puffed out a breath that fluttered her hair and reached up to push it away from her face. "Wow," she mumbled.

A smile tugged at his mouth. He liked that he'd left her befuddled. It almost made up for his confusion.

He let his hand wander now, exploring the long, taut line of her back and the delicate string of vertebrae. All of her bones felt fine to him, almost fragile compared to his.

Hard not to remember how easily his had shattered. Hers...no. He wouldn't let anyone hurt her.

"How do you stay in such good shape?" Probably not the most romantic thing to have said, but he was curious.

Her nose scrunched up. "Gym. Self-torture."

He laughed. "You could find a sport you enjoy, you know."

"Oh, I have. I do. I love riding, and swimming is okay, but the most effective is the elliptical and the treadmill. I'd probably run outside, but around here it's either too hot or too miserably cold. Not much in between."

"Ever tried racquetball?"

"I don't like things flying at me."

They had something in common; Gabe definitely didn't like bullets flying at him.

He chuckled, rubbed his face against her head to feel the sleek silk of her hair and decided not to ruin a good moment by worrying. He could enjoy, couldn't he?

Except she sighed, a puff of air he felt on his chest, and said, "I should go back to my bed."

Gabe quit breathing, just held himself still. "Why?"

"Chloe will be scared if she wakes up to find herself alone."

"She's used to being alone in bed for a couple of hours before you join her." What was he arguing for? Her to stay the night? To keep this casual, it would be better if she didn't.

Trina was quiet for a minute. "Can I ask you something?"

Immediately wary, he said, "Is this a 'get in my head' question?"

"Well, kind of. No, more me wanting to know you."

Because of Joseph, he knew quite a bit about her childhood. The loving parents, the tight family. His past was a blank to her.

"You can ask," he said after a minute.

"Do you have family? People you stay in touch with, who worry about you?"

He didn't talk about this. But… Trina was different. Throat tight, he said, "No."

"I guess I knew that." She sounded sad.

Was he going to do this? "Never even knew who my father was," he said hoarsely. "My mother was an addict. She died when I was five. I barely remember her."

"I'm so sorry." She turned her head enough to press a kiss to his chest. "I don't suppose you were adopted."

"No." He hesitated. "A rancher took me on as a foster kid when I was fourteen. I stayed until I graduated from high school. He was a quiet guy. I thought he needed some extra labor. But…"

"But?" she prodded, when he didn't finish.

"He died when I was in my early twenties. Left me the ranch." Gabe stared up at the rafters. "It wasn't a huge place, but it had a year-round creek running through it. Two neighboring ranchers bid each other up, and I came out of it with enough money to let me pay for half of this place, when the chance came."

"You didn't expect anything from your foster father."

It wasn't a question; she knew. But he shook his head anyway. "No. I wish I'd known—" His throat seized up.

"That he loved you?"

Had he? Gabe still didn't know.

He felt something warm and…wet? She wasn't crying, was she? He touched her face to find she was.

"I haven't been a kid for a long time, Trina."

"But you intend to stay alone, don't you?"

A spasm seemed to close his throat completely, when he should be saying yes. Reminding her that this was recreational sex. But somehow he couldn't speak at all.

Which was fortunate, because for the first time in his life, he wasn't sure what he'd have said. What he thought was, *That's what I always figured.*

Past tense.

He was stunned to realize that the unexpected, unwelcome feelings he had for this woman had him in a tighter grip than he'd imagined. He wanted her to worry about him. He wanted to know she was waiting at home for him. And *this* felt like home: him, her, the ranch, his cabin…and Chloe.

In a panic, he stayed silent. Instead, he rolled on his side and kissed her, until neither of them could think about past or future. Only now.

TRINA WAS SOUND ASLEEP and really wanted to stay that way, but the mattress bobbed like a wave-tossed boat. She groaned, pried open her eyelids and found Chloe jumping on the bed about a foot from her.

"Go 'way," she mumbled.

"Uh-*uh*. Gabe says to tell you it's breakfast time."

Trina whimpered and buried her face. Chloe kept bouncing.

Well, at least she wasn't mute and sad. Why wasn't she, given yesterday's terrifying events?

Probably, Trina realized, because she hadn't really known what was happening. Chloe had to have heard the gunshots, though. Was there any chance they hadn't triggered panic because whoever killed her family had used a silencer?

Sad to say, Trina realized, she was definitely awake. "Okay, okay."

Once Chloe was satisfied that Trina was really getting up, she scampered away. A shower mostly finished the job. When she got out, though, she saw herself in the foggy mirror and froze. Grabbing the hand towel, she swiped at the glass and kept staring. There were an awful lot of…not bruises, but red spots. Probably from Gabe's stubble, she thought in chagrin. At the time, it had felt good.

So good, in fact, that her whole body tingled as she remembered their lovemaking.

Even the weight of his silence after her question didn't squelch the tingles.

Trust, she reminded herself. He had talked to her. And he hadn't said, *Yeah, I'm a loner.* His silence gave her hope she could change his mind.

And wasn't that typical female idiocy, believing she could change a man? But that wasn't it; she liked him, could even love him, exactly the way he was. If only…

She made a horrible face at herself in the mirror and got dressed.

When she went downstairs, Gabe gave her a hard, searching look that she returned with a feeble smile. Creases formed on his forehead.

She ate the pancakes he put in front of her, and produced a short grocery list for him when he reminded her that he was going shopping. Since he'd shopped Saturday, she didn't need anything, but it wouldn't hurt to have him pick up some fresh veggies, not to mention milk. They were going through an awful lot of it.

Chloe watched them. "You don't hafta work?"

Trina did a little better with this smile. "Nope. I'm taking a vacation."

The little girl brightened. "Can I ride Mack today?"

"Yep," Gabe promised. "Later. I have to do errands this morning."

"We could ride and then you could do errands," Chloe said slyly.

He laughed, came around the breakfast bar to swing her in the air. Depositing her back on the stool, he said, "Good try, but no."

"Well, poop."

He only laughed again, kissed Trina on the cheek and left, after extracting a renewed promise that they stay inside and not answer the door. Fingertips pressed to the exact spot on her cheek that he'd kissed, she watched as his truck passed the cabin, then turned toward the ranch proper rather than the highway.

He was on his way to borrow yet another pickup truck from a ranch hand, and presumably took along another of those burner phones he'd bought as if every man kept a selection on hand.

Because while he did intend to grocery-shop, he also planned to call Risvold.

Trina's skin felt too tight the whole time he was gone. What if someone came to the door? What would Detective Risvold say after Gabe told him about the ambush?

Would Gabe want her to spend most of the night in his bed again?

At six minutes past eleven o'clock, Trina saw the borrowed truck pass out on the ranch road. Not that she was watching or anything. But thank goodness, he'd only been gone two hours.

A few minutes later, he returned in his truck. She hovered in the kitchen, waiting for him. He walked in the back door laden with bags from a grocery store and Target, and glanced around. "Where's Chloe?"

"Living room. She loves those puzzles you bought."

His smile formed lines in his cheeks. "I noticed." He hefted one of the bags. "Four more."

After he plopped them down on the counter, Trina delved into the bag and saw, in delight, that his choices were perfect. The one on top was a unicorn. But, bless his heart, he'd also bought a puzzle with pirates, one with an animal alphabet and a barnyard puzzle.

"Thought we'd go for the dinosaur puzzle next time, and maybe the big trucks."

How could he possibly believe he shouldn't have a family, that he wouldn't make a wonderful father?

After thanking him, she asked, "Did you reach Detective Risvold?"

Gabe went to the refrigerator and grabbed a bottle of water before he pulled out a stool and half sat, one foot braced on the floor. "No, I talked to Detective Deperro instead. Risvold was out. Deperro seemed a little less… aggressive."

"I had the same impression. Did you tell him about the ambush?"

A glint in Gabe's eyes, he said, "I didn't share every detail, but yes. I said two vehicles, four men, tried a pincer move on us. They barricaded the highway, shot at us. I'd swear he was genuinely stunned, although he could have been playing me."

"Did you give him the license plate number?"

They'd talked about this before he left this morning. He had a friend who was a cop in Portland, and Gabe had intended to ask him to run the number.

Gabe's forehead furrowed, but he said, "I'm not sure I would have if it had been Risvold, but…yeah. Doesn't mean I won't tap my friend, too. We can call this a test. In fact, I'll call Alan this morning."

Trina told him her speculation that Chloe hadn't actually heard gunshots when her parents and brothers were killed.

"Not a silencer, a suppressor," Gabe said absently. "That's a good thought, although I'm not sure knowing one way or the other helps us identify the killer."

"Most normal people wouldn't have one. In fact, aren't they illegal or something?"

"Not in Oregon, although theoretically you have to get BATF approval to buy one." He paused, interpreted her expression accurately. "Bureau of Alcohol, Tobacco and Firearms."

"Oh." She frowned. "Do you have a permit for that handgun?"

"Don't need one in this state. For concealed carry, you do." His lips twitched. "I haven't bothered yet. I'm not spending that much time here, and until I met you, I didn't have any need to carry a weapon at all."

"Oh. I'm sorry."

"Don't be," he said brusquely. "Truth is, I was feeling pretty damn useless until you came along."

Trina blinked at that, and wasn't surprised when he turned his back to put groceries away. The conversation was over.

Her temper spiked. No, it wasn't. "What did Detective Deperro *say*?"

Gabe dumped several plastic bags with vegetables into the refrigerator and closed it before facing her again. "He wanted to know who I am. Swore he wasn't trying to track down you and Chloe."

She snorted, sounding an awful lot like his horse.

"He didn't say much, but his frustration came through loud and clear. I didn't get the feeling he's happy with how the investigation is going. Or not going. I asked about the random guy wandering through the neighborhood. He told me straight-out that they'd never taken that seriously."

"Then why did Risvold try to feed that crap to me?" she exclaimed.

"Because he didn't like the idea of you expecting information to go two ways?" Gabe suggested. He leaned against the counter and crossed his booted feet at the ankles. "I'm damn sure he didn't want you to know if they were looking at Pearson or anyone else close to the family."

"I've worked with children involved in a criminal investigation twice before. That detective trusted me enough to be frank. Of course, being a woman, she probably doesn't have the same territorial issues."

Gabe grinned, startling her into instant, intense awareness of him lounging there not three feet from her. Even with that big body ostensibly relaxed, she didn't make the mistake of believing she could catch him off guard. Nope, she'd seen a demonstration of how lightning fast his reflexes were.

"You might be right," he said, the smile lingering on his mouth. For a moment, they just looked at each other. Then he pushed himself away from the cabinet. "Hey. Come here."

She sneaked a peek toward the living room. "I should check on—"

"Can you hear her?"

"Hear?" She concentrated. He was right—Chloe was singing softly to herself. Trina smiled and stepped forward into his arms, which folded around her. Splaying her fingers on his chest, she said, "She'll be in here any minute demanding to ride your horsie, because you said 'later' and it *is* later."

He laughed, and nuzzled her cheek. "Sure, but she isn't here yet. And why waste an opportunity?"

He captured her mouth and made good use of their time.

Chapter Ten

Gabe decided to call his friend Portland police detective Alan Cullen before he did a single other thing. Fortunately, Alan returned Gabe's call within ten minutes.

"You're the last person I expected to hear from," he said. "I thought you were still in rehab at Fort Benning."

Sitting out on the front porch in an Adirondack chair, Gabe grimaced. Alan had been a good enough friend, he should have gotten in touch sometime in the last year. Loner that he was, he'd resisted even depending on Boyd. "I've been at the ranch for a couple of months. The damn rehab has dragged on."

"Then what's with the license plate number?"

Gabe gave him a synopsis of events, and even that took a few minutes. Voice changing as he shifted into cop-mode, Alan asked a few questions.

"Damn," he said at last. "Joseph Marr's sister. Lucky you were available. Although I suppose Joseph could have called Boyd instead."

Feeling instant resistance, even repugnance, Gabe ground his teeth before forcing himself to say, "I guess so." He'd seen the way Boyd looked at Trina the first time he and she had met. Hell. What if she and Boyd—

He shook off the possibility because it made him so angry.

"Okay, what's the license plate number?" Alan asked.

Gabe read it off.

"I can run it right—" The silence didn't last long. "Huh."

"What's that mean?"

"It's tagged. Belongs on a charcoal gray Audi RS7. Was it fast?"

"Oh, yeah."

"Six hundred and five horsepower engine." The remark was absent; it wasn't what Alan was really thinking about. "Registered owner is a guy named Craig Jarvis. He's ostensibly an importer, but the DEA has their suspicions about him."

Drug Enforcement Administration? Gabe felt as if a critical puzzle piece had been inserted. Dark corners were suddenly bathed in harsh white light.

"Does he live on this side of the mountains?" he asked.

"Yes, Bend." Alan paused. "You know central Oregon has become a hotbed of drug trafficking, don't you? Lots of small airfields, rural sheriffs' departments that don't have the manpower to monitor odd comings and goings. There are several drug task forces over there, although—" he paused "—it doesn't look like your county is included. Attention has focused on the major highways—I-5, of course, but also Interstate 84 and highways 97 and 20. You're not on any of those, but a county with so little population might be ideal for bringing drugs in from Mexico and Central America. Distribution could be tricky, though."

"I have a good idea how the drugs are getting distributed," Gabe said tightly. He told Alan what he was thinking, and how drug trafficking might well have led to the murders.

"You need to contact the Oregon HIDTA Investigative Support Center. They coordinate information for federal, state and local law enforcement within their counties."

"Granger County is outside their jurisdiction."

"You think they won't jump on this?"

"Maybe." Sometime during this conversation, he'd risen to his feet, too tense now to sit. He stood at the porch railing, looking at the dry forest surrounding his cabin. "I need to think about this. Tell me you don't have any obligation to contact anyone."

There was a short silence. "What's your hesitation?"

"First, why hasn't Sadler PD brought in some help?"

"You so sure they haven't?" Alan asked.

"Not positive," Gabe admitted with reluctance. "I did pass on the same license plate tag to one of the detectives. But damn it, there hasn't been so much as a hint that they're considering a drug trafficking angle. Even I'd begun to feel uneasy when several people mentioned the conflict at Open Range Electronics over whether they ought to maintain their own trucks versus shipping through other companies."

"What's your real problem?" That was like Alan—get to the point.

"Trina and Chloe," Gabe said without hesitation. "If either of us talks to any law enforcement agency, they're going to get right back to the investigators in Sadler. With my name. It would mean moving Trina and the girl, at the very least. I'm not letting them out of my sight. So then all three of us would be AWOL and hunted, and I'll tell you, Alan, I think Sadler PD has a leak."

"It wouldn't be a shock if a major trafficking organization had bought themselves a cop or two," his friend conceded. "But…hell. How are you going to handle it on your own?"

"Don't know yet. No, I realize we'll have to trust someone, sooner or later, but right now all I have is speculation. If those two detectives aren't wondering the same thing you and I are, then they're even more incompetent than I believed."

"I'll give you that." Alan gusted a sigh. "This is your call, not mine. But if I can do anything, I will, even if it's bailing you out of jail."

Gabe's grunt was almost a laugh. "What are friends for?"

"Keep me informed."

They left it at that. Gabe stayed where he was for a long while, even though Chloe must be bouncing off the walls with impatience for the promised horseback ride.

What if Michael Keif had somehow discovered that his company trucks were being used to transport illegal drugs? Drugs that might even be packed in O.R.E.-labeled boxes? Everything he'd worked for would be at risk of going down if even one truck was searched and the drugs were found. The feds would have descended like army airborne troops on a known terrorist hideout.

Pearson was the executive whose responsibilities included the trucking fleet. He was also the one who resisted suggestions that it was too expensive to maintain compared to alternatives.

Gabe also had to consider the possibility that someone lower on the org chart had set up a deal with traffickers. It didn't have to be Pearson.

Either way, Russell Stearns could have learned what

was going on, and wanted a slice of the pie. He might have felt confident that if Keif were out of the picture, he'd be asked to take his place—and would then be in a position to enrich himself by abetting, or at least turning a blind eye to, any and all illegal activities, for a payoff.

Damn, Gabe wished he trusted either of the two detectives. He'd had a better feeling about Deperro...but not enough to risk giving away Trina and Chloe's whereabouts.

Maybe Boyd knew of someone well-placed whom he trusted. Worth asking. Otherwise... Gabe gave his head a hard shake, trying to stir thoughts, worries, ideas, in hopes they'd resettle in a new arrangement.

They didn't.

His next step...

The front door opened behind him and a small voice said, "Can't we ride *now*?"

He gave a rueful smile. Keeping a promise came next.

TRINA ENJOYED TODAY'S RIDE even more than she had the other day. Gabe chose a different route, one that allowed them to ride side by side much of the time. They passed through several gates and pastures, cows and calves watching them from a distance. Apparently, he'd decided that since neither had been sore from the last ride, they were up to a longer one today.

They hadn't had a chance for him to tell her about the conversation with his cop friend. She'd worried when he first came back into the cabin with Chloe, though. The lines scored on his forehead looked permanent, and she'd swear the grooves in his cheeks hadn't been that deep before. But he had gradually relaxed after saddling the horses, lifting Chloe up and then swinging up behind her.

He proved willing to talk about the ranch, and even a little bit about his teenage years in Texas. "Hooked me on the life," he admitted. "I'd hate being trapped indoors every day, stuck behind a desk."

Trina learned this was an enormous operation, and Boyd and Gabe fully intended to expand it. Literally, since they were keeping an eye out for any land bordering theirs to go on the market, and also because both men were interested in breeding and training horses on a larger scale than they were currently doing.

"Boyd's waiting for you to retire?" she asked.

"Yeah." Gabe paused, perturbation momentarily reversing the relaxation she'd seen on his face. "No hurry, though."

This wasn't a man who'd let a mere injury stop him, she realized anew. That grim determination was to her benefit right now, hers and Chloe's, but it also meant he wouldn't let a hookup with some woman prevent him from returning to what really mattered to him.

Her trust that he might actually feel more for her than he wanted to admit dissipated into near nothingness.

"*I* want to be a horsie rancher," Chloe announced, proving she'd been listening. "'Cept, I've never seen a baby horse."

"They're called foals," he said, with a gentleness that always made Trina's heart feel as if it were developing fissures. "And since they're usually born in the spring, we have some right now. We can go look at the mares and foals tomorrow, if you want."

Planning happy activities laid a veneer over the reality that they were hiding out, waiting for… Trina hardly knew anymore. Chloe to tell them who had killed her daddy? Would they really be safe once that happened?

She realized they'd made a gradual circle and were nearing Gabe's cabin and barns again. Probably just as well; her thighs were starting to ache.

Today, Gabe let her unsaddle her borrowed mount and turn him out in the paddock. Still holding the bridle, Trina heard a distant buzz. Puzzled, she swiveled in place, trying to identify the source of the sound. It was a motor of some kind. An ATV, maybe? She knew that ranchers did sometimes use them in place of horses to herd cattle.

"Into the barn," Gabe said suddenly. *"Now."*

The sound was increasing in intensity and volume. Maybe it was the crack of his voice, maybe some subliminal fear, but she scooped up Chloe and ran. Gabe was right behind. In seconds, they reached the shadowy interior of the barn that had several stalls, hay storage above and a tack room.

He pulled the sliding door almost closed, leaving a three-inch gap to admit sunlight and give him a view out.

"It's a helicopter," Trina whispered, as if they might be overheard.

"It is." He stood where he could see out, his face set, his body still but the furthest thing from relaxed. This was the soldier, coiled to take action.

An unarmed soldier, she realized in sudden alarm. Trina clutched Chloe tight.

Gabe started to swear, not quite under his breath, but then he glanced at Chloe and clamped his mouth shut.

The sound of the whirling rotors became deafening. Chloe cried out and clapped her hands over her ears. Trina held her breath, as if she were a small animal caught in the open when the shadow of a falcon swept over her.

Gabe never moved, but she swore the band of light dimmed. Was the helicopter hovering right overhead? Or landing? Images from war movies flickered in her head. No wonder that sound had seemed so ominous.

And then the roar began to recede. Trina sagged, stepping back to allow herself to lean against the rough board wall of the tack room.

"Where's it going?" Her voice was too loud.

"The ranch center." He sounded remarkably normal. "Let's dash for the cabin."

Trina smiled for Chloe's benefit. "Okeydoke. That was noisy, wasn't it?"

Trembling, Chloe asked, "What was that?"

Halfway across the open ground, Gabe reached for Chloe and lifted her into his own arms. "It was a helicopter passing overhead. Have you ever seen one?"

Puckers appeared in the high, curved forehead. "I think so," she said uncertainly. "It landed on top of the hospital. Daddy—" her voice hitched "—said sometimes sick people ride in one 'stead of an ambulance."

"That's right." Gabe had the back door open and ushered Trina in. She heard the dead bolt *snick* behind them. "Helicopters are faster than ambulances. They fly right over stop signs and red lights."

Chloe decided then and there that she needed the bathroom. Trina hurried her to the one on this floor, then settled her with one of her new puzzles, promising lunch in a few minutes.

Just as she returned to the kitchen, Gabe's phone rang.

"Oh, yeah," he said, seconds into the call. "Did you get a look at it?"

Boyd, she realized. Unfortunately, Gabe's end of the conversation wasn't very illuminating.

He concluded the call and dropped the phone on the counter. Standing a few feet from her, he said, "The helicopter stampeded some cattle and horses. Boyd is seriously pissed. He grabbed binoculars but insists there were no visible markings. The windshield was tinted. Had to be private. I've seen the sheriff's department search and rescue helicopter. It's bigger than this one, white with green stripes and the department logo. Medic helicopters are conspicuously marked, too. I've sure never seen one locally that was black."

"Black seems sort of…" Trina searched for a word.

"Covert?"

"Well, yes."

"It definitely was. All aircraft are required to have what's called an 'N' number painted in a conspicuous place. There are rules about how tall the letters and numbers have to be. Boyd thinks the number must have been taped or painted over."

She was almost surprised to see that her hand was steady as she chopped hard-boiled eggs in preparation for making egg salad sandwiches. "So, does that mean they know we're here?" *They* were more frightening because they remained faceless, their numbers unknown. Bad enough when she'd thought there was a killer, singular.

Gabe touched her, his knuckles light on her cheek. She let herself lean into the touch, just for a minute.

"No," he said huskily. "Boyd made some calls. We know for sure the damn thing flew over several other ranches out here, at least. Could have been a dozen or more. Having it go over that low scared the crap out of a lot of cattle and horses. The sheriff's department and the FAA are getting some irate phone calls." He smiled slightly. "Boyd is joining them."

"Good!"

"Won't do any good, of course, when nobody can identify the damn thing. Whoever was flying it had to know there'd be an uproar. My guess is the helicopter will be grounded for a while."

"I wonder if O.R.E. has one for the executives."

"That's an excellent question." Gabe leaned against the cabinet. "I'll do some research. If they do, it has to be registered."

"This is my fault." She looked toward the kitchen window but was aware of it only as a bright rectangle. She'd already been brooding about this but had comforted herself that the men would have no way of narrowing their search. She'd been wrong. If Gabe had left his truck outside today, or had been returning from one of his expeditions, they'd have been located. "They know Chloe and I are hiding out near here because I insisted on going to work. It was so stupid." Shaking her head, she rinsed her hands, then stood with them dripping into the sink. She hated having to see his expression but finally turned her head. "You didn't have a gun out there. If they'd landed…"

His eyes were warm, nothing like she'd expected. Gripping her shoulders, he said, "Okay, one thing at a time. First, I've been keeping a rifle in the barn. If that damn thing had looked like it was settling on the ground, I'd have had the rifle in my hands. I didn't want to scare Chloe."

"Oh. Okay."

He drew her toward him, not seeming to care that the hands she flattened on his chest were still wet. She was vaguely surprised they didn't steam, given his body heat.

"Second," he said sternly, "yeah, they have a geographic fix on us because you and I were going back and forth to town. But we were doing that for good reason. Two reasons. You do good working with those kids, Trina. And something I didn't tell you. Risvold claimed if you didn't show up for work, he'd assume you'd skipped the area. He made some threats. No matter what, if I hadn't agreed that the risk was justified, I'd have said no."

Guilt morphed into annoyance, even though she should be glad he was accepting responsibility, too. "So I had no real say?"

"You had a say. My decision would have been final."

"Does the word *arrogant* ring any bells?"

He smiled slightly.

She was being absurd. This wasn't a battle of the sexes. It was survival.

"Will you show me where you keep that rifle?" she said steadily, stepping back. "In case…"

"Yes." Gabe frowned. "Damn, I should have already done that. Have you ever handled a gun?"

"Are you kidding? Joseph has done his best to prepare me for any of life's eventualities. Riots, earthquakes, muggers, zombies, you name it, I'm ready." But not a house fire, she thought. Not arson. And he hadn't covered the unit on evasive driving.

Leaning a hip against the cabinet, Gabe laughed, as she'd intended. "I don't suppose you target-practice?"

She wrinkled her nose. "I haven't in a while. Brother dear would disapprove if he knew how lax I've been. But I do know what I'm doing with a hunting rifle or a handgun."

"Good." Leaning forward, he brushed his lips over

hers, kissed her forehead and released her. "I hear the munchkin coming."

"Oh! I need to get these sandwiches made."

Quietly, he said, "I'll show you while she's napping."

Trina became aware of the tension between her shoulder blades and creeping up her neck. They wouldn't be making passionate love during Chloe's nap time, they'd be inspecting available armaments.

Because this was war, wasn't it?

GABE TOLD TRINA the combination to the gun safe, then had her handle the smallest handgun he owned, the one best suited to a woman, as well as a black hunting rifle. She loaded magazines and unloaded them. He'd have liked to have her do some shooting, but they couldn't afford for anyone to hear the barrage of gunfire, so he settled for satisfying himself that she appeared competent with a weapon in her hand.

Then, unhappy, he vowed to do his damnedest to be here 24/7 to protect her and Chloe. For all he knew, Trina had the skills of a sharpshooter, but he had a lot of trouble imagining her pinning a man in her sights and pulling the trigger. She was a woman of warmth and compassion, one who'd chosen to work with traumatized children. He suspected she would be able to pull that trigger if she believed it was the only way to save the little girl she so obviously loved. And then she'd have to live with what she'd done.

Gabe had killed often enough, he ought to be utterly hardened to the necessity and the aftermath. In one way, he was. He'd learned to compartmentalize, a term one of those damn therapists at the army hospital liked to throw around. It wasn't a bad description, he'd decided.

For the most part, he put those memories in a drawer rarely opened. He'd never discussed it with any of his friends and teammates, but he suspected they did the same, whatever imagery they used.

That didn't mean he didn't dream, wasn't blindsided on occasion by a memory of the face of a man just before he died—or *as* he died, which was worse. His drawer didn't seem to have a secure lock holding it closed.

If Trina had to shoot to kill, she'd be haunted by what she'd done for the rest of her life. She wasn't him. She saw the humanity in everyone, believed in the possibility of goodness.

The minute the gun safe was securely locked, he left her. He didn't let himself look back, even though he knew she watched him go. He could work out and still be close by if someone showed up. Slacking off the way he had been wasn't acceptable. Nothing had changed. He had a goal.

Once in the makeshift gym in the other half of the outbuilding where he parked his truck, Gabe warmed up, then did some squats and lunges while holding weights. He welcomed the burn of straining muscles and ignored the deeper, more ominous pain in his pelvis and thigh. He added ten pounds to the barbell, lay back on his weight bench and began a methodical series of presses, sweat stinging his eyes and soaking his shirt.

Finally, he let the barbell crash onto its stand and swore, long and viciously. His ability to focus had always been unshakable. So why couldn't he get Trina out of his head?

Chapter Eleven

Gabe had trouble looking away from Trina during dinner, even though he could tell he was making her uncomfortable. After his earlier brooding, he tried to understand his physical fascination with her. He studied every changing flicker of expression on her face, the tiny dimple that formed to the right of her mouth when she tried to suppress a smile, the rich depths of her eyes, the way light reflected off her hair. He liked that her ears stuck out a little bit, that her upper lip had a deep dip in the center.

Yeah, he'd gotten in over his head, all right.

He'd known beautiful, leggy, curvy women before, which meant that calling his obsession with Trina physical might not be right. It was definitely part of it, though. Man, he hoped she planned to join him in his bed tonight.

The way she chattered with Chloe, he wondered if she was feeling shy with him. Would he need to ask? Beg? His chest felt tight, his belly in a knot. The vegetarian chili she'd made was great, but he ate mechanically, his appetite not really there.

He hadn't lived with a woman and child since he was a kid himself. The proximity with Trina and yeah, the little girl, too, was doing a number on him. If anything, he disliked leaving them alone even more now, after the helicopter had damn near skimmed the peak of the cabin roof. If they'd been outside while he ran errands, he could have come home to find them gone. Just like that.

Or dead. One of those sons of bitches in the helicopter could have showered them with bullets, left them sprawled in the dirt.

Gabe suddenly realized the other two were staring at him, as if waiting for something. Had he noticeably shuddered? No, he knew better than that. He never gave away his emotions.

Trina or Chloe must have asked a question. He felt some warmth at the jut of his cheekbones.

"Sorry," he said. His voice came out a little husky. Shutting down the dark images he'd just seen wasn't easy. "My mind was wandering."

"I asked if you'd like more chili." Trina nodded at his empty bowl.

"Oh, uh, thanks. I don't think so. It'll make a great lunch tomorrow."

She nodded and smiled at Chloe. "Ready for a bath?"

"Yes!" The little girl scrambled off her chair. When she hit the floor, her shoes flashed with neon pink lights. Gabe had bought them for her, thinking she'd like them. He'd seen her dance, staring entranced at her feet until she tripped over them and went down, giggling.

"Okay, just let me at least get started on cleaning up—"

"Nope." Gabe pushed back his chair. "You cooked, I clean."

"You'll put the chili away?"

He raised an eyebrow. "Don't trust me?"

A strange, almost frightened expression crossed Trina's face. But then she bit her lip, met his eyes and said, "Of course I do."

Disturbed, he watched as she hustled Chloe out of the kitchen. Exactly what kind of trust had they been talking about there?

TRINA DIDN'T KNOW what had gotten into her. This was ridiculous. She and Gabe had had great sex. Why not have more of it? She'd known from the beginning that she'd be risking heartbreak, but would another night, even another week's worth of nights, leave her more wounded than she'd already be?

Probably not. An involuntary sigh escaped her as she sank down on the edge of the tub and started the water running, then poured in the fragrant liquid that immediately frothed into giant, iridescent bubbles.

"Where's my mermaid?" Chloe stared in dismay at the array of toys in the basket beside the tub. Her worry ratcheted up. "I want my mermaid!"

For a man who'd never had kids or, from the sound of it, a little sister, Gabe had flawless taste in toys and clothes. Chloe loved everything he'd bought her. Trina might have suggested going for somewhat less girly, but then he'd brought the barnyard and alphabet puzzles. Before their ride this morning, he'd said in a low voice, "Do you think she'd like cowboy boots?"

Trina had rolled her eyes and said, "Is pink her favorite color?"

He'd laughed, the wonderful, deep rumble that had begun to sound less rusty than it had when they first came here.

Oh, heavens—were there such a thing as pink cowboy boots? Of course there were.

Trina delved in the basket, spotted a bit of yellow—why did mermaids never have plain brown hair?—and plucked out the rubber mermaid. "Voilà!"

Chloe seized her toy and stood obediently still while Trina peeled off her sweatshirt and pink overalls. Lifting them, Trina took a whiff. "Do I smell horse?"

The three-year-old giggled again. "I rode Mack today!"

"So you did. Hmm. Do you think I smell horsie?"

Chloe leaned toward her and sniffed ostentatiously. "Uh-huh."

"I bet Gabe does, too." Trina wondered if he'd shower before he went to bed, or wait until morning. She might discourage him. Horse was a nice addition to essence of man.

Chloe climbed into the tub and played contentedly while Trina watched her and tried to figure out what she could do or say to persuade her to talk about what she'd seen when her father was killed in front of her hideout.

What if, after all this, she said she'd seen a man, but she didn't know him? Maybe offered a vague description of brown hair that wasn't *almost* black like her daddy's, except, well, she couldn't really remember?

Except… Trina didn't believe that's what would happen.

Hearing a murmur of voices, Trina tensed, then realized Gabe must have turned on the TV. To watch the local news, undoubtedly. She made a habit of diverting Chloe so he could watch. The last thing they wanted was for her to see a recap of the awful crime that remained unsolved and had people in Sadler double-checking the locks on their doors.

Maybe Detective Risvold was right, and she should be

pushing this child harder than she had been. Her instincts said no, but... Chloe had bounced back remarkably well, was exceptionally verbal for her age and seemed to have emerged from the shadow of fear.

Tomorrow, Trina decided. She'd come right out and ask. Did you see who hurt your daddy?

GABE FROWNED AT the television, entirely missing the by-play between the local news anchors. The pain that arced from one hip to the other told him he'd pushed too hard today in his workout. The last time he'd seen the physical therapist, the guy had lectured him.

"Some pain is productive, Gabe, but not all. You can do damage if you don't listen to what your body tells you."

He was damned if he'd listen. Because what his body was telling him was unacceptable. He'd worked through pain plenty of times before, and he would again this time.

A segment on the news caught his attention. A car had been turned into an accordion by a telephone pole. No way anybody in that vehicle had survived.

"Police don't yet know whether alcohol or drugs played a part in this tragedy," the reporter on scene told them earnestly. The flashing lights on police cars gave an eerie look to the backdrop. She gestured toward the torn hunk of metal that hardly resembled a car anymore. "It seems likely the driver far exceeded the speed limit, perhaps reaching eighty to a hundred miles an hour. As you can see—" the camera panned to the empty highway "—the road does curve here, which may explain why the driver lost control."

Gabe would have felt more pity if he hadn't thought how lucky it was that the dead man hadn't hit another car when he was flying down the highway. At least he hadn't killed anyone else.

Nothing else of interest came up. He paid attention to the weather report, but it held no surprises. He turned off the TV just as Trina hesitated at the foot of the stairs.

"Come and sit with me," he said.

She did, settling down on the sofa within the circle of his arm. Relieved, he bent his head to nibble on the rim of her ear. "Something's bothering you tonight."

"Oh… I guess I'm just frustrated." She told him what she'd been thinking, about pushing Chloe harder.

Gabe couldn't disagree, even as he felt reluctance he didn't understand. He wanted the two to be safe…but once an arrest was made, they wouldn't need to stay with him. His bodyguard stint would be done.

Or would it? Troubled, he thought about how ruthless drug trafficking organizations tended to be. Even if the killer was arrested, the trial wouldn't happen for months to years. What about the men who'd tried to shoot Gabe and his passengers out on the highway? He doubted the killer had been in that helicopter, either. Would those men ever be identified? There was some serious money behind this hunt for the little girl who could put away a man willing to murder to protect his illicit profits.

Assuming, he reminded himself, that the trafficking theory was accurate.

"What are you thinking?" Trina asked.

"If these are drug traffickers, I'm concerned that arresting the one man Chloe saw won't be enough."

He was sorry he'd said anything when he saw her face…and when his own thoughts took him to a logical conclusion.

He made sure he held Trina's gaze when he said, "I

take that back. If we're right that Pearson, Stearns or anyone else at Open Range is involved in transporting drugs, the traffickers will fold up their tent and find another way to move the drugs to markets. Right now they're trying to protect the guy who was useful because he'd developed a slick operation that may have been working for a long time. Who knows? Maybe even years. But reality is, once he goes down, the DEA will be all over O.R.E. The traffickers may already be trying to erase any footprint they've left there, just in case. If Chloe speaks out and can identify her father's killer, it's all over."

Trina's body jerked. "Maybe I should go wake her up and demand answers right this minute. Take her by surprise."

Gabe turned enough to wrap both arms around her. "You'd scare her. That wouldn't be a good start, and you know it."

She closed her eyes and let her head fall against his head. "I know. I keep thinking about this, though. If she'd seen a stranger, I'll bet Chloe would be able to tell us. She's talked about some really scary stuff."

"I think you're right," Gabe said. "On some level, she's torn. Whoever she saw, he's been around enough that she can't make herself believe—or accept—that he would hurt her daddy."

"Or she."

He inclined his head. "I may go back and talk to the neighbor who's attended parties at the Keifs' before. Who from O.R.E. was a regular at that house?" He remembered the woman saying that Ron Pearson had been at one time—but not recently.

Trina stirred. "Given that Michael fired him, probably not Russell Stearns."

Gabe made an acknowledging noise in his throat, even as he wasn't thinking as sharply as he'd like. His hands had started roving, and he wanted to kiss her instead of continuing to talk. Would Trina be offended if he silenced her with his mouth?

With a small cry, she turned in his arms, pushed herself up so she was kneeling and pressed her mouth to his.

Urgency rose in him, hot and fast. He felt the sting of her teeth on his lip, and returned the favor. He gripped her butt and lifted her to straddle him. When she whimpered, he found her breast and kneaded. Damn, he was ready. It was like body-surfing a tsunami. Too powerful to be denied. Resenting any delay, he found himself struggling with the button and zipper on her chinos. He could free himself in seconds, but he had to get her out of her pants...

With a raw sound, Gabe ripped his mouth away from hers. "Chloe would see us if she came to the top of the stairs."

Those haunting eyes dazed, Trina blinked. Comprehension appeared slowly. "Oh, no."

"We have to make it upstairs."

She sat back on his thighs and traced the ridge under his zipper with one hand. "Think you can make it?"

When he snarled, she laughed.

"You'll pay for that," he muttered, rising with her clasped in his arms.

Her legs locked around his hips. "That sounds like fun."

He kissed her and, somehow, strode toward the stairs at the same time. If there was any buried pain left from his brutal workout, he didn't feel it.

EARLY THE NEXT AFTERNOON, Trina sat at the kitchen table rather than in the living room. She'd just put Chloe down for her nap and didn't want her voice drifting up the stairs to wake her.

Gabe had given her one of his burner phones, deciding it would be safe for her to make some calls with it, so long as she didn't contact the detectives. "Or," he'd added sternly, "anyone else who might possibly feel obligated to call them."

She knew he was restless. He wanted to be out there investigating in person, rather than from a distance. Prowling the trucking division of O.R.E., for example, or interviewing the woman who'd lunched with Russell Stearns. He had succeeded in identifying her from a photo on the company website. Julie Emmer, thirty-five, blonde and buxom, worked in accounting, a position that suggested the possibility she was using her creativity to disguise costs and income that the IRS, among others, might question. Trina had pointed out that Julie wasn't in a position to have masterminded illegal use of the trucks. If Michael had suspected she was up to anything, why would he have hesitated to confront her, fire her—and call the cops?

Gabe hadn't disagreed. "When the feds step in, they're going to find a nest of vipers," he said. "No one man—or woman—is making this happen."

When he'd started pacing that morning, Trina suggested he borrow yet another vehicle and go do some detecting.

"We can't keep on this way, doing nothing but waiting," she'd exclaimed in frustration.

He'd scowled. "I don't see you leaning on Chloe yet."

"I just…had second thoughts." After last night's vehemence, she was embarrassed to have backpedaled today. "But when I see the right moment, I will."

"We've done more than wait," he argued. "I'd say we've made significant progress. Anyway, detectives spend most of their time on the phone and computer, not busting down doors or slamming suspects into walls."

Trina rolled her eyes. "At the very least, maybe you should talk to one of our favorite detectives again. You could tell him what you suspect. They might be willing to open up to you."

His scowl deepened. "I'm not leaving you alone."

Two hours later, he produced the phone. "Let me know the minute you're done. I'll destroy it."

She knew he'd talked to Boyd this morning, too. Boyd had been willing to be Gabe's legs on this, but they shared the concern that either could unintentionally lead the cops, if not the bad guys, right to the ranch.

Trina decided to call Vanessa again to ask about the helicopter. Gabe had determined online that the company did own two for the use of executives. He'd been unable to find a photo or description.

"The helicopters?" Vanessa sounded momentarily surprised. "Does this have anything to do about the one buzzing ranches?"

"I'm probably freaking about nothing, but when I saw the uproar on the morning news, I had to wonder if it could have anything to do with Chloe. You know why I'm worrying."

"I'll check with Bob and get back to you," the other woman said without questioning her further. "Oh, speaking of the news. Did you see anything about the guy who died when his car smashed into a telephone pole? He'd been a truck driver for O.R.E., and had quit his job that day. They're talking suicide."

"Really? There wasn't much of an update this morning."

"Online, there is. I saw his supervisor being interviewed by a reporter with News Channel 21," Vanessa informed her. "The supervisor tried to sound sorrowful, although I couldn't tell if it was genuine. He claimed Glenn Freeman had had an apparent breakdown, storming into the offices, talking wildly, threatening to kill himself and quitting. He acted like he was either drunk or stoned on something. The supervisor insisted he'd called Freeman's wife to express his concern. It was such a tragedy that the man took his own life before he could get help."

"Wow. I saw a mention of his death but not where he worked." Coincidence, anyone? "What did the wife have to say?"

"She was outraged. Glenn had been angry about something the previous evening, but he wasn't a heavy drinker and certainly didn't do drugs. She didn't believe for a minute that he'd have killed himself. Of course, spouses always do say that."

"True. It's interesting, though."

That was big enough news that Trina ventured out to find Gabe. Apparently, Boyd had produced the mysterious somebody who'd arrived this morning to replace the shattered window in Gabe's truck.

The two stood out by a white pickup talking. Boyd caught a glimpse of her coming out the back door and made a quick gesture. She retreated inside before the other man could see her.

She heard the sound of an engine, and Gabe followed her into the kitchen a minute later.

"Wasn't he supposed to see me?" she asked.

"I'm sure he's a good guy, but there's no point in taking chances."

Fine. "I just learned about something I thought you should know." She took a soda from the refrigerator and popped it open as she reminded him who Vanessa was, then asked if he'd read or seen anything about the high-speed car accident.

His attention sharpened. "I did last night, yeah."

"Well, Vanessa says he worked as a truck driver for O.R.E. The supervisor says he threw a scene when he quit, like he was drunk or on drugs. Now there's speculation that he drove himself into a telephone pole on his way home."

"That could be convenient for somebody."

"Apparently, the wife says he wasn't a heavy drinker, didn't use drugs and wasn't suicidal. She claimed he'd been upset or mad about something the evening before."

"Damn. I'd like to talk to her."

"Surely she'll tell the police if she knows anything. Plus, won't his car be examined to be sure it hadn't been tampered with?"

"It was destroyed. A mechanic might have trouble so much as finding a brake line."

"But why would he have been driving so fast?"

"I can think of a good reason," Gabe said softly.

Her breath caught. "Someone was in pursuit." She remembered the high speeds Gabe had reached, before he realized the enemy was in front of them as well as behind.

"Makes sense, doesn't it? Given whatever he likely

spilled when he came in to quit, they couldn't afford to let him even make a phone call."

The poor man. Or maybe she should save her pity. It was possible he'd been knowingly transporting illegal drugs but made his employers mad by demanding more money, and even been foolish enough to try to blackmail a dangerous organization.

Her phone rang. Surprised, she saw that the caller was Vanessa. She mouthed the name to Gabe, who nodded.

"I made an excuse to call Bob," the other woman said, without preamble. "I mentioned what I saw about a helicopter flying low over local ranches and stampeding cattle, and he said the pilot must have been crazy to fly that low. I wondered where the helicopter could have come from, and he said, well, not from O.R.E. He's used company helicopters a couple of times to get to meetings in Portland. Theirs are white with the logo covering both sides."

Trina had seen the logo plenty of times. It had what looked like a Texas longhorn bursting through a circle. "Um…he didn't get curious about your interest?"

"No, he kind of volunteered the information. Besides the search and rescue and medic helicopters, the only other one he knew of belongs to the company that takes tourists sightseeing. You've seen it, haven't you?"

"I'd forgotten, but yes. It was painted bright orange, as I recall."

"Really garish," Vanessa agreed. "Listen, if there's anything else I can help with…"

They ended up leaving it at that. Once Gabe trashed this phone, Vanessa would have no way to reach her again. Of course, Trina hadn't told her that.

Setting the phone on the table, Trina said, "It has to be about O.R.E., doesn't it?"

"It's looking that way." His blue eyes never left her face. "You know what you have to do, Trina."

"Can we go see the foals first?" she begged. "Once she wakes up?"

He'd made excuses not to ride this morning. Out of Chloe's hearing, he said, "They're zeroing in on us. I'm reluctant to take you and Chloe out where you'd be exposed."

Now she thought, *Open range*. There was an irony.

After a moment he nodded. "I did offer. But…do you really expect her to be that traumatized by a few questions?"

"You saw her last time."

"I did, but she was downright perky by the time she'd had breakfast the next morning."

Trina slumped. "I'm a coward. I don't even know why! I work every day with kids and adults like her. I know we won't get anywhere until they tell me what's at the heart of their fear or depression. When they finally do, it's a cleansing hurt. It will be for Chloe, too. Even so—" She couldn't finish.

Gabe reached across the table to enclose her hand in his much larger one. "Sure you know why," he said, voice deep and comforting.

Her vision a little blurry, she tried to smile. "I love her."

"It makes all the difference."

A hard squeeze in her chest made her wonder. How did he know that, if he'd never let himself love anyone?

Was there any chance at all that *she'd* made a difference?

Chapter Twelve

Cross-legged on the sofa in the living room, Trina faced a child who sat with her head hanging. Chloe had been so joyful since seeing the dams and foals, helping hand out carrots and even touching the soft, inquisitive lips of a nearly snow-white foal. With just a few words, Trina had erased all that happiness. And yet how could she back off?

"Chloe, this is really important." For all that she was trying for her usual warmth and calm, urgency leaked through. "You saw somebody with your dad that morning, didn't you? The police don't know who hurt your mom and dad and brother."

Chloe sneaked a desperate peek at her before ducking her head again.

"We won't be able to go home until you tell me."

Right. Guilt would help.

Regretful, Trina cupped the little girl's chin, nudging it upward. "Honey?"

Suddenly, Chloe threw herself backward. "I don't got a home!" she screamed, rolled off the couch and ran.

She wouldn't go outside by herself, would she? Adrenaline flooding her, Trina leaped up, too. Chloe had raced into the kitchen. The sound of a scraping at the back door electrified Trina. She came in sight just in time to see Gabe coming into the house, and scooping up Chloe, who'd aimed for the opening.

His alarmed gaze met Trina's. He didn't have to ask what had happened, because he knew what she intended when she led Chloe to the living room.

"Hey." He bounced her in his arms. "Hey. It's okay. It's okay."

Trina got a heart-stopping glimpse of Chloe's face, wet with tears…even as not a single sound escaped her lips.

Déjà vu.

GABE WOULD HAVE SWORN the kid had shrunk, and she'd already been tiny enough. She sat at the kitchen table only because Trina had plunked her down on her chair. She might as well have been a rag doll. She hadn't so much as glanced at the macaroni and cheese on the plate in front of her.

"Please, will you eat?" Trina begged. "It's your favorite food."

They all knew that. Earlier, she had promised to make Chloe's favorite dinner. She'd served peas tonight, too, another favorite.

And damn it, Gabe was hungry, and he liked macaroni and cheese, too, especially Trina's homemade version, but eating when Chloe looked so woeful didn't feel right. Trina hadn't taken more than a few bites, either.

Finally, she sighed. "If I dish up some ice cream, will you eat that?"

There wasn't a twitch to acknowledge her.

As protective as he felt for both of them, this was killing him. The little girl, shoved back into silence. The misery on Trina's face. She shouldn't have to shoulder responsibility for something they'd agreed needed to be done. Should he have joined her when she tried to get Chloe to open up? Maybe his presence would have reassured the scared child.

Or not.

He thought some nasty swear words. Now what? A bath? Would Chloe just sit in the water, instead of splashing happily the way she usually did? Would she sleep tonight, or huddle in darkness, feeling as if she were back in that cupboard waiting for her mommy to say it was okay to come out?

He cleared his throat. "Hey, munchkin. I need to give Mack some grain. Would you like to come out with me while Trina dishes up ice cream for all of us? Oats are Mack's idea of dessert, you know."

Chloe shook her head without looking at him.

Well, at least she was present. Gabe lifted a shoulder to say, *I tried.*

"You know what?" asked Trina, trying for false cheer. "I'm going to put your mac and cheese back, since you didn't touch it. There'll be plenty for us to have for lunch tomorrow."

"I wouldn't mind that ice cream," he said. "I bought chocolate mint, didn't I?"

Chloe pushed her lower lip out a fraction, just to be sure he didn't think he could soften her up. A hint of amusement lifted the weight in his chest by an ounce or two. He admired stubbornness.

Gabe rose to dish up the ice cream while Trina cleared the table, covered the casserole dish and put it in the fridge. When they passed each other, he kissed her on her cheek. "I predict a recovery by morning," he murmured.

Hope and doubt mixed on her face. "You think…?"

"She's going to be really hungry." He raised his voice. "Shall I dish some up for you, Chloe? Nope? Okay."

The kid held out and didn't watch the two adults eat their ice cream, but he had no doubt she was aware of every delicious, chilly bite going into their mouths. Once Trina held out a spoonful.

"Want a taste?"

Chloe crossed her arms and turned her face away.

Relief was beginning to loosen his unhappiness. He'd have called this a sulk, if Chloe's earlier panic and grief hadn't been obviously genuine. Nevertheless, he suspected that he and Trina were now being punished.

Sad to say, he thought ruefully, her attempt was working.

Twenty minutes later, Trina gave up and put on a movie for Chloe, then came back to the kitchen. "I can't believe I blew it so badly!"

Gabe wrapped her in a comforting embrace and kept his voice low. "You keep saying that, but I don't know why. Maybe she's not ready to talk. That doesn't make asking questions wrong."

"It's the way I did it. I let my frustration get to me. I know better. I do."

Feeling a smile growing on his face, Gabe said, "Hadn't occurred to me before, but I think I used the same technique Chloe did to get rid of those damn therapists at the hospital that kept trying to make me open up about my feelings."

Trina pushed back from him. "You became catatonic?"

"No, I got sullen."

"Did it work?"

"Absolutely." Somewhere, he found a grin, even though the subject had been a sore one and this day had sucked. "I wasn't real enthusiastic about you, you know, once Joseph told me what you did for a living."

"I did notice," she said tartly.

"Although—" his smile faded and he found himself looking into her eyes "—somehow you've gotten a lot further than any of them did."

"Really?" It was a whisper.

"Really." He cleared his throat for the second time this evening, and for the same reason. Emotions trying to choke him. What was he going to do about her?

"I might have wanted to get into your head," she said, still so quietly he barely heard her, "but I've never tried to offer therapy."

"Do you think I need it?"

She frowned but shook her head. "No. And certainly never from me."

It felt like a promise. An important one. Gabe thought about saying something but finally settled for a nod. Trina gave him a shaky smile and retreated.

"I hate to say this, but I think I should stay with her tonight. I don't like the idea of her being alone."

He didn't want to be alone, either, but he was a lot less fragile than Chloe, so he nodded.

When Trina took Chloe upstairs for her bath a few minutes later, he didn't follow, even though he wanted to. He liked listening to Chloe playing in the tub, Trina teasing her. More often than he'd want Trina to know, he stood in the hall and listened to her read picture books and fairy tales aloud, taking on the voices of characters. He'd have liked to see the expressions on her face, too.

If he'd gone in to join them, would she have felt too silly to squeak and rumble and whisper?

Tonight, it felt damn lonely down here.

USUALLY, CHLOE WAS a snuggler. Even sound asleep, she made her way across the bed when Trina got into it. Maybe she was only drawn to warmth, Trina didn't know.

Tonight, Chloe had curled up on her side facing the window. When Trina gently rubbed her back beneath the covers, she'd subtly arched away, reminding Trina of how a cat shrank from a touch.

"I'm sorry," Trina whispered. "I know I got really pushy today. I wish I could see what you saw, and never have to ask you." She waited, hoping Chloe would do or say something, but the small lump didn't move. "While you're falling asleep," she murmured, "think about the horses. Wasn't that foal beautiful? You heard Gabe say he'll end up dappled and gray the way his mommy is, but that's beautiful, too. I think the foal was curious, because you were small like him."

Closing her eyes but knowing sleep would be slow coming, Trina saw Gabe's face instead of horses. And his big, graceful body. She was almost painfully conscious of him whenever he was near. She'd thought actually having sex would vent some of the tension, but it hadn't.

Twice in her life—leaving out early teenage crushes— she'd thought she was in love, but those feelings hadn't been anything like this deep longing, physical and emotional. She knew she was probably deluding herself to think he felt something similar, that he might be questioning the certainties about his future that he'd thought rock solid.

Her mood bleak, she wondered if she might be sorry if she got what she was wishing for. If they were serious about each other, what would she do? Move to the army base where he was stationed, try to find work and then wave a falsely cheerful goodbye every time he shipped out? Wait for weeks and months and even a year at a time for him to come back to her, haunted the entire while by fear that he'd be injured again—or come back in a box to be buried? Even if she loved him, was that a life she could endure?

He'd said himself that he wouldn't be an active-duty Ranger for that much longer. But what did that mean? Two more years? Five? Ten?

Yet if she loved him, how could she not accept him for what he was, be waiting when he came home?

And, of course, all this agonizing was absurd when she didn't have the slightest idea how he felt about her, or whether any new emotions had the slightest impact on his determination to rejoin his unit. Trina didn't even know why he loved being a Ranger so much. Was it the sense of mission? The danger, the exhilaration of cheating death? The tightness with his teammates? Would he ever talk to her about it?

Sleep sneaked up on her. She roused when Gabe came up to bed, listened to every small sound from his bedroom, even toyed with the idea of slipping out of bed and going to him. But her eyelids were so heavy, and tonight she didn't want Chloe to wake and find herself alone.

She must have slept like a log, because her next conscious awareness was of morning light seeping around the edges of the blinds. And of the bony knees pressing against her stomach, and the warm little girl who'd wormed her way beneath Trina's arm.

Trina's lips curved as she stayed absolutely still. Yesterday had been a setback, that's all. Everyone made mistakes; everyone got scared sometimes. She remembered Gabe predicting a recovery by morning. Oh, she hoped he was right!

Finally, her bladder drove her to get up. Inevitably, Chloe woke up, too, blinking sleepily at her.

Trina swooped down to kiss her cheek, said, "Good morning, sunshine!" and dashed across the hall to the bathroom. On the way back, she glanced at Gabe's door, ajar, but couldn't tell if he was still in bed or long since up.

Returning to the bedroom, she found Chloe sitting on the side of the bed, clutching her plush unicorn. Still cheerfully, she said, "I'll bet you're hungry, aren't you?" Her own stomach was growling. "Let me get dressed, and let's go make breakfast. How about oatmeal? That'd fill us up."

Predictably, Chloe wrinkled her nose. "Can we have waffles?"

Trina's heart felt as if it was swelling to fill her rib cage. "Yep. If you want to help, you need to get dressed, too."

Chloe scampered to the bathroom first. On her return, she picked out red corduroy overalls and a pink shirt, a combination that made Trina wince, but what the heck? "Can we ride *today*?" she asked, while sitting on the floor putting on socks.

Trina looked for Chloe's shoes. "I don't know. I think Gabe is nervous because of that helicopter coming overhead. Since we're hiding here, he wants to make sure nobody sees us."

A sock halfway on, Chloe went still. Yesterday, Gabe hadn't been honest with Chloe about why they couldn't go, but creative excuses would collapse eventually. Right now she and Trina were pretty much cabin-bound, and Chloe already knew why, more or less.

The little girl looked up. "Why can't *this* be home?" she asked, voice small and plaintive. "Can't we stay here? With Gabe?"

Oh, God. Trina wanted that so fiercely the pain held her silent for a moment. Finally, she swallowed, crouched beside Chloe, and kissed her on the forehead. "I like it here, too. But…your grandma might want you to live with her. Remember?"

"I don't wanna go live with her!" Chloe wrapped her arms around Trina's calf and held on tight. "I want you to be my mommy!"

I want to be your mommy, too. But she couldn't say that, because it might not be possible. Probably wouldn't be. Chloe *had* relatives.

Had it been another, terrible mistake, letting herself love this child, when she knew she wouldn't be able to keep her?

Maybe. But it wasn't one she'd take back if she could. No, she thought, on a wave of peace salted with pain, loving Gabe wasn't something she'd take back, either.

Struggling to calm herself, she said, "You know I love you, sweetie. Right now we're sort of…waiting to see what will happen. I can't make you promises, except that, if you go live with your grandma or your aunt and uncle, I'll come see you as often as I can. Okay?"

Chloe's face crumpled, but she nodded.

"Waffles," Trina declared, spotting the missing shoes tucked just beneath the bed.

As Gabe and Mack loped toward Boyd's house, he was stuck on thinking about what Trina had told him. Chloe's extreme reaction had happened not because she was afraid to talk about the bad man, but because she didn't want to go "home."

"That was a stupid thing for me to say, anyway." Trina was way too quick to berate herself for anything she viewed as a screwup. "Even *I* don't have a home. Chloe knows that. Hers is just a nightmare. She must have been thinking she was safe here, but that once we leave, she'll have to go live in a strange house with a relative she doesn't know that well."

It bugged Gabe to know that might well be true. How could Trina combat it if family wanted to take her in? His heart had done some strange acrobatics when he heard that Chloe wanted them to stay here, with *him*. So far, he was mostly ignoring the small voice in the back of his head that said, *They could if you retire.*

If he surrendered to a damn injury, was what he meant. The idea was unthinkable to a man who'd made himself without a lot of encouragement or support from anyone else. He didn't *quit.*

Except…hell. He really didn't like imagining the day Trina thanked him and he had to hug her and Chloe goodbye because they were going on with their lives.

Alone under an overcast sky, he said a word he had had to swallow a few times recently because he didn't want a three-year-old kid to hear it…and because he was old-fashioned enough not to like using it around a woman, either.

When he reached the bustling heart of the ranch, he rode Mack into a barn, dismounted and tied him there, in the relatively cool, dim aisle lined by stalls. He had to stop and talk to a man holding a horse out front while a farrier bent over working on a front hoof. Then he walked toward the house, where Boyd expected him.

"You made it," his partner said, letting him in.

"You thought I'd get lost?"

"Hey, you never know. Haven't seen much of you around here."

"You know why," he said, too sharply, when he knew Boyd was only kidding. Man, this never-ending tension was getting to him, in large part because he wanted to take action. He wanted to find the bastard who was behind all this crap, not wait to *be* found. And yeah, he didn't like that Boyd had been able to go out and do things he couldn't, even though this was another kind of teamwork.

He accepted an offer of iced tea, and the two men sat in the enormous living room. Gabe felt uncomfortable in such a large space. He'd be curious to see whether Trina preferred this showplace of a log home.

Boyd said abruptly, "The Keifs' neighbor didn't recognize Julie Emmer." She was the accountant Gabe had seen having lunch with Russell Stearns. "I showed her the photo on my phone, and she kept shaking her head. This Julie hadn't been to any of the same parties she had."

He nodded.

"I may have left Mrs. Freeman thinking I was a reporter. When I said I had questions about her husband and his death, she let me in without asking for ID."

Not smart, but not uncommon, either. The woman's life had just been smashed.

"She insisted Glenn hadn't told her what was worrying him about his work, but something was. She said it had started two or three days before he died. He'd had a short run—Seattle—and came home really upset. She thought something might have happened on the road, but he said not. He told her he couldn't keep working for O.R.E., that he was sorry because they might have to move and the kids would hate getting pulled from school."

Gabe winced. The television reporter had described him as "a married father of two children," but he hadn't really thought of the poor kids. "What about her interviews with the cops? Did they sound aboveboard?"

"I'm going to say no." Boyd's expression was grim. "She said the detective asked only whether Glenn had been drinking too much, whether he'd sought counseling. Could he have had a car accident he hadn't told her about, maybe a string of tickets? That might have made him fear he'd be fired. Did he sometimes speed?"

"In other words, this detective steered away from anything that might point to a problem at O.R.E."

"You got it. In fairness, the company is the biggest employer in the county, by a long shot. I'm going to guess local government in general tiptoes around O.R.E. issues."

Gabe grunted. That was, of course, an explanation for some of Risvold's problems investigating the Keifs' murders.

"When I raised the subject of drugs," Boyd continued, "she flipped out. What was I talking about? And then she got mad and said Glenn wouldn't have been involved with anything so vile." He grimaced. "She showed me the door."

"Damn. If only he'd told her what he'd discovered."

"That would be nice," Boyd countered, "except that if there'd been any hint he had in her first response to the news about her husband, I doubt she'd have lived long."

"No, you're right." Gabe stretched out his legs and gazed broodingly at his booted feet. "Her obvious shock and ignorance saved her."

Boyd stayed silent, a frown pulling at his eyebrows. After a while, he said, "So, what's next?"

"Hell if I know." Gabe told him about Trina's attempt to put some pressure on Chloe, and how it had backfired.

Sounding tentative, unusual for him, Boyd began, "If you three just stay hunkered down…"

Gabe swore and surged to his feet. Glaring down at his friend, he said, "Until Chloe's ready to start kindergarten? I think Trina's partners might have kicked her out of the practice by then, don't you? And what happens after my physical?"

He made a rough sound and shoved his fingers through hair that was way past regulation length, bracing himself to be called out on the dramatics.

All Boyd said was, "You still working out?"

His glare probably intensified. "Of course I am!"

"And?"

"And what?" Gabe snarled, but he knew. Would he pass the physical? He hated feeling conflicted about the possible outcome. Damn, did he *want* to fail, because of these inconvenient feelings for a woman?

His buddy smiled faintly. "Okay."

"I've got to get back. I don't like leaving them." He'd just felt a tug, as if he were attached with a tether.

"I understand." Without further comment, Boyd walked him out.

Gabe mounted, trotted Mack out of the barn and kicked him almost immediately into a gallop.

TRINA TOOK THE containers holding the peas nobody had eaten last night and the mac and cheese, too, from the refrigerator. This was one meal that couldn't be easier. Of course, she shouldn't get ahead of herself, assuming Gabe would rush home. He and Boyd might have a lot to talk about—

A neigh from outside drew her to the window, where she could see the paddock, where the gelding she'd been riding called eagerly over the fence. Yes! Coming into sight, Mack answered, and Gabe leaned forward to slap him on the neck.

She went into the living room, unnerved when she didn't immediately see Chloe. She rushed to the downstairs bathroom, calling, "Chloe?"

The bathroom was empty. Trina spun to go for the stairs but spotted Chloe crawling out from behind a hefty leather easy chair.

"It scared me when I didn't see you. Were you hiding?"

"Kinda." Her eyes were red, her hair stringy and falling out of the ponytail.

Trina sank down on the chair and held out her hand. "Will you come and cuddle with me?" To heck with lunch.

The little girl sniffed, nodded and, with a little help, scrambled up onto Trina's lap. Trina tucked her in close and resolved not to ask any more questions. The comfort of an embrace was enough.

Chloe mumbled something Trina didn't hear. She bent her head closer, even as she half listened for the back door to open.

"I sawed Uncle Ronald."

It took a few seconds for the words to sink in. Chloe had sawed—seen—a man she called "uncle." Ronald.

"'Cept, *he* wouldn't hurt Daddy!" she exclaimed passionately. "He leaned over so I sawed him. He musta been going to help Daddy get up, only…only he didn't."

"Oh, honey."

Chloe sounded younger, as if she'd regressed in the past few minutes to a time when her language was less well developed. The tear-wet, freckled face peered up at Trina in bewilderment.

"I *almost* went out, but then I 'membered Mommy saying to wait, no matter what, so I didn't."

Trina sent a prayer of thanks winging upward. She wished Chloe's mother could know that she had saved her. Maybe…maybe she did.

"I'm so glad," she whispered. "So glad."

Chloe muffled a sob against her.

The creak of a floorboard brought Trina's head up fast. Gabe stood in the opening from the kitchen, his expression arrested. Swallowing the agony and the hope, she nodded.

Chapter Thirteen

"Call me paranoid," Gabe growled, "but I don't trust Risvold in particular. He may have innocent reasons for his behavior and his excuse for an investigation, but I can't forget that he or his department had a leak." Remembering the burns on Trina's back spiked his temper. That fire had come damn close to claiming two victims, ensuring that the Keif murders were never solved.

Despite all Gabe had seen and done, he had to shake his head over this guy. Ronald Pearson had to be unbelievably cold-blooded and ruthless. The same could be said about the terrorists Gabe hunted, but they at least committed atrocities out of idealism, however mistaken, not greed.

"You're right," Trina said in response to his reminder. "But…a detective? I did some research online, and he's been with the Sadler Police Department for twelve years."

"Detective for six of those. I know. And he might have been accepting kickbacks for those same twelve years," Gabe pointed out. "Longevity and integrity aren't synonymous."

She made a face. "What are you going to tell them, then?"

Gabe rolled his shoulders to release some tension.

"To start with, I'll call Deperro, not Risvold. I won't accuse his partner of anything, but I'll express our concern about the past leak that was damn near fatal for you and Chloe." Concern being such a pallid word for what he really felt.

Trina shivered. "Yes, it was."

"I'll set up a meeting for them to ask Chloe their questions." They both knew the cops couldn't make an arrest based on the word of an anonymous caller. Not Trina's word, either. No, they'd insist on interviewing the three-year-old witness.

Sounding uneasy, Trina said, "You mean, take her to town?"

"Not a chance." He made his voice solid granite. "They could grab her and we couldn't stop them. I'm thinking at Boyd's place. We can make sure there are too many witnesses for them to be able to get away with anything."

Her fingers bit into her palms. "Does that mean we can stay here, then? Until it's all over? I mean, they wouldn't know the cabin is here, or your name…"

"I'm on the deed and there's a permit on file for the cabin," he said, almost gently. "And don't forget the fly-over. It wouldn't take a genius to realize that, if we know Boyd, this or one of the other ranch houses is a good possibility for the hideout."

Her anxiety wasn't as well hidden as she probably thought it was, but she only nodded. "Then we'll have to figure out something else."

Moving fast, he shoved back his chair and rounded the table. Gripping her upper arms, he tugged her to his feet. "I won't abandon you."

She blinked a couple of times in quick succession,

nodded and softened, letting herself lean against him. He wanted to share his strength with her but knew that wasn't why she needed him. This was a gutsy woman. Despite the intense compassion that allowed her to reach terrified children, she'd do whatever she had to.

She straightened and stepped back, even managing a smile of sorts. "Thank you. I…had faith that you wouldn't. So, are you going to Bend again?"

He'd rather still be holding her but respected her decision to stand on her own two feet. "Yeah, I think so. If they've ever traced one of my calls, with luck they'll think we're in that area."

"Okay. I'd tell you to get groceries, too, but we don't need anything."

"Good. I don't want to be away that long." He smiled crookedly. "Although I do appreciate my home-cooked meals."

She chuckled. "Are you running out of phones yet?"

"Nope, I pick one up every time I go in the right kind of store. Better not to be remembered as the guy who purchased ten phones. Speaking of, I'm going to leave one with you, in case of an emergency. I'll enter my number, Boyd's and Leon Cabrera's. One or both of them may be closer than I am."

Whether he liked it or not, the possibility was real that bad stuff could go down at any time.

"You'd better get going," she suggested.

"Yeah." After entering the numbers, Gabe handed a phone to her. Then he kissed her, quick and hard, and went out the door. He heard her lock it behind him before he strode to the outbuilding where he garaged his truck.

Having decided not to take the time to switch out vehicles, Gabe spent the drive second-guessing himself.

Would a recording of Chloe's testimony be sufficient? That's all a jury would see, anyway. No one would put a preschooler on the stand. Or was there a safer place for a meet, one that wouldn't give away their location?

But he shook his head at that. It wouldn't surprise him if the cops already knew where they were. To give them a strong suspicion, all they'd have had to do was succeed in tracing one of those assorted license plates to a guy now working at the ranch.

He really did believe that the rats would desert the sinking ship the minute cuffs closed around Ronald Pearson's wrists. He and Trina would need to stay on guard for a while, sure, but—

A Deschutes County Sheriff's Department car passed him going the other direction, a sight that snapped him back to the awareness of his surroundings. He knew better than to brood at the wrong time and place.

Ten minutes later, he parked, facing out, in the Home Depot lot.

His call was put through to the detective, who answered brusquely. "Deperro."

"Detective, this is Dr. Marr's friend."

"Damn it, what's with the secrecy?"

"You know as well as I do," he snapped. "You have a leak. If you know how word got out about Chloe starting to talk and where she was living, you should have told Dr. Marr or me. As it is, I don't figure I can talk to either of you without assuming what I say may be passed on."

"That's insulting."

Gabe's radar hummed. Deperro should have spoken sharply; *sounded* insulted. Instead, he'd said what he ought to, but without conviction.

"I have news," Gabe said abruptly. "Chloe told Trina

and me who she saw that morning. It was the partner, Ronald Pearson." He heard only silence. Stunned? "'Uncle Ronald' is what she called him. He bent over her father's body, so she got a good look at his face. She thought he was going to help her daddy get up, but he didn't."

"Damn," Deperro muttered.

Gabe could think of stronger words. "If you're doing your job, by now you know the likelihood that drug traffickers are using O.R.E.'s fleet of trucks to transport their products to market. Chances are that Michael Keif found out somehow, and they had a confrontation."

"Risvold doesn't believe in the drug angle, but I was heading that direction."

"Good to know. Okay. I'm assuming you need to talk to Chloe yourself before you can make an arrest."

"Yeah." The detective's voice sounded hoarse. "We do. Man. I've never arrested anyone based on the word of a kid that age."

"Now that you know, you'll find plenty of other evidence. I hope you have the DEA ready to close in on Open Range the second you've arrested the bastard."

Possibly irritated, the guy only said, "Will you bring the girl here? The sooner, the better. What time?"

"Not there. I need better security than you can give us." He mentioned the local rancher he knew, who had agreed to allow them to meet at his house. "We can do this afternoon. We'll need an hour or two to get there, be prepared."

They agreed on four o'clock. Gabe glanced at the dashboard clock. Yeah, that gave them plenty of time. He named Boyd and the ranch, then ended the call.

Once again, he dumped the phone on his way out of

the parking lot, this time in a small, wrinkled bag left from an order of burgers and fries. Then he steered a route to the highway.

TRINA DID A lot of pacing even as she listened for any sound from Chloe upstairs. She felt again as if her skin had shrunk, only worse.

It wasn't as if there was any reason to think they were in danger, unless… Was he right, that the detectives might have figured out how to find them? If so, they'd displayed more patience than she would have anticipated. Their initial impatience had been understandable. How frustrating would it be to have a single witness and she was not only mute but couldn't communicate by writing, either? Had they actually come to grasp how traumatized Chloe was? Remembering her last conversation from Risvold, she made a face.

Not feeling any calmer, Trina went from window to window, stealing looks out. The only movement was in back, where the horses wandered from the paddock into the shade of an overhang where Gabe kept a manger and a tub of water. Finally, surrendering to this edgy feeling, she opened the gun safe. She could just leave it standing open… No, she couldn't. What if she didn't see Chloe come downstairs? Okay, then, she'd take out the black rifle Gabe had let her handle as well as the smallest handgun, and set them up high on the bookshelves, where she could snatch them quickly at need. She knew he'd checked, and rechecked, to be sure they were loaded and ready if she needed them.

She felt a little better once she had the guns out and had closed the safe again securely. Then she went back to her route, window to window, and to clock-watching.

Gabe would have made his call and started back. More than that—he'd surely be home in fifteen to twenty minutes, if he hadn't been held up. Say, he'd had to wait to reach the detective.

Ten minutes later, the sound of an engine came to her. Trina almost slumped in relief, but she went to the front window and opened a slit in the blinds to see out. Dust rose on the cutoff to Gabe's cabin. The vehicle was big and black…but something didn't look quite right. Wary, she waited.

It was an SUV that pulled up in front, one with the kind of antennas that police cars had. And a row of lights inside, at the top of the windshield. A man got out.

Detective Risvold. She could make out his face clearly, see the badge on his belt and the holstered gun at his hip. Why would he have just showed up here like this?

Apprehensive, Trina took out the phone, went to Gabe's number, then changed her mind. Boyd was closer. Her thumb hovered over the screen.

"Ms. Marr!" Risvold called. At least he had the sense to wait by his SUV. "I know you're in there. I'm here to talk to the girl."

He couldn't know anything of the kind, not for sure.

Ignore him? Crack the door and tell him he had to wait?

Call Boyd. But for a second, she hesitated. Had she heard something upstairs? *Don't let Chloe come down, not now.*

"Damn it, Miss… *Dr.* Marr." He leaned on the "doctor." Sneering? Or pacifying her? "I'm short on patience. There's a killer walking free. I can't do anything about that until I hear what the kid has to say."

All true.

Ring. Ring. Ring. Finally, "Chaney here."

"It's Trina," she whispered, then realized there wasn't any reason not to speak in a normal voice. "Detective Risvold is standing out front demanding I let him in to interview Chloe."

"What?" Boyd said. "How the hell did he find you? Never mind. Damn, I'm on horseback, probably ten minutes from home, longer to get to you. Where's Gabe?"

"He drove to Bend to call. He told you what Chloe said?"

"Yeah. Shit. Don't let the guy in. I'll call Leon. He may be nearer to you."

"Okay. Thank you. Gabe should be back anytime."

"Good. You armed?"

"Yes, but… I can't shoot a police officer!"

"You can if he takes out a window or tries to break in," he said grimly. "Go for a warning shot. That ought to have him retreating out of range."

Her smile wobbled. "Okay. Thanks, Boyd." She sidled over to the bookcase and grabbed the rifle. She was more comfortable with it. Then she scrolled to Gabe's number, just as more dust rose outside as another vehicle approached fast. Was he back…?

No, this was a dark gray sedan with, she saw as it got closer, the same kind of antenna.

She pushed Send.

GABE'S HANDS CLENCHED in frustration on the steering wheel as he sat in his truck in the scant shade of a lodgepole pine. After leaving Highway 97, he'd driven only a few miles on the secondary road before spotting a police car parked on a dirt pulloff ahead. Probably there to catch a few speeders, but he couldn't risk sailing by. It was unlikely the deputy would notice the distinctive dents made by bullets, but a BOLO with the description of Gabe's truck or the license plate might conceivably have gone out. Gabe had been lucky enough to see a dirt lane turning off to the left half a mile before he reached the cop, and he'd taken it.

A dusty plume rose behind the truck. He'd driven only until he passed out of sight over a rise before he braked and maneuvered until he was facing back the way he'd come. Then he drove slowly until he could see the damn cop.

Waiting, he felt his gut seething. He kept glancing at his phone. He could call Trina, but all he'd do was scare her.

On the highway, a pickup pulling a stock trailer passed. Not a likely speeder. The police car stayed where it was.

His phone rang. He looked down at the strange number and knew. Trina.

IT WAS DETECTIVE DEPERRO who got out of the second car, Trina saw in surprise. Why wouldn't they have come together?

Advancing on his partner, Deperro didn't even glance at the house. He looked mad, she realized. Wanting to hear what they were saying, she grabbed the rifle and unlocked and cracked open the front door.

"…shouldn't have come." That was Risvold.

"We have a meeting set up. You know that. This—" the other detective's sweeping gesture including the cabin, the SUV and Risvold himself "—doesn't look good."

Risvold was sweating profusely. Half-turned as he

was to face his partner, she thought he said, "I tried to keep you out of this."

Her uneasiness crystalized and she fumbled with the safety, then raised the barrel of the rifle, but too late. Risvold pulled his gun and shot Detective Deperro in the chest. Shock on his face, Deperro staggered back, fell.

Furious but also feeling weirdly calm, Trina sighted and shot out the window of the SUV. "Drop the gun!" she yelled.

Risvold wheeled toward her and fired. The *crack* and *thud* when the bullet plowed into the heavy wooden door seemed simultaneous.

She fired back, probably a little wildly. The bullet skimmed the side of the SUV. Risvold swore viciously and leaped behind it.

She suddenly realized she couldn't see Deperro. Which meant he wasn't dead. He must have crawled, because he sure hadn't jumped to his feet; she'd have seen that. Maybe he and Risvold were *both* taking refuge behind the rear of the SUV, which wouldn't be good.

Gabe, please hurry. Boyd, where are you? But she knew, in some part of her mind, that hardly any time had actually passed.

"Trina?" A scared voice came from behind her.

Oh, God, of course the gunshots had awakened Chloe.

"Honey, I need you to—" No, no, she couldn't tell her to hide, to not come out until Trina or Gabe told her so. Once in a lifetime was enough. Except—Trina desperately wanted her to *have* a life. "Get down behind the couch," she said. "A man is shooting at the house, and I don't want him to hit you by accident."

The second she saw the little girl duck behind that hefty leather sofa, Trina turned back to peer through the crack again. Risvold…no sight of him. But Detective Deperro had somehow gotten up. Emerging from the other side of the SUV, he bent over and ran toward the far corner of the cabin.

Another shot rang out. He hit the ground, rolled and grabbed his thigh. Trina fired again, this time aiming through the nonexistent windshield and out a side window, she hoped very close to where Risvold must be crouched. Right above his head would be good.

She heard swearing and fired again. Deperro staggered to his feet and kept going.

She had to ignore the whimper from behind the couch.

I'll run out of bullets, she realized, not quite as calmly. Gabe had said the Savage Model 110 had a four-cartridge box. Five shots, with one already loaded. She counted. How many times had she already fired? Three? No, four. One more. Then she'd have to go for the handgun.

A pounding at the back door had her lurching around. *Oh.* It had to be Boyd or Leon. She hesitated only an instant, made sure Risvold was still out of sight, closed and locked the door.

Ignoring the whimper from behind the sofa, she ran.

GABE DROVE LIKE a madman.

The sheriff's department car had suddenly pulled out onto the highway and accelerated. The rack of lights came on, red, white, blue, rotating. Boyd had said he'd call 911. Gabe hoped this deputy was on his way to the ranch.

But damn it, he turned off on a lonely crossroad and raced up over a rise.

From that moment on, Gabe floored it. He didn't slow down even when he groped for his ringing phone.

"Leon's out in hell-and-beyond to rescue a steer tangled in barbed wire," Boyd reported tensely. "I'm on my way, but close to ten minutes out. I'm hearing shots."

Gabe breathed a word that might have been a profanity or a prayer. Or both. "I might beat you there," he said. "I'll pass the cutoff, and approach from behind the cabin."

"Don't shoot me." Boyd was gone.

If that was meant to be funny, it missed its mark. The urgency driving Gabe left no room for humor.

THE KITCHEN DOOR had a glass inset. Rifle raised in firing position, Trina peered around the corner from the living room.

It was Detective Deperro looking to one side, then turning suddenly, as if he'd heard her, to stare right at her.

He raised a fist and mimicked knocking, even as he darted another look toward the far corner of the cabin.

Queasy, Trina couldn't help wondering if the fight out front had been a setup, designed to make her trust one of the two partners and let him in. What if that first bullet had been, she didn't know, a blank? But the second one…no, she'd seen blood blossom on Deperro's leg.

Wait. He must be wearing a bulletproof vest. That's why the shot had knocked him down but not injured him significantly.

Make a decision.

It wasn't any kind of decision, she realized almost immediately. He could use the butt of his gun to knock out the glass so he could let himself in. In fact, he could have done that already, instead of waiting politely despite the stress and pain he must be feeling. Her only other option was to shoot him. Of course she couldn't do that.

A thought floated absurdly through her head. Gabe hadn't built his cabin to withstand a siege. She'd bet he was going to be sorry.

She rushed forward and unlocked the door, throwing it open.

Deperro flung himself in, and she saw that the leg of his cargo pants was soaked with blood.

"Oh, no. Did it hit an artery? You should lie down and elevate your leg." She sounded, and felt, hysterical.

His dark eyes met hers. "No, I wouldn't have made it this far if the artery was spurting. It hurts like a mother—" He censored himself. "But I'll live. Listen, we don't have time for this."

"No." Trina sprinted for the living room. Seeing Chloe huddled in a small ball, she stopped. "Sweetie, please go upstairs to the bedroom."

Except for the shivers, Chloe didn't move, didn't respond. Didn't even lift her head. Trina wanted to go to her but couldn't.

She hated that the closed blinds didn't let her see out front at all. After grabbing the handgun, she leaned the rifle against the wall beside the door.

A dragging footstep behind her was followed by the detective saying softly, "Well, hello, little one." Then, obviously speaking to Trina, "Where's the guy who's been calling me?"

"On his way. Here any minute." She had to believe that. She pressed her back to the door. "What happened?"

"Damn. You got some towels or something else I can use?"

"There's a bathroom under the staircase."

She watched him go, then undid the dead bolt, gripped the Colt and cracked the door, ready to shoot. Nothing happened. She peered out. No movement. But Risvold could be on the porch already. Without sticking her head out, she wouldn't see him if he was off five feet to one side or another. Holding her breath, she listened. The silence was absolute.

"I'm making a mess," Deperro said. "I'm sorry."

She checked over her shoulder. He'd ripped a towel lengthwise and somehow tied half of it around his thigh, the other half folded to provide a pad.

Her laugh broke. "That's the least of our problems."

"Yeah, it is." He was staring at the thin band of sunlight. "I've been wondering about Risvold, but…damn, I still can't believe he's crooked. I told him what your friend said, that we were meeting at four, and a couple of minutes later he made an excuse and sidled out. I followed him."

"But…what can he do by himself?"

Those eyes were now black, the set of his mouth grim. "I don't think he'll be by himself for long."

Suddenly light-headed, she wheeled to peer through the crack again, and saw a cloud of dust out on the road.

GABE'S TRUCK ROCKETED down the dirt road. He'd lowered the windows but didn't hear any shots. What if he was too late? What if he found Trina and Chloe—No, damn it! He wouldn't even think that.

He passed the cutoff to his cabin, drove another two or three hundred yards, then steered off the road, bumping over rough ground. He parked, leaped out and ran. He wasn't halfway to the cabin when he saw a cloud of dirt rising where his had just settled. Reinforcements?

Bad enough that Trina was already having to face down two armed, experienced cops.

Unless she was dead, taken out by one of those shots.

He willed the fear away. With luck, Boyd had beaten him here.

He broke from the trees behind the paddock and barn. An engine—no, more than that, at least two—announced the approach of more vehicles. Mack and the gelding were snorting, moving restlessly but sticking close to the barn. Smart. Stepping lightly, Gabe eased around the corner to where he could see the back of the cabin. Nothing there. The door was still closed, the window intact.

A voice behind him said softly, "Yo, it's me."

He spun in a shooting position, his brain catching up in time to keep his finger from tightening on the trigger. Sweat darkened Boyd's hair and his T-shirt, creating a sheen on his face. He carried a handgun that he must have had with him in case of trouble.

"Has she called again?" Boyd asked.

"Not a word." Gabe pulled his keys from his pocket. "Ready?"

They didn't run, just moved as quietly as a pair of ghosts, sweeping the surroundings with their guns as they went. At the back door, Boyd covered him while Gabe unlocked it. They stepped inside. He immediately heard a man's voice. Son of a bitch.

He didn't even look at Boyd, just walked toward the living room without making a sound.

First, he saw Chloe, squeezed to try to make herself invisible. He evaluated her with lightning speed. Her whole body trembled. She didn't even look up. Scared out of her skull, but alive. Then he saw the man's back.

Hair as dark as Leon's, but this guy was a lot bigger. He clearly hadn't heard the man approaching behind him.

Gabe measured the distance.

Chapter Fourteen

"It's an SUV." Trina spoke tensely. "Another one's coming behind it."

"Crap," Deperro muttered. "Why don't you let me take the front, you get where you can see the back door?"

"Don't shoot," a dark, deep voice said.

Trina spun and saw that Deperro had done the same. "It's Gabe!" she cried, having to stiffen her knees to keep from crumpling to the floor in relief.

His eyes met hers fleetingly, the expression so raw her heart skipped a beat. The next second, her personal warrior stared hard at the detective. "What's *he* doing here?"

The two of them tried to talk over each other. Trina fell silent and let Detective Deperro tell his story.

"Hey, honey," another man said. Then, "Who is *he*?"

Trina's sinuses burned, but damned if she'd let herself cry. "Boyd. You came."

He offered his charming smile. "Always."

She had the feeling he meant that literally.

Then she paid attention to what was happening out front. Two SUVs slammed to a stop, doors flying open as men jumped out. Four, five, six… eight. And Risvold, who must have scurried bent over as far as the rear of the sedan, straightened to meet his army.

"Eight men," she reported. "Nine, with Risvold. And…they're armed." Carrying what she was afraid were semiautomatic—or even fully automatic?—rifles that made the bolt-action Savage she'd been shooting seem useless. She focused on one of the men. "I think that's Ronald Pearson."

Gabe swiftly edged her aside and took a look. "In person," he murmured, before snapping out his next order. "Go unlock the gun cabinet."

She hustled. Once it was open, Gabe told her which of the remaining rifles he wanted.

Voice a little husky, he said, "Good, thanks," when she brought it to him.

Without asking, Boyd chose another for himself.

"You have something I can borrow?" the detective asked.

Boyd scrutinized him. "You any good with a rifle?"

"Trained as a sniper. Army," he added.

Boyd relaxed subtly. "All right, then."

Deperro hobbled over and took the last rifle. Watching Gabe's unrevealing back, Trina heard the bolt slide and knew Deperro was verifying that the weapon was loaded.

"Can somebody trade out the magazine for me?" she asked, hoping none of the men heard the tremor in her voice. "It should still have one cartridge loaded."

Boyd moved a lot like Gabe did, she suddenly realized. Both were almost uncannily graceful. Power was visible in their strides, but leashed. She doubted either ever broke so much as a twig underfoot.

"They're spreading out to surround us," Gabe said in a voice so level it raised the hair on the back of her neck. "Looks like a couple of them are carrying AK-47s, or something similar. Crap, there's either an AR-15 or an Omega 9mm. Boyd, did you call 911?"

"Yes. The sheriff's department doesn't have a great response time, but somebody should have been here." He muttered something under his breath. "I'd better call back. It wouldn't be good if a lone deputy rolled up right now."

"No."

He took his phone out.

"Just before I got here, I called a buddy with the DEA." It was Deperro speaking up. "Told him what I thought was happening."

"Did he take you seriously?" Gabe asked.

"Sounded like it. I wondered if they weren't already looking that direction."

"They likely to show up out here, or raid O.R.E.?"

"They'd damn well better show up," he growled.

Without so much as an acknowledging nod, Gabe said, "Trina, take Chloe upstairs. Tuck her in the bathtub. Ought to provide some protection. Then come down and take up a position behind the sofa. That'll make you central, and you'll be able to back any of us up."

She didn't argue. All three men were far more prepared for the ensuing battle than she could ever be.

Chloe's small body was stiff in her arms. She hurried upstairs, diverted to her bedroom to grab the comforter and the stuffed unicorn, then carried her into the bathroom. On her knees after settling the little girl in the tub, she stroked the soft red-gold hair. "I know this is scary, sweetie. But we'll be fine. I'll leave the door open so you can hear us. Okay?"

Chloe shivered harder, but her head did bob.

"Good. You're such a brave girl." Trina kissed her,

then tore downstairs. The rifle and handgun lay behind the sofa, where Gabe wanted her.

Deperro knelt at the end of the short hall, where he could see into a room Gabe hadn't even furnished. A home office? In his fleeting visits, he wouldn't need anything like that.

Even in profile, she saw that the detective's skin tone was closer to gray than his usual bronze. The towel around his thigh was soaked. Blood dripped onto the polished plank floor.

"What's your first name?" she asked in a low voice.

He gave her a startled look. "Daniel."

A barrage of gunfire broke out, seemingly coming from all directions. Trina jerked as glass shattered. She could see only Deperro, who thrust the rifle around the doorframe and fired. Once, twice, again. She desperately wished she could see Gabe, but she heard him swearing as he fired.

Silence fell, interrupted by a phone ringing.

It was apparently Boyd's, because he said a few words she couldn't make out.

Then he raised his voice slightly. "Leon's set up in back."

"Anybody injured?" Gabe. "Should have said, any new injuries?"

The other two men both answered, "No."

"Trina?" he said sharply.

"I'm fine."

"Okay. My preference would be to hold them off without killing—not sure what my command structure would think about me taking out a bunch of drug traffickers while I'm rehabbing—but it's not looking like we're going to have any choice."

"My presence lends some legitimacy." Deperro's voice—Daniel's voice—came out thin.

Alarmed, Trina saw him close his eyes, wipe a forearm over his face.

"Let's trade places," she said, starting to crawl forward.

"No." He waved her back and resolutely squared his shoulders. "I'm good."

"You seeing any activity?" Boyd called.

"Zip." Gabe, sounding grim.

Barely seconds later, another burst of sound deafened Trina. Gunfire, and more. Deperro seemed to be yelling. An explosion powerful enough to shake the floor beneath Trina's knees sent the detective flying backward. He slammed into the wall, his rifle sliding along the floor toward Trina.

A second, equally powerful explosion came from the kitchen, a third from the front porch.

Terrified, Trina scrambled from the shelter of the sofa to flatten herself against the wall next to the hall. Gabe spared one look over his shoulder to see her, then resumed firing. She drew a deep breath for courage, leveled the rifle and spun to see the hall.

A bullet slammed into the wall inches from her chest. Her first shot took a man down, sending his handgun flying. He pushed himself to his knees and lunged forward for the gun. She shot again, hitting the floor in front and to one side of him.

"Flat on the floor!" she ordered. "Don't move or you're dead."

GABE HAD NEVER fought in a battle with his attention divided. But not once had he been able to quash his awareness of Trina. He hated knowing they needed her, that he couldn't tuck her away upstairs with Chloe. After hearing a bark that had to be her rifle, he called, "Trina?"

He was betting she'd never be fine again. But he'd been right; in the moment, she'd been willing to kill to ensure that those men wouldn't get their hands on Chloe.

Seeing no movement out front, Gabe risked turning. Trina stood with the barrel of the rifle alternately pointing at the man who lay flat on the floor and the open doorway beyond.

Thank God, Deperro stirred, shook his head. Blood dripped down one side of his face, but gradually he regained his wits. Showing his teeth, he torturously got to his knees, crawled forward and planted a knee in the middle of the guy's back. From a pocket, he produced plastic cuffs.

As he wrenched one hand behind the man's back, then the other, the guy glared at Trina, his face twisted in hate. Just for that look, Gabe wanted to shoot him. The son of a bitch didn't know how lucky he was that Gabe still held on to a modicum of self-control. Or was that sanity?

He had an almost amused thought. So much for those overanxious therapists back at the hospital. He'd gotten through surreal circumstances all but guaranteed to trigger flashbacks.

It's not over yet.

He turned his head and scanned the front. Because he'd pinned them there, he knew at least two men were crouched behind the row of SUVs, probably more. Pearson, for sure. He didn't seem to have joined the battle. Did he really think he could stay safe while everyone else took the risks? Too bad one of the traffickers hadn't gotten irritated and popped him.

Given what appeared to be another lull, Gabe raised his voice. "How many down?"

"I've got one who looks dead," Boyd reported. "There's another guy out by the barn. One of Leon's, shots, I think. He's alive, but the way he's writhing, I'm guessing he took a bullet in his knee."

"I shot one." Trina sounded almost numb. "Daniel's hurt worse, but he handcuffed the guy."

"Deperro, did you take another bullet?"

"Just stunned," Deperro said coolly. "Grenade."

"Yeah, those were no flash-bangs," Gabe agreed. "I have a couple down, too. That leaves only four. I'm thinking they may run for it."

"Won't do Pearson any good to run," Boyd commented.

"Or Risvold." Deperro sounded utterly cold. Betrayal did that to a man.

They all heard an engine start. Gabe swore. "Looks like they don't mind leaving their buddies behind."

"Wouldn't it be good if…if they do leave?" For the first time, Trina's voice trembled.

About ready to expose himself to shoot some tires, Gabe cocked his head. "Sirens."

"Helicopter, coming fast," Boyd called from the back.

"Good guys or bad guys?"

"It's white with…can't see the insignia."

Good guys. Not that Gabe allowed himself to lose focus or let relief shut down the adrenaline, not yet. He'd seen men killed when they dropped their guard prematurely.

Flashing lights appearing through the trees. Two, three…four law enforcement vehicles. Doors open, men taking position behind them with rifles pointed.

A voice boomed through a bullhorn. "Drop your weapons. Stand up slowly, hands in the air."

A second voice blasted from somewhere behind the cabin, too.

What looked like SWAT officers raced forward, yanked one man after another from behind the line of vehicles. Planted their faces against the side of the black SUVs, hands on the roof. With pleasure, Gabe watched Detective Risvold, Ronald Pearson and two other men being frisked.

At last, he lowered the Remington, leaned it against the wall and said in a rough voice, "Trina? Come here."

She flew to him. He yanked her too hard against him, afraid he was hurting her but realizing that for the first time in his damn life he was shaking and couldn't help himself. Yet she held him just as hard, and maybe it wasn't him who was shaking after all.

Finally, he touched his forehead to hers. "I've never been so scared before," he murmured. It was a minute before he could make himself release her and open the front door.

GABE DISLIKED DEALING with the aftermath as much as he had defending his cabin as if it were a plot of ground in Afghanistan. He sent Trina upstairs to take care of Chloe, and walked out beside the wheeled gurney carrying Deperro.

Just before he was lifted into the first ambulance, Gabe held out a hand. "Thank you, Detective. We might not have made it without you."

Deperro shook, offering a wan smile. "Daniel."

Gabe didn't trust easily, but this cop had proved himself. "Daniel," he said with a nod. "We'll be talking."

He waited until the ambulance doors closed before he looked around in astonishment. The four uninjured men, including Pearson and Risvold, had been hauled away immediately, behind the cage in two police cars. Gabe had watched as Pearson, face florid, had argued furiously as he was cuffed. Risvold hadn't said a word, blanched by shock until he looked like the walking dead.

The two men Gabe shot were being evaluated and treated here in front, along with the one Deperro had cuffed inside. Medics had trotted around back to look at the others. All waited their turns in other ambulances as they arrived.

Two DEA agents in body armor and the SWAT lieutenant closed in on him. "I'm told you're Gabe Decker," one of the agents said.

Boyd crossed the porch and came to join him. When one of the DEA guys looked askance at him, Gabe said shortly, "We co-own the ranch."

Boyd glanced over his shoulder. "Looks like they did a number on your cabin."

They all swept appraising looks at the front of the building. The porch railing and some of the boards were shredded. Jagged bits of glass clung in window frames. The door was badly scarred, as were sections of the log walls.

"Bullets would have ripped right through the walls if they hadn't been so solid," one of the men commented.

Gabe grunted. That wasn't why he'd built out of logs, but being bulletproof had certainly turned out to be a secondary benefit. "The grenade blasts inside did a lot of damage, too. Especially to the kitchen." But miraculously, none of them besides the detective had been injured. That's what mattered.

Trina and Chloe were safe. He had a feeling Trina could have held off the whole damn attack force alone if she'd had to. His heart beat out of rhythm as he pictured her at the top of the stairs, spraying bullets.

"We need you to tell us what happened, step by step," the same DEA agent said. They'd introduced themselves earlier, but it took Gabe a minute to summon his name.

Philip Zepeda, that was it. And the taller, older agent was Todd Carter.

"Anybody killed?" Gabe asked first.

"I'm told one of the two out back is in critical condition," the SWAT lieutenant said. "We have a Life Flight coming for him. Otherwise, they'll all recover to stand trial."

"Okay." Gabe suddenly realized both his thigh and one hip ached fiercely. To hell with pride. "You mind if we sit?" he asked. Without waiting for an answer, he walked over to take a seat on a porch step.

The older DEA guy joined him.

"Don't know if Detective Deperro had a chance to talk to you."

Zepeda's mouth tightened, but he finally nodded. "Briefly."

Boyd and Gabe told the story in turns, starting with the original murders and progressing through the leak that led to the arson fire and Trina's decision to go into hiding with Chloe. Gabe didn't offer details as to how he'd evaded notice when he drove Trina to and from work, but he did describe the attack on the highway as well as the black helicopter buzzing the ranch buildings. He talked until he was hoarse: Chloe finally telling them what she'd seen, his own trip to call Detective Deperro, what Deperro had said about why he'd followed his own partner out to the ranch and the confrontation that had left him with a bullet in his thigh.

Boyd put in his bits here and there. They'd considered leaving Leon out of this, but the bullets would be matched to weapons, so it was better to be honest.

When he finished, the SWAT lieutenant ran a hand over his close-shaved head. "Hell of a thing."

Boyd gave the DEA agents a hard stare. "I assume you didn't give the traffickers a chance to clean house at Open Range Electronics."

They exchanged a glance. Zepeda was apparently elected to be the mouthpiece, because he said, "The possibility that the company played any part in drug trafficking is still speculation." He cleared his throat. "However, we had a warrant in hand, and acted on it immediately after Detective Deperro's call. He and I have worked on drug enforcement task forces together in the past, so I placed a high reliance on his word."

His phone rang, and when he stepped away, the gathering broke up. Gabe knew these had been only the first of multiple interviews. It might be an eon before his weapons were returned to him. Every one that had been fired had been gathered as evidence. He was indifferent to that; he hadn't so much as opened the gun safe until Joseph's call asking him to keep his sister safe.

Gabe hoped Trina was with him when the time came to tell brother Joseph the whole story.

BY BEDTIME, GABE had hardly spoken to Trina since he and she had packed up everything they'd need for a day or two and taken Chloe to Boyd's larger ranch house. Boyd had labored without a lot of help to maintain some conversation at the dinner table. Gabe spoke up only when asked a direct question. Trina would have been furious with him if not for his tenderness toward Chloe, who'd burrowed in his arms as often as she had in Trina's. Boyd's cook had had the sense to serve a child-friendly meal, and while Chloe had picked at her food, she *had* eaten.

It had taken longer to get her to sleep than usual, too. Trina went back downstairs to join the men but quickly wondered why she'd bothered. She was in that unpleasant state of being wired still and exhausted, too. Chatting with Boyd while Gabe watched her broodingly wasn't what she needed.

Suddenly having had enough, she jumped to her feet. "I think I'm ready for bed. I'll see you both in the morning."

Gabe rose, too. "I'll do the same."

As stirred up as she was, she almost wished he'd stayed downstairs. Once upstairs, she turned into the bathroom and shut the door practically in his face. Only, her skin prickled as she showered and brushed her teeth. Aroused, mad, hopeful, she opened the door. If he'd gone on to bed…

He was waiting. Any indignation she'd felt was washed away instantly at the expression on his face. He started kissing her before she had a chance to take a breath. Her desperation rose to meet his, and they barely reached his room before they made love with frantic, silent need. The second time was no less urgent.

In the wake of the astonishing pleasure, she concentrated on his heartbeat, on the warm chest beneath her hand. She had to keep her mouth shut. She had to. Whatever she wanted to believe, she really didn't know how he felt about her.

And, oh, she hated knowing that trying to push him would be the absolute wrong thing to do.

Once certain he was asleep, Trina slipped out of his bed and between cold sheets to join Chloe. She needed to be here when Chloe woke up. She hadn't the slightest doubt that the police would insist on hearing Chloe's testimony themselves, and soon. As in, tomorrow.

Morning found Chloe still frightened but, thank heavens, not mute. Accordingly, at midmorning a detective and the detective division lieutenant arrived to speak to her. Trina was permitted to sit on the sofa, but an arm's length from the little girl. She did understand that they needed to be certain she wasn't sending signals with her touch. Gabe had taken up a stance right behind the sofa, probably ready to glower if anyone dared upset Chloe.

Trina would have been a lot more apprehensive if this detective wasn't the woman she'd worked with before. This time, there were no snapped questions, no veiled impatience. Detective Melinda McIntosh got Chloe chattering about Mack and the foals here on the ranch, until she was relaxed and animated.

When the important question came, she said clearly, "I saw Uncle Ronald. I heard him and Daddy yelling before. Then there was a bang and Daddy fell down. And… and some more bangs. Uncle Ronald leaned over Daddy, only he didn't help Daddy up."

Only a few questions later, it was over. Boyd ushered the cops out while Gabe told Chloe the housekeeper had made something yummy just for her.

Trina stayed where she was, almost numb. There was no more reason to be afraid. She had her life back. She could rebuild her town house, or buy a different place. Go back to work. Talk to Chloe's grandmother.

So why didn't she even want to stand up?

She was staring blankly at the view through the enormous front window when Gabe walked in front of her. Then, of course, she couldn't see anything but him. Her gaze slowly lifted.

"Can we talk?" he asked.

He'd never said when his physical would take place. Had he put it off because of his promise to her brother?

"Oh, sure. If you'd like to sit down…"

"No, I don't want to be interrupted. Do you mind going for a walk?"

She nodded, rose to her feet as if she'd been preparing to bounce up any minute and verified that the housekeeper would keep an eye on Chloe.

Gabe didn't touch her, but outside he nodded toward a small stretch of wooded land, beyond which was a white-board fence enclosing a pasture. A small herd of horses grazed a distance away.

"What are you thinking you'll do now?" Gabe asked, after a couple of minutes of silence.

"Oh— Get new ID. Decide whether I want to rebuild or find someplace else to live. You know. Everything I had to put off." Striving to sound bright, she asked, "You?"

"I don't have any choice but to take my physical," Gabe said slowly. "I have another ten months on this enlistment."

Her heart sank.

They had reached the fence. Instead of leaning on it, he stopped and took her hands. "I don't want to leave you."

"I'm…not sure what that means."

"You may not feel the same…you probably don't. I

don't have the education you do, or—" His vivid blue eyes showed stunning vulnerability. "You're nothing I ever expected, but... Damn." He blew out a long breath. "I'm in love with you, Trina. If you'd wait for me... You could stay in the cabin, so you wouldn't need to get another place. Once it's fixed up, I meant." Now he was talking fast, persuasively. "And that's only if I pass the physical."

The awful tightness in her chest had released as suddenly as a stretched rubber band, leaving her wobbly on her feet like a one-day-old foal.

She could ask him what he envisioned for his future, but she'd realized something in the past twenty-four hours. The powerful need to protect, to serve, was part of what she loved about him. There was no way she'd ask him to give up being a Ranger.

"I love you, too," she said simply. "Only...there's something you should know."

He had started to draw her closer but stopped. "What's that?"

"Chloe's grandmother or another relative may want her now, but I'm going to ask if they'd let me adopt her. I'd do everything I could to allow them to maintain a relationship with her, but... I love her."

Gabe groaned and pulled her into his arms. "I assumed we'd try to keep her. Don't keep scaring me."

"Having a child means—"

"I want you to marry me." Every word came out gritty. "Soon. So I'll know you're here, waiting for me."

Her vision blurred. "We could come with you, you know."

"I don't think I'll pass the physical," he told her. "If

I do, I'll finish my enlistment, but then I'm done. The time was coming anyway. I'm ready to be a rancher."

"You're not saying this because you think it's what I want?"

Gabe shook his head. "No," he said quietly, bending to brush his mouth softly over hers. "I want to breed and train horses, help Boyd build this into the most successful ranch in Oregon."

Her smile felt luminous. "How would you feel about breeding a kid or two?"

This laugh was new, joyous. His guard had come crashing down. "I might have to look into your bloodlines…"

"Try telling that to Joseph."

He grunted as if she'd hit him. "He'll be my brother-in-law."

"Yes, he will."

"Lucky I already liked him," he said, just before he kissed her. And kept right on kissing her.

* * * * *

WYOMING COWBOY PROTECTION

NICOLE HELM

To my husband, who always asks,
"Do you need time to write?"

Chapter One

August

Addie Foster watched from the car's passenger seat as a whole new world passed by her window. If she'd thought Jackson Hole was like nothing she'd ever known, Bent, Wyoming, was an alien planet.

She'd grown up in the heart of Boston, a city dweller always. Occasionally her family had traveled up to Maine for quaint weekends or vacations in little villages, enjoying beaches and ice-cream shops.

This was not that. This wasn't even like those dusty old Westerns her grandpa had loved to watch as he'd reminisced about his childhood being a Delaney in Bent, Wyoming—as if that had ever meant anything to Addie.

It meant something now. Seth fussed in his carrier in the back seat and Addie swallowed at the lump in her throat. Her sister had died trying to protect this sweet little man, and Addie had spent the past nine months struggling to protect him.

The baby's father hadn't made it easy. Addie had been able to hide Seth for three months before Peter

Monaghan the 5th had discovered her sister's deception, and *no one* deceived Peter Monaghan the 5th.

For six months, Addie had crisscrossed her way around the country, running out of false identities and money. Until she'd had to call upon the only person she could think to call upon.

Laurel Delaney.

Addie had met Laurel at Addie's grandpa's funeral some twenty years ago. They'd taken an instant liking to each other and become pen pals for a while.

They'd drifted apart, as pen pals always did, once the girls got into high school, and Addie never would have dreamed of calling Laurel out of the blue until desperation led her to think of the most faraway, safe place she could imagine. Someplace Peter would have no reach. Someplace she and Seth would be safe from his evil crime boss of a father.

"Don't worry," Laurel said pleasantly from the driver's seat as Seth began to cry in earnest. "We're only about five minutes away. I'm sorry I can't have you stay with me, but my place is pretty cramped as it is, and Noah needs the help."

Noah Carson. Addie didn't know anything about him except he was some relative of Laurel's boyfriend, and he needed a housekeeper. Addie didn't have experience keeping anyone's house, let alone a ranch, but she needed a job and someplace to stay, and Laurel had provided her with both. In the kind of town Peter would never dream of finding on a map, let alone stepping foot into.

She hoped.

"I'm going to have to apologize about Noah, though," Laurel said, maneuvering her car onto a gravel road off the main highway. "This is kind of a surprise for him."

"A surprise?" Addie repeated, reaching into the back and stroking her finger over Seth's leg in an effort to soothe.

"It's just, Noah *needs* the help, but doesn't want to *admit* he needs the help, so we're forcing his hand a bit."

Addie's horror must have shown on her face, because Laurel reached over and gave Addie's arm a squeeze, her gaze quickly returning to the road.

"It's fine. I promise."

"I don't want to be in anyone's way or a burden, Laurel. That isn't why I called you."

"I know, and in an ideal world Noah would hire you of his own volition, but we don't live in an ideal world. Noah's cousin, who used to do most of the housekeeping, moved out. Grady—that's Noah's other cousin—tried running an ad but Noah refused to see anyone. This, he can't refuse."

"Why?"

Laurel flicked a glance Addie's way as she pulled in front of a ramshackle, if roomy-looking, ranch house.

"Addie, I know you're in trouble."

Addie sucked in a breath. "You do?"

"I could be reading things wrong, but I'm guessing Seth's father isn't a very good man, and you need to get away from him."

Addie swallowed. It was the truth. It wouldn't be a

lie to tell Laurel she was right. Seth's father was a terrible man, and Addie desperately needed to get away from him.

"I'm a cop, Addie. I've dealt with a lot of domestics. This is the perfect place to get away from a guy who can't control himself. You're safe here. In Bent. At the Carson Ranch, and with me looking out for you." Laurel smiled reassuringly.

"I just…" Addie inhaled and exhaled, looking at the house in front of her. It looked downright historical. "I need a fresh start. I'd hate to think it's built on someone who doesn't want me around."

"Noah might not want you around, but he needs you around. The way I see it, you two need each other. Noah might be quiet or gruff, but he's not a jerk. He'll treat you right no matter how much he doesn't want you to be here. I can promise you that."

"And the baby?"

"I've never seen Noah hurt anyone, and I've known him all my life and worked in law enforcement here for almost ten years. But most especially, I've never seen him be cruel to anyone, even Delaneys. He's not an easy man to read, but he's a good man. I'd bet my life on that."

The door to the house opened and a big, broad, bearded man stepped out. He wore jeans and a T-shirt, the lines of a tattoo visible at the sleeve. His grin was like sin, and all for Laurel. So this couldn't be the quiet, reserved Noah she was apparently ambushing.

"That's your man?" Addie asked, watching him

saunter toward where they were parked. She'd never seen two people just look at each other and flash sparks.

Laurel grinned. "Yes, it is. Come on. Let's get you introduced."

NOAH GLOWERED OUT the window. Damn Grady. More, damn Laurel Delaney getting her Delaney nose all up in his Carson business. Since he wasn't the one sleeping with her, Noah didn't know why he had to be the one saddled with her relative.

But saddled he was.

The young woman who got out of the passenger seat looked nothing like a housekeeper, not that a housekeeper had ever graced the uneven halls of the Carson Ranch. He came from hardscrabble stock who'd never seen much luxury in life. Never seen much purpose for it, either.

Noah *still* didn't, but all his help had moved out. Grady was off living with a Delaney. Vanessa, who'd once taken on much of the cleaning and cooking responsibilities—no matter how poorly—had moved into town. His brother, Ty, came and went as he pleased, spending much of his time in town. Any time he spent at the ranch was with the horses or pushing Noah's buttons. Noah's teenage stepcousin was as helpful as a skunk.

Noah was running a small cattle ranch on his own, and yes, cleaning and cooking definitely fell by the wayside.

Didn't mean he needed an outsider lurking in the

corners dusting or whatnot. Especially some wispy, timid blonde.

The blonde pulled a baby out of the back seat of the car. And she had a baby no less. Not even a very big-looking baby. The kind of tiny, drooly thing that would only serve to make him feel big and clumsy.

Noah's scowl deepened. He didn't know what to do with babies. Or wispy blondes. Or people in general. If only the horses could housekeep. He'd be set.

The door opened, Laurel striding in first. Noah didn't bother to soften his scowl and she rolled her eyes at him.

Noah was a firm believer in history, and the history of Bent, Wyoming, was that Carsons and Delaneys hated each other, and anytime they didn't, only bad things came of it. Noah didn't know what Laurel had done to Grady to change Grady's mind on the importance of the feud, but here they were, ruining his life. As a couple.

It was a shame he liked Laurel. Made all his scowling and disapproval hard to hang on to.

The blonde carrying the baby stepped in behind Laurel, followed by Grady.

"Noah," Laurel said with one of those smiles that were a clear and sad attempt to get him to smile back.

He didn't.

"Noah Carson, this is your new housekeeper, Addie Foster, and her son, Seth. Addie, this is Noah. Ignore the gruff Wyoming cowboy exterior. He's a teddy bear underneath."

Noah grunted and Grady laughed. "Ease up there, princess. No one's going to believe that."

Laurel shot Grady a disapproving look. "The point is, Noah will be a fair and, if not pleasant, a *kind* employer. Won't you, Noah?"

He grunted again. Then looked at the blonde. "Thought you were a Delaney."

"Oh, well." Addie smiled, or tried to. "Sort of. My grandfather was one." She waved a nervous hand, her eyes darting all around and not settling on any one thing.

"I'll show you to your room, and Noah and Grady can bring in the baby stuff," Laurel said cheerfully, already leading Addie and baby down the hall like she owned the place.

"Come on, let's get the stuff," Grady said once the women were gone.

"Remember when this was my house because I was the only one willing to work the ranch full time?" Noah glanced back at where the two women had disappeared. "Your woman's going to get baby ideas," he muttered.

Grady scoffed, but Noah noted that he didn't argue.

Which was to be expected, Noah supposed, but Noah hated change. Especially uncomfortable change. People change.

"You don't have to be prickly about it. You're going to have a clean house and a few home-cooked meals. Try a thank-you."

"You know me a lot better than that," Noah returned as they opened the trunk to Laurel's car.

Grady sighed, grabbing a stroller. "Laurel thinks Addie's in a bit of trouble."

"What kind of trouble?"

"Laurel's theory? Abusive husband."

"Hell," Noah grumbled. He didn't know what to do with babies, and he definitely didn't know what to do with a fragile woman who'd been the victim of abuse.

"She just needs a fresh start is all. Somewhere she feels safe. I'll keep an eye out for any other jobs that'll work while she's got the baby, but this is important. And it isn't like you don't need the help."

"It isn't that bad."

Grady looked at him dolefully as they hefted a menagerie of baby things out of Laurel's trunk and headed toward the house. "Pretty sure you were wearing that shirt yesterday, cousin."

Noah looked down at the faded flannel work shirt. "No, I wasn't." Maybe. He didn't mind doing laundry, but he hated folding laundry, and then the clean and dirty sometimes got a little mixed up if they weren't muck clothes.

Grady stepped inside, but Noah paused on the stairs. He looked back over his shoulder at the mountains in the distance. Clouds were beginning to form and roll, and there'd be a hell of a storm coming for them soon enough.

On a sigh, Noah stepped inside. This was his idea of a nightmare, but he wasn't a jerk who couldn't put his own wants and preferences on the back burner for someone in trouble. If the woman and the baby were really running from some no-good piece-of-trash ex…

He'd suck it up. He might be growly and taciturn, but he wasn't a bad guy. Not when it came to things like this. She might be related to a Delaney, but he knew what violence could do to a family. Carsons couldn't help but know that, and he'd promised himself he wouldn't be like them.

Somehow it had worked out. This generation of Carsons wasn't half as bad as the last, if a little wild, but he and Grady and Ty stood up for people who couldn't stand up for themselves. He wouldn't stop now.

Even if the woman and her baby did have Delaney in their blood.

Noah walked down the hall and into the room where Grady was already setting up all the baby gear for Addie while Laurel cooed over the baby in her arms. Noah gave Grady a pointed look but Grady ignored it.

"Well, we better get going and let you have some settle-in time," Laurel said, looking around the room as if inspecting it. "You can call me day or night. Whatever you need, or Seth needs."

"Thanks," Addie said, and Noah tried not to frown over the tears shimmering in the woman's eyes. Hell, female tears were the worst thing. Laurel and Addie hugged, the baby between them, before Grady and Laurel left. Laurel paused in front of Noah.

"Thank you," she mouthed, holding a hand over her heart.

Noah merely scowled, but the annoying thing about Laurel was she was never fooled by things like that. She seemed to be under the impression he was the nicest one of the lot.

Noah hated that she was right.

"So, I'll leave you to settle in," Noah offered, not expressly making eye contact considering this was a bedroom. "Need anything, let me know."

"Oh, but... Shouldn't I be saying that to you? I

mean, shouldn't we go over duties? Since Laurel and Grady set this up, I… I'm not sure what you expect of me." She bounced the baby on her hip, but Noah figured it was more nerves than trying to keep the boy from fussing.

He tried to smile, though even if he'd accomplished it he knew it was hard to see beyond the beard. "We can do it in the morning."

She blinked at him, all wide blue-eyed innocence. "I'd like to do it now. This is a job, and I should be working it."

"It's Sunday. Rule number one, you don't work on Sunday."

"What do I do then?"

"I don't care, but I'll cook my own meals and clean up after myself on Sundays. Understood?"

She nodded. "What's rule number two?"

Timid. He did not know what to do with timid, but he was being forced. Well, maybe he needed to treat her like a skittish horse. Horse training wasn't his expertise, but he understood enough about the animals to know they needed a clear leader, routine and the opportunity to build their confidence.

Noah glanced at the hopeful young woman and tried not to grimace.

"I have a checklist," she blurted.

"A checklist?"

"Yes, of duties. Of things I do for people. When I'm housekeeping. I… You…"

The sinking feeling that had been plaguing him since Grady announced his and Laurel's little plan that morning sank deeper. "You haven't done this before, have you?"

"Oh." She looked everywhere around the room except him. "Um. Well. Sort of."

"Sort of?"

"I… I can cook, and clean. I just haven't ever been on a ranch, or lived in someone else's house as their employee. So that's, um, well, it's super weird." She glanced at the kid in her arms. "And I have a baby. Which is weird."

"Super weird," he intoned.

She blinked up at him, some of that anxiety softening in her features. "If you tell me what you want me to do, I promise I can do it. I'm just not sure what you expect. Or want."

"I'll make you up a checklist."

She opened her mouth, then closed it, then opened it again. "I'm sorry, was that a joke? I can't exactly tell."

Noah's mouth twitched of its own accord. "Settle in. Get the baby settled in. Tomorrow morning, six a.m., kitchen table. We'll discuss your duties then."

"Okay."

He turned to go, but she stopped him with a hesitant "um."

He looked over his shoulder at her.

"It's just, could you give us something of a tour? A map? Smoke signals to the bathroom?"

Noah was very bad at controlling his facial features, half of why he kept a beard, so the distaste must have been clear all over his face.

"I'm sorry, I make jokes when I'm nervous."

"Funny, I just shut up."

Those big blue eyes blinked at him, not quite in horror, but not necessarily in understanding, either.

"Sorry," he muttered. "That was a joke. I joke when I'm nervous, too."

"Really?"

"No. Never," he replied, chastising himself for being prickly, and then ignoring his own chastisement. "Follow me. I'll show you around."

Chapter Two

September

Addie liked to use Seth's afternoon nap for laundry folding and listening to an audiobook, then dinner prep. She'd been at the Carson Ranch for a full month now, and while she couldn't claim comfort or the belief she was truly safe and settled, she'd developed a routine, and that was nice.

She found she liked housekeeping, much to her surprise. As an administrative assistant in the family business—a franchise of furniture stores Grandpa had moved to Boston to run when his father-in-law had died suddenly back in the fifties—she'd hated waiting on people, keeping things and meetings organized. She'd taken the job because it had been expected of her, and she hadn't known what else to do with her life.

So, the fact keeping everything neat and organized at Noah's house, making meals and helping the ranch run smoothly felt good was a surprise. Maybe it was the six months of being on the run and not having a house or anything to care for except Seth's safety.

Maybe it was simply that she felt, if not safe here, like she *fit* here.

Addie worked on chopping vegetables for a salad, the baby monitor she'd bought with her first overly generous paycheck sitting on the sill of the window overlooking the vast Carson Ranch. She hadn't needed a monitor in any of the previous places she'd been. They were all hotel rooms or little one-room apartments where she could hear Seth no matter where she went.

Now she had a whole house to roam, and so did Seth. They had these beautiful views to take in. For as long as it lasted, this life was *good*.

Some little voice in the back of her head warned her not to get too attached or settle in too deeply. Peter could always find her here, although it was unlikely. She hadn't shared anything with her father since he'd cut off Kelly long before Seth, and she'd been on shaky ground for *not* cutting Kelly off as well.

As for the rest of her friends and family, she'd sent a cheery email to them saying she'd gotten an amazing job teaching English in China and she'd send them contact information when she was settled.

If anyone had been suspicious, she'd been long gone before she could see evidence of it.

Addie didn't miss Boston or her cold father or even the furniture store that was supposed to be her legacy. That was also a surprise. Boston and her family had always been home, though not exactly a warm one after Mom had died when Addie'd been a kid. Still, striking out and starting over as a faux single mom had been surprisingly fulfilling. If she discounted the terror and constant running.

But she wasn't running right now. More and more, she was thinking of the Carson Ranch as *home*.

"You are a hopeless idiot, Addie Foster," she muttered to herself.

She startled as the door swung open, the knife she'd been using clattering to the cutting board from nerveless fingers.

But it was only Noah who swept in, looking as he always did, like some mythical man from a Wild West time machine. Dirty old cowboy hat, scuffed and beaten-up cowboy boots. The jeans and heavy coat were modern enough, but Noah's beard wasn't like all the fashionable hipster ones she was used to. No, Noah's beard was something of an old-fashioned shield.

She found herself pondering a little too deeply what he might be shielding himself from. Snapping herself out of that wonder, she picked up the knife. "You're early," she offered, trying to sound cheerful. "Dinner isn't ready yet."

It was another thing she'd surprisingly settled into with ease. They all three ate dinner together. Noah wasn't exactly a talkative guy, but he listened. Sometimes he even entertained Seth while she cleaned up dinner.

He grunted, as he was so often wont to do, and slid his coat and hat off before hanging them on the pegs. She watched it all through her peripheral vision, forcing herself not to linger on the outline of his muscles in the thermal shirt he wore.

Yes, Noah had muscles, and they were not for her to ogle. Though she did on occasion. She was *human*, after all.

"Just need to call the vet," he said.

"Is something wrong?"

"Horses aren't right. Will there be enough for dinner if Ty comes over?"

"Of course." Addie had gotten used to random Carsons showing up at the house at any time of day or night, or for any meal. She always made a little extra for dinner, as leftovers could easily be made into a lunch the next day.

Gotten used to. She smiled to herself as Noah grabbed the phone and punched in a number. It was almost unfathomable to have gotten used to a new life and think she might be able to stay in it.

Noah spoke in low tones to the vet and Addie worked on adding more lettuce to the salad so there would be enough for Ty. She watched out the window at the fading twilight. The days were getting shorter and colder. It was early fall yet, but the threat of snow seemed to be in the air.

She loved it here. She couldn't deny it. The mountains in the distance, the ramshackle stables and barns. The animals she didn't trust to approach but loved to watch. The way the sun gilded everything gold in the mornings and fiery red in the evenings. The air, so clear and different from anything she'd ever known before.

She felt at *home* here. More so than any point in her life. Maybe it was the circumstances, everything she was running from, how much she'd taken for granted before her sister had gotten mixed up with a mob boss. But she felt it, no matter how hard she tried to fight it.

She could easily see Seth growing up in this amazing place with Noah as something like a role model. Oh, it almost hurt to think of. It was a pipe dream. She couldn't allow herself to believe Peter could never find them here. Could she?

Noah stopped talking and set the phone back in its cradle, looking far too grim. Addie's stomach clenched. "Is everything okay?"

"Vet said it sounded like horses got into something chemical. Poison even," Noah said gruffly with no preamble.

Any warmth or comfort or *love* of this place drained out of Addie in an instant. "Poison," she repeated in a whisper.

Noah frowned at her, then softened that imperceptible amount she was beginning to recognize. "Carsons have some enemies in Bent. It isn't unheard of."

It was certainly possible. The Carsons were a rough-and-tumble bunch. Noah's brother, Ty, could be gruff and abrasive when he was irritated. Grady was certainly charming, but he ran a bar and though she'd never spent any time there since the ranch and Seth took up most of her time, Laurel often spoke disparagingly of the clientele there.

Then there was Noah's cousin Vanessa. Sharp, antagonistic Vanessa would likely have some enemies. Or Grady's troublemaking stepbrother.

The problem was none of them lived at the ranch full-time. They came and went. Noah could be grumpy, but she truly couldn't imagine him having enemies.

She, on the other hand, had a very real enemy.

"Are you sure?" she asked tentatively.

"Look, I know you've had some trouble in your past, but who would poison my horses to get at you?"

He had a point. A good point, even if he didn't know the whole story. Peter would want her and Seth, not Noah or his horses. He'd never do something so small and piddly that wouldn't hurt *her* directly.

"Trust me," Noah said, dialing a new number into the phone. "This doesn't have a thing to do with you, and the vet said if he gets over here soon and Ty helps out, we'll be able to save them." Noah turned away from her and started talking into the phone, presumably to his brother, without even a hi.

Addie stared hard at her salad preparations, willing her heart to steady, willing herself to believe Noah's words. What *would* poisoned horses have to do with her?

Nothing. Absolutely nothing. She had to believe that, but everything that had felt like settling in and comfort and routine earlier now curdled in her gut.

Don't ever get too used to this place. It's not yours, and it never will be.

She'd do well to remember it.

October

NOAH FROWNED AT the fence. Someone had hacked it to pieces, and now half his herd was wandering the damn mountains as a winter storm threatened in the west.

He immediately thought of last month and the surprise poison a few of his horses had ingested. The vet had saved the horses, but Noah and Ty had never found the culprits. Noah liked to blame Laurel and her precious sheriff's department for the crime still being unsolved, even though it wasn't fair.

Whoever had poisoned the horses had done a well enough job being sneaky, but not in creating much damage. For all he knew it was some kids playing a dumb prank, or even an accident.

This right here was no accident. It was strange. Maybe it could be chalked up to a teenage prank, but something about all this felt wrong, like an itch he couldn't reach.

But he had to fix the fence and get the cows before he could worry about wrong gut feelings. Noah mounted his horse and headed for the cabin. He'd have to start carrying his cell to call for help if these little problems kept cropping up.

What would Addie be up to? She'd been his housekeeper for two months now, and he had to admit in the quiet of his own mind, he'd gotten used to her presence. So used to it, he relied on it. She kept the cabin neat and clean, her cooking was better and better, and she and the boy… Well, he didn't mind them underfoot as much as he'd thought he was going to.

Maybe, just maybe, he'd been a little lonely in that house by himself earlier in the summer, and maybe, just maybe, he appreciated some company. Because Addie didn't intrude on his silence or poke at him for more. The boy was loud, and getting increasingly mobile, which sometimes meant he was crawling all over Noah if he tried to sit down, but that wasn't the kind of intrusion that bothered him. He found he rather enjoyed the child's drooly smiles and screeches of delight.

"What has happened to you?" he muttered to himself. He looked at the gray sky. A winter storm had been threatening for days, but it hadn't let down its wrath yet. Noah had no doubt it would choose the most inopportune time possible. As in, right now with his cows scattered this way and that.

He urged his horse to go a little faster. He'd need Grady and Ty, or Vanessa and Ty if Grady couldn't get away from the bar. Maybe even Clint could come over after school, assuming he'd gone today. This was an all-hands-on-deck situation.

But as he approached the cabin, he frowned at a set of footprints in the faint dusting of snow that had fallen this morning. The footprints didn't go from where visitors usually parked to the door, but instead followed the fence line before clearly hopping the fence, then went up to the front window.

A hot bolt of rage went through Noah. Someone had been at that window watching Addie. He jumped from the horse and rushed into the house. Only when he flung open the door and stormed inside did he realize how stupid he looked.

Addie jumped a foot at her seat on the couch, where she was folding clothes. "What's wrong? What happened?" she asked, clutching one of his shirts to her chest. It was an odd thing to see, her delicate hands holding the fabric of something he wore on his body.

He shook that thought away and focused on thinking clearly. On being calm. He didn't want to scare her. "Somebody broke the fence and the cows got out."

Addie stared at him, blue eyes wide, the color draining from her dainty face as it had the day of the poisoning. He'd assured her *that* had nothing to do with her, and he believed it. He believed this had nothing to do with her, too, but those footsteps and her reaction to anything wrong or sudden…

He wondered about that. She never spoke of Seth's father or what she might be fleeing, and her actions always seemed to back up Laurel's theory about being on the run from an abusive husband. Especially as she now glanced worriedly at Seth's baby monitor, as if she could see him napping in his room through it.

Noah shook his head. He was being paranoid. Letting her fear outweigh his rational mind. He might have a bit of a soft spot for Addie and her boy, which he'd admit to no one ever, but he couldn't let her fears become his own.

She was his employee. If he sometimes caught himself watching her work in his kitchen… A housekeeper was all he needed. Less complicated than some of the other things his mind drifted to when he wasn't careful.

Luckily, Noah was exceedingly careful.

"Going to call in some backup to help me round them up."

"Shouldn't you call Laurel?" She paused when he scowled, but then continued. "Or anyone at the sheriff's department?"

She had a point, but he didn't want to draw attention to repeated issues at his ranch. Didn't want to draw the town's attention to Addie and that something might be going on, if it did in fact connect to her.

Maybe the smarter thing to do would be keep it all under wraps and then be more diligent, more watchful, and find whoever was pulling these little pranks himself. Mete out some Carson justice.

Yeah, he liked that idea a lot better.

"I'll handle it. Don't worry."

"Does this have to do with the poisoning? Do you think—"

Noah sent her a silencing look, trying not to feel guilty when she shrank back into the couch. "I'll handle it. Don't worry," he repeated.

She muttered something that sounded surprisingly sarcastic though he didn't catch the words, but she went back to folding the laundry and Noah crossed to the phone.

He called Ty first, then let Ty handle rounding up whatever Carsons could be of help. He didn't tell Ty about the footsteps, but a bit later when Ty, Grady and Clint showed up and Noah left the cabin with them, he held Grady back while Ty and Clint went to saddle their horses.

"What's up?" Grady asked. "You think this is connected to the poison?"

"I think I can't rule it out. I don't have a clue who's doing it, but part of me thinks it's some dumb kid trying to poke at a Carson to see what he'll do."

Grady laughed. "He'd have to be pretty dumb."

"Yeah. I don't want Addie to know, but..." He sighed. He needed someone besides him to know. Someone besides him on the watch, and Grady ran the one bar in town. He saw and heard things few other people in Bent did. "There were footprints at the window, as if someone had been watching her."

Grady's jaw tightened. "You think it's the ex?"

"I don't know what it is, but we need to keep an eye out."

Grady nodded. "I'll tell Laurel."

"No. She'll tell Addie. She's just calmed down from the poisoning—now this. I don't want to rile her more."

"Laurel will only do what's best. You know that."

Noah puffed out a breath. "Addie's settled from that skittish thing she was before. Hate to see her go back."

"She's not a horse, Noah." Grady grinned. "But maybe you know that all too well."

Noah scowled. "I want to know who poisoned my horses. I want to know who ran off my cattle, and I damn well want to know who's peeping in my window."

Grady nodded. "We'll get to the bottom of it. No one touches what's ours. Cow, mine or woman." Grady grinned at the old family joke.

Noah didn't. "No woman issues here," he grumbled. But Grady was right in one respect. No one messed with the Carsons of Bent, Wyoming, and walked away happy or satisfied about it. For over a century, the Carsons had been pitted on the wrong side of the law. The outlaws of Bent. The rich, law-abiding Delaneys had made sure that legend perpetuated, no matter what good came out of the Carson clan.

It was a good thing bad reputations could serve a purpose now and again. He'd do anything to protect what was his.

Addie wasn't his, though. No matter how he sometimes imagined she was.

He shook those thoughts away. "Will you stay here and watch out?"

"You could," Grady suggested.

"Addie'd think that's weird. I don't want her suspicious."

"That's an awful lot of concern for a Delaney, cousin," Grady said with one of his broad grins that were meant to irritate. Grady had perfected that kind of smile.

Noah knew arguing with Grady about the cause of his concern would only egg Grady on, so Noah grunted and headed for the stables.

Addie Foster was not his to protect personally. Grady'd do just as good a job, and Noah had cows to find and bring back home.

When that weird edge of guilt plagued him the rest of the night, as if his mission was to protect Addie and asking for help was some kind of failure, Noah had the uncomfortable feeling of not knowing what the hell to do about it.

When Noah didn't know how to fix a problem, he did the next best thing. He ignored it.

Chapter Three

November

Addie hummed along with the song playing over the speaker at the general store. Seth happily slammed his sippy cup against the sides of the cart as she unloaded the groceries onto the checkout counter.

"I swear he grows every week," Jen Delaney said with a smile as she began to ring up Addie's items.

"It's crazy. He's already in eighteen-month clothes." Addie bagged the groceries as Jen handed them to her.

It was true. Seth was growing like a weed, thriving in this life she'd built for them. Addie smiled to herself. After the horse poison and the fence debacle, things had settled down. She'd been here three months now. She had a routine down, knew many of the people in town and mostly had stopped looking over her shoulder at every stray noise. Sometimes nights were still hard, but for the most part, life was good. Really good.

Noah had assured her time and time again those two incidents were feud-related, nothing to do with her, and she was finally starting to believe him. She trusted Noah. Implicitly. With her safety, with Seth.

Laurel had been right on that first car ride. Noah wasn't always easy to read or the warmest human being, but he was a *good* man.

Which had created something of a Noah situation. Well, more a weirdness than a situation. And a weirdness she was quite sure only she felt, because she doubted Noah felt much of anything for her. On the off chance he did, it was so buried she'd likely not live long enough to see it.

"Addie?"

Addie glanced up at Jen. The young woman must have finished ringing everything up while Addie was lost in Noah thoughts. Something that happened far too often as of late.

Addie paid for the groceries, smiling at Jen while she inwardly chastised herself.

Noah Carson was her boss. No matter that she liked the way he looked or that she got fluttery over his gentle way with the horses and cows. And Seth.

She sighed inwardly. He was so sweet with Seth. Never got frustrated with the boy's increasing mobility or fascination with Noah's hat or beard.

But no matter that Noah was sweet with Seth, or so kind with her, he was off-limits for her ever-growing fantasies of good, handsome men and happily-ever-afters.

She glanced down at the happy boy kicking in the cart. Sometimes Seth gave her that smile with big blue eyes and she missed her sister so much it hurt. But it always steadied her, renewed any resolve that needed renewing.

She would do anything to keep him safe.

She pushed the cart out of the general store to where her truck was parallel parked, but before she reached it, a man blocked her way.

She looked at him expectantly, waiting for him to move or say something, but he just stood there. Staring at her.

She didn't recognize him. Everything about him was nondescript and plain, and still he didn't move or speak.

"Excuse me," she finally said, pulling Seth out of the cart and balancing him on her hip. "This is my truck."

The man moved only enough to glance at the truck. Also a new skill for her, driving a truck, but Noah had fixed up one of the old ones he used on the ranch for her to use when she had errands.

The strange man turned his gaze back to her and still said nothing. He still didn't move.

Addie's heart started beating too hard in her chest, fear seizing her limbs. This wasn't normal. This wasn't...

She turned quickly, her hand going over Seth's head with the idea of protecting him somehow. This man was here to get her. Peter had finally caught up with them. She had to run.

She could go back in the store and...and...

"Oof." Instead of her intended dash to the store, she slammed into a hard wall of man.

"Addie."

She looked up at Noah, whose hand curled around her arm. He looked down at her, something like concern or confusion hidden underneath all that hair and stoicism.

"Everything okay?" he asked in that gruff voice

that suggested no actual interest in the answer, but that was the thing about Noah. He gave the impression he didn't care about anything beyond his horses and cows, but he'd fixed up that truck for her even though she hadn't asked. He played with Seth as if people who hired housekeepers usually had relationships with the housekeeper's kid. He made sure there was food for Ty, room for Vanessa and Clint, and work if any of them wanted it.

He was a man who cared about a lot of people and hid it well.

"I just..." She looked back at where the strange, unspeaking man had been. There was no one there. No one. She didn't know how to explain it to Noah. She didn't know how to explain it to anyone.

The man hadn't said anything threatening. Hadn't done anything threatening, but that hadn't been normal. "I thought I saw someone..." She looked around again, but there was no sign of anyone in the sunshine-laden morning.

"As in *someone* someone?" Noah asked in that same stoic voice, and yet Addie had no doubt if she gave any hint of fear, Noah would jump into action.

So she forced herself to smile. "I'm being silly. It was just a man." She shook her head and gestured with her free hand. "I'm sure it was nothing." Which was a flat-out lie. As much as she'd love to tell herself it was nothing, she knew Peter too well to think this wasn't *something.*

She blew out a breath, scanning the road again. There was just no other explanation. He knew where she was. He knew.

"Addie."

She looked back at Noah, realizing his hand was still on her arm. Big and rough. Strong. Working for Noah had made her feel safe. Protected.

But this wasn't his fight, and she'd brought it to his door.

"I'm sorry," she whispered, closing her eyes.

"For what?" he asked in that gruff, irritable way.

Seth lunged for Noah, happily babbling his favorite word over and over again. "No, no, no." Addie tried to hold on to the wiggling child, but Noah took him out of her arms with ease.

"Aren't you supposed to be back at the ranch? You know I get groceries on Wednesdays. I could have picked up whatever for you."

"It's feed," Noah said. "Couldn't have loaded it up yourself with the baby." He glanced at the grocery cart behind her. "We'll put the groceries in my truck."

"Oh, I can handle…"

"He always falls asleep on the way home, doesn't he?" Noah asked as if it wasn't *something* that he knew Seth's routine. Or that he was letting Seth pull the cowboy hat off his head, and then smash it back on.

Noah moved for the cart, because you didn't argue with Noah. He made a decision and you followed it whether you wanted to or not. Partly because he was her boss, but she also thought it was partly just him.

"Let's get home and you can tell me what really happened." Noah's dark gaze scanned the street as if he could figure everything out simply by looking around.

She knew it was foolish, but she was a little afraid he could. "I swear, nothing happened. I'm being silly."

"Well, you can tell me about that, too. At home." He handed her Seth and then took the cart.

Home. She'd wanted to build a *home*. For Seth. For herself. But if Peter had found her...

She couldn't let herself get worked up. For Seth's sake, she had to think clearly. She had to formulate a plan. And she couldn't possibly let Noah know the truth.

Noah didn't think running away was the answer, that she knew after listening to his lectures to Clint.

Beyond that, regardless of his personal feelings for her—whether they existed deep down or not—he had a very clear personal code. That personal code would never let a woman and a baby run away without protection.

Which would put him in danger. Very much because of her personal feelings, she couldn't let that happen.

"Okay. I'll meet you back at the ranch." She smiled pleasantly and even let him take the cart of groceries and wheel it down to where his truck was parked on the corner. She frowned at that. "If you were in town to pick up feed, why are you here?"

Noah didn't glance at her, but he did shrug. "Saw the truck. Thought you might need some help loading." Then he was hidden behind his truck door, loading the groceries into the back seat.

Addie glanced down at Seth. "I really don't know what to do with that man," she murmured, opening her own truck door and getting Seth situated in his car seat. She supposed in the end it didn't matter she didn't know what to do with him. If someone was here...

Well, Seth was her priority. She couldn't be a sitting

duck, and she couldn't bring Noah into harm's way. This wasn't like the poison or the fence. This was directed at *her*. That man had stared at *her*. Whether or not those first two things were related didn't matter, because *this* was about *her*.

Which meant it was time to leave again. She slid into the driver's seat, glancing in her rearview mirror, where she watched Noah start walking back toward the store to return the now-empty cart.

Addie had become adept at lying in the past year. She'd *had* to, but mainly she only had to lie to strangers or people she didn't know very well. Even that initial lie to Laurel, and the past three months of upholding it with everyone, hadn't been hard. Pretending to be Seth's biological mother was as easy as pie since he was hers and hers alone these days.

But finding a new lie, and telling it to Noah's face— that was going to be a challenge. She changed her gaze from Noah's reflection to Seth in the car seat. She smiled at him in the mirror.

"It's okay, baby. I'll take care of it." Somehow. Someway.

NOAH HAD UNLOADED the groceries at the front door, and Addie had taken them inside, the baby monitor sitting on the kitchen table as they quietly worked.

He should have insisted they talk about what had transpired at the general store, but instead he'd gone back out to his truck and driven over to the barn to unload the feed.

Then he'd dawdled. He was not a man accustomed to dawdling. He was also not a man accustomed to *this*.

Every time something bad had happened in the first
two months, he'd been the one to find it. Little attacks
that had been aimed at the ranch.

Whatever had shaken Addie today was about her.
What she'd seen. He could attribute her shakiness to
being "silly" as she said, or even her previous "situation" with her ex, but he didn't know what that was.
Not really. He certainly hadn't poked into it. He was
not a poker, and Addie was not a babbler. It was why
this whole thing worked.

But she'd eased into life at the Carson Ranch. So
much so that Noah, on occasion, considered thanking
Laurel and Grady for forcing his hand on the whole
housekeeper thing. She'd made his life easier.

Except where she hadn't. Those uncomfortable
truths he'd had to learn about himself—he was lonely,
he liked having someone under his roof and to talk to
for as little as he did it. He liked having her and Seth
in particular.

Which was his own fault. She didn't carry any responsibility for his stupid feelings. Even if he'd had
a sense of triumph over the fact Addie didn't jump at
random noises anymore, and she didn't get scared for
no reason. Both with the poison and the fence, she'd
walked on eggshells for a few days, then gotten back
to her old quietly cheerful self.

He'd never told her about the footprints and they'd
never returned. So maybe he'd overreacted then.
Maybe *he'd* been silly, but whatever had rattled her
at the store was something real. Which meant they
needed to talk about it.

But he wasn't the *talker*. He was the doer. Grady

or Ty went in and did all the figuring out, and Noah brought up the rear, so to speak. He was there. He did what needed to be done, but he was no great determiner of what that thing was. He left that to people who liked to jack their jaw.

Which was when he realized what he really needed. He pulled his cell phone out of his pocket and typed a text. When he got the response he'd hoped for, he put his phone away and got back to his real work. Not protecting Addie Foster and whatever her issue was, but running a ranch.

He worked hard, thinking as little about Addie as possible, and didn't reappear at the main house until supper. He stepped up onto the porch, scraping the mud off his boots before entering.

The blast of warmth that hit him was an Addie thing. She opened the west-facing curtains so the sun set golden through the windows and into the kitchen and entryway every day. Whenever he stepped in, she had supper ready or almost.

Seth slammed his sippy cup against his high-chair tray and yelled, "No!" Noah was never sure if it was a greeting or an admonition.

Noah grunted at the boy, his favorite mode of greeting. He sneaked a glance at Addie to make sure she still had her back to him, then made a ridiculous face that made Seth squeal out a laugh.

Noah advanced closer, but he noted Addie was slamming things around in the kitchen and didn't turn to face him with her usual greeting and announcement of what was for dinner.

It all felt a little too domestic, which was becoming

more and more of a problem. He couldn't complain about being fed nightly by a pretty woman, but sitting down with her and her kid for a meal every day was getting to feel normal.

Integral.

Noah hovered there, not quite sure what to do. Laurel had assured him via text she'd come in and figure out whatever was up with Addie after he'd contacted her, but Addie did not seem calmed.

He cleared his throat. "Uh. Um, need help?" he offered awkwardly.

She turned to face him, tongs in one hand and an anger he'd never seen simmering in her blue eyes.

She pointed the tongs at him. "You, Noah Carson, are a coward. And a bit of a high-handed jerk."

He raised an eyebrow at her, but Addie didn't wilt. Not even a hint of backing down. She crossed her arms over her chest and stared right back at him. In another situation he might have been impressed at the way she'd blossomed into something fierce.

"Because?"

She huffed out a breath. "You went and told Laurel I was having a problem when I told you I was not."

"But you were."

"No. I wasn't." She pointed angrily at the table with the tongs. "Sit down and eat."

He'd never seen much of Addie's temper. Usually if she got irritated with him she went to some other room in the house and cleaned something. Or went into her room and played with Seth. She never actually directed any of her ire at him.

He didn't know what to do with it. But he *was* hungry, so he took his seat next to Seth's high chair, where the kid happily smacked his hands into the tiny pieces of food Addie had put on his tray before Noah walked in.

She slammed a plate in front of Noah. Chicken legs and mashed potatoes and some froufrou-looking salad thing. Usually she didn't *serve* him, but he wasn't one to argue with anyone, let alone an angry female.

She stomped back to the kitchen counter, then to the table again. She sat in a chair opposite him with an audible *thump*.

Her huffiness and sternness were starting to irritate him. He didn't have much of a temper beyond general curmudgeon, but when someone started poking at him, things tended to… Well, he tended to avoid people who made him lose his temper. Addie'd never even remotely tested that before.

But she sure was now.

"I can handle this," she said, leveling him with her sternest look. She shook out a paper towel and placed it on her lap like it was an expensive cloth napkin and they were in some upscale restaurant.

"What? What is this thing you can handle?" he returned evenly.

She stared right back at him like he was slow. "It's nothing. That's why I can handle it."

Noah wanted to beat his head against the table. "You were *visibly* shaken this morning, and it wasn't like it used to be."

Her sharp expression softened slightly. "What do you mean?"

Noah shrugged and turned his attention to his food.

"When you first got here you were all jumpy-like. This was not the same thing."

She was quiet for a few seconds, so he took the opportunity to eat.

"I didn't know you noticed," she said softly.

He shrugged, shoveling mashed potatoes into his mouth and hoping this conversation was over.

He should have known better. Addie didn't poke at him, but she also didn't leave things unfinished. "I need you to promise you won't call Laurel like that again. The last thing I need is well-meaning people…" She trailed off for a few seconds until he looked up from his plate.

Her eyebrows were drawn together and she was frowning at her own plate, and Noah had the sinking, horrifying suspicion those were tears making her blue eyes look particularly shiny.

She cleared her throat. "I'll handle things. Don't bring Laurel into this again." She looked up, as if that was that.

"No."

"What did you say?" she asked incredulously.

"I said no."

She sputtered, something like a squeak emanating from her mouth. "You can't just…you can't just say no!"

"But I did."

Another squeaking sound, which Seth joined in as if it was a game.

Addie took a deep breath as if trying to calm herself. "A man stood in my way and wouldn't move. He said nothing, and he did nothing threatening. It was nothing. Calling Laurel, on the other hand, was something. And I did not appreciate it."

"If what happened this morning were nothing, it wouldn't have freaked you out. What did Laurel say?"

"She said you're an idiot and I should quit and move far away."

"No, she didn't." He didn't believe Laurel *would* say something like that, but there was a panicked feeling tightening his chest.

"Noah, this isn't your problem," Addie said, and if he wasn't crazy, there was a hint of desperation in her tone, which only served to assure him this *was* his problem.

"You live under my roof, Addie Foster. You are my problem."

She frowned at him as if that made no sense to her, but it didn't need to. It made sense to *him*. The people in his family and under his roof were under his protection. End of story.

Chapter Four

Addie ate the rest of her dinner in their normal quiet companionship. Quite honestly, she was rendered speechless by Noah's gruff, certain proclamation.

You are my problem.

He had no idea what kind of problem she could be if she stayed, and yet no matter how many times she'd chastised herself to pack up and leave *immediately*, here she was. Cleaning up dinner dishes while Seth crawled in and out of the play tent she'd placed on the floor for him.

You are my problem.

She glanced at the door. Noah had stridden back outside right after dinner, which he did sometimes. Chores to finish up or horses or cows to check on, though sometimes she thought he did it just to escape her.

She sighed heavily. Noah made no sense to her, but she didn't want to be his *problem*. He'd been nothing but kind, in fact proving to her that her sister's determination after Peter that all men were scum wasn't true in the least.

Noah might be hard to read and far too gruff, but he was the furthest thing from scum she'd ever met.

She glanced at Seth, who popped his smiling face out of the tent opening and screeched.

"Except for you, of course, baby," Addie said, grinning at Seth. Growing like a weed. It hurt to look at him sometimes, some mix of sorrow and joy causing an unbearable pain in her heart.

He'd settled in so well here. Their routine worked, and what would she do when she left? Where else would she find this kind of job where he got to be with her? Even if she could find a job that would allow her to afford day care, they wouldn't have the kind of security she needed. Seth always needed to be with her in case they needed to escape.

Like now.

She squeezed her eyes shut. She was in an impossible situation. She didn't want to put Noah—or any of the Carsons—at risk of Peter, but if she ran away without thinking things through, she risked Seth's well-being.

"No! No! No!" Seth yelled happily, making a quick crawling beeline for the door.

Addie took a few steps before scooping Seth up into her arms, a wriggling mass of complaint.

"He's not back yet," Addie said gently, settling Seth on her hip as she moved to the windows to close the curtains for the night. Sometimes, though, she and Seth stood here and watched the stars wink and shimmer in the distance while they waited for Noah's last return of the evening.

It felt like home, this place. Even with a man whose life she didn't share and was her boss living under the same roof. It was all so *right*. How could she leave?

And how can you stay?

She shook her head against the thought and closed the curtains. As she stepped back toward the kitchen to gather Seth's tent, she noticed something on the floor.

An envelope. Odd. Dread skittered through her. Noah always brought the mail in when he came to grab lunch. He always put it in the same place. Which was most definitely not the floor.

Maybe it had fallen. Maybe someone had managed to shoehorn the envelope through the bottom of the door; most of the weather stripping was in desperate need of being replaced.

Her name was written in dark block letters. With no address. She swallowed, her body shaking against her will.

Seth wiggled in her arms and it was a good anchor to reality. She had a precious life to keep safe. Somehow. Someway. She was the only one who could.

She forced herself to bend down and place Seth gently on the floor. He crawled off for the tent, and with a shaking hand Addie picked up the envelope.

Slowly, she walked over to the table and sat down. She stared at it, willing her breathing to even and her hands to stop shaking. She'd open it, and then she'd know what her next move would have to be.

She forced one more breath in and out and then broke the seal of the envelope and pulled out the sheet of paper. Feeling sick to her stomach, Addie unfolded the paper until she could see text.

I see you, Addie.

She pressed her fingers to her mouth, willing herself

not to break down. She'd come this far. She couldn't break down every time he found her. She just had to keep going, over and over again, until he didn't.

She wanted to drop the paper. Forget it existed. But she didn't have that option. She folded it back up and slid it inside the envelope, then pushed it into her pocket. She'd keep it. A reminder.

He wanted her scared. She didn't know why that seemed to be his priority when he could have her killed and take Seth far away.

There was no point trying to rationalize a sociopath's behavior. She knew one thing and one thing only: Peter wouldn't stop. So neither could she.

If she'd been alone, she might have risked staying in one spot. Just to see what he would do. But she wasn't alone. Now she had to protect Noah and the Carsons and Delaneys who'd been so kind to her.

She stood carefully, walking stiffly over to Seth. She pulled him out of the tent, much to his screaming dismay.

She patted his back. "Come on, baby. We don't have much time." She glanced at the windows where the curtains were now pulled. Was he out there? Waiting for her? Was it all a lure to get her to come out?

Were his men out there? Oh, God, had they hurt Noah? True panic beat through her. She could escape. She'd had enough close calls—a landlord letting her know a man had broken into her apartment, noticing a broken motel window before she'd stepped inside—to know she could find her way out of this one.

But what if they'd hurt Noah? She couldn't leave him. She couldn't let them…

Seth was bucking and crying now, and Addie closed her eyes and tried to think. She couldn't rush out without thinking. She couldn't escape without making sure Noah was okay, which was not part of any of the escape plans she always had mapped out in the back of her mind.

She should call Laurel. She hated to call Laurel after yelling at Noah for doing so, but this wasn't about her pride or her secrets. It was about Noah's safety.

Seth was still screaming in her ear, kicking his little legs against her. Addie retraced her steps, perilously close to tears.

She made it to the kitchen and fumbled with the phone. She was halfway through dialing Laurel's number when the front door squeaked open. Addie dropped the phone, scanning the kitchen for a weapon, any weapon.

If she could make it two feet, there was a butcher knife. Not much of a weapon against a gun, but—

Noah stepped inside, alone, his dark cowboy hat covering most of his face as he stomped his boots on the mat. When he glanced up at her, her relief was short lived, because there was a trickle of blood down his temple and cheek.

Addie rushed over to him, Seth's tantrum finally over. "Oh, my God, Noah." He was okay. Bleeding, but okay. She flung herself at him, relief so palpable it nearly toppled her. "You're okay," she said, hugging Seth between them.

"What the hell is wrong with you?" Noah grumbled, a hard wall against her cheek.

Which was when she realized she'd miscalculated deeply. Because he would know everything was wrong now, and she had no way of brushing this off as being silly.

HE FELT ADDIE stiffen against him and then slowly pull away. She did not meet his gaze, and she did not answer his question.

He was a little too disappointed she wasn't holding on to him anymore. "Addie," he warned, too sharp and gruff. But the woman affected him and he didn't know how to be soft about it. "What is it?"

"You're…bleeding," she offered weakly, still not looking at him.

"Yeah, one of my idiot cousins left a shovel in the middle of the yard and I tripped right into the barn door. What's going on? And don't lie to me. Just be honest. I'm not in the mood to play detective."

"Are you ever in the mood for anything?" she muttered while walking away from him, clearly not expecting him to catch her words.

"You'd be surprised," he returned, somewhat gratified when she winced and blushed. Still expressly not looking at him. It grated. That she was lying to him. That today was one big old ball of screwy.

That when she'd thrown herself at him he'd wanted to wrap his arms around her and hold her there. Worst of all, her *and* the kid.

"So, I just thought… I thought I heard something and—"

"Bull." Did she have any idea what a terrible liar she was? It was all darting eyes and nervous hand-wringing.

"Well, I mean, maybe I didn't hear anything, but when I was closing the windows there was a bird and—"

"Bull."

She stomped her foot impatiently. "Stop it, Noah."

"Stop feeding me bull and I'll stop interrupting."

She frowned at him and shook her head and heaved an unsteady exhale. She looked frazzled and haunted, really. Haunted like she'd been when she'd first gotten here, but he'd never seen her look panicked.

She walked over to the tiny kitchen, where Seth's tent was on the floor. She crouched down and let the boy crawl inside. She watched the kid for a second before walking over to a drawer and pulling out a washcloth. She wet it at the sink, then moved to the cabinet above the oven where they kept a few first aid things and medicine. She grabbed a bandage before returning to him.

She stood in front of him, gaze unreadable on his. She stepped close—too close, because he could smell dinner and Seth's wipes on her. That shouldn't be somehow enticing. He wasn't desperate for some domestic side of his life.

But she got up on her tiptoes and placed the warm cloth to where he'd scraped his forehead on the edge of the door. She wiped at the cut, her gaze not leaving his until she had to open the bandage.

Her eyebrows drew together as she peeled it from its plastic and then smoothed it over his forehead, her fingertips cool and soft against his brow. She met his gaze again then, sadness infusing her features.

"Noah, I have to leave."

He studied her, so imploringly serious, and, yeah, he didn't think that was bull. "Why?"

She glanced back at Seth, who was slapping his hands happily against the floor. "I just do. I can't give any kind of notice or time to find a new housekeeper. I have to go now." She glanced at the window, vulnerability written into every inch of her face that usually would have made Noah take a big old step back. He didn't do fragile, not a big, rough man like him.

But this wasn't about smoothing things over. This was about protecting someone who was very clearly in trouble.

"You're not going anywhere. You just need to tell me what's going on and we'll figure it out."

She looked back at him, expression bleak and confused. "Why?"

"Why?" He wanted to swear, but he thought better of it as Seth crawled over to his feet and used Noah's leg to pull himself into a standing position. Addie needed some reassuring, some soft and kind words, and he was so not the man for that.

But he was the only man here, and from everything Laurel and Grady had told him, and from Addie's own actions, Noah could only assume she'd been knocked around by Seth's father and feared him even now.

Softness might not be in him, but neither was turning away from something a little wounded.

"You're a part of the house. You've made yourself

indispensable," he continued, trying to wipe that confused bleakness off her face.

"No. No. No," Seth babbled, hitting Noah's leg with his pudgy baby fingers.

Noah scooped the kid up into his arms, irritated that Addie was still standing there staring at him all big-eyed and beautiful and hell if he knew what to do with any of this.

"You didn't just take a job when you came here— you joined a family," he said harshly. "We protect our own. That wasn't bull I was feeding you earlier. That is how things work here. You're under Carson protection."

"I've never known anyone like you," she whispered. Before that bloomed too big and warm and stupid in his chest, she kept going. "Any of you. Laurel, Grady. Jen, Ty. The whole lot of you, and it's so funny the town is always going on about some feud and Grady and Laurel cursing everything, but you're all the same, all of you Carsons and Delaneys. So good and wanting to help people who shouldn't mean anything to you."

"You've been here too long for that to be true. Of course you mean something to us." He cleared his throat. "Besides, you're a Delaney yourself by blood."

She looked away for a second, and he couldn't read her expression but Seth made a lunge for her. One of his favorite games to play, lunging back and forth between them. Over and over again.

Addie took Seth, but she met Noah's gaze with a soft, resigned sadness. "I'm not safe here. More importantly, Seth isn't safe here. We have to go."

"Where?"

"What?"

"Where will you go that you'll be safe?"

"I…" She blew out a breath, that sheen of tears filling her eyes, and if this hadn't been so serious, he would have up and walked away. He didn't do tears.

But this was too big. Too important.

"I don't know," she whispered, one of the tears falling over her cheek. "I'm not sure anywhere will ever be safe."

Noah had the oddest urge to reach out and brush it away. He tamped that urge down and focused on what needed to be done. "Then you'll stay."

"Noah."

"If you don't know where to be safe, then you'll stay here where a whole group of people are ready and willing to protect you and Seth."

"I can't put any of you in this, Noah. It's dangerous."

"Not if you tell us what we're up against." Not that it'd change *his* mind. He'd fight a whole damn army to keep her here.

Because she was useful. Like he'd said before. Integral. To his house. To the ranch. That was all.

"Promise me you'll stay put." They were too close, standing here like this. Even as Seth bounced in her arms and reached for his hat, their eyes didn't leave each other.

But she shook her head. "I can't, Noah. I can't promise you that."

Chapter Five

Addie knew the next step was to walk away. Run away, but Noah's gaze held her stuck. She was afraid to break it, that doing so might break her.

She'd been strong for so long, alone for so long. She had to keep being that, but the allure of someone helping… It physically hurt to know she couldn't allow herself that luxury.

"Here are your choices," Noah said in that low, steady voice that somehow eased the jangling nerves in her gut. "You can try to run away, and I can call every Carson, hell, *and* Delaney, in a fifty-mile radius and you won't get two feet past the town limits."

Irritation spiked through her. "Noah, you—"

"Or you can sit down and tell me what's going on and we can fight it. Together."

Together.

She couldn't wrap her mind around this. Protection and together. Because she was his employee? Because she lived under his roof? It didn't make any kind of sense.

Her father had cut off Kelly when she'd dropped out of school and refused to work at the furniture store.

Then when she'd asked him for help in Kelly's final trimester when the depth of her trouble with Peter was really sinking in, he'd refused to help.

He'd told Addie to never come home again if she was going to help Kelly.

If a father had so little love for his daughters, why was a friend, at best, so willing to risk himself to protect her?

"Telling me would be much easier," Noah said drily.

It sparked a lick of irritation through her. She didn't care for this man of such few words ordering her around. "You don't get to tell me what to do. You aren't my keeper. You aren't even…" She trailed off, because it wasn't true. No matter how quiet and stoic he could be, he *had* become her friend. Someone she relied on. Someone she worked *with* to keep the Carson Ranch running. It had given her so much in three short months, and she'd pictured Seth growing up here, right here. A good man.

Just like Noah.

Noah *was* her friend. Something like a partner, and wouldn't that be nice? Wouldn't that make all this seem possible? Which was why she couldn't. She just couldn't. She'd made a promise to herself. No one else got hurt in this.

"Noah, the truth is, I care about you." Far more than she should. "I care about all of you—Laurel and Grady and Jen and…the lot of you who've made me feel like this was home." She glanced toward the window, but she'd closed the curtains. Was someone out there? Waiting? Would they attack? "But the kind of danger I'm in is the kind I can't bring on all your heads. I couldn't live with myself."

"I don't think that's true," he said, still standing so close and so immovable. Like he could take on the evil that was after her. "I think you'd do anything, risk anything, to keep Seth safe."

Her chest felt like it was caving in. Because he was right. She would do anything. She didn't want to bring the people who'd been so good to her into the middle of it, but what if it was the best bet to keep Seth safe?

"And so would I," he continued. "No little kid deserves to live in the shadow of the threat of violence, so we don't run. *You* don't run. We fight it. But I need to know what I'm fighting."

What was there to do in the face of Noah's mountain wall of certainty and strength? She didn't have any power against it. Not when she could all but feel the determination coming off him in waves. Not when he let Seth gleefully fall into his arms, and there was so much danger outside these walls.

"Seth's father is a dangerous man," she whispered. She knew *that* was obvious and yet saying it out loud…

"He knocked you around."

He said it like a statement, and maybe she should treat it like a question and refute it. But what was the point? "He's a mobster." She laughed bitterly. "I didn't believe it the first time someone told me. As if mobsters are real."

"But he is."

Noah's voice was serious. Not a hint of mocking or disbelief. Which hurt, because when Kelly had told her about Peter's criminal ties, over a year ago, Addie had laughed it off. Then, she'd figured they'd call the cops. It had taken Kelly's death for Addie to finally get it through her head.

Kelly had been talking about going to the cops, telling them what little she knew. The very day after she'd told Addie that, she'd been shot and killed on her way home from the drugstore.

A mugging gone wrong, the police had told Addie.

But Kelly had been certain she was in danger and in that moment Addie had finally gotten it through her thick skull that Peter was not the kind of man who was ever going to pay for his crimes or listen to reason.

He was a murderer and she couldn't stop him.

Kelly had kept Seth a secret, or so Addie had thought. But she'd gotten Peter's first note ten minutes after the police had left her apartment informing her of Kelly's murder.

Too bad.

She hadn't understood at first. Then she'd gotten the next a month later.

We're watching.

She'd taken it to the police, but they'd decided it was a prank.

The next month's letter arrived and had prompted Addie's flight reflex.

We're coming for my son. And you.

Peter was dangerous, and there was nothing...*nothing* she could do to stop him. Laws didn't matter—the police had never helped her, and once he'd involved Seth she couldn't trust law enforcement not to take Seth away from her.

Right or good certainly didn't matter when it came to Peter *or* the law.

"He could have me killed and Seth taken away with the snap of a finger. But he doesn't. I don't know what game he's playing. I only know I have to keep Seth safe. I thought we'd be safe here. Too isolated for even him to find, but I was an idiot. And now we have to leave."

"You won't be leaving."

She looked up at him, wondering what combination of words it would take, because he didn't understand. Maybe he wasn't scoffing at the idea of the mob, but he didn't truly get it if he thought he could keep her protected. "Noah, the cops couldn't help…" She almost mentioned Kelly, but she couldn't tell him about Kelly. Couldn't tell him she couldn't go to the police regarding Seth because she technically had no rights over her sister's child. "…me. I tried. Who are you to stop him? I realize you and the Carsons fancy yourselves tough, Wild West outlaws, but you cannot fight the *mob*."

"I don't see why not."

She blinked at him. "You have a screw loose."

His mouth quirked, that tiny hint of a smile she so rarely got out of him, and usually only aided by Seth. All hopes of more of Noah's smiles were gone. Dead. She had to accept it. She couldn't let him change her mind.

"I don't want you hurt," she whispered, all the fear welling up inside her. "I don't want anyone getting hurt."

"Same goes, Addie." He had started to lean back and forth on his heels as Seth dozed on his shoulder.

It was such a sight, this big, bearded, painfully tough

man cradling a small child to his chest. They were both in so much danger and she didn't know how to fix any of it.

"It's late. Let's get some sleep tonight. I'll call up Grady and Ty in the morning and we'll plan."

"Plan what?"

"How to keep you and Seth safe." He rubbed his big, scarred hand up and down Seth's back.

"They're here, Noah." Her voice broke, and she'd worry about embarrassment later. "They left me a note. They're *here*. We don't have time for plans."

She hadn't realized a tear escaped her tightly and barely held control until Noah reached out, his rough hand a featherlight brush against her cheek, wiping the tear away.

"Then we'll have to fight."

TRUTH BE TOLD, Noah didn't know what a man was supposed to do when a woman told him the mob was after her, but he'd learned a long time ago that in the face of a threat, you always pretended you knew what you were doing.

"Show me the note."

She backed away then, though not far. He didn't think even at her most scared she'd back away from the baby sleeping in his arms. Seth was a nice weight. Warm and important.

"Show me the note," he repeated, in the same quiet but certain tone. The kind of tone he'd employ with a skittish horse and not, say, how he'd speak to his teenage cousin who annoyed the piss out of him.

She inhaled sharply, but he watched the way she let

it out. Carefully. Purposefully. She was scared witless, but she was handling it. Though he'd grown to know her, respect her even, the way she was handling this without falling apart was surprising him.

She reached behind her and pulled out an envelope. "It was…" She paused and cleared her throat. She'd cried a few moments ago, just a few tears, and it cracked something inside him. But she was handling it now. Holding her own. Against the threat of a *mobster*.

"It was on the floor. I assume slipped under the door." Her face paled. "God, I hope that's how it got in here."

Noah kept his expression stoic and his gaze on her, though now he wanted to search the house from top to bottom. Too many nooks and crannies. Too many…

One thing at a time. That's how things got built and solved. One thing at a time.

Her hand was shaking as she held out the envelope. He could see her name written there. Addie Foster. Yet it didn't matter what was in the letter. It mattered that Addie get it through her head he was going to protect her.

He put his hand over her shaking one. "Let's go to your room. We'll put Seth down, and then I'll make sure the house is secure." He'd call Laurel, and she could decide how involved the police needed to be. "You know Laurel's a cop, right? A good one." He nudged her toward the hall.

"I'm sure she is," Addie replied, gaze darting everywhere as they walked back toward the bedrooms. "But the law can't touch him."

"That might be true back where you're from, but it ain't true here."

She looked at him bleakly as they stepped into her room. "It's true everywhere."

Noah was not a demonstrative person by any stretch of the imagination, but he had the oddest urge to pull her to his chest. Let her nestle right there where the baby was sleeping.

Instead, he turned to the crib and transferred Seth onto the mattress. The baby screwed up his mouth, then brought his thumb into it and relaxed. Within moments his eyes drooped shut and his breathing evened.

Noah glanced around the room. Nothing was amiss, and he knew for a fact the window didn't open. It'd accidentally been painted shut two years ago, and they'd left it that way so they had a room to put Clint in he couldn't escape without going through one of the main thoroughfares.

The joy of teenagers.

So, one room checked out and safe. Addie stood next to her bed, arms wrapped around herself, envelope clutched in one hand. She shook from head to toe. And why wouldn't she? She'd been running from a mobster for how long?

Noah'd be damned if she ran another mile.

He eased the note from her grasp and then pulled the letter from the envelope.

I see you, Addie.

He muttered something particularly foul since the baby was too fast asleep to hear him. "I'm going to call Laurel." She opened her mouth to argue, no doubt, but he kept going. "I'm going to check out the house.

I want you to stay put, door locked, until I'm sure everything is secure." She wanted to argue, he could see it all over her, so he played dirty. "You're in charge of Seth. Stay put."

"I know you want to help," she said, her voice raspy with emotion. "I also know you think you *can* help." She shook her head. "You don't know what you're up against."

It poked at the Carson pride he didn't like to put too much stock in, but Carsons had survived centuries of being the poor-as-dirt underdog in the fight. Carsons always found a way to make it work, and even a mobster wouldn't make that different. "And you don't know what or *who* you've got in your corner."

She visibly swallowed. "I'm afraid, Noah, and I don't know how not to be. He killed my sister. Seth's father had her *killed*. I've taken his son from him. I'll be lucky if all he does is kill me, too."

He couldn't stomach the thought, and it was that horrible, clutching panic that moved him, that had him acting with uncharacteristic emotion. He touched her, too-rough hands curling around her shoulders. His grip was too tight. She was too fragile, and yet she didn't wince or back away.

Because she wasn't actually fragile. He thought of that first moment he'd seen her, when he'd been so sure. He'd been wrong. She was brave and bone-deep strong.

She looked up at him, all fear and hope.

"He will not lay a hand on you," Noah growled. "Not a finger. This is Bent, Wyoming, and we make some of our own rules out here. Especially when Carsons and Delaneys are involved. Now, you sit. Maybe make a list of all the players so Laurel knows who she's looking for, and try to remember in detail everything that's happened with Seth's father so far. I'm going to search the house and once I know we're safe in here, we'll come up with a plan to stop him where he stands."

"If we escalate, he escalates," Addie said miserably.

"Then we'll escalate until it's finished. You're done running, Addie Foster. You belong right here." He'd do whatever it took to make that true.

Chapter Six

Addie's eyes were gritty from lack of sleep and her throat ached from talking. Far as she could tell, she'd told her story—well, a version of it—four times. Noah first, then once to Laurel and Grady, once to Noah's brother, Ty—who apparently had been an Army Ranger. Then she'd spouted the story all over again to a youngish-looking deputy in uniform.

She left out the fact Seth wasn't hers. If Peter being in the mob didn't matter here, maybe Seth's parentage didn't, either.

After the whole endless rehashing of it, Laurel and the other deputy, followed by Noah, Grady and Ty, had gone out to search the property. Noah's cousin Vanessa had arrived to watch after Addie.

"You're babysitting me," Addie said, watching the woman move around the kitchen.

"Babysitting happens when you've got a mobster after you, I think."

Fair enough.

Addie imagined Vanessa Carson was the kind of woman who'd know how to handle this on her own. She looked as infinitely tough as her brother, Grady, and male cousins. She had the same sharpness to her features, and there was the way she held herself. Like she knew she was right and she'd fight to the death to prove it.

Addie wanted so badly to believe the Carsons could take on Peter and his thugs.

But *why*? No matter how often Noah told her he'd protect her, she couldn't figure out *why*.

"This is an awful lot of manpower for the maid," Addie said, a comment she might have swallowed if she hadn't been exhausted, nerves strung taut. She stared miserably at Seth's monitor. He'd wake up soon, and how was she going to take care of him without falling apart?

The same way you've been doing for the past year. You're strong, too, whether you feel that way or not.

She liked to think of that as her sister's voice urging her on, but she knew it was just herself. Kelly had always had more of a glass-is-half-empty outlook on life.

"But you aren't just a maid," Vanessa said, as if it wasn't even a question. "Noah runs the ranch, you run the house. That's a partnership, at least—Noah'd see it that way. Noah doesn't just *employ* people. He collects them."

When Addie only stared at Vanessa, trying to work that out, Vanessa sighed and walked over to the table, taking the seat across from Addie.

"Noah's got a soft heart. I think that's why he hides it all with beard and grunts. I think some people were just born that way. Protectors. He doesn't see it as a debt to be paid, or an inconvenience. Once you're in his orbit, you're his. Even if he doesn't like you much."

"That doesn't make any sense."

Vanessa laughed, low and rumbly, just like the rest of the Carsons. "I've never thought Noah made much sense, so I agree. But it doesn't have to. It's who he is. It's what he does. You know, Noah's a firm believer in this feud business between the Carsons and the Delaneys. Delaneys are always out to get us, and messing with that is a historical recipe for disaster."

"But—"

Vanessa held up a hand. "When Laurel was in some trouble before you moved here, Noah jumped right in to help. When Grady announced he and Laurel were shacking up…" Vanessa shuddered. "He was the only one who didn't make a loud, raucous argument against it."

"I think they're sweet," Addie whispered, staring at the table. Even though it wasn't the point. Even though her heart beat painfully in her chest. Noah was unlike any man she'd ever known.

How differently things would have turned out for her and her sister if they'd had more honorable men in their lives.

"Of course you do," Vanessa returned. "You're a Delaney."

Addie looked up at Vanessa's sharp face, because she didn't particularly consider herself family. "I guess, along the line, but—"

"Here? Along the line counts."

"So Noah thinks I'm cursed, but he'll protect me anyway?"

"He will."

"But he'll never see beyond the fact I'm a Delaney?"

Another thing she shouldn't have said. What did it matter what he saw her as? She was just his maid, even if that meant she'd fallen into the path of his protection.

"Now, that is an interesting question," Vanessa drawled. "If we weren't worried about mobsters and such, I'd probably—"

A faint sound staticked through the monitor. Both Vanessa and Addie looked at it. Then another sound.

"It sounds like someone's—"

"Breathing," Vanessa finished for her, and then they were both on their feet, scrambling toward the room.

It could have been Seth, having a bad dream, puffing out those audible gasps of air. But she knew what her baby sounded like. Knew what odd noises the monitor picked up. This was not that.

Vanessa reached the door first, pulling a small gun out of the inside pocket of her jacket. "If someone's there, you let me deal. You get the baby and get out."

Addie nodded as an icy, bitter calm settled over her. She didn't have time to be afraid. She could only focus on saving Seth.

Vanessa quietly and carefully turned the knob, then flung open the door in a quick, loud movement.

There was a figure in the window. Addie didn't have time to scream or panic. She rushed to Seth's crib and pulled him into her arms. She couldn't hear anything except the beating of her heart as she held Seth close, too close. He wiggled and whimpered sleepily.

It was only with him safely held to her chest that Addie realized there was shouting coming from outside. Vanessa was standing on the rocking chair, peering out what appeared to be a hole cut in the glass of the window.

"What happened?" Addie asked, her voice no more than a croak. Safe. Safe. Seth was safe. It was paramount.

Vanessa glanced back at her. "They got him. Laurel's arresting him."

"Who—"

Noah barreled in through the door, all gasping breath and wild eyes. Addie had never seen him in such a state, and she didn't even get a word out before he grabbed her. *Grabbed* her, by the arms, searching her face as Seth wriggled between them. It was the most emotion she'd ever seen on the man.

"You're both all right?"

Addie nodded wordlessly. She didn't know what to say to him when he was touching her like this, looking at her like this. It was more than just that stoic certainty that he'd protect her. So much more.

"I'm good, too," Vanessa quipped.

"Shut up," Noah snapped, seeming to remember himself. He dropped Addie's shoulders as though they were hot coals. He stepped back, raking a hand through his hair, his face returning to its normal impassive state.

It was as if that simple motion locked all that *feeling* that had been clear as day on his face back down where it normally went.

If there weren't a million other things to worry about, she might have been thrilled to see that much emotion geared toward her.

"Who was it? What happened?" Addie asked, cradling Seth's small head with her hand.

"As to who, we're not sure. He's not talking. No ID. We'd canvassed the buildings. Ranch is too big in the dark to find anyone. We were coming back when I caught the figure at your window. We all ran over, pulled him out, Laurel cuffed him. She'll take him down to the station now. She wanted you to come out and see if you could ID him first."

It was all so much, and she knew they wouldn't understand it was only the beginning. This was only the first wave. Peter would keep coming, wave after wave, until she had no strength or sanity left. That's when he'd take Seth. When she was at her weakest.

She swallowed against the fear, the futility. She wouldn't let it happen.

She was a Delaney, apparently, and she had a Carson—or four—in her corner. Noah—all that worry and fear and determination and vengeance flashing in his eyes for that brief minute—was in her corner.

They would keep Seth safe. *They* could.

HE DIDN'T WALK Addie outside to ID the guy. Couldn't manage it. Not with all the awful things roiling in his gut. If he went out there, he wasn't certain he'd control himself around the man who'd been breaking into his house.

So he sent her with Vanessa. He held Seth, the boy back asleep again despite the commotion. Noah studied the room he'd thought was safe, glared at the window where a carefully cut circle gave adequate access for a small man to try to crawl through.

She couldn't sleep here tonight. It wasn't safe. No room with windows was safe, it seemed, and *all* the rooms had windows. Nothing was safe.

He ran his free hand over his face. What a mess.

But it wasn't an insurmountable mess. They'd caught this guy, and Noah was under no illusions it was the mobster after Addie and Seth, but he worked for him. He had to have information, and with information, they could keep Addie safe.

She had two families ready to take up arms and keep her and the kid safe. He had to let that settle him.

Addie returned, clearly beaten down. "It wasn't the same man from the store. So Peter has two men here. Usually he only sends one." She looked exhausted and all too resigned to a negative fate.

Not on his watch.

"You can't stay here," he said when she didn't offer anything.

Her entire face blanched in a second. "But you said…" She looked around the room desperately, then straightened her shoulders and firmed her mouth. "Well, fine, then, better to have a running start."

"Running?" He stepped toward her, lowering his voice when Seth whimpered into his shoulder. "Where the hell do you think you're going?"

She fisted her hands on her hips, that flash of temper from before at dinner. He was glad to see it now. Better than resigned.

"You just told me I can't stay here!"

"*Here*. In this room."

She blinked. "Oh." She cleared her throat. "Be more specific next time."

That she could even think he was kicking her out…

Everything in him ached, demanded he touch her, but he kept the impulse in check. "Nothing that happens is going to change the fact that we're in this together."

"Noah…" She bit her lip and took a few steps closer to him. She seemed to be studying him. His eyes. His mouth.

My damn soul.

"You were so worried," she said, her voice hushed and nearly awed. "When you came in here. About me. About Seth."

"Of course I was. A man was climbing in your window. You were being threatened in *my* house. What man wouldn't be worried?"

"Because it's your house?"

She was fishing, he realized with a start. Fishing for more. It was his turn to swallow, and he was man enough to admit he backed away. Sometimes a man had to tactically retreat.

She didn't let him. She took those steps he'd backed off, closing the necessary distance between them. He thought for a blinding second she was going to reach out to touch him.

Instead, her fingertips brushed Seth's cheek. "I wish I understood you." She looked up, dark blue eyes too darn perceptive for any man's good. "I wish I understood what makes a man think people are his possessions to control, to warp, to let live and die at will, and what makes a man protect what isn't even his."

You are *mine.*

It was a stupid thought to have and he needed to get rid of it.

"We need to figure out what we're going to do. We need to formulate a plan. This house isn't safe, but I don't know where else would be safe."

Addie turned away from him then. He wished he could erase her fear. But he knew even when you were afraid and had someone protecting you, someone helping you, it couldn't eradicate fear. Fear was a poison.

But it could also be the foundation. He'd lived in fear and learned to protect out of it. So he would figure out a way to protect her.

"There's a cabin," he continued. "It's well-known Carson property and it's entirely possible that since someone tracked you here, they could track you there. But it's smaller. We could protect it better."

"We?" She turned around again. "Noah, what about the ranch?"

"Grady and Ty can take care of the ranch. And Vanessa, if necessary. I have plenty of help to carry out the day-to-day, and to keep an eye out in case any other uninvited guests show up."

She shook her head vigorously. "You can't leave your ranch. It's your work. It's your home."

It was. His heart and soul. But he could hardly send her off alone, and he'd be damned if he sent her with anyone else.

"We'll go. Until we get some information from Laurel about who this guy is and what he's doing. We'll go. You'll be safe there. Seth will be safe there, and we'll figure something out. A plan."

"Now?"

Noah nodded firmly. "Pack up whatever you need for yourself and for Seth. I'll make arrangements."

"Noah."

He told himself one of these days he would get that wary bafflement off her face. But for now, there was too much work to do.

"I don't know how to thank you. I don't know how to…" Her gaze moved from his face to the little boy in his arms. "You've been so good to us."

"It sounds like you deserve a little of people being good to you."

She nodded. "Deserve." She blew out a breath and he could see the exhaustion and stress piling on top of her, but she was still standing. He remembered that first moment, when he'd been irritated Grady and Laurel had thrust someone fragile on him.

But Addie had turned out to be something else entirely, and he would do whatever it took to ease some of that exhaustion from her. Get her out of here now, and then once they got to the cabin she could sleep. Rest. He'd take care of everything.

"I will keep you safe. I promise you." She didn't believe him yet. He didn't need her to, but he'd keep saying it until she did.

She stared up at him and reached out. He thought she was going to take Seth, or gently brush the baby's cheek again, but this time she touched *him*. Her fingertips brushed his bearded jaw. "I know you want to."

"I will. I don't make promises I can't keep."

Her mouth curved the slightest bit, but Noah couldn't catch a breath because she was still touching him. She traced the line of his jaw to his chin, then back up the other side, and no amount of stoicism he'd adopted over the years could keep the slight hitch out of his breathing.

Her smile grew. "I believe that," she said, watching her own hand as it traveled down to rest on his chest, just above his heart.

She looked up at him from underneath her lashes, and it wasn't the first time in three months he'd wanted to kiss her, but it was the first time in three months it seemed right. Possible. Infinitely necessary.

He shifted Seth easily, carefully, and if he leaned toward Addie's pretty, lush mouth, well, he was a man, damn it. Who could deny this attraction when they were both exhausted and scared to their boots?

The door swung open and Addie jumped back. Noah had some presence of mind. He simply glared at their intruder.

"Hey, you guys ever com…" Ty trailed off, looking from Noah to Addie, and then back again with a considering glance. "Sorry to interrupt."

"Weren't," Noah returned, that one word all he could manage out of his constricted throat at first. "I'm going to take Addie to the cabin."

Ty nodded. "Good idea. Safer. Less room to watch. Grady, Vanessa and I will handle things here."

Noah jerked his head in assent. "Let's move fast."

Chapter Seven

Addie slept like the dead. No matter how many fears or worries occupied her brain, she'd been up for nearly twenty-four hours by the time they reached the isolated Carson cabin.

And, she supposed, as she awoke slowly in an unfamiliar bed in an unfamiliar house, knowing Noah was nearby keeping her safe had made sleep easy.

She stretched in the surprisingly comfy bed. Surprising because everything about the Carson cabin was rustic and sparse, but the bed was nice.

She had to get out of it, though, because Noah would need some sleep. He'd probably been up before her yesterday, and now he'd spent who knew how long taking care of Seth and keeping them safe.

She pressed her hand against her chest. It simply ached at how much that meant. How much she'd wanted to kiss him last night. Or this morning. Whatever moment in time. He'd been about to. She'd almost been sure of it.

Almost.

She pushed out of the bed. She hadn't even changed out of her jeans and T-shirt last night. She'd fallen into that bed, making noises about when Seth would wake up and need a diaper change, and Noah had hushed her, and that was the last thing she remembered.

She ran a hand through her hair. It'd be good to tidy up, but she had no idea how long she'd slept. There was no clock in here, the window was boarded up and she had no idea where she'd left her phone.

She opened the bedroom door and stepped into basically the rest of the cabin. A small living room, an even smaller kitchen that attached, and a bathroom on the other side. There was another door she had to assume was another bedroom.

The diminutive size of the place made it far more secure than the ranch. Just as isolated, of course, but there wasn't much in Bent by way of bustling cosmopolitans.

She frowned at the empty room. The front door was locked shut. Multiple times. A door lock, a dead bolt, a padlock on some latch-looking thing. It was dark because all the windows were boarded up. Surely Noah couldn't have done all that while she was sleeping.

And where *was* he?

It was then she heard the faint snore. She pivoted so she could see the front of the couch, and there was all six-foot-who-knew of Noah Carson, stretched out on a tiny couch, a cowboy hat over his face, while Seth slept just as soundlessly in the little mobile crib, Noah's arm draped over the side—his fingertips touching Seth's leg.

It was too much, the way this big, gruff cowboy had taken to a small child who wasn't even his. But Addie understood that. Seth was her nephew, not her own, but he was hers now. All hers.

Noah wanted to protect her and Seth, but he was putting himself in danger to do so. He was even changing his life, for however brief a time, to do so.

So she would protect him right back. Take care of him as much as he'd allow.

She tiptoed to the kitchen and started poking around the cabinets seeing what kind of provisions they had. She knew Noah had packed a lot of things before they'd loaded up Vanessa's small car—an attempt at throwing anyone who might be watching off the scent—and drove up the mountains in the starry dark to this place. Vanessa had driven off so no evidence would be left that the cabin was occupied, and then it'd just been her and Noah and Seth.

She blew out a breath. *Breakfast.* She needed to focus on the here and now, not what came before and not what would come after. She looked around for her phone, found it on the small kitchen counter.

She flipped it open, searching for the time, only to see the text message from a Boston-area number.

Her stomach turned. She'd gotten a new burner phone in every city she'd stayed in for a while, but Peter somehow always found out what her number was.

She wanted to delete the message before looking at it, because she knew it would say something awful. Something that would haunt her. She remembered each and every one of his previous messages, and how many had made her run again.

All the words of the terrible things he was going to do to her once he found her that she'd read months and months ago swirled around in her head. She couldn't erase them.

But she could erase this message.

"What's wrong?"

Addie jumped a foot, not having realized Noah had woken up and was peering at her over the back of the couch.

"Nothing," she said automatically.

"Addie, I know you're scared, but you have to be honest with me if we are going to do this. There can't be any lies between us anymore."

She glanced at the crib where Seth was still sleeping. Was the fact that Seth wasn't her child a lie? How could it be? He was hers now. One way or another.

Then she glanced at the phone in her hand.

"It might be nothing," she said hopefully. She didn't believe it was nothing. There wasn't anything *nothing* about a Boston area code texting a number she'd given no one except Carsons and Delaneys.

Noah stood. He skirted the couch and raked fingers through his hair. It was sleep tousled and all too appealing. Even with the awful fear and panic fluttering in her breast, she looked at him and there was this soothing to all those awful jitters. They still existed, fear and worry, but it was like they were wrapped up in the warm blanket of Noah's certainty.

Noah's certainty, which existed around him like his handsomeness. Funny in all of this mess, she could finally admit to herself that she wanted him. Not just a little attracted, not just a silly little crush because he'd given her a home.

No, she *wanted*. Maybe it had to do with that moment last night where she'd thought he was about to kiss her, because he'd never given any inclination of interest before. So surely his reciprocating feelings was her silly fantasy life taking over because a man like Noah… Well, he knew what he wanted. In all things. If he wanted her, he would've said something.

Probably. Unless there was some noble reason in his head he thought he shouldn't. There was no reason to wish for that. Except, she *wanted*.

She had to push all these thoughts and feelings away, though, because right now Noah was standing there, frowning at her. And she was going to protect him and take care of him right back, so that meant not irritating him.

Which apparently meant the truth.

"There's a text message," she managed to say, reluctantly holding her phone out to him. "From a Boston area code."

"That's where this bastard is?" Noah demanded, his voice hard as he took the phone out of her hands.

Addie nodded. "I don't want to open it. It's always some vile thing." At the spark of Noah's temper moving over his face, she quickly continued. "Whenever he finds me, he texts me threats. This is the first one I've had here. I think he likes making me scared."

Something in him closed up. That anger vanished off his expression, but she could still feel it vibrating under that stoic demeanor. "Some people like knowing they're in your head. That you're running scared. Gives them a thrill."

"Yes," Addie agreed, feeling sick to her stomach. "He could have had Seth by now. So, what he's doing isn't just about getting him back. I mean, I think he wants him back, but he wants me to suffer for as long as possible. I think. I don't know. He doesn't make any sense. That's why I have to run." She wanted to sink to the floor, but she leaned against the wall and it held her up.

"You're done running," Noah said forcefully, as if it was his decision to make. "Now we go after him."

NOAH ANGRILY PUSHED a button on the phone. Though he heard Addie's intake of breath, his anger was too close to a boiling point to worry about comforting her. Besides, he wasn't any good at comforting. He had learned how to protect, and that's what he would keep doing.

He read the text message grimly.

Hello, Addie. Wyoming. Really? Going to ride a few cowboys? Are you about to get lassoed? Maybe we'll have ourselves a little standoff. You, me and the baby. Who will live? Only time will tell.

He hit a few buttons, finding a way to forward the text message to Laurel with the number on it. Then he deleted it from Addie's phone, since he didn't want her looking at it.

"Has *he* ever come after you? Or is it always his goons?"

"Uh, goons, as far as I know. Usually only one per town."

Noah nodded. "We'll need to get him here, then."

"Noah, he *killed* my sister. Well, he had her killed. If he comes here, he will have more people killed. Not just me or Seth, but you and your family. He's capable, if he wants to be."

"You don't know how deeply sorry I am about that, Addie. Sorry you had to go through it, sorry someone lost their life. But if you run away, it doesn't end. As long as he has something to come after, he's coming after you. Stopping him is the only answer."

"What if we can't?" There wasn't just a bleak fatality in her tone, there was genuine question.

"I have stopped bad men before. I am not afraid to do it again. We have good and right on our side."

"Good doesn't always win."

"It will here." Because he'd made a promise to himself, growing up in the midst of all that *bad*, that he would make sure good prevailed once he had the power. "Now, instead of arguing, let's discuss our plan."

Addie pushed her fingers to her temples and he took stock of how much sleep had helped her. She wasn't shaking and didn't look as pale. While there were still faint smudges under her eyes, they weren't that deep, concerning black they had been early this morning when they'd arrived at the cabin.

She was more mussed than usual, but that didn't detract from how pretty she looked in the middle of the dim cabin. Like a source of light all herself.

Get yourself together.

She dropped her hands from her temples. "Before we plan, you need to sleep. I don't know what time it is, but I—"

"I caught a few hours once Seth settled," he said, nodding toward the portable crib they'd brought. "I'm fine."

She stared up at him, much the way she'd been doing since he'd told her she was under his protection. Not as if she didn't believe him, but as if he were some mythical creature.

He wanted to be able to be that. Someone she could trust and believe in. Someone who could save her from this. He only prayed he could be.

"Are you hungry? Let me make breakfast. Or dinner. Or whatever meal. I'll make something. That'll be the first step."

"Addie." He gently closed his fingers around her arm as she passed. "You're not the housekeeper here, okay? You don't have to cook or clean."

She looked at his fingers on her arm, then slowly up at him. "If I'm not the housekeeper here, what am I?"

Mine. That stupid word that kept popping unbidden into his head. She stepped closer to him then, like last night, when he'd thought he could kiss her and it would be okay. When he'd been driven by relief instead of reason.

She reached up with her arm not in his grasp. He should let her go. He didn't. She touched his jaw as she had last night, her fingertips lightly brushing across his beard.

Her tongue darted out, licking her bottom lip, and oh, hell.

"You *were* going to kiss me last night before Ty came in," she said on a whisper. A certain, declaratory whisper. "Right?" she added, and if he wasn't totally mistaken, there was *hope* in that "right?"

He might have been able to put her off if not for the hint of vulnerability. Because what was hope but a soft spot people could hurt and break? He cleared his throat, uncomfortable with the directness of the question. "I was thinking about it."

"So, you could do it now."

His gaze dropped to her mouth, no matter how much his conscience told him not to give in to this. Protecting was not taking advantage of. Fighting evil with good was not giving in to something he didn't have any right to want.

But she was close, the darker ring of blue around her pupils visible. The hope in her eyes too tempting. Her lips full and wet from where she'd licked them.

It didn't have to be a distraction. It didn't *have* to be wrong. It could be the start of something.

What? What are you going to start on this *foundation? What do* you *have to offer?*

Since the last question sounded a little bit too much like his father, he pushed it away. He wouldn't be driven by his father's voice.

He leaned closer, watching in fascination as her breath caught, and then she, too, leaned forward.

His phone trilled, which startled him back to reality. They were in a serious, dangerous situation with her child sleeping a few feet away. She was scared and out of sorts.

Now was not the time for nonsense. He glanced at the caller ID, frowned when it was Laurel's number. "It's Laurel."

Addie nodded.

"What?" Noah greeted.

"Bad news," Laurel said in her no-nonsense cop tone. "He's gone."

Before Noah could demand to know what that meant, Laurel continued.

"We did some questioning, but two armed men broke into the station. We're small and understaffed and… Well, three deputies were injured. Badly. They're…" She paused, and though she kept talking in that same efficient cop tone, Noah could tell she was shaken.

"Are you okay?"

"I'd gone to get dinner for everyone," Laurel said bitterly. "Hart got the worst of it. He's in surgery. The other two should be okay, but it'll be… Well, anyway, I need you to be on guard. Three men, at least, are now on the loose and likely after Addie and Seth. I've called in more men, but we don't have an endless supply of deputies."

"We're boarded up. Armed. You keep your men."

"There could be more of them."

Noah tried not to swear. "I'll be ready."

"Everyone in Bent has been told to be on the lookout for out-of-towners and immediately report it to us. Aside from Carsons and Delaneys, no one has the full story—I didn't want anyone doing anything stupid. So you'll have warning if someone's coming your way, but I'm stretched so thin now here and—"

"I'll handle it."

"We'll all work together to handle it." She paused again. "You know, my brother—"

"No Delaneys."

She sighed heavily. "Addie *is* a Delaney, moron. We're all in this together. If you dare bring up the feud right now, I swear to God…" Then she laughed.

"Oh, you did that on purpose to get me riled up about something else."

"I don't know what you're talking about," he muttered. Except she'd sounded *sad*, and sad wasn't going to do anyone any good. "I gotta go."

"Keep your phone on you, and be careful."

"Uh-huh. Keep me updated."

"Will do."

Noah hit End and looked at Addie, who'd moved into the kitchen, her back to him, as she hugged herself. He wasn't sure how much she'd heard, but clearly enough to be concerned. He could try to put it lightly, but he thought after the whole almost-kiss thing, they needed the straightforward truth. "He escaped."

Addie leaned against the tiny slab of countertop in the minimalist kitchen. "How?" she asked, her voice strangled.

Noah didn't want to tell her. He even toyed with the idea of lying to her. But in the end, he couldn't. If they were going to win this, they needed to be open and honest with each other.

"Someone helped him. A few deputies were hurt in the process."

She whirled on him then, all anger and frustration. "I can't have this, Noah. I cannot have people's lives on my head."

"They're on the mob's head. Beginning and end of that story."

She shook her head and marched over to the living room, purposefully keeping as much room between them as possible in the tiny cabin. "I'm packing Seth up and we're running. You can't stop me."

She paused over Seth's crib, clearly warring over the idea of picking him up when he was sleeping.

Noah parked himself in front of the door, picking up the rifle he'd rested there. "You're not going anywhere."

She glanced back at him, her expression going mutinous. "You can't keep me prisoner here."

"Watch me."

Chapter Eight

Addie was so furious she considered walking right up to him and punching him in the gut.

Except Noah was so big and hard her little fist couldn't do much damage, if any. And that was the thing that had dogged her for a year.

She had no strength and no power. She couldn't win this fight. She could only put it off a little while.

And everyone trying to help her was going to die.

Her knees gave out and she fell with an audible *thump* onto the couch, guilt and uselessness washing over her.

"Don't... Don't cry. Please." Noah grumbled.

Which was the first time she realized she *was* crying. Not little slipped-out tears. Huge, fat tears. She sobbed once, tired and overwhelmed. It was easier when it was her and Seth against the world. She didn't have to deal in hope or guilt. All she had was *run*.

"Addie, honey, come on." She felt the couch depress and Noah's arm go around her shaking shoulders. "Please. Please stop crying. You're not a prisoner. You're just... We're just lying low, that's all. Together. Hell, you have to stop crying. It just about kills me."

He sounded so desperate, she wished she could stop. But she was just so *tired*, and the truth was she wanted to let Noah handle it. Believe him. But the man who'd tried to steal Seth away had escaped, and people had been hurt, and all those people would have been fine if she'd never come here.

"Those men are hurt because of me. You're in this cabin because of me. You should have let me run. I'm only trouble."

His strong arm pulled her tighter. "You're not trouble. You've been a victim, and you've been brave and strong for a long time. Let someone take the reins."

"I'm hardly brave. I'm sitting here crying like a baby."

"You escaped a madman for how long?"

She blew out a breath. "But I can't beat him."

"Maybe not alone. Together we will, and I don't just mean me. You've got Laurel and Grady and everyone. The whole town is with us. That doesn't make what you've managed to do less. Addie, look at him," he said, gesturing toward the crib and Seth. "He's perfect."

"He is."

"You did that."

"No, I didn't." *He's not mine.* The words were on the tip of her tongue, but Noah's rough hand cupped her cheek.

"Promise me you won't try to run off. Promise me you'll trust me on this. We are in this together, until you're both safe."

He was touching her so gently, looking at her so earnestly, asking for a promise she didn't want to give.

She even opened her mouth to refuse the promise, but something in the moment reminded her of before.

Noah believed her. From the beginning. Without hesitation. If she had done that with Kelly, maybe everything would be different.

Grief threatened to swamp her, but she couldn't change the past. What she could do was change her future.

Trusting him to help was what she had to do. And maybe anyone who got hurt along the way… She hated to even think it, but it was true.

She would sacrifice a clean conscience for Seth, so if people got hurt, as long as Seth was safe, she couldn't let it matter.

"Okay. Okay." She nodded, even as his hands stayed on her cheek. "I promise we're in this together." No matter what guilt she had to endure. It was for Seth. If she could remember that…

It was hard to remember anything with Noah's big, rough hand on her face. She'd long since stopped crying, but he was still touching her. And he was not a man given to casual touches.

Yet it didn't feel like the other two moments. Those moments that had been interrupted, where everything in her had stilled and yearned. There was some lack of softness on his face.

But unlike those other two moments, this time he did close the distance between them. His mouth touched hers, and for all the ways Noah had *clearly* resisted this moment, there was nothing tentative about it.

He kissed like a man who knew what he was doing. His lips finding hers unerringly, no matter how much beard separated them. There was nothing she could have done to prepare herself for that wave of feeling. Something so warm and sweet and bright she thought she couldn't name it.

But the word *hope* whispered across the edges of her consciousness as she reached out for him, wanting to hold on to something. Wanting it to be him.

When he pulled away, all too quickly in her estimation, he searched her face, relaxing a millimeter, and somehow she understood.

It wasn't a real kiss. It wasn't loss of control because passion so consumed him. "You did that to distract me," she accused. She should be angrier, more hurt, but all she could really be was bone-deep glad he'd done it.

Now she knew how much *more* was worth.

He pressed his mouth together, though she thought maybe under the beard was some kind of amused smile. "Maybe," he rumbled.

She crossed her arms over her chest huffily. "It didn't work."

His mouth quirked that tiny bit. "Yes, it did."

Her heart fluttered at his easy confidence. She didn't understand this man. Gruff and sweet, with so many walls, and yet he could kiss like he'd been born to do it and *knew* what kind of effect he had on her.

She was torn between kissing him again—much deeper and much longer this time—and eliciting more of this almost-smiling, certainly half-teasing man out of him.

But a loud *bang*, something like an explosion outside, had them both jumping. Addie was afraid she'd screamed, but in the end it didn't matter. Noah was on his feet, rifle in his hands, and she had already swept Seth up against her chest.

Noah's mouth was a firm line under his beard. Without a word he took her by the arm and propelled her around the couch. He shoved a narrow table against the wall out of the way, and then as if by magic, pulled up a door in the middle of the floor. An actual door.

"It's a cellar. Cramped and dark, but it can keep you safe if you're quiet. Go down there."

"But what about you?"

"I'll handle it. I promise."

"There could be—"

He slapped his phone into her palm. "Call or text everyone. You stay here and safe and let them come to my rescue, got it?"

Remembering her earlier promise to herself—*anything for Seth*—she swallowed and nodded. She turned to the dark space the pulled-up door allowed and did her best to ignore fear of dark or cramped or not knowing as she felt her way down a shaking length of stairs.

Seth wiggled and fussed against her, but was mostly content when she held him hard and close.

"Good?" Noah asked.

"Peachy," she muttered, and then she was plunged into darkness.

NOAH'S HEART BEAT too hard and too fast, but he focused on keeping his breathing even. He kept his mind on the facts he had.

Someone was outside and trying to get in. Addie and Seth were safe in the cellar if he kept them so. The boarded-up windows made no entrance into the cabin undetectable. *He* had the tactical advantage.

Except he couldn't see who was out there or how many, and though he knew the general vicinity that loud bang had come from, he didn't know exactly what had caused it or what kind of weaponry the undetermined number of men had.

He knew how to fight bad men, but he'd never had to fight off a possible group of them. He'd have to figure it out. Seth and Addie were counting on him.

The door shook in time with another large bang. And then another. He realized grimly there was also a banging coming from the back of the cabin, so there were at least two of them. Trying to get into the cabin from two different directions.

He needed to create some kind of barrier and he needed to make sure he kept both men—if it was only two—far away from Addie and Seth. He didn't want to leave them alone to draw the men away, but if she called Laurel, there would be help on the way.

Because the cabin had been used as a hideout for the Carson clan for over a century, it had all sorts of hidden places and secret exits. Maybe he could sneak out and pick off whoever was out there. Based on the banging, he had a better idea of where they were than they had of where he was.

It was a chance he'd have to take. He couldn't let them get inside. There would be too many ways he could be cornered, too many ways Seth making noise might give Addie away. And he had to know more about what he was dealing with so he wouldn't be caught unaware.

He strode to the kitchen, gripped the rifle under his arm and gave the refrigerator a jerk. He didn't push it all the way out, in case he needed to hide this little secret passageway quickly. Instead, he yanked the wallboard open and shoved his body through the narrow opening.

There was a crawl space that would lead him outside—one of the sides he hadn't heard banging against. And if he miscalculated, well, he pulled his rifle in front of him. He'd use that to nudge the door open, shoot first and ask questions later. Whatever would keep Addie and Seth safe.

On his hands and knees, pushing the rifle in front of him, he squeezed his too-big body through the too-small space. He nudged the door with the gun, then frowned when it didn't budge.

After a few more nudges—harder and harder each time—he finally got the small door to move, but just enough to see what was blocking it.

Snow. Far too many inches of snow. He pushed the rifle behind him, army-crawled up to the slight opening he'd made and got as close to the crack as possible so he could look out.

The world was white. He couldn't even see trees. Just snow, snow and more snow. On the ground, still falling from the sky, accumulating fast.

The chance of help coming was about as remote as it'd ever be. Even if Addie got through to Laurel or a Carson, it'd take extra time.

Which meant he had to get back inside the cabin. There'd be no trying to lure the men away when he didn't have much hope for quick backup.

He turned and pushed himself through the crawl space after pulling the door to the outside closed. He twisted his body this way and that, getting out behind the refrigerator, trying to come up with a new plan.

He was breathing heavily, but he heard the distinct sound of something. Not pounding anymore.

Footsteps.

He didn't have time to push the refrigerator back in place, because a man dressed in black stepped out from the room Addie had been sleeping in just hours before.

Noah raised his rifle and pulled the trigger without even thinking about where the bullet would hit. The most important thing was stopping him.

The man went down with a loud yowl of pain, but another gunshot rang out in the very next moment. Noah only had the split second to realize it wasn't his own gun before a pain so bright and fierce knocked him to his back. His vision dimmed, and damnation, the pain threatened to swallow him whole.

He stared up at the ceiling, a blackness creeping over him, but he fought it off, clinging to consciousness with everything he had in him.

He had to keep Addie safe.

He tried to move, to do anything, but he felt paralyzed. Nothing in his body worked or moved. It only throbbed with fire and ice. How was it both? Searing licks of heat, needling lances of cold.

When a man stood over him, hooded and dim himself, it gave Noah something external to focus on. The man's black coat, not fit for a Wyoming winter, was covered in melted snow droplets. He had his face covered by a bandanna or hat. His eyes were a flat brown.

Evil eyes that were familiar—not because he knew this man, but because Noah had stared evil in the face before.

"Where's the baby?" the man rasped, pointing his small handgun at Noah's head.

Noah groaned, more for show, though the pain in his side was a blinding, searing fire. He'd heard Addie scream, but apparently the man hadn't, or just couldn't figure out where they were.

Noah thought of Addie and Seth and pretended to roll his eyes back in his head. He could hear Seth crying now, which distracted the man's attention. Noah took that brief moment to gather all his strength and kick as hard and groin-targeted as he could.

Chapter Nine

Addie listened to the persistent thumping. She knew it was people trying to get in. People trying to get her and Seth.

She knew Noah would fight them with all he had, but would it be enough? The horrifying worry that he was only one man and there were at least two men out there curdled her stomach.

She reminded herself she'd texted every last Carson and Delaney Noah had in his phone. Even though she hadn't had a response, the messages showed as sent, which meant she only needed one person to see it.

She could not think about what it might mean if no one was looking at their phone. If no one came to help them. So she paced the cellar, trying to work off all her nerves while at the same time keeping Seth happy. She needed to feed him. Even if Noah had fed him while she'd been asleep, he'd be getting hungry again.

She glanced above at the light footsteps. She knew Noah was moving around carefully and quietly on purpose and *God* she just could not think about what he was doing up there.

She used the weak light from Noah's tiny phone

screen to illuminate her surroundings until she found a large flashlight sitting at the base of the stairs. She clicked it on, relief coursing through her when a strong beam popped out.

Clearly the Carsons used this cabin at least somewhat frequently, because there were a few shelves lined with provisions. Mainly canned foods, but if she could find one with a pop-top, she could at least give Seth a little something to keep him happy.

No matter that her arms shook and she felt sick to her stomach, she forced herself to read through all the labels. She found a can of pears, one of Seth's favorites.

"Okay, little man, let's get you a snack." She looked around the cellar again with Noah's flashlight. She needed a blanket or something she could put Seth on.

She poked around a pile of old furniture in the corner. Broken chairs, a bent mattress frame. Tools of some sort. A conglomeration of rusty, broken crap.

And a crib. She blinked at it. The legs had been broken off of it, and there was no mattress, but it had once been a crib.

"Something is going our way, Seth," she murmured, glancing warily above her as things got eerily quiet.

Quiet was good. Quiet had to be good.

Balancing Seth on her hip, she carefully picked through the debris of nonsense and pulled the crib out. She studied it, then the room around her. If it was even, and she could push the broken side up against a wall, it could act as an effective playpen if she wanted to go check on Noah.

She heard footsteps again, tried not to think too hard about what that silence might have meant.

She shrugged out of her sweater and placed it in the bottom of the crib. Quickly she ran her fingers around the wood and didn't find any exposed nails or sharp edges. She set Seth down and searched around for other soft things.

She found a stack of folded dish towels and sniffed them gingerly. A little musty, but not terrible. She started placing them over the corners of the crib. A little softening to—

The gunshot was so loud, so close, she screamed. Seth began to wail and she grabbed him to her chest, trying to muffle both their cries as another gunshot almost immediately rang out.

Two gunshots was not good. She didn't have a weapon, but she did have this pile of tools. She bounced Seth until he stopped crying, and she tried to keep her own tears at bay as she heard another thump, then more thumps. Grunts.

No gunshots.

She scrambled to the pile of debris and grabbed the heaviest, sharpest-looking tool she could find. She'd pushed the crib against the wall sort of behind the stairs, and that would work in her favor if she could keep Seth quiet.

The food. The food. She set the tool down by the crib and grabbed the can she'd dropped. She transferred Seth to the little crib and made silly faces to keep him distracted and quiet as she opened the can.

Seth gurgled out a laugh at one of her faces, but it didn't assuage any of her shaking fear, because something scraped against the floor right above her. She could hear someone fiddling with the floorboard. Oh, God, it wasn't Noah. Noah knew how to open it.

On a strangled sob she popped the can of pears open and grabbed one without thinking twice. She handed it to Seth. Usually she didn't give him such big pieces, but she needed time. She needed to keep them both safe.

She clicked off the flashlight just as the door opened and light shone in. Addie grabbed the tool and gripped it in both hands as she stepped back into the shadows.

The tool was sharp. It would cause serious damage even with her limited strength. Her stomach threatened to revolt, but she refused to let it.

She was done running, cowering and giving in. She'd made that choice to stand and fight up there with Noah. So she would do whatever it took. Whatever it took to fight for him. Fight for Seth.

She was done being a victim.

She swallowed the bile that threatened to escape her throat as some man who was most definitely not Noah took the stairs. He didn't have a flashlight, which put her at an advantage. Seth was liable to make a noise any second, so she had to be ready.

She quietly lifted the tool above her head and just as Seth murmured happily over a piece of pear, the man turned.

She brought the tool down onto his skull as hard as she could, and he strangled out a scream and fell in a heap. Her stomach lurched as she realized the tool was lodged in his skull as it fell with him.

But she couldn't worry about her stomach. She needed to get to Noah, and if no one was coming at the sound of the man's scream, he had to be acting alone.

Or someone else is hurting Noah.

She picked Seth up, much to his screaming dismay, and scurried around the motionless body on the floor.

Oh, God, had she killed him?

Had *he* killed Noah?

She climbed the stairs, Seth screaming in her ear. She stumbled up into the living room, desperately searching for Noah.

Then she saw him lying on the floor. And blood. Too much blood.

"Noah. Noah." She dropped to her knees next to him, not even worried she was getting bloody herself as long as she kept Seth out of it. "Noah. You have to be alive, Noah."

"No! No!" Seth said gleefully, clearly not understanding the scene around them.

Addie had to focus. Focus on what was in front of her. He'd clearly been shot. Blood pooled on one side of his body, but not the other. His face was ashen. But, oh, *God*, his chest was moving. Up and down.

"Noah." She wasn't sure what to do with a gunshot wound. Pressure. That's what they did in the movies, right? Apply pressure.

"Not dead," he muttered, though his eyes stayed closed.

"Oh, thank God you're awake." She pressed a kiss to his forehead and his eyelids fluttered, but they didn't fully open.

"No!" Seth squealed again.

"Where's he?" Noah demanded.

She assumed he meant the man she'd... "I... Well, he came down and I think I killed him." She'd still need to close up the door, cover it with something really heavy to keep him down there just in case. But for now she had to focus on Noah.

"Good," Noah replied, his voice firm for the first time, though his eyes remained closed. "I killed the other one. Must be it or they'd be in here."

"For now."

Noah grunted.

"I have to… I have to get you help." She pawed at her pocket for the phone Noah had given her earlier. She had a text from Laurel and as she clicked to read it, Noah said almost the exact thing.

Blizzard. Can't get up. Grady and Ty trying with horses. Will be a while.

"Blizzard. No help."

Addie closed her eyes in an effort to try to think. "We need to focus on you right now." She stood and crossed to the travel crib. It was upended, but she righted it and set Seth inside, cooing sweet reassurances at him as she gave him a toy.

She went through the next few steps as though it were a to-do list. Get as many blankets, towels and washcloths she could. Put a pillow under Noah's head. Peel the bloodied shirt away from his side. Try not to throw up. Gently wash out the terrible wound.

Noah hissed out a breath, but that just reassured her he was *alive*. "Is there a first aid kit anywhere?"

"Bathroom maybe," he muttered.

She was on her feet in an instant. Seth fussed but not a full-blown cry…yet. She had to get Noah some semblance of patched up. She wished she could move him to a bed, but who would lift him? Her and what army?

She jerked open the cabinet under the sink and rummaged. Soap, extra toilet paper, a box of condoms. Her cheeks warmed, but she kept looking until she found a flimsy canvas pouch with the red first aid cross on it.

She hastened back to Noah's side. His eyes were open so she tried to smile down at him. "Well, we survived."

His mouth didn't move and he looked so pale even under all his hair and beard. "For now," he managed in the same tone of voice she'd used earlier.

Wasn't that the truth?

She studied the wound again, and it was bleeding once more. She tried not to let despair wash over her. The only way Noah survived this was her somehow making it so.

So that's what she'd have to do.

It was a strange thing to be shot. Noah would have thought just the bleeding part of his body would hurt, but everything hurt. He kept losing consciousness, awakening who knew how long later on the cold, uncomfortable floor.

He tried not to groan as he forced his eyes open. He looked around the quiet room. The only sound he recognized was Seth sucking on a bottle.

It was a little bit of a relief to know things were business as usual for the baby.

Addie appeared in his wavering vision, and she knelt next to him, a tremulous smile on her face. "Oh, good, you're really awake this time."

"Was I kind of awake before?"

She nodded down at his chest and he realized that under the blanket draped over him he was shirtless and bandaged. "You came to a few times when I was bandaging you up best as I could. Well, I called Laurel and she patched me through to a paramedic. You're lucky because it didn't seem to make any kind of...hole."

No, the bullet seemed to have grazed him. Badly, but no holes and no bullets floundering around in his body. It was good and it was lucky.

He was having trouble feeling it.

"I need to get up," he said. Lying there was making things worse. If he got up and moved around he could hold on to consciousness. He tried to push himself into a sitting position. His head swam, his stomach roiled and the pain in his side *burned*. Addie's arms came around him, though, surprisingly sturdy, and she held him up.

He was so damn dizzy, even if he had the strength he wasn't sure he could get to his feet. It was unacceptable. This was all unacceptable. Because he did need stitches, and there was no way to get them. Which meant he was going to halfway bleed to death and be a weak, useless liability to Addie and Seth.

No, he wouldn't be that.

"We need to secure the place. They got in through your room—"

"I dragged the man you shot outside," Addie said flatly. "I boarded up the bedroom window again best as I could. I've locked the room from the outside— since we won't be spending any more time in separate rooms, we don't need it. I also barricaded the cellar just in case the man I…hurt isn't dead."

He stared. "You did *all* that while I was out?"

"It's much better than sitting here fretting that you're dead. Or waiting. Grady and Ty are still trying to get to us with the horses, but the blizzard set them back quite a bit. Apparently Ty knows some battlefield medicine or *something* and can stitch you up when he gets here." Addie shuddered.

"I don't know what to say." Or feel. Or do. She'd handled it all. He was a burden now, but somehow she'd handled it all.

"Let's get you to bed and then you're going to lie down and stay put. You need to rest and not aggravate the bleeding until someone can get up here to help." She glanced over at Seth's travel crib. "Let's do it now before he finishes that bottle and starts yelling."

He wasn't sure he could get to his feet, but he wasn't about to admit that to her. There had to be *something* he could handle. Something he could do.

He rolled to the side that wasn't injured and tried desperately not to groan or moan as he struggled onto his feet. The world tipped, swayed, but he closed his eyes and with Addie's arms around him, he managed to stay upright.

Because slight little Addie—the woman he'd deemed fragile the first time he'd met her—held him up as he swayed.

She pulled the blankets that had been around him over his shoulders, then held tight, leaning her body against his tipping one as he took a step.

He walked, and noted she moved slower than he might have tried to. She was holding him back. Making him take it easy. He should have worked up some irritation, but mostly he could only concentrate on getting the interminable distance from the kitchen floor to his bed.

But they inched their way there, no matter how awful he felt. Somehow he got his feet to keep moving forward. Managed to ease himself onto his bed, with Addie's help.

Once he was prone again, he managed a full, painful breath. She was already tucking blankets around him, though she paused to inspect the bandage, the strands of her hair drifting across his chest. Somewhere deep down there was the slightest flutter of enjoyment and he figured he had a chance of surviving this yet.

"You need to rest. No getting up without help. No pushing yourself. Do you understand me?"

He grunted irritably. He hoped she considered it assent, even though it wasn't. Not a promise, because why would he promise that?

"You need to try to get something to eat. Keep up your strength. I'm going to—"

He grabbed her, unmanned at the fact there was a beat of panic at the thought of her leaving him. It was the aftereffect of shock. Had to be.

She patted his hand reassuringly, and it was that something like *pity* in her gaze that had him withdrawing his hand. He wasn't to be pitied. Yeah, he'd been shot trying to save *her*.

And she saved herself, didn't she?

"I'm just going to get Seth. Grab you some soup I already warmed up. Trust me, Noah, the three of us are plastered to one another's sides until this is all over."

She slid off the bed, and still that panic inside him didn't disappear. "How'd you kill him without a gun?" he asked. Anything to keep her here. Here where he could see her. Where he could assure himself they'd come out this on the other side.

For now. What about the next other side?

Addie fiddled with the collar of her T-shirt, eyes darting this way and that. "Well." She cleared her throat. "Th-there were a bunch of tools down there so I just picked up the sharpest, biggest one and when he came down the stairs I hid in the shadows, then bashed him over the head." She let out a shaky breath. "I've never…hurt someone. I've never had to. I don't know how to feel."

"You feel relieved you were able to defend yourself," he said, hoping even though he felt weak and shaky and a million other unacceptable things she could feel that in her bones. "You took the relief of saving your-self or someone else—it was all you could do." He should know.

She cocked her head, those blue eyes studying him. He might have fidgeted if he'd had the energy. "You've hurt people? I mean, besides today?" she asked on a whisper.

Part of him wanted to lie or hedge, but he was too tired, too beat down to do either. "When I've had to."

"Like when?"

"It isn't important now. What's important is surviving until Grady and Ty get here. What's important is coming up with the next step of our plan."

"What on earth is the next step going to be?"

The trouble was, he didn't know.

Chapter Ten

Watching Noah search for an answer to that question hurt almost as much as watching him suffer through what must be unbearable pain. Even though the paramedic she'd talked to who'd walked her through sterilizing and bandaging Noah's wound had assured her that Noah would survive for days as long as he rested and kept hydrated, Noah looked terrible. From his ashen complexion to the way he winced at every move.

Seth began to fuss in the main room and she forced herself to smile at Noah. "Be right back."

She wasn't sure if it was fear or something else written all over his face. He clearly didn't want her to leave, but she had to get Seth and try to feed Noah.

It was strange, and maybe a little warped, but knowing Noah was hurt calmed her somehow. Much like protecting Seth, it gave her a purpose. She couldn't cry. She couldn't fall apart. She had to be strong for her men.

Noah is not your man.

Well, she could pretend he was. It might get her through this whole nightmare, and that was the goal. Coming out on the other side.

She moved into the living room and smiled at Seth. He made angry noises, though hadn't gone into full-blown tantrum yet. He'd been up for a solid eight hours now, and was fighting a nap like a champ. But he was otherwise unaffected by everything that had happened, and she could only be grateful for that. It soothed.

She picked up the toy he'd thrown out of his travel crib and handed it to him. He took it, though he didn't smile. When she picked him up, he sighed a little and nuzzled into her shoulder.

Oh, he was getting so big. And somehow she had to make sure he grew up. When she stepped into the room, she laid Seth in the middle of the bed next to Noah.

He fussed, then rolled to his side, cuddling up with Noah's not-shot side.

Noah looked slightly alarmed, but Addie didn't have time to assure him Seth would be okay for a few minutes. She went back and folded the travel crib, then set it back up in the room before heading to the kitchen.

She ladled out some soup she'd been keeping warm for when Noah woke up. She went through the very normal motions of making Noah dinner, then went through the not-so-normal motions of taking it to him.

In bed.

With a sleeping baby between you and a gaping wound from a bullet in his side and who knows how many psychopaths after you.

She darted a look at the door, the many locks, then the windows and all the boarding up they'd done. She'd found a heavy metal cabinet in a back mudroom and moved it over the door to the cellar. None of these things would permanently keep bad people out, but it would slow them down and give her and Noah warning.

Besides, she had the snow in her favor now. Unless there'd been other men with the two they'd killed who were lying in wait, any more of Peter's men would have to contend with the same weather Grady and Ty were facing.

She straightened her shoulders and breezed back into Noah's room, hoping she looked far more calm and capable than she felt.

She lost some of that facade, though, when she caught sight of the big, bearded cowboy with his arm delicately placed around the fast-asleep baby. Something very nearly *panged* inside her, but she couldn't allow herself to dwell on any pangs.

"You need to try to eat as much of this as you can," she said quietly. She placed the bowl of soup on the sturdy, no-nonsense nightstand. "I'll go get a chair," she said, searching the room. "Then I can feed you."

"No."

"Noah—"

"Just need to sit up, and I can do it myself," he said through clenched teeth as he worked to move himself into a sitting position, pain etched all over his face.

She stood over him, fisting her hands on her hips. "You shouldn't. Don't make me stop you from moving."

He winged up an eyebrow at her, and something in that dark expression had her faltering a little bit. Because it made her think of other things she shouldn't be thinking of with Seth asleep next to him and the gaping wound in Noah's side.

"You're not feeding me," he said resolutely as he struggled to get into a sitting position in the bed.

She wanted to push him back down, but she was afraid she'd only hurt him more, so she tried to take a different approach. "It wouldn't be any problem to do it. You're injured. Let me take care of—"

"You're not feeding me," he repeated.

Maybe she was reaching, but his complexion didn't seem quite as gray, even as he managed to lean against the wall...because in this sparse, no-nonsense room there was no headboard.

She frowned at him, then at the soup, then back at him. "Fine. You've worn me down. Let it cool while I move Seth to—"

"He's fine. Give me the soup."

"Noah."

"Addie, you killed a man. Saved us. Boarded up windows and talked to paramedics. Give me the soup and take a sit."

You killed a man. She was trying so very hard not to contemplate that. So she handed him his soup.

"What part of take a sit did you not understand?" Noah asked, and though his tone was mild she didn't miss the harsh thread of steel in his tone.

"What part of *I killed a man* don't you understand? I might snap and kill you, too, if you keep bossing me around."

Noah smiled then. Actually smiled. "I'll take my chances."

"I want to be relieved you're feeling good enough to smile, except you so rarely smile, I'm just prone to think you have a fever or some kind of horrible brain sickness."

"If I do, you should probably sit down because your fluttering around is stressing me out."

Addie frowned. "I'm not... I don't *flutter*." This time he didn't smile, but his lips *did* quirk upward. She slid onto the bed, Seth's sleeping body between them. She sighed heavily. "If I sit still, all I think about is all the ways things can go wrong."

He reached over and touched her arm, just a gentle brush of fingertips. "We'll get through this."

Addie blew out a breath. "We're stuck in a room in a tiny cabin that people have already infiltrated in the middle of a blizzard with no medical help or backup."

"But we fought off two armed men."

She frowned. "You've been *shot*, that's not exactly a victory."

"Not dead, though." He gave her arm a little squeeze, and though he tried to hide it, she noticed the wince. "Why don't you try to sleep while I eat? We need to take the opportunities to rest while we can."

"Noah..." Only she didn't know what to say or ask. She glanced down at Seth, who was sprawled out between them, blissfully unaware of everything going on around him.

She had to make sure he stayed that way, and this ended. "Noah, when you said you'd hurt people before this because you'd had to, what did you mean?"

He opened his mouth, most definitely to change the subject, but she needed to know. Needed to know how to go on from here. How to deal with the fact she'd hurt someone. "Tell me."

Noah brought the spoon to his mouth, slowly, carefully. Not because his body hurt, though it did, but because every part of him recoiled at the idea of telling her that. It would likely change her opinion of him, and more than that, he didn't want to tear down all those walls that kept it firmly in the past.

But maybe she needed to hear it. She needed to understand how to justify it so she could accept the things a person had to do to keep the people she loved safe.

She was so tense, sitting there on the opposite side of his bed. Eyes darting everywhere, hands clasping and unclasping. It was an interesting dichotomy: the woman who'd managed to do *everything* while he'd been unconscious, and this nervous, afraid-to-sit-and-think woman sharing a bed with him.

With a baby between you, idiot.

"My father wasn't a particularly kind man." Understatement of the year. "Ty and I were capable of withstanding that, but sometimes his targets weren't quite as fair or equal to the task."

"I'm not sure a son should ever have to be equal to the task of an unkind father."

"It was fine. We were fine, but Vanessa came to live with us for a bit when she was in high school. Her dad had died, and she'd gotten kicked out of her mother's house when her mother's new husband hadn't treated her so well. It was the only place to go, and we figured we'd keep her safe."

"From what? Unkindness? Because *safe* sounds like more than an unkind father."

"I suppose it was. It most certainly was when it came to Vanessa. Dad drank, more once Mom was gone, and she was by this point. Once Dad decided someone had the devil in them..."

"What does that even mean?"

Noah shrugged, trying not to think too deeply on it. Trying not to remember it as viscerally as he usually did, but it was a bit too much. Seth and Addie. This cabin. The pain throbbing at his side.

He took another spoonful of the soup, trying to will all this old ugliness away with the slide of warm soup down his throat. It didn't work. Instead the black cloud swirled around him like its own thick, heavy being.

But Addie slid her hand over his forearm. Gentle and sweet, and the black cloud didn't depart, but that heaviness lifted.

"He was a hard man. A vicious man. Made worse when he was drinking. He decided Vanessa had the devil in her and it was his job to get it out. I never quite understood it. He was not a religious man. No paragon of virtue. A Carson villain as much as any that came before."

"So you hurt him to protect Vanessa?"

Noah shouldn't have been surprised Addie could put it together, though it shamed him some. It must be obvious, the mark his father had made on him no matter how many years he'd striven to do good, *be* good.

"I guess."

"You *guess*?"

"I mean, that's the general gist."

"Then what's the actual story? I don't just want the gist."

He glanced at her then, the frown on her face, the line dug across her forehead. He didn't quite understand this woman, though he supposed he'd very purposefully tried *not* to understand her. To keep his distance. To keep everyone safely at arm's length.

But she'd slid under that at some point, and he didn't think she'd even really tried. She'd shown up at his door looking fragile and terrified, and he'd been certain it would be easy or she'd disappear or something.

She'd killed a man. In self-defense. Of herself, her son, of *him*. And her hand rested on his arm, a featherlight touch, soft and sweet.

But she was stronger than all that. It was probably the blood loss, but he wanted to tell her now.

"Sometimes he'd whale on us," Noah offered, lifting a shoulder. "We were big enough to take it. Vanessa wasn't. I couldn't let him hurt her. Not just because she was my cousin and family, but because she hadn't done anything wrong. She didn't deserve it."

"Then neither did you or Ty."

But they'd weathered their father's many storms and Noah had never felt... It had felt like his lot in life. The way things were. He wasn't a philosophical man. He'd always played the cards he'd been dealt. Bitterness didn't save anyone.

But violence could. "He went after her one day. Really went after her." Noah tried to block it out. The sound of Vanessa sobbing, how close his father had come to hurting her. In every way possible.

"I wanted to kill him. To end it. Part of me wanted that." Still, even years after Dad had died in a cell somewhere. He wished he'd killed him himself.

"And that weighs on you," Addie said, as if she couldn't understand why even though it was obvious.

"He was my father. Everything he was weighs on me."

"But you're you." Her hand slid up his arm to cup his cheek. She even smiled. How could she possibly smile at *that*? "A good man. A noble one. I didn't think they existed, Noah. Not outside of fairy tales."

"I'm no fairy tale."

Sheer amusement flashed in her eyes, and it sent a pang of longing through him he wasn't sure he'd ever understand.

"No. You're no fairy tale, but you remind me good exists in the real world when I most need to remember that." She leaned across the sleeping baby and gently brushed her mouth across his bearded cheek. "Thank you," she whispered.

Maybe if they weren't on the run, if she hadn't killed a man, if he wasn't bleeding profusely where a man had shot him, he might have known what to do with all that. As it was, all he could do was stare.

"You should rest," he managed to say, his voice rusty and pained.

She sighed, dropping her hand from his cheek and settling into the pillows underneath her head. She stared at the ceiling rather than him. "So should you."

"Food first for me, which means you rest first. Just take a little nap while Seth does, huh?"

She yawned, snuggling deeper into the pillows. "Mmm. Maybe." She turned her gaze to him, so solemn and serious. "Noah…"

"We're going to make it out of here. I promise." If he of all people could make her believe in good, he could get her out of here. He would.

"No, it isn't that. It's just… Seth's not—"

A loud pounding reverberated through the cabin. Noah bit back a curse as he tried to jump into action and the move caused a screaming burn in his side. He put a hand on Addie's arm as he glanced at her pale face.

Three short raps later and Noah let out a sigh of relief. "It's Ty."

Chapter Eleven

Addie scurried out of the bed and toward the front door, hoping Seth would stay asleep and Noah would stay put.

Even though Noah had seemed so abundantly sure it was Ty at the door, Addie hesitated. What if it was a trick? What if Noah was hallucinating? She frantically searched the living room and kitchen for a weapon. For anything.

Before she could grab a knife from the kitchen, she heard Noah's footsteps and labored breathing. She turned and glared at him.

"You should have stayed in bed."

He didn't say anything, just carefully maneuvered himself to the door. He pounded on it, and it was only then she realized he knew it was Ty because they were pounding in some secret code.

"You could have explained."

Noah merely grunted.

"Move this?"

Addie hurried to move the couch away from the door, Noah reaching out to open the locks on the door as she did.

Irritably, she slapped his hand away and undid the last lock herself before yanking the door open.

Ty stood there, his hat pulled low and the brim dusted with snow. He had to step up and over to get through the snowdrift that had piled up outside the door.

"What the hell are you doing on your feet, idiot?" Ty demanded the moment he stepped inside and his eyes landed on Noah. He quickly started pushing Noah back toward the room he'd only just come from.

"Where's Grady?" Noah said.

"Shoveling out some room for the horses in the barn. We'll search the area once I've got you patched up," Ty returned. With absolutely no preamble he turned to Addie. "Boil water, find me all the bandages or make-shift bandages you can, and a few towels. Bring them to the bed."

"Seth's asleep in the bed," Noah muttered as Ty kept pushing him toward the bedroom.

Without even stopping, Ty barked out another order Addie's way. "Move the kid out of the bed."

"You'll be respectful," Noah said in that stern, no-nonsense tone.

Ty rolled his eyes. "Leave it to you with a bullet hole in your side to worry about respectful."

"It's fine. The most important thing is patching Noah up," Addie said resolutely, passing them both into the room and carefully maneuvering Seth from the bed to the mobile crib.

She stood there for a second looking at her baby as he squirmed, scowled, then fell back to sleep. She'd been so close to telling Noah he wasn't hers, which had been so silly. What did it matter? In every important way, Seth was hers.

No one needed to know that she had no legal claim over him. That would complicate everything.

On a deep breath, she turned to Ty, who was disapprovingly helping Noah into a prone position on the bed.

"Boiling water, bandages, towels. Anything else?"

"That'll do," Ty returned, lifting Noah's makeshift bandages she'd put on him herself. "You're one lucky son of a gun," Ty muttered to his brother, and it was in that moment Addie realized Ty's gruffness and irritation all stemmed from worry and fear.

It softened her some, and steadied her more. This family was like nothing she'd ever known, and she'd do whatever she could to help them, protect them. She just had to remind herself every now and again she didn't really belong to them, no matter what it might feel like when Noah touched her so gently, kissed her to distract her or smiled at her despite the bullet wound in his side.

As Addie marched to the kitchen, Grady came inside. He stomped his snowy boots on the mat as he latched the front door with the variety of locks. He looked pissed and dangerous, and yet it didn't make her nervous or even guilty. It made her glad this man was on her side.

"I saw the dead one outside. Nothing of any interest on him," Grady said roughly as Addie prepared a pot to boil water in. "Laurel said there were two."

"I… There's one in the cellar," Addie said, nodding toward the metal cabinet she'd dragged across the door. "I think… I think he's dead." Dead. She'd killed a man and kept *telling* people about it and she wasn't sure how to feel about it...except Noah had said she should be relieved. Glad she'd protected herself and Seth. *And him*.

"If he's not dead now, he will be," Grady said, so cool and matter-of-fact it sent a shiver of fear through Addie.

Grady pulled a small gun from beneath the jacket he still wore. Whatever stabs of guilt from before the attack were gone now, because she could only be relieved she had people to help her.

Grady moved the cabinet off from the cellar door and eased his way down. Addie grabbed a knife from a drawer and eased her way close to the cellar. While she thought the man was dead, she'd absolutely jump to Grady's defense on the off chance the man was alive and got the better of him.

But Grady returned, grim-faced and serious. "Dead," he said stoically, and yet she could tell he was searching her face for signs of distress.

Addie straightened her shoulders. "Good." She wanted it to be good. She headed back for the kitchen and the boiling water.

"Laurel's beating herself up over this."

"She shouldn't," Addie said resolutely. "They're mobsters. Escaping police custody and doing the most damage possible is part of their job."

She grabbed some towels out of the drawer, trying to force her face to look calm and serious. Like Laurel herself. In charge and ready for anything.

Grady smiled ruefully. "And just think, you and Noah managed to stop a few. I wish I could convince Laurel she's not to blame, but what we feel and what's the truth isn't always the same. Not much we can do about it. Though Laurel will try, till she's blue in the face and keeling over. We're all going to try to put an end to this."

"Noah thinks we need to lure Peter here. I think he'll just keep sending men. After all, we know at least one more is out there. I can only imagine more are coming to do more damage."

"We'll handle it."

"Are all you Carsons so sure of yourselves?"

Grady grinned. "Damn right we are. You don't survive centuries of being on the wrong side of history without knowing how to face the bad guy."

But Peter was so much more than a *bad* guy. Addie thought he was evil incarnate. Even a rational man would have taken Seth long ago. Instead, he wanted her in a constant state of fear. She had no doubt Peter would take away everything she loved before he was done.

She had to find some Carson bravery and surety. She had to believe in her own power, and theirs.

Peter couldn't win this, if she had to sacrifice herself to make sure he didn't.

"Grady, I have a plan." The scariest plan she'd ever considered. Dangerous. Possibly deadly. But if she had to face that to keep everyone she loved safe, well, then so be it.

NOAH WOULD NOT admit to anyone, even his own brother, he was feeling a little woozy. Part the loss of blood, and part the fact that someone stitching him up while he was unmedicated wasn't really that great of a time.

"That should do it," Ty said, and because Noah

had spent his childhood shoulder-to-shoulder with his brother and knew all the inflections of his voice, he knew Ty was struggling with all this.

He also knew the last thing Ty would want was to talk about it.

"How often you have to do that in the army?"

"Don't worry about it."

So Ty didn't want to talk about that, either. Well, lucky for Ty Noah didn't have the energy to push. "When am I going to feel normal?"

Ty raised an eyebrow as he cleaned up the mess he'd made. "You got shot and patched up by passable emergency stitches at best. You need a whole hell of a lot of rest. Worry about that, not when."

"I have to keep her safe. *Them* safe."

"You have to rest first."

"I don't have time to rest."

Ty sighed heavily and Seth began to move around. A few little whimpers escaped his mouth, but he was still half-asleep.

"There is too much at stake," Noah said in a whisper. "Don't you see that?"

"Of course I see that. I also see that you've been shot. You're going to have to let some people step up and do the protecting here. We're all on it. Carsons. Delaneys."

"What good has that ever done?"

"You're still alive, aren't you?" Ty returned.

"Thanks to Addie."

"Well, she's a Delaney herself."

Noah scowled, well, much as he could with this terrible exhaustion dogging him. "You're not hearing me."

"I'm hearing you just fine. Enough to know you're getting mixed up with her."

"I'm protecting her," Noah replied resolutely. He was not mixed up in anything, because Addie was… well, whatever she was. *Strong. Vibrant. Everything.*

"Whatever you want to call it," Ty said with a shrug, having cleaned up all the stitching debris. "You need to rest before you can do more of it."

Seth began to whimper in earnest and Ty looked at the baby with something like trepidation in his gaze. "I'll get Addie."

"He won't bite you, you know," Noah offered irritably.

"I'll get Addie," Ty repeated, hurrying out of the room.

"Coward," Noah muttered, smiling over at Seth. "I'd pick you up, but I think I'd get in a little bit of trouble, kid." He painfully adjusted so Seth would be able to see him over the edge of his crib.

"No!" the boy demanded, pounding his little stuffed animal against the sides of the crib.

"I'd be in a whole heap of trouble."

"No," he repeated forcefully, and Noah had to smile. A year old and he already had Addie's spirit. A no-non-sense certainty, but with it a certain headstrong quality that wasn't Addie at all, and still Noah admired it. Because it would serve the boy well as he grew up.

Seth was damn well going to grow up somewhere where Noah could protect him.

"Awake already, baby?" Addie swept in, smiling at Seth as she scooped him into her arms. She turned to Noah. "You okay?"

"I'll live."

"Well, that is encouraging," she returned. Her voice was…odd. A little high. Not exactly panic, but nerves threaded through it. He watched as she moved around the room, collecting Seth's diaper change supplies.

Something was wrong. He'd learned in the past few months that poking at it would only make her insist everything was fine. He had to be sneakier in getting the information out of her.

Too bad he didn't have any idea how to be sneaky.

"Everything okay out there?"

"Oh, you know." Addie's hand fluttered in the air as she laid Seth down on the bed, preparing to change his diaper. "The guy in the cellar is definitely dead. Laurel is blaming herself." She hesitated a second, only a second, before she said the next part. "Grady and I devised a plan."

Noah could tell by hesitation he wouldn't like the plan at all. Besides, why was she devising plans with Grady?

"What kind of plan?" he asked, hoping his voice sounded calm and not accusatory.

She smiled sweetly at him. Too sweetly as she expertly pulled the used diaper off Seth's wriggling body and wiped him up before replacing it with a new diaper.

"You need to rest. We'll catch you all up when you're feeling a little more up to things." She finished changing Seth's diaper and pulled the boy to his feet, tugging his pants back up.

"Catch me up now."

"Everything is fi—"

When he started to get up, she hurried to his side

of the bed, Seth bouncing happily on her hip. She slid onto the bed next to him, pressing him back into the pillow. Not forcefully enough that he *had* to lie back down, but he didn't like the idea of fighting her. Not when she was touching him and looking at him with such concern in her expression.

"Don't get up." She didn't say it forcefully like Ty had, but plaintively, worry and hurt swirling in her blue eyes. He didn't want to admit it might come from the same place—care.

"No!" Seth grabbed Noah's nose. Hard. And squealed for effect.

Addie gently pried Seth's fingers off his face. "You need to rest."

"Now is not the time to rest. I can rest when this is over."

"Ty's worried. I can tell he's worried. Can't you be a good patient? For your brother?"

Noah grunted.

"I'll take that as a yes." Addie smiled. "I'm going to go get Seth something to eat. Why don't you try to rest?"

"No! No! No!" Seth lunged at him, smacking his pudgy hands against Noah's cheek.

"Gentle," Addie said soothingly.

It was all too much, these two people who'd come to mean so much to him no matter how hard he'd tried to keep them out. He'd told Addie the worst parts of himself, and she was still here, wanting to protect him and get him better. That little boy *knew* him and *liked* him for whatever darn reason.

He had to protect them, not just because it was the

right thing to do, but because he cared. He needed them, much to his own dismay and fear.

But dismay and fear were no match for determination. He took Addie's free hand, gave it a squeeze as her blue gaze whipped to his, looking surprised by the initiation of physical contact.

Which was a little much. He had kissed her before everything had blown up. Maybe he'd used the distraction excuse, but that didn't mean…

Well, none of it meant anything until she and Seth were safe. "Tell me what the plan is, Addie. I care too much about you to pretend I'm not worried about this."

She blinked, clearly taken aback by the mention of care, and maybe he should have been embarrassed or taken the words back, but he was too tired. Too tired to pretend, to keep it all locked down.

"You won't like it, Noah. I'm sorry. But you have to understand, it's what I have to do. For Seth. Once and for all."

"Explain," he growled.

"I'm going to be bait."

"Over my dead—"

"It'll get Peter here, and if we plan it out right, Laurel will have grounds to arrest him and transfer him to the FBI, which means he won't be able to escape this time."

"You don't know that."

He could tell that doubt hurt her, scared her, but she clearly needed both so she'd start thinking clearly.

"Or maybe I kill him, Noah. Maybe I do that. I don't know. What I do know is I can't keep running. You said so yourself. He has to come here. He doesn't want Seth, not really. He wants to cause me pain. So, I give him the chance."

"We can make that happen without you being bait."

"Yes, it's gone so well so far," she said drily, pointing to his bandaged side.

Which poked at his pride as much as the fear settling in his gut. That she would put herself in a situation where she could be hurt, or worse.

"I won't allow it."

She scoffed, shoving to her feet. Seth complained in his baby gibberish but Addie only paced. "I don't know why you insist on acting as though you have any say, any right. You don't get to tell me how to live my life, Noah Carson. You don't get to boss me around. This is my problem. Mine."

"And I don't know why you insist on acting as though that's true when I have told you time and time again it's mine, too. I'm here. I'm injured. I've killed to protect you and Seth. It is *our* problem."

She closed her eyes briefly before sitting back down on the bed. "I know. I know. I just… We have to work together but that doesn't mean… You're hurt, Noah. We have to play to our strengths. You have to watch over Seth for me. You'll have to protect him and keep him safe. That's what I need from you. What *we* need from you."

"Addie," he all but seethed.

"I'm counting on you, so you have to do it."

"I'll be damned if I let that madman touch you. If I have to fight you *and* Grady to make sure that's the case."

"It's the only way. You're the only one who can keep

Seth safe. I need you to do that for me, Noah. You're the only one I can trust with him."

"I can't let you do this, Addie."

"I know you must think I'm weak or stupid to have gotten mixed up in this thing—"

"I don't think that at all."

"Then you have to *trust* me." She took his hand in hers, Seth still happily slapping at his face while tears filled Addie's eyes. "Noah, I need you to protect him. He is the most important thing in the world to me. You're the only one who can do it. I know this kills you, but I wouldn't ask if it wasn't the only way. I can handle Peter as long as you can keep Seth safe."

He couldn't do this anymore. He was too tired. His head was pounding. Everything hurt, throbbed and ached. He couldn't fight her like this. He needed to build up his strength first. "We'll discuss it more tomorrow."

She sat there for a few seconds looking imperiously enraged before she let out a slow breath. "Fine." She seemed to really think over tomorrow. "We can talk more tomorrow. You need to rest."

"Yeah."

She started to move, but she still had her hand on his, so he grabbed it. Squeezed it. He needed her to understand that plans where she went off and put herself in danger just weren't an option. Not because she was weak. Not because of anything other than a selfish need to keep her close and safe.

Addie's and Seth's blue eyes peered at him, and he looked at them both, some brand-new pain in his chest. Not so much physical, this one.

"You're both important to me," he said resolutely. As much as he'd wanted to keep care and importance to himself, it was getting too dangerous to keep it bottled up. Too dangerous to try to keep her at arm's length. She had to know. "So important."

Some ghost of a smile flittered across her mouth before it was gone. Then she pressed her lips to his forehead, warm and smooth and somehow reassuring. "You're important to us," she whispered. "Now get some rest."

He wanted to fight it, but exhaustion won as Addie slipped out of the room, and Noah fell into a heavy sleep.

Chapter Twelve

Seth's schedule was so off it was nearly two in the morning before he was down for the night. Ty was asleep in the other bed in the cabin, having fixed up all the broken-in areas from earlier. Grady was asleep on the couch, snoring faintly.

Addie slipped into Noah's room and carefully laid Seth in his crib, watching him intently.

She would sacrifice anything for this boy. Including herself. It hadn't been an option before, but now she had people she could trust. People she could *entrust*.

Noah would protect him. The Carsons and Delaneys would give him love. Stability. Family.

She turned to Noah, asleep on the bed.

Knowing what she was going to do tomorrow she had to accept this might be the last time she spoke with him. She wouldn't allow herself to consider she might not survive, but she had to consider the fact that Noah might be so angry at her he'd never speak with her again.

She had to do what she had to do. For Seth, and for the only opportunity for a future that didn't involve running, losing or fighting for her life.

She slid onto the empty side of the bed, her heart beating a little too fast no matter that she was sure. Sure what she was going to do tonight, and sure what she was going to do tomorrow.

Noah stirred next to her and instead of staying on her own side, she scooted closer to him. The warmth of him, the strength of him. It was such an amazing thing that time and luck had brought her this man who wanted to protect her.

"Morning?" he murmured sleepily.

"No. Middle of the night." She should let him sleep. She should insist he rest. But she only had this one moment. She couldn't waste it. She pressed her mouth to his bearded cheek. "Would you do something for me?"

"In the middle of the night?"

"Well, it's a naked kind of something. Night seems appropriate."

She felt his whole body go rigid, and she was almost certain she could feel his gaze on her in the darkened room.

"Am I dreaming?" he asked suspiciously.

She allowed herself a quiet laugh and slid her hand under the covers and it drifted down his chest, his abdomen and then to the hard length of him. "Feels pretty real to me."

"That's a terrible line," he muttered, but he didn't shift away. Which might have been because of the injury on his opposite side, except he didn't shrink from her intimate touch. If anything he pushed into it.

"Noah, I want to be with you." She kissed his cheek, his jaw. "I've been pretending I don't, but it seems so silly to pretend with all of these horrible things going on. I don't want to pretend anymore, but if you don't want me—"

His mouth was on hers, fierce and powerful, before she could even finish the sentence. He carefully rolled onto his good side and his arms wound around her, drawing her tight against his body, trapping her own hand between them.

"I shouldn't," he said against her mouth. "God knows I shouldn't." But he didn't let her go, and his mouth brushed her lips, her cheeks, her jaw.

"Why not?" she asked, if only because he hadn't stopped touching her, holding her, kissing her.

"You're too…" He trailed off.

When he never finished his sentence, she cupped his face, holding him there, a tiny inch away from her mouth. "I'm just me," she whispered before kissing him, something soft and sweet instead of intense and desperate.

That softness lingered, all those furtive glances they'd hidden over months of being under the same roof. All the hesitant touches immediately jerked away from. Longing glances behind each other's backs.

It had seemed so necessary then, and now it was stupid to have wasted all that time. Time they could have been together—getting to know each other, touching each other. And they hadn't only because she'd been certain he was too good and honorable to even look at her twice, and he'd been convinced she was too… *something*.

But they were just them, and for a little while they could be together. She tugged at his T-shirt, trying to pull it off him without hurting him. Carefully, she rid him of the fabric and discarded it on the other side of the bed.

His calloused hands slid under her shirt, the rough texture of his palms scraping against her sides and sending a bolt of anticipation through her. He lifted her shirt off her and dropped it.

"I closed the door, but Seth's asleep in his crib. We have to be quiet," she whispered.

He exhaled, something close to a laugh. "You think?" His breath fluttered across her cheek, his hands tracing every curve and dip of her body, cupping her breasts.

She groaned, trying to arch against him, bring him closer.

"Shh," he murmured into her ear, something like laughter in his voice.

Her heart squeezed painfully, because she wanted all of Noah's smiles and all of Noah's laughter and she was putting all of that in jeopardy. He was too noble, too sure to ever forgive her for going out on her own.

But that didn't change the fact that it needed to be done.

She trailed her hands across the firm muscles of his abdomen, sighing happily as she reached the waistband of his shorts. She moved to pull them down and off, give her full access to him, but he hissed out a breath and Addie winced, pulling away from him.

"I don't want to hurt you." No matter how much she wanted this, the thought of him in pain—

"I'll live. Keep touching me, I'll live."

She might have argued with him if his hands weren't on her. Tracing, stroking, pulling responses out of her body she didn't know were possible. She felt as though her skin were humming with vibrations, as though the room were filled with sparkling light instead of pitch-black.

They managed to remove the rest of each other's clothes without causing Noah any more pain—at least that he showed. Addie straddled his big, broad body, her heart beating in overtime, her core pulsing with need and something deeper in her soul knowing this was something meant. Elemental.

Noah was hers, and maybe she even loved him. She'd probably never get to explore that, but at least she got to explore this. Something she'd never felt, certainly not with this bone-deep certainty it was right. *They* were right.

She kissed him as he entered her, a long, slow slide of perfect belonging. His arms held her close and tight, and when he moved inside her, she sighed against his mouth and he sighed against hers.

He took her as though he was studying every exhale, every sigh, and making sure she did it again. And again, and again, with a kind of concentration and care no one had ever shown her. Until she was nothing but shaking pleasure, dying for that fall over into release.

"Noah."

"Addie."

It was the way he said her name, low and dark, full of awe, that propelled her over that sparkling edge of wonder. Noah pushed deep and held her tight and they lay there for who knew how long.

It didn't matter, because she wanted time to stop. Here. Right here.

But life didn't work that way. She slid off him, curling up into his good side. He murmured something, but she couldn't make it out.

"Sleep," she whispered, brushing a kiss below his ear.

"You, too," he murmured, holding her close.

She should. Sleep and rest, because tomorrow she would have to face a million hard things she'd been running from for too long.

So she gave herself this comfort. Noah's arms around her, his heart beating against hers. The fact that he'd been as desperate for her as she'd been for him, and out of something horrible that may change her life forever, at least she'd gotten this little slice of rightness.

It would give her strength, and it would give her purpose, and tomorrow she would find a way to end this all.

NOAH AWOKE TO the sound of a woman's voice. But it was all wrong. It wasn't Addie.

He opened his eyes, glancing at the woman sitting next to him on his bed.

"What the hell are you doing here?" he grumbled, his voice sleep-rusted and scathing against his dry throat. His body ached, just *ached*, and yet there was something underneath all that ache. A bone-deep satisfaction.

Except Addie wasn't here, and his cousin was.

"Good morning to you, too, sunshine," Vanessa offered cheerfully, bouncing Seth in her lap. "I don't know what the hell you do with these things, but he's a pretty cute kid."

"Where's Addie?"

"Can you hold him, or will that hurt your stitches?"

"Where the hell is Addie?"

Vanessa sighed gustily. "I know you've been shot and all, but there's no need to be so grumpy and demanding."

"Don't make me ask again, or you will regret ever stepping foot in this cabin."

Vanessa raised an eyebrow, and it was the kind of warning he should probably heed, but panic thrummed through his body, making it impossible to heed anyone's warning.

"You're hurt, so I'll give you a pass on that, Noah, but don't ever speak to me that way."

He struggled to get himself into a sitting position.

"Geez, you really are hurt." She wrinkled her nose. "Please tell me you're not naked under there."

He glared at her as Seth made a nosedive for him. With a wince, Noah caught the boy. Poor kid was too cooped up. He needed to crawl around and move, but the cabin wasn't the place for it.

And where the hell is Addie?

"I am not naked." At some point he'd pulled his boxers back on last night.

Vanessa clucked her tongue and shook her head. "First Grady. Now you."

"Now me what?"

"A Delaney, Noah. Really?"

"She's not a… Not…really. Where is she?"

"Well, she and Grady went somewhere."

"Where?" he growled.

"Sworn to secrecy, sorry."

The only thing that kept Noah's temper on a leash was the fact that if he started yelling at Vanessa, he'd likely scare Seth. And then Vanessa would make him pay for the yelling later. He took a deep breath, doing everything in his power to keep his anger from bubbling out of control.

"I know you don't like this, but you're hurt, and Addie had an idea and… Look, Grady promised he and Laurel would keep her safe. Ty's out seeing if he can get a truck up here to take you to the doctor. We're on baby patrol. It isn't so bad."

She'd done it anyway. After last night, after saying they'd talk about it, she'd gone and done some stupid, dangerous thing anyway. "She's going to put herself in harm's way. How is that not bad?"

"She's the one who brought this mob mess to your doorstep, Noah. You'd be at your ranch, unharmed, if it weren't for her."

"She's not responsible for that. The man who's after her is."

"A man she had a kid with, Noah."

Slowly, because he couldn't believe Vanessa of all people would say that, he turned his head to face her. "You didn't just say that."

Vanessa shrugged, crossing her arms over her chest, adopting that pissed-off-at-the-world posture that seemed to propel her through life. "Well, it's true. You're paying because of the choices she made to get involved with someone awful. And yeah, the awful guy is at fault, but that…" She looked away, and Noah noticed a flicker of vulnerability he understood only because he'd once saved her from the abuses of his father.

"You're hurt," she said forcefully. "I get to be a little put out about my cousin being hurt."

He softened, only a fraction. "She's been hurt, too. You should be able to find some sympathy. You of all people."

Whatever vulnerability that had been evident in the cast of her mouth disappeared into hard-edged anger. "Then you need to understand that sometimes, not always but sometimes, people need to fight their own battles. Without you."

Which hit far too many insecurities of his own. He looked down at Seth, who was happily pulling at his chest hair. It might sting when he gave a strand a good tug, but it had nothing on knowing Addie was out there trying to fight her own battles.

She'd done that enough and he'd promised her no more, they were in this together, and she'd just ignored it. "I should have known what that was," he muttered.

"What *what* was?"

"Nothing. Never mind." But it had been a goodbye, plain and simple. And worse, so much worse, she'd chained him here under a responsibility he couldn't ignore. He scooted out of bed, hefting Seth onto his good side. "He needs to eat."

"No!" Seth tugged at his hair, making a sound Noah had a sneaking suspicion was his attempt at the word *hat*.

Noah strode out into the living room, Vanessa at his heels. Ty pushed in the door at the same moment, grim-faced and blank-eyed.

"We can't get out quite yet."

"How'd you stab me in the back and get Addie out of here?"

"They took the horses," Ty said with a shrug, clearly not worried about the backstabbing.

Figured.

"Give me your hat," he demanded, holding out his hand to Ty.

Ty cocked his head, but handed the Stetson over after shaking some of the snow off it. Noah handed it to Seth, who squealed happily.

"If anything happens to her," Noah said, deadly calm, because he didn't have any other choice of what to be— he had to protect Seth—"God help all of you." With that he strode into the kitchen to get Seth some food.

Chapter Thirteen

Addie sat in the Carson ranch house for the third boring, alone day in a row and tried not to cry. None of this was going like it was supposed to.

The plan had been to install her at the Carson Ranch, making it look like she had Seth with her, and wait for the next ambush. They'd moved her, faked Seth's presence and acted as though they were trying to be sneaky while laying all sorts of clues that this is where they were.

But it had been three days. No matter how often she talked to Laurel on the phone about how sure Addie was that having Grady or one of the sheriff's deputies be a lookout was clearly keeping Peter away, Laurel insisted they keep going without Addie attempting to make personal contact with Peter.

Better to wait him out, Laurel insisted. Let him feel like he was the one making the moves, not being lured.

Addie was learning that arguing with Laurel was absolutely pointless. The woman would do whatever she wanted, whatever she thought was best. Noah was like that. Grady, too. All the Carsons and all the Delaneys so sure they knew what was best and right.

Her included. She smiled a little at the thought. She was here because she'd been certain her being bait was the *only* way. She hadn't let Noah stop her.

But thinking about Noah only hurt. She missed him. She missed Seth like an open, aching wound. All there was to do in the silence of the Carson ranch house was miss them and worry about them and think about how mad Noah must be at her. If she managed to get over that she could only fret over the way it kept snowing and snowing and snowing.

She stared at her phone, trying to talk herself out of the inevitable panic call to Laurel. But she couldn't do it. This couldn't keep going. How long would she survive this endless, crazy-making waiting?

What awful things was Peter planning? He'd already proved he could wait as long as he pleased. He'd let her get settled here, hadn't he? Oh, she was now certain he was behind the poison and the fence-breaking. Little hints he was on the way, but enough doubt to cause her to wonder and worry, then talk herself out of it and settle in. Something like psychological warfare, and Peter was a pro.

She hit Call on Laurel's number in her phone, determined to talk Laurel out of the lookouts. She had to do this alone, without help or watchdogs. Maybe if she was persistent enough with Laurel—

"Addie, if you're calling me to tell me you can't do this—"

"I can't do this."

Laurel sighed. "Look, we've got some stuff brewing."

Addie straightened in her seat at the kitchen table.

Noah and Seth missing like limbs she didn't know what to do without. "What does that mean?"

"Give me a sec."

Addie waited, trying not to think too hard about what *brewing* might mean.

"There. Some privacy. Listen, we've had five brand-new visitors to Bent in the past three days. That never happens. Now, none of them match the FBI's description of Peter, but that doesn't mean they don't work for him."

"I can't wait around for Peter if he's just going to send people. Maybe I should go to Bost—"

"You're not going anywhere." Laurel said it with the same kind of finality Noah had said it with days before. Addie hadn't listened to him. Why should she listen to Laurel?

"But Peter hasn't left Boston." If she went there. If she confronted him… She might die, sure, but maybe…

"According to the FBI, but who knows what they know."

"Laurel, they're the FBI. Maybe if I worked with them—"

"They clearly don't care enough. When I spoke with an agent all he could talk about was some other organized crime group they're infiltrating as part of the Monaghan case. They want a case. We want you safe. It's personal for us. Look, there was this guy at Grady's bar last night. He didn't match any of the descriptions we have on file as Peter's men, but maybe that's good. Maybe he sent someone new. He disappeared somewhere out of town last night, but if he comes back we'll be ready to tail him."

"What did he look like? Peter isn't big on hiring new men. His goons are all either friends from childhood or people his father used."

"Red-haired guy, about six foot maybe. Green eyes. Little scar next to his eye."

Addie's heart stopped, or at least it felt as though it did. "Laurel," she managed to whisper.

"You recognize him?"

"Laurel, that's Peter."

"What?"

"You just described Peter," Addie repeated, something like panic and relief swelling inside her chest. Thank God they could move forward. Peter was here.

And what would he do to her? She couldn't think about that. She had to think about the future. About ending this.

"No. The description we have of Peter is six-four, two forty, dark hair, blue eyes, with a tattoo on his wrist."

"No. No, that's not Peter. That's not Peter at all. He's shorter. Wiry. Red hair. Green eyes. The scar. I would know, Laurel. I would know."

Laurel swore. "So much for the damn FBI. Okay, I've got to radio this new description out to my men. Because he's here, Addie, and things are going to go down soon. Be smart. Be safe. Keep everything on you. Phone. Gun. Everything. Got it?"

Addie nodded before remembering she was on the phone. "Yeah, yeah, I got it." She didn't like carrying the gun around, so she'd started keeping a sheathed awful-looking knife in her pocket and the gun hidden in the kitchen. But she'd go get the gun. She'd be safe. She'd end this.

"I'll call again soon. Be safe." And with that the line went dead.

Addie took a deep breath. This was what she'd left Noah for. This was what she needed to do to keep Seth safe once and for all. She got to her feet, shaky with nerves, but filled with righteous determination.

Peter was here. Which meant he'd be *here* soon enough. They'd made it look like they were trying to keep her safe, but the locks were paltry and the windows weren't boarded. It'd be easy for anyone to sneak in.

When someone did, she'd have a deputy at her door, or Grady, or someone to save her and arrest Peter. If she could keep calm. If she could think clearly and make sure Peter made his intent known.

He would. She was sure he would.

"God, please, please, let that all be true," she whispered.

A loud smacking sound startled a scream out of her. She whirled at the sound of clapping, and her knees nearly buckled when Peter stepped around the corner, applauding as he smiled that horrible dead-eyed, evil-infused smile.

"Impressive performance, Addie."

She stood straighter, reminding herself to be strong. Reminding herself what she was doing. Saving Seth. Saving herself.

"Really, that was impressive," Peter said, gesturing at the phone clutched in her hand. "You should thank me for such a compliment."

"Go to hell."

Peter sighed heavily. "Always so rude. Your sister at least had some manners."

"Don't talk about her."

Peter rolled his eyes. "Well, this has gone on quite long enough, hasn't it? Though your fear and running has kept me quite entertained, and this darling little *family* you think you've created here. I can't decide if I want to kill them all and let you live with the guilt of *that* or something else entirely."

Addie smiled, some inner sense of calm and rightness stealing over her. Any second now, she'd be rescued and Peter would be put in jail. "Good luck, Peter," she offered faux-sweetly.

Any fake smiles or pretended enjoyment on his face died into flat, murderous fury. "I don't need your luck. I wonder if my son is old enough to remember watching me kill you."

Addie lifted her chin. "You'll never touch him."

There was a commotion somewhere in the back and Addie let out a shaky breath. They'd gotten his murder threat, which meant the deputy was coming to arrest Peter.

Except Peter's mouth twisted into a smile that sent ice down her spine. "Oh, you think that's your savior? You think your sad little plan was going to work on me? You're even dumber than your sister, Addie."

"She wasn't so dumb. She got Seth far away from you, didn't she?"

Peter lunged, grabbing her around the throat. She fought him off, and he didn't squeeze her hard enough to cut off her oxygen. He simply held her there, glaring at her with soulless green eyes no matter how she punched and kicked at him.

"It was fun while it lasted. Watching you run. Watching you settle in and convince yourself you were safe, bursting that bubble over and over again, but you stopped running. That really ruins my fun, Addie."

"Good," she choked out.

"Good indeed. I suppose it's time to find my son. I'm going to kill whoever has him in front of you. No one's going to save you, Addie, because right now in the back of this property a man who looks an awful lot like me is forcing a woman who looks quite a bit like you at gunpoint toward the mountains. And while your friends follow *him*, we'll be going in the opposite direction." He stuck his mouth right up against her ear. "No one's going to find you, Addie, and Seth will be all mine."

In a low, violent voice she cursed him. In the next second she felt a blinding pain, and the world went dark.

THE CONTINUOUS RAGE that had begun to exist like a tumor in Noah's gut never, ever let up in the three days of being stuck in the Carson cabin knowing Addie was somewhere out there without him to keep her safe. The only thing that kept him from exploding was the boy. Not just Noah's job to keep him safe, but watching Seth take hesitant steps from couch to wall and back again was…something. It eased a part of the horrible anger inside him, and he thanked God for it.

"No," the boy said, grinning happily up at him. Noah held out his hand and Seth slapped it with enthusiasm. Noah had taught a kid to high-five, and even amid the worry and anger, there was some joy in that. Some pride. Silly, maybe, but it was good. This was good.

This he would protect. "Gonna be a bruiser, aren't you, kid?" Noah murmured.

"Ma?"

Noah didn't let that rage show on his face. He kept his smile placid. "Mama will be home soon." Which was a promise he wasn't about to take lightly. Three days had healed his stitches well enough. He wasn't dizzy anymore, and he felt much stronger. Everything still hurt like hell, but it was bearable.

He was going to get out of here soon. Whether Ty and Vanessa wanted him to or not. He just had to formulate his plan and make sure Ty and Vanessa had the ability to protect Seth. So he could protect Addie.

Noah glanced over at Ty. Every morning and afternoon he went tracking out down the road in the vain hopes it was clear enough to get them all down the mountain.

They still had Vanessa's horse, but it couldn't carry them all, and Seth was too little to be traveling in this kind of weather, anyway.

Laurel checked in with Ty every evening, but no one would ever talk to Noah. The minute he grabbed the phone or tried to use his own, they hung up. Everyone refused to communicate with him, and it made the rage bigger, hotter. Rage was so much better than fear.

Every person in his life was a coward, and what was worse, he *felt* like one. No matter that watching Seth and protecting him was a noble pursuit. It felt like a failure not to be protecting Addie, too.

Vanessa was in the kitchen complaining about making dinner even though she was by far the best cook out of the three of them, and had insisted they stop trying as it all tasted like "poison."

Noah wasn't convinced his reheating a can of soup could poison someone, but Vanessa was happiest when she was complaining so he just let it go. Let her pound around and pretend she didn't like taking care of all three of them.

"No. Ha." Seth smashed Noah's hat onto his head. Noah tried to pay attention to their little game and not the fact that Ty's phone was trilling about two hours earlier than Laurel's usual check-in.

"Yeah?" Ty asked gruffly into his phone.

Seth continued to play his favorite game of taking the hat on and off, though he'd now added putting the hat on his own head to the mix.

"I see," Ty said, his voice devoid of any inflection.

Noah looked over at him, a heavy pit of dread in his stomach. He tried to reason it away, but it stuck like a weight, because Ty's expression was as blank as his voice.

In anyone else, Noah might have said he couldn't read that practiced blankness. Ty hadn't had it growing up, but he'd come home from the Army Rangers with the ability to completely blank all expression from his face.

It was just in this situation Noah knew the only reason he'd have to do that was if Addie'd been hurt.

"What happened?"

Ty didn't speak for a moment as he slowly placed his phone back in his pocket. But his gaze held Noah's. "The guy's in Bent."

The guy. Noah got to his feet, carefully maneuvering around Seth. "The guy's in Bent. Where's Addie?"

Ty stayed where he was. Still and blank. "It's all part of the plan."

Which did absolutely nothing with the way the dread was turning to fear, which he'd channel into fury. "Where is Addie?"

Ty blew out a breath. "If you can calm yourself, I'll explain it to you."

Calm? How was anyone *calm* knowing that a person he'd vowed to protect was just wandering around out there? A target. Aided by his family. He didn't know what was worse, that she'd made love to him and left to face evil alone, or that his family had helped her.

"They put Addie up at the ranch. Alone, but under the watch of either a deputy or Grady or even Laurel, depending on the time of day."

"Let me guess. It went so well. The bad guy's caught and Addie is one hundred percent safe."

Ty scowled. "The guy created a bit of a diversion. Instead of just trying to take Addie, he had another guy with him who made it look like *he'd* taken Addie. So, two guys with a woman apiece went in opposite directions. Since only one deputy was watching, he had to make his best guess on which one was actually Addie."

Noah laughed bitterly. Idiots. All of them. He strode for his rifle, which was hung up on the wall out of reach of Seth. He started gathering what he'd need. His coat, a saddlebag, a first aid kit.

"Noah, you can't just leave," Vanessa said.

"Like hell I can't."

"What about Seth?" Vanessa demanded.

"You'll keep him safe."

"Addie asked *you* to do that."

"And I asked you all to keep Addie safe. She's not. She's with a mobster who's been chasing her for a year, who will very likely kill her once he finds out where Seth is. Who in this damn town is a better tracker than I am?" he demanded, glancing back and forth from Ty to Vanessa and back again.

"I'm not half-bad," Ty said. "Army Ranger and all. Besides, the deputy is tracking one of them. It could be Addie."

"And it could not be. Regardless, a mobster and his buddy have two women. Both are likely going to end up dead if someone doesn't do something."

"Let me do it," Ty said. "I can track as well as you. And I don't have a gunshot wound."

"You can't track as well as I can *here*. *I'm* the one who knows Bent and those mountains better than anyone. *I* helped track Laurel down when she was kidnapped. No one, and I mean *no one*, is better equipped to do this thing than I am. Not Laurel's idiot deputies, and not you or Grady. So I am taking that horse. You are arming yourself to the teeth. You die before you let anyone harm that child. And I will die before I let anyone harm Addie."

"You're hurt, Noah."

"I'll damn well live." Because he didn't think he could if something happened to Addie. So he couldn't let that happen.

Chapter Fourteen

Addie woke up groggy, her head pounding. It felt like a hangover, but in painful detail she remembered all too well what it was.

Peter had hit her with something and knocked her out. Nausea rolled in her gut, and she wished she knew more about head trauma or concussions. Was she seriously hurt? Was she going to die?

You will not die. Not until Seth is safe. Seth. Noah. She had to hold on to the belief that she could end this for them.

She took a deep breath in and slowly let it out. She took stock of her body as she looked around her surroundings.

She was cold. So cold. She smelled hay and horse. The walls were slats of wood and… She was in the stable. In one of the horses' individual pens. Tied to the wooden slats and sitting in the hay. Cold without a coat on in the middle of winter, head throbbing from who knew what kind of head trauma.

But she was not far from the Carson Ranch. At least, she didn't think. This didn't look exactly like the stables close to the house. Everything out here was a little dilapidated, and the hay certainly wasn't new. It was gray and icy. She knew for a fact someone had been doing Noah's chores around the ranch to keep the horses and cows alive.

So maybe she wasn't at the Carson Ranch at all.

She couldn't panic. Even as it beat in her chest like its own being, she couldn't let it win. She had to be smart. She had to *think*.

She was tied to the wooden slats of the stables with a rope. The wooden slats didn't look particularly sturdy, but the rope on her wrists was tight and rough.

She gave her arms a yank and the wooden slat moved. She paused and listened, but there were no sounds except the howling wind. Was Peter around?

She gave her arms another yank. Again the wooden slat moved, even creaked a little as though she'd managed to splinter it. She tried not to let the hope of it all fill her with too much glee. She had to focus. Listen for Peter. Be smart. She had to be smart.

Still there was nothing but silence. No footsteps. None of Peter's nasty comments. She didn't feel the oppressive fear of his presence. So she kept yanking. Harder and harder with fewer pauses between times. Each time Peter didn't appear, she felt emboldened to move faster.

She lost track of how many yanks, of the burning in her wrists from the way the rope rubbed, because all she could think about was escape. She could outrun Peter in the snow. While he fancied himself a hunter and an outdoorsman, she knew from her sister he did it in upscale lodges with guides doing most of the work.

She'd been living in Wyoming for months now,

doing somewhat physical labor by keeping house. She wasn't soft like Peter. She could outrun him. She knew at least some of the area. She could win.

She had to believe she could win.

She gave another hard yank and it was followed by the sound of wood splintering. Her momentum sent her forward, and since she didn't have the arms to reach out and catch herself as her wrists were tied together, she maneuvered to her side and fell that way.

She blew out a breath, not moving for a few seconds as she lay on the icy hay. Peter still didn't come running.

She laughed out a breath. She'd done it. She'd actually done it. But she had to focus and be careful and smart. Peter could be anywhere, and with her hands tied behind her back and a piece of wood dangling from the rope, she couldn't fight him off. Her only option right now was to escape.

And go where?

It was winter in Wyoming and she had no coat. She had some kind of head injury and her hands were tied behind her back.

Taking her chances with the elements was a much better option than taking her chances with Peter. Someone would find her. They knew she'd been taken, diversion or not. Someone would find her. She had to believe that.

She got to her feet, leaning against the wall as dizziness washed over her. She was definitely not 100 percent, but she could do this. Her legs were fine.

Once the dizziness settled, she took a step away from the wall. She wasn't completely steady on her feet, but it would have to do. Maybe Peter had tied her up and left her to die from exposure, but she had a bad feeling he wasn't done with her yet.

If she escaped now she could press charges. She could tell the FBI everything she knew and they'd have to arrest him for all the other things as well. She'd never had any evidence he'd killed Kelly, but she had proof that he'd tried to kill *her* in the here and now.

It had to be enough.

Carefully, she poked her head out of the stall she'd been in. The entire stable was empty. Ramshackle. She had no idea where she was. She'd never seen this building before. All of the buildings she'd seen on Carson property were certainly old and a little saggy, but cared for. No holes in the sides or roofs caving in like this building had.

So, not on Carson property, but people were looking for her. So all she had to do was run.

And hope she didn't end up in the mountains. Alone. Overnight.

There was a giant door on one side of the stable, but she wasn't stupid enough to go out that way. If Peter was still around, he'd see that. So she needed a window or a loose board or something. It was still dangerous, but she'd cut down as much chance of detection as she could.

She searched the stable and found two long-ago-broken windows. There wasn't an easy way to leverage herself up and out with the jagged edges of glass, the height, or her hands tied behind her back. So she went to the holes in the walls, poking and prodding at the wood around them as best she could without the full use of her arms.

It wasn't easy going and frustration was threatening, but she couldn't let it overwhelm her. Couldn't let—

She frowned as the faint smell of gasoline started to filter through the air. She hadn't seen any machinery in the stables that might be leaking old fuel. Panic tickled the back of her throat, but she swallowed it away. Maybe it was a side effect of the head injury.

Except then she heard laughter and everything inside of her roiled with futility as Peter's face appeared in the hole she'd been working on.

"Here's Johnny!" he offered all too happily before kicking at the loose boards around the hole—creating an even bigger one. The debris flew at her and she tried to move back so it wouldn't hit her, but she lost her balance and fell back on her butt, unable to stop from falling all the way onto her back since she couldn't use her hands to hold her up.

Peter stepped through the large hole he'd kicked and loomed over her. "Did you think you'd escape?" Peter laughed as if this was all just fun for him, to torture someone. To hurt someone. What had been warped in him to feel good at another's misfortune?

The smell of gasoline got even stronger, and Addie tried not to let fear destroy all the courage she had inside her.

But Peter calmly pulled a lighter out of his pocket, flicking the small flame to life in the frigid air between them, and the smell of gas was only making her feel even more dizzy than she already had.

"Actions have consequences, Addie. Your sister

learned that. The hard way. I thought you might have more sense, but I see I was wrong. You stopped running. You tried to fight. No one fights me and wins."

"I've been doing an okay job. You don't have Seth."

"But I will. The question is whether I let you die here, or in front of him."

The smell of gas was making her sick to her stomach. The flick of the lighter. He was going to kill her.

She breathed through that fear, because he would want to save himself. He'd want to be far enough away before he set this place on fire. It would give her a chance. It had to give her a chance.

"If you tell me where he is, I might just let you out. Let you run again. If not…" He shrugged and flicked the lighter again.

"You'll never find him. Ever."

"I guess you're dead, then." And he dropped the lighter.

HORSEBACK TOOK TOO damn long. Especially with the snow and the isolation of the cabin. Carson Ranch was too far away. Everything was stacked against Noah, including the pain ricocheting through his side where he might have already busted his stitches.

He wouldn't let any of that stop him.

Besides, if he'd been in a vehicle he would have to go down through Bent. On horseback—slower or not—he could cut up through the valleys where there weren't any roads and enter the property through the northeast pastures. It'd be more of a surprise approach, and maybe he'd even catch Peter with Addie trying to get out.

The closer he got to Carson property, the less he let his brain move in circles. He was focused. He was determined. For Seth and for Addie, he'd do whatever it took.

"Stop!"

The order seemed to have come out of nowhere, and Noah would have ignored it if not for the glint of a gun from behind the tree line next to him. He brought his horse to a stop, surreptitiously eyeing his surroundings, what options he had.

"Carson?"

Noah stared at the glint of gun. He couldn't see the person and he didn't recognize the voice, but whoever it was continued on.

"Get behind the trees. Now."

He followed the harsh order if only because if it was someone out to hurt him, they would have done it by now. He nudged his horse back into the trees and eyed the man.

Crouched behind a rock was one of the Bent County deputies. He looked more like a boy to Noah, but Noah dismounted and looped the reins of the horse to the closest tree. He crouched next to the *kid*, ignoring the throbbing pain in his side.

"I've got one of the fugitives in my sights," the deputy offered. He held out a hand. "Deputy Mosely. Laurel made sure we knew what all the Carsons looked like so we didn't actually hurt the wrong person." He frowned. "She didn't tell me you'd be coming as backup, though."

Noah shook the man's hand and said nothing. He was more interested in scanning the valley below the rocks. There were two lone figures standing next to a ramshackle building that had been an outhouse long before Noah's lifetime.

He couldn't make out faces or even heights, but his stomach sank. "That's not Addie," Noah said flatly. Even from this distance he knew that wasn't the shade of her hair. It was too white blond, not honeyed enough.

"What? How… You don't know that." The man shifted in his crouch and brought a pair of binoculars to his eyes.

"I know that," Noah replied, striding back to his horse. He didn't even need to take a look through the binoculars. "Which way did the other couple go?"

"I don't… The opposite. You can't just…" The kid straightened his shoulders, adopting what Noah supposed was meant to be an intimidating look. "Mr. Carson, I would kindly suggest you don't try to get in the way of the Bent County Sheriff's Department's actions."

Noah snorted and didn't stop moving. "The Bent County Sheriff's Department can go to hell."

Deputy Mosely sputtered. Hell, was this kid just out of the academy or something?

"What are you going to do?" Noah demanded, gesturing toward the couple in the valley.

"Not that it's your business, but I'm going to radio Deputy Delaney and follow her orders to—"

Noah rolled his eyes. No damn way was he letting this go even more wrong. He lifted his rifle and pointed it toward the couple below.

"Sir, put the weapon down immediately…"

Noah looked through the sight, saw his target—

the man's arm, because he wasn't an idiot or scared of doing the wrong thing while in uniform—and shot, ignoring the fact that the deputy had pulled his gun. The kid wasn't going to shoot a fly, let alone Noah himself.

"You…" The man gaped at him, like a damn grounded fish.

"Well, go arrest him," Noah ordered, putting his gun back in its soft case. "Get her back wherever she came from. Send everyone you've got available in the *opposite direction of*…" He trailed off as he noticed something not quite right in the horizon. Weirdly hazy.

He whirled around and there was a billow of smoke off to the west. "There," he said, already moving for Vanessa's horse. "Send everyone there. North point of Carson property. Follow the smoke."

"You can't just—" the deputy called after him.

Noah urged his horse into a run. "I just did." Vanessa's horse sped through the snow, agile and perfect, and Noah thanked God they had the kind of animals who could handle this.

Now he just had to make it across the entire north pasture to whatever was on fire and hope he could get there quick enough to save Addie, because he had no doubt she was somewhere in the middle of it.

God help the man who hurt her.

Chapter Fifteen

It turned out Addie had learned something in school. Stay low during a fire. Cover your mouth. Use your hands to feel out a possible escape route.

It was difficult to nudge her shirt over her nose with only the use of her chin and neck, but she managed after a while. Crawling was even more difficult with her hands tied behind her back, but she forced herself through an awkward, careful crab walk.

It didn't matter, though. There was no escape. There was only smoke and heat. Everything around her was burning. *Burning.*

She held on to the insane hope Peter had set himself on fire in the blaze instead of only trapping her inside. Even as the roaring of the fire creaked and crackled. Even as she had no idea where she was in the stables, let alone if she was close to some escape.

But she kept moving. Kept blinking against the sting of the smoke, kept thinking past the horrible sounds around her. She could lie down and die, but where would that leave Seth?

And Noah? What would happen to Noah?

She had to keep fighting.

So she scooted around, even as it got harder and harder to breathe. Even as she was almost convinced she was crawling in endless circles she'd never escape. But anything was better than stopping, because stopping would be *certain* death instead of just maybe death.

She thought she heard her name, and she was more than sure it was in her head, but she moved toward it anyway. It was either death or some guardian angel.

"Addie."

Some unknown voice above the din of the fire, and still she crawled toward it. She paused in her crawling. She tried to call back, but nothing came out of her scorchingly painful throat except a rusty groan muffled by her shirt.

Useless. She resumed crawling. Toward that faint sound.

"Addie."

"Noah." It came out scratchy and sounding nothing like his name and really she had to be hallucinating, because how would *Noah* be here? He was watching Seth.

Oh, God, he had to be watching Seth. She crawled faster, ignoring the way she couldn't see, the way her whole body felt as if it were swaying. She moved toward Noah's voice. Whether it was a hallucination or not, it had to be her escape.

She tried to keep her breathing even, but it was so hard. Tears stung her eyes, a mix of emotion and stinging from the flames around her. It was a searing, nauseating heat and she kept crawling toward it. Toward salvation.

Or is it your death?

Out of nowhere, arms were grabbing her, and there was somehow something cool in all the ravaging heat. Then it was too bright, and she had to squeeze her eyes shut against all that light.

For a moment she lay there in the foreign icy cold, eyes squeezed shut, almost certain she'd died.

But hands were pulling her to her feet, and then to take steps, and she let whoever it was lead her. Wherever they were going, it was away from that horrible fire.

"Just a ways farther."

She opened her eyes even though they burned like all the rest. "Noah." She could hear the fire raging behind them, even as he pulled her forward in the drifts of snow.

"Come on, sweetheart, a little ways farther."

"Am I dreaming?"

He glanced back at her, but continued to pull her forward. "Feels pretty unfortunately real to me," he said. There was no hint of a smile, and yet she wanted to laugh. Those were her words.

This was real. The misty gray twilight that hurt her eyes after the dark smoke of the stable. Noah, *Noah*, leading her to safety.

"Where's Seth?" Her voice sounded foreign to her own ears, scraped raw and awful, but she only barely felt the seething pain beyond the numbness. Still, the words were audible somehow.

"He's safe. That I promise you. Where's Peter?"

"I don't…" They reached the tree line and finally Noah allowed her to stop walking, but she was pulled into the hard press of his chest. He swore ripely, over and over again even as his hands methodically moved over her body.

"I don't think we have time for sex," she said, attempting a joke.

"I'm checking you for injuries," he replied, clearly not amused.

Her arms fell to her sides as Noah cut the rope holding her hands together.

"No broken bones," he muttered. "I imagine you have some kind of smoke inhalation." He pulled her back, studying her face intently. "What hurts?"

"I don't…" She couldn't think. All she could see was the blazing fury in his gaze. "How are you here?"

"I wasn't going to let him take you, and apparently I'm the only one in this whole world with any sense. You running off. Laurel having *children* watch you who follow the wrong damn people." His hands gripped her arms, his eyes boring into her. "I swear to God if you ever do anything like this again, I'll lock you up myself."

He was so furious, so violently angry, and yet his grip was gentle, and he kept all that violence deep within him. This man who'd been shot trying to keep her safe, and was now pulling her out of burning buildings.

"Noah…" She didn't know what to say, so she leaned into him and pressed her mouth to his. Everything hurt except that.

His hand smoothed over her hair and he kissed her back, the gentleness in the kiss the complete antithesis of everything she could tell he was feeling.

She'd believed she could take Peter on alone—well,

with the help of Laurel and Grady and the deputies, but mostly on her own. And she knew, even now with a bullet hole in his side to tell him otherwise, Noah thought he could take Peter down bare-handed.

But in this moment, and in his kiss, Addie realized something very important. They could only survive this *together*.

"You don't have a coat," he murmured, immediately shrugging out of his and putting it around her. She didn't even know how her body reacted to it. She felt numb all over, but somehow she was standing.

"You'll be cold now."

"I have more layers on," he returned, scanning the horizon around him. "Where'd he go?"

"I don't know." She pulled away and looked back at the burning stable, feeling an unaccountable stab of grief even with her renewed sense of purpose. "I was hoping he'd burned himself up."

Noah squinted down at the building. "Not likely. There." He pointed at something. Addie squinted, too, but she saw nothing.

"Tracks," Noah said flatly. "Coming and going."

"How can you see that? It's been snowing and—"

"I can see it." His gaze returned to her. "You need a doctor."

"Over my dead body are we separating ever again, Noah Carson. It's you and me against Peter, or you're going back to Seth right this instant."

He opened his mouth and she could tell, just *tell*, he was going to argue, so she gave his chest a little push until he released her. "We don't have time to argue, and if you can't see that the only way we survive this, the only way we *win* this, is together, I don't have time to convince you."

"You're right we don't have time to argue," he muttered, taking her hand. "But you better keep up until we get to Annabelle."

"Who's Annabelle?"

"Our ride."

NOAH WASN'T SERIOUSLY worried about Peter being on the run.

At first.

After all, Addie was safe with Noah, and Ty and Vanessa together could take care of any lone psychopath who clearly wasn't as good of a criminal as he fancied himself. So far Peter'd had ample opportunity to really hurt Addie and he hadn't done it. He kept giving her opportunities to escape. Maybe he expected her to die in the fire, but he certainly hadn't made sure.

Maybe he didn't want to hurt Addie. Maybe he just wanted his son back. Noah would never let that happen, but it soothed him some to think maybe this could all be settled without Addie getting hurt.

He glanced back at where she sat behind him on Annabelle's back. Her face was sooty and her breathing sounded awful. She was clearly struggling, and still she watched the ground and the trail of Peter's footprints they were following on horseback.

Any magnanimous thoughts he'd had toward Peter Monaghan obliterated to ash. He had left Addie to die in that fire. A painful, horrible death. No, he was no kind-hearted criminal who couldn't bring himself to end her life on purpose. He wanted her tortured. He was evil.

He needed to be stopped. Ended. So Seth never had to grow up and truly know what it was like to have that kind of soullessness in a father.

Noah would make sure of it.

He led Annabelle next to Peter's footprints, shaking his head at how easy this all was. Scoffing at the FBI and everyone else who hadn't caught this moron.

Until he realized that the footprints doubled back and followed Noah's original ones. Back to where he'd stopped with Deputy Mosely. Then carefully going along the trail of his horse's prints.

It had snowed, but lightly. There'd been no major wind. Since the snow had been a crusty, hard ice, the horse's stuck out.

With a sinking nausea, Noah realized Peter was going to use Noah's own damn trail to lead Peter to Seth.

"How did Peter get a horse?" Addie wondered aloud, her voice still low and scratchy.

Noah tensed and tried to think of a way to explain it that wouldn't lead her to the conclusion he'd drawn. Not that Peter had gotten a horse, but that he was following Noah's horse's tracks. Noah tried to think of how to hurry without drawing attention to the fact that they needed to hurry.

Vanessa and Ty could handle Peter, but Noah was slowly realizing Peter had more in his arsenal than Noah had given him credit for.

"Noah," she rasped in his ear. "Tell me what you're thinking."

He swore as the footprints stopped and suddenly vehicle tracks snaked out across the snow. Peter clearly wasn't alone anymore. He had what Noah assumed was some kind of snowmobile, and at least one man helping him.

A vehicle that could traverse the snow better and faster than his horse. Following his tracks back to the cabin. The only hindrance would be trees, but that wouldn't make the tracks unfollowable on foot.

"Noah... Noah, please tell me this isn't what I think it is," Addie said, her voice shaky from cold or nerves, he didn't know.

He couldn't tell her, so he kicked Annabelle into a run. He didn't want to push the horse this hard, but they had to get to Seth. "What do you think it is?" he asked through gritted teeth as wind rushed over them, icy and fierce. If he was cold without his jacket, fear and determination kept him from feeling it.

Addie didn't answer him. She held on to him, though, the warmth of her chest pressing into his back. She was careful to hold him above his wound, but sometimes her arm slipped and hit him right where it already ached and throbbed.

But the pain didn't matter. What Addie thought didn't matter. All that mattered was getting to Seth before Peter did.

Addie held on tight as they rode hard toward the Carson cabin. Much like his desperate ride in the opposite direction, the land seemed to stretch out in never-ending white, and there was no promise in the beautiful mountains of his home. There was only danger and failure.

Still, Noah urged Annabelle on, and the horse, bless her, seemed to understand the hurry. As they got closer to the cabin, Noah eased Annabelle into a slower trot. The snowmobile tracks veered one way, but if Noah went the opposite they could sneak up on the back of the cabin through the wooded area.

"Why are we slowing down? He's got so much time on us if he was in a vehicle. We can't let him get to Seth."

"Vanessa and Ty will fight him off."

"He isn't alone," Addie said flatly. "Someone had to bring him that snowmobile."

Noah ducked and instructed her to do so as well as they began to weave their way through the trees, bobbing around snow-heavy limbs. He didn't need the snowmobile's tracks anymore. "They couldn't cut through the trees with the vehicle. It looks like someone walked this way and instructed them how to get around this heavily wooded part. So they didn't approach the cabin this way as a group. That's good."

"Is it?"

"Ideally, it gives us the element of surprise, but that can't be all. We need to slow down, think and plan. We need to end this."

She laughed bitterly. "I keep thinking that and we keep running this way and that."

"You said we needed to work together. Well, here we go. Peter must think you're dead. He has to." Which got Noah thinking… "Addie, if he thinks you and Seth are dead…"

"How could we possibly do that? What would it solve? We'd always be in danger if he found out."

"Not if he's in jail, which is the least of where he be-

longs. Convincing him you're dead would just be insurance. A layer of safety on top of all the other layers."

"I… I guess, but do we have time to figure out how
to do that? We have to make sure Seth is safe."

"All you have to do is make sure Peter doesn't see
you."

"I don't give a… We just need to get Seth. That's
all I care about."

Noah understood that, whether he wanted to or not.
But he couldn't let fear or panic drive him. That's what
had led him to the Carson Ranch, and yes, he'd saved
Addie in the process, but he'd also led Peter straight
to Seth.

"You're going too slow," Addie insisted, desperation tingeing her voice.

"I can't imagine what it must be like, the fear and the
panic, but we can't let it win. You know I wouldn't let
anything…" He trailed off, because he *had* let things
happen to her and Seth. "We have to end this, which
means we have to be smart. Leading with emotion,
with fear, with letting someone else call the shots, is
what got us here, Addie. If we'd fought straight off, if
you'd stayed in the cabin, if I hadn't flown after you
half-cocked… We're mucking things up right and left,
and we can't keep doing it. Because Seth *is* at stake."

He felt as much as heard Addie's sharp intake of
breath, feeling bad for speaking so harshly to her, but
it was all true. They couldn't keep *reacting*, they had
to plant their feet and act.

"Maybe you're right," she said softly into his ear
as he brought Annabelle to a stop. They were deep in
the woods, but he knew exactly where the cabin was

though he couldn't see it though the snow and thick trees. About a hundred yards straight ahead.

"So, let's figure out a plan. A real plan. A *final* plan. One that brings you both home safe."

"Home?" she echoed.

"Bent is your home, Addie. Yours and Seth's. From here on out, it'll always be your home." He'd fight a million battles and risk life and limb to make it so.

Chapter Sixteen

Addie let Noah help her off the horse. The horse was panting heavily, and Addie couldn't help but breathe in time with her. Too shallow. Too fast.

But Noah was right. No matter that she wanted to tear through the woods screaming, shooting at anyone who got in her way with Noah's rifle, until Seth was safely in her arms. It wouldn't do the thing that needed to be done.

Seth. She needed Seth's *permanent* safety at the top of her list. Not just these snatches of time with it-didn't-matter-how-many people protecting him. She needed to give him safety, stability, a *home*.

Bent is your home. She hadn't realized how desperately she wanted that to be true until Noah had said it, had held her gaze steady and sure. Underneath all that surety, she'd seen...she was sure she'd seen the kind of bone-numbing fear and fury she felt in her soul at Seth being in direct line of danger.

"If we're going to convince him Seth's dead, we have to get Seth away first."

Noah nodded, his jaw set. She could see the way he

thought the problem through. She could see the same thing she felt.

How? How? How?

"I'm not usually the one with the plan. I'm the one who acts," he muttered.

"Well, the other plans haven't worked. Maybe you need to be."

He flicked a glance at her, eyebrows drawing together. "We don't know how many men he has."

"There were only tracks to one vehicle, right? So it can't be more than a couple. Maybe four of them altogether. And there's four of us. It's a fair fight."

"Really," Noah replied drily.

"It's close, anyway."

"We'll go with four men," Noah said, staring through the trees. "Armed, probably better than us." Noah glanced at her again. "Do you think he meant to kill you?"

"I don't think he cares either way. He wants me hurt and scared, but what he really wants is Seth."

"You don't think he has some kind of feeling for the mother of his child?"

Addie had to look away. She should tell him. Explain the whole thing. Except they didn't have time for that right now. "It's complicated."

Noah rubbed a hand over his beard. "There's a secret passageway into the cabin. The guy who shot me saw me come out of it, but surely he couldn't relay that information back to Peter considering you killed him."

Killed him. She'd killed a man. And she was prepared to kill another. If the opportunity arose, she needed to be willing to kill Peter. Seth's father.

She steeled herself against that soft spot. Yes, Peter was Seth's father, and maybe Seth would never fully understand the threat his father posed. She prayed he didn't. That he'd never fully understand. Even if it meant he grew to hate her.

Seth was the most important thing. His life. His future. His happiness.

"So, we'll create a diversion," Noah said, steel threaded through his voice. He might not be used to being the one making the plans, but he was certainly used to being in charge. "I'll be careful and try to sneak in the cabin, but the most important thing is getting you into the secret passage. If I can get to Ty and Vanessa, we can work out how to get Seth to you through the passage. If we can, we'll get Vanessa, too, and you two can figure out how to make it look like something happened to Seth while Ty and I fight them off."

"That leaves you vulnerable. Four against two."

"We don't know they have four, and I'd bet on me and Ty anyhow."

"You said yourself they probably have better weapons."

"You can't beat the bad guy without taking some risks, Addie. I think we can both agree Seth is the most important thing, right? It's why you left. It's why you let yourself be bait. I lost sight of that, took Seth's safety for granted in the face of a danger to yours, and look where it led. Right here. It's my fault Peter figured out how to get to Seth, because I lost sight of that one thing. Well, not again. I'd die before I let anything happen to him."

Addie blinked back the tears that stung her eyes.

She'd come to that same conclusion, too, and as much as the idea of losing Noah physically hurt, Seth... Seth was the priority.

"All right," Addie managed, though her voice was scratchy from the fire, from the cold, from emotion. "We'll go up to the cabin, scope it out. You'll show me the secret passageway. We'll get me in, then I'll wait."

"I'll see if I can get to Ty or Vanessa without detection. You stay in that secret passageway until we get you Seth, or we can get Vanessa and Seth in. We'll keep the rest occupied."

"What if—"

"That's the plan. We focus on the plan. If we get there and we can't get to the secret passageway, we'll come back here and reevaluate. Now we move. We have to be silent. They can't know we're there yet, but most especially they can't catch sight of you."

"Most important after Seth, that is."

Noah nodded. "We'll promise each other, here and now, everything we do is to protect that boy." He held out his gloved hand.

Dwarfed and warmed by his coat, she slid her hand out of the sleeve and shook Noah's. "Agreed."

Noah turned to the horse, pulled some things out of the bags that hung off the saddle. Feed and water. A blanket. He took those few minutes to make the horse comfortable. "If you and Vanessa get out, you need to be able to make your way back to Annabelle. We're going to cover our tracks, so you have to be able to get back here blind."

Addie swallowed. She didn't know the area at all, especially out here. "How?"

Noah considered the question, then pulled a small Swiss Army knife out of his pocket. "We'll mark the trees." He gave her a once-over. "I don't have a gun to give you, so you'll have to take this once we're done. You need some kind of protection."

Protection. She pulled out the knife she'd managed to stick into the back of her pants back at the ranch. It hadn't helped her against Peter because she'd been trying to lure him, not hurt him, and then he'd knocked her out.

She wouldn't be so stupid next time.

"I have this."

Noah raised his eyebrows, since it was a pretty impressive knife she'd found with a bunch of hunting supplies in one of the supply closets at the ranch. It had been the easiest-to-conceal weapon she'd been able to find that had a kind of sheath that would keep her safe from the blade.

"That'll do. Let's get started." With that, Noah began a path toward the cabin, carefully marking a network of trees with little *x*'s a person would have to know were there to find, while Addie carefully covered their tracks in the snow.

When they could start to see the cabin through the trees, their pace slowed, but they didn't stop. As silently as they could, they crept forward, still working, always watching.

Addie could make out the snowmobile, empty and parked to the side of the cabin. But as her gaze searched the space around the cabin, the woods around her, she saw no sign of any men. Only their footprints around the snowmobile.

Noah nodded toward the cabin and she followed him, wordlessly stepping into the bigger prints he left. They didn't have time to cover these. Not yet.

With one last look around the yard and tree line, Noah stuck his fingers into some crevice Addie hadn't even seen and seemingly magically pulled, amassing snow in a large hill behind it, until a very small door opened.

He gestured her forward, and even though it was dark and who knew what all lay inside, Addie knew she had to crawl in there. So on a deep breath, she did. Squeezing through the opening and contorting her body into the dark space that was some hidden part of the cabin. She re-sheathed her knife and shoved it where it had been down the back of her pants.

"Stay inside," Noah said, worry reflecting in his dark eyes even if it didn't tremble in his voice. "On the opposite side is another door, but it's covered by the fridge. If we can get Seth, or Vanessa and Seth, to you, it'll be through there. There's a peephole here." He pointed to a hole in the wall that allowed her to see out into the backyard. "But there's no way to see inside."

"Okay." She tried to keep her mind on those instructions. On the plan they'd created together.

"Stay put until one of us gets you. Promise?"

She didn't want to promise that. There were so many what-ifs in her mind.

"The only exception to that promise is if you know Seth is in immediate danger. Okay? Deal?"

She still didn't love that deal, because she wanted to protect him, too, but... Well, they'd seen how well that worked out when Noah had rushed to protect her. She was glad to be alive, and Peter probably would have found Seth eventually, anyway, but…

But Seth had to come first. "Deal."

Noah nodded and started to push the door closed, then he swore roughly. Addie jumped, thinking they'd been caught, but he only reached forward and pulled her to him.

"Do you want your coa—"

Then his mouth was on hers, rough and fierce. A kiss of desperation, anger and, strangely, hope.

"I love you, Addie," he murmured against her mouth.

And before she could even think of what to say to *that*, Noah pushed the door closed with an audible *click*.

She was in the dark and alone, and she had to sit with *that* and wait.

I love you.

What kind of man said I love you before he closed you into a secret passageway while mobsters were after you and the baby in your care?

But neither anger nor bafflement took hold quite like she intellectually thought they would. Instead, she felt only the warm glow of *love*. Love. Noah—taciturn, grumpy, sweet, good Noah—had said he *loved* her.

After she'd spent so much of the time before Peter had come being afraid to even think he might look at her with more than blind disinterest, Noah *loved* her.

She couldn't possibly predict what would happen with all this, if they'd all survive unscathed or not, but Noah loved her, and Seth needed her.

For Seth, she could endure anything. With love, she could face any challenge.

NOAH MADE QUICK work of covering up the snow around the door and his tracks to and from the secret passageway. He searched his surroundings, listening for any faint hint at where everyone was. It left a terrible feeling in his gut. Everything was too quiet.

He moved soundlessly through the trees to make a circle around the cabin, checking the perimeter. Once he was satisfied there was no lookout on this side, he focused on the tracks around the cabin.

There were quite a few sets of footprints, though he could assume the shallow ones were old and filled with new snow. The heavy ones… He counted, tried to make out different footwear, tried to decide who was who based on where they'd come from.

Three men, it looked like, though looks could be deceiving. There was the pair of tracks that had followed Noah's original ones. They came out of the woods, then went down the road. Then the vehicle tracks.

Only one set of footprints went toward the cabin. The other two fanned out down the road.

So they had two men watching the road for intruders, and one man—probably Peter, though he couldn't be sure—on the inside.

His odds were good, because if he only had men looking out from the road, the Carsons could kill Peter before he could make a peep.

But Noah wouldn't be that cocky this time around. He'd still be careful. Cautious. He glanced at the snowmobile. No one was getting away on that thing. He didn't want Addie to be seen, and Seth wouldn't be safe on it. So it was useless to him.

He needed to make it useless to them as well. Moving as quickly but as quietly as he could, he lifted the panel to the engine and then used his Swiss Army knife to snap any wires or tubes he could find. He paused, waiting for someone to fly out of the trees or a bullet to come whizzing by, but nothing happened.

He crept closer to the cabin. The windows were boarded up, so there was no way to see in. He frowned at the door, because it appeared to be cracked open.

Noah moved toward it, gaze still darting behind him and at the road. The closer he got, the more he realized he could hear someone talking in there.

"You lot seem to think you're awfully tough."

Noah reached for the rifle on his back. Still, no matter how he maneuvered himself, he couldn't see inside the crack of the door. He could only hear.

He was tempted to bust in and start shooting, but he couldn't do it without knowing what was on the other side. He couldn't risk his brother or his cousin any more than he could risk Seth.

"Tougher than some pissant who has to hide behind a mob to make himself feel like a big strong man. What are you compensating for, buddy?" Ty's voice drawled the question lazily and Noah shook his head. You'd think a former Army Ranger would have more sense than to poke at the enemy with people's lives on the line, but Ty had never been what Noah would consider predictable.

"The only reason I haven't shot you in the head, you miserable sack of nothing, is that I'm waiting on one of your loved ones to show up so they can watch the life drain out of you. That might be avoidable if you tell me where the boy is."

Ty laughed and Noah nearly sagged with relief. They'd hidden Seth somehow. In the cellar maybe? It'd be impossible to get him out of there without Peter seeing him and Vanessa, if she was down there with him.

Noah winced as a flash of light hit his peripheral vision. He did a quick scan of the tree line, but he didn't see anyone or any sign of a gun. He turned his attention back to the cracked door of the cabin, but the flash of light persisted. *Flash. Flash. Flash.*

Noah studied the tree line, over and over again, seeing no sign of anyone. Another flash, and he finally got it.

It was coming from the barn, and since it seemed purposeful rather than the precursor to being picked off, Noah moved toward it.

He wouldn't lead Peter to Seth again, so he took a long circuitous way that involved using some of the other men's tracks to hopefully throw anyone off the scent, then his own back into the woods. Once hidden in the trees, he took off on a dead run.

When he reached the back of the barn, he gave three short raps against it. When they were returned in double time, he rounded the corner. He kept his body close to the barn, dragging his feet hoping to make the trail simply look like melted snow runoff causing a rut in the snow.

When he reached the barn opening, which had no closure anymore as the barn was almost never used and falling apart, he slid inside.

Vanessa was holding a very frightened-and-bundled-up-looking Seth. She had a quilt around them that had hay stuck all over it, and he assumed Vanessa had hidden them in a pile of old hay.

Noah winced, but he didn't have time to worry about whether Seth was comfortable. He had to keep the boy alive. "What's going on?"

"We heard them coming. Ty sent me to the barn. I have no idea what's going on aside from that. I've been trying to stay hidden, but Ty's been in there so long…" She bit her lip, sending an uncharacteristic worried look toward the cabin.

"I heard him. He's holding his own, it appears. They've got men watching the road, but none watching the cabin. I don't think they expected to be followed, but maybe they're expecting police to show up. They think Addie's dead. She's in the secret passageway. I need you to go get her. She'll lead you to Annabelle, then you take the quickest route to Bent."

He started pulling Vanessa toward the opening, glancing every which way before he nodded toward the back of the cabin.

"What about you?" Vanessa asked as she ran.

"Ty and I will take care of it." He did his best to hurriedly cover the tracks they were making. "Get Addie and go. Now."

"If either of you die, I swear to God I'll find a way to make you pay," Vanessa said angrily, eyes suspiciously shiny.

"Love you, too, Van," Noah muttered, pulling the rifle off his back. "Now get him and her the hell out of here."

With one last angry look, she gave a nod and pulled

the door open. Noah kept watch, ready to shoot anyone who might appear and try to intercept.

Addie scooted out, wide-eyed, and then immediately held out her arms and Seth fell into them, crying faintly. Addie soothed him, and Vanessa encouraged her into a run toward the trees.

She never even looked his way.

Chapter Seventeen

Addie wished she could go faster, but following the small marks on the tree back to Annabelle wasn't as easy as it had sounded an hour or so ago. Though she could somewhat follow the disturbance in the snow that was her and Noah's covered tracks from earlier, the wind and fading daylight had made that difficult as well.

Vanessa had a thin, weak flashlight out and Addie was using her fingers to feel the bark of the trees for the heavy slash of a cut. But Seth clung to her, whimpering unhappily, and that kept her going regardless of the frustration.

"It's okay, baby," she murmured, searching the trees, every pain and ache in her body fading to a dull numbness.

"Here's the next," Vanessa announced. They'd been trying to cover their tracks, at the very least obscure how many people had run away from the cabin. It was all getting so tiring, and she needed to get Seth somewhere warm, even if he was bundled to the hilt.

"Man, you guys sure made a trek," Vanessa mumbled as they searched the next grouping of trees.

"Noah wants them to think I'm dead."

In the dim twilight Vanessa looked back at her. "Dead? Well, that's smart. I'd prefer *him* dead, but that'd do, too."

"And Seth."

Vanessa's eyebrow winged up as she went back to searching the trees. "How's that going to work?"

"I don't know. I'm taking ideas." Addie sighed and stood to her full height. "Here's the next."

A huffing sound caught both women's attention and they looked toward it. Addie nearly cried from relief as Vanessa ran the few yards to Annabelle.

"There you are, sweetheart," Vanessa offered to the horse, running a hand over her mane. "I bet you're cold. Let's get you home, yeah?"

Addie approached as Vanessa pulled some feed out of the saddlebag and fed it to Annabelle by hand. Vanessa looked at her and Seth and then pressed her lips together.

"This is going to be tough and slow going. We're going to have to do this bareback so we all fit, and go slow so Seth is safe."

Addie swallowed at the lump in her throat. "Do you think we'll make it?"

"We won't know until we try. Once we get somewhere warm, we'll figure out a way to make it look like Seth's… Well."

Addie didn't like to say it, either, even if it was just a ruse they were planning. It felt too possible, too real, especially on the run from Peter.

"The dark is going to be a problem," Vanessa said flatly.

"I could maneuver Bent blindfolded and turned around, but these forests and mountains? It's another story."

"Can't we make our way to the road?" Addie asked as Vanessa unbuckled the saddle and dropped it to the ground.

"Noah thinks Peter has men on the road. Any ideas on where to hide the saddle? If we're trying to hide the fact more than just me and Seth escaped, we can't leave this lying around."

"We'll bury it," Addie said resolutely.

"It'll take time."

"I think it's time we have." She had to hope it was time they had. As long as Peter wasn't after them, they had to do everything they could to hide the fact that she was still alive. "We could use it maybe. Make it look like the horse threw you and Seth and the saddle. A horrible, bloody accident. Then we see if Laurel can get someone at the hospital to forge records or something."

"Far-fetched. A horse couldn't throw a saddle, and that's only for starters."

"Peter wouldn't know that. He'd see a saddle and blood and then we'll leave the horse's prints and go straight for town. Get someone, anyone, to drive us to the hospital and see what we can fabricate from there."

Vanessa considered. "We'll need blood."

Addie shifted Seth onto her hip, then pulled the sheathed knife out of the back of her pants.

Vanessa swore under her breath. "You aren't really going to cut yourself open for this, are you?"

"Better me doing the cutting than Peter." Addie grimaced at the thought. "Well, you might have to do the cutting."

Vanessa swore again. "I don't know how you got into this mess, Addie, but boy do you owe me once we're through it."

"Then let's get through it." With that, Addie set about to create quite the fictional scene.

NOAH WANTED TO give Addie and Vanessa as much time as possible to get a head start before he engaged with Peter and his men, but the longer Ty stayed in there at the mercy of a mobster, the less chance his mouthy brother had of escaping unscathed.

When Noah had returned to the door after watching Vanessa, Addie and Seth disappear into the woods, it had been closed so there was no hope of overhearing more. Maybe he could sneak down the road and try to pick off Peter's men? Then there'd be no one to come running if he and Ty overpowered Peter.

But the problem remained: he couldn't see inside the cabin. He had no idea what weapons Peter had or what he might have already done to Ty.

And how much longer did he give Addie and Seth and Vanessa before he stepped in and helped his brother?

He frowned at a faint noise. Something like horse hooves off in the far distance. Couldn't be Addie and Vanessa, because the sound was more than one horse. Could they have reached help already?

Noah stayed where he was, scrunched into a little crevice in the outside logs of the cabin that gave him some cover. A horse came into view, but it wasn't anyone Noah recognized, which meant it had to be one of Peter's men.

How the hell did he get a horse? Noah seriously considered shooting the stranger, but he stopped himself. He didn't know what Peter was doing to Ty in that cabin, and he couldn't risk his brother's life.

The man dismounted stiffly if adeptly. Almost as though he'd been given rote instruction on horseback riding but hadn't had much practice. He went straight for the snowmobile, far too close to Noah for any kind of comfort.

But the man didn't look his direction. He tried to start the vehicle and was met with silence. He swore ripely, then pulled a walkie-talkie out of his coat pocket.

"Snowmobile's been tampered with," the man said flatly into the radio.

Static echoed through the yard and Noah tried to think of some way to incapacitate the man without making sound.

"Leave it. Search the woods on horseback. Someone has my kid and is trying to get to Bent. We can't let them." It was Peter's voice, Noah was fairly sure.

Noah didn't have time to worry anymore. He had to act. As silently as he could, he pulled his rifle out of the back case. He couldn't risk shooting the man and having anyone hear the gunshot, so he'd have to use it as a different kind of weapon.

He took a step out of his little alcove, and the man was too busy fiddling with the snowmobile to notice. Another step, holding his breath, slowly raising the rifle to be used as a bludgeon.

Without warning, the man whirled, his hand immediately going for the gun he wore on his side. Noah had been prepared for the sudden movement, though, and used the rifle to smack the gun out of the man's hand before he could raise it to shoot. Noah leaped forward and hit the butt of the weapon against the man's skull as hard as he could.

The man fell to his feet, groaning and grasping the ground—either for his own weapon or to push himself up, but Noah pressed his boot to the back of the man's neck. The man gurgled in pain.

Before Noah could think what to do next, the front door was flung open and Noah raised his rifle, finger on the trigger, a second away from shooting.

But Ty was the one who emerged, and immediately hit the deck upon seeing Noah's rifle.

"Help me out here," Noah ordered.

"Thought I was going to die at my own brother's hand," Ty muttered, and it was only as he struggled to get to his feet that Noah realized he was tied up.

"What the hell is going on?"

"Oh, that idiot burst in and I let him think he had the upper hand so Van could get the kid away. He tied me up. Yapped at me till I thought I was going to die of boredom, but he was searching the house the entire time."

"Where's he now?" Noah asked, pushing his boot harder against the squirming man's neck.

"He found the passageway," Ty muttered disgustedly. "Smarter than he seems. He's got radio contact with his men. Somehow they got horses. Can't imagine they know how to ride them, but the idea was to start searching the tree perimeter. He's got some fancy

GPS and all sorts of crap. They're out there, looking for them."

"Get over here."

Ty complied. When the gasping man on the ground grasped for his leg, Ty kicked him in the side.

Noah retrieved his Swiss Army knife, then used it to cut the zip ties that were keeping Ty's hands together and behind his back.

"Managed to get out of the ones around my feet, but the hands were a bit harder."

"Thought Army Rangers could escape anything."

"I'd have done it eventually. But I heard a commotion. Figured I didn't have much time. Luckily it was just you."

"And Peter is out there."

"Van'll keep Addie safe."

Noah glanced down at the man, who was still struggling weakly against his boot. "Addie's dead," Noah said flatly.

"What?" Ty demanded on an exhale.

Noah brought a finger to his lips, mimed being quiet, and his brother seemed to catch on. "Peter set a fire on the property. She died in it."

"Then he'll pay," Ty said, his voice nothing but acid, which Noah wasn't even sure was all for show.

"Yes, he will. Get me something to tie this garbage up with."

Ty nodded and disappeared back inside. He returned with some cords. "These will have to do."

They worked together to tie the man's hands and legs together around an old flagpole in the front yard.

He fought them, but weakly, and in just a few minutes he was tightly secured to the pole.

Noah moved to the back of the cabin, searching the perimeter for any signs of Peter or his men. Peter had left tracks from the back of the cabin to the trees, so that was something.

"We're outnumbered," Ty said from behind Noah. He slid the other man's gun into his coat pocket. "We've got one horse and no vehicle. How are we going to catch this guy?"

Noah looked around at the trees and the mountains as shadowy sentries in the dark. The moon shone above, bright and promising. The night was frigid, but he and Ty had survived worse. "Wyoming is how we're going to catch this guy."

Chapter Eighteen

Addie's arm burned where she'd had Vanessa cut it. Without warning or discussion, Vanessa had subsequently made a rather nasty-looking cut on her own arm.

"Sure hope we can get a tetanus shot or something at the hospital," Vanessa had muttered before grabbing a handful of snow and mixing it with the blood.

Seth was pretending to ride the saddle that they'd placed in the snow as Addie and Vanessa worked to make two arm cuts look like enough blood to have been blunt force trauma to the head. Once they'd done as much as they could and were teeth-shatteringly cold, they bandaged each other up with the first aid kit that had been in Annabelle's pack.

Addie shot Seth worried glances as they did all this, because despite the layers he was wearing, the snow would make him wet and it was nightfall. The temperature had been dropping steadily, seemingly every minute.

Vanessa used her weakened flashlight to survey their supposed accident scene. It didn't look nearly as gruesome as Addie had hoped, even in the mix of sil-

very moonlight filtering through the trees and faded
yellow glow of a too-small flashlight. "How will they
even see it?"

"I imagine they're a little better equipped than we
are. High-powered flashlights, headlights if they can
get that snowmobile out here. Besides, they might not
even be after us yet. Maybe they won't start looking
till daylight."

"True." But if that was the case, they might not see
it at all, and all this work for nothing. She shook her
head. She couldn't think like that. As long as they got
to safety without Peter knowing she was alive, they'd
succeeded. The rest of the plan could still work.

She scooped Seth off the saddle, much to his dismay. He began to kick and scream. "He needs food.
A diaper change."

Vanessa nodded, then moved the faint glow of her
flashlight to Annabelle. "Let's get going, then. I think
we've done the best we can."

It was some doing getting back on the horse without a saddle and getting Seth situated between them,
but eventually they were on their way. Seth fussed
and fidgeted, small mewling cries in the middle of a
dark forest.

But moonlight led their way, and Addie focused on
the hope. She didn't allow herself to consider if Noah
and Ty were okay, if Peter knew what was going on.
She didn't think about the future any further than them
reaching Bent without problem.

Seth was beginning to doze, something about the
rocking motion of the horse soothing him enough to be
taken over by sleep. Addie was feeling a little droopy

herself, but holding on to Vanessa and Seth between them kept her from nodding off.

Addie wasn't sure how long they trotted through the freezing cold night. The wind was frigid and rattled the trees. The moon shone high and bright and yet gave off no warmth and very little hope.

Seth finally went totally limp in her arms, asleep despite all the danger around them—from people and from the elements. Every once in a while Addie thought it'd be simpler to just lie in the snow and sleep. She was so tired—exhausted physically, tired of fighting a man who'd never give up.

Then Vanessa slowed the horse on a quiet murmur. "Are we there?"

Vanessa shook her head. "I hear something," she said quietly. Moonlight glinted her dark hair silver, but the dark shrouded her face so Addie couldn't read her expression.

Then Addie heard it, too, and they both winced as a beam of light glanced over the trees. Faint, far in the distance, but coming for them.

"Maybe it's Noah," Addie whispered.

"Not with that kind of light."

Which Addie knew, but she'd just wanted something to hope for. But what would false hope get her? Dead probably. All of them dead. "Let me off. Take Seth. I'll create a diversion."

"No."

"It's the only way. They'll catch us, and I can't let Peter ever get his hands on Seth. I just can't."

"He's supposed to think you're dead."

"Then it'll be even more of a diversion when I'm

not. I can't control the horse, Vanessa, and even if I could you have a much better chance of finding Bent than I do. Let me off. I'll scream bloody murder while you ride fast as you can to town."

"They'll kill you, Addie."

"Maybe." She'd made her peace with that in the burning building. She would die for Seth. She had to be willing. "Seth is the most important thing. That was an agreement Noah and I made when we came back here. Peter doesn't care much whether I live or die. I'm a game for him, but he does want Seth or at least convinced himself he does if only to punish me. So we do everything not to give him what he wants. I'll scream—you ride toward town. I'll lead them back to our little scene saying Seth is dead. If I don't make it, I trust you Carsons will make sure Seth is safe."

"Addie…"

But she could tell Vanessa was relenting, so she shifted Seth until she could push him forward into Vanessa's lap. Seth began to whimper and Addie awkwardly slid off the horse. "There's no time. They can't hear him crying. Go. Fast. As fast as you can."

"Cut the little bastard open with that knife of yours. Do whatever you have to do to stay alive. I'll send all the help here the minute I get to town."

"Just go," Addie said. "Keep my baby safe."

Vanessa hesitated. "I'm going to keep Annabelle walking slow and quiet until I hear you scream. Then we'll gallop. Scream as loud and long as you can and hopefully they won't hear me. If you see any split off and come after me, scream 'bear.' It might be enough of a distraction to give me a leg up."

"Okay," Addie agreed. The thought of one of Peter's men breaking off and going after Vanessa scared her to her bones, but splitting up was the best way. The only way. She'd wail and scream and pretend Seth was already dead and pray to God it didn't turn out to be true.

Vanessa urged Annabelle into motion, a quiet walk the opposite direction of the murmuring noise and moving lights. They were definitely closer, but a ways off.

Addie started to walk toward them. Her heart beat hard in her chest, and fear and cold made it hard to move through the snow, but she marched forward. Closer and closer until the swath of light started to hit her.

Then she began to scream.

NOAH WAS TIRED of the wound on his side holding him back, and yet he couldn't seem to push himself or the horse beneath them harder than he already was. He had no idea where Peter's man had gotten this horse, but it wasn't as adept as his horses back at the ranch.

The snow was deep and the air frigid cold, and while he'd been used to cold his whole life, something about the fear of losing the people he loved made it heavier, harder.

Or was that the gunshot wound to his side that he may or may not have accidentally ripped the stitches out of?

He didn't mention that to Ty. He didn't mention anything to Ty as they rode on, following the trail of Peter's men.

"Don't know where this horse came from, but it's not used to this kind of weather or terrain," Ty said grimly.

"Maybe not, but we've covered more ground than we would've on foot." Noah surveyed the tracks in front of them. Peter's tracks converged with two pairs of horse's tracks not too far from the cabin. They'd been following the horse tracks back down toward the road, but then the tracks abruptly turned back into the trees toward the mountains.

"You think these idiots have any idea what they're doing?" Ty asked disgustedly.

"Doesn't look like it. Doesn't mean they're not dangerous."

"True enough."

Out of nowhere, causing both Noah and Ty to flinch in surprise, a bloodcurdling scream ripped through the night.

They didn't even exchange a glance before they leaned forward in tandem on the horse, urging it to move toward the scream as fast as it could. The horse might not have been experienced or used to the terrain, but it seemed to understand panic.

There was moonlight, but far in the distance an unnatural light moving around as well. And the scream. It just kept going, with only minimal pauses for the screamer to breathe.

He tried not to think about who the screamer was, though there were only two possibilities, and he knew it wasn't Vanessa. But he couldn't allow himself to ponder what Addie might be screaming about, or why.

He only had to get to her. To the screaming, whoever it might be and for whatever reason.

"Stop," Noah ordered abruptly.

"What?" Ty demanded, but he brought the horse to a stop.

"I'll go on foot and sneak around the opposite direction. They have more men, more weapons. We need the element of surprise."

"Agreed, but I should be the one on foot. You're favoring that side, brother."

"I'll live."

"You keep saying that."

"And it'll keep being true." Noah dismounted without letting Ty argue further. "You go straight for the lights, slow and quiet. I'll circle around. I promised Addie we'd keep that baby safe, so he's our first priority. We don't risk him, and you don't risk you."

"But you can risk you, I'm assuming."

"I won't do anything stupid." But if he had to make some sacrifices, then so be it. "Go."

Ty nodded grimly in the moonlight, and Noah took off in a dead sprint. He circled the light instead of going for it, using the moonlight as his guide and the trees as his protection.

Everything in his body burned. His wound, his lungs, his eyes. Still, he pushed forward, adrenaline rushing through him.

He was finally close enough to see people, so he slowed his pace, hid behind a tree and watched the morbid procession of shadows.

Between moonlight and their flashlights, he could make out the odd scene moving toward him. He tried to make sense of what he was seeing. Peter was pushing Addie through the snow, while two men on horseback followed with their guns pointed at her. But they were *following* her, and she was leading them somewhere most definitely not in the direction of the cabin or Bent.

Where was Vanessa? Seth? Had Addie sacrificed herself? Had they escaped undetected? Or had something horrible happened?

Addie slowed, stumbled, and fell to her hands and knees in the snow.

"Get up," Peter ordered. "Or I'll really give you a reason to fall."

Addie struggled to her feet and it took everything in Noah not to jump forward and gather her up in the safety of his arms. But that would only get them both killed.

Still, he and Ty had the element of surprise. They could take out three guys, if they were careful. If they were smart.

"Move!" Peter ordered in a booming yell.

"I'm lost. I don't know where…"

"You better figure it out because if you don't show me the boy's dead body, I'm going to think you're lying, Addie. Then you'll be dead and I'll make sure that boy has the most hellish life you could ever imagine."

"He's your son. He's dead. Don't you have any compassion?"

Dead. Seth, dead. Addie wouldn't be walking let alone coherent if that were true, so it was all part of the plan. To make Peter think Seth was dead, but why hadn't Addie stayed out of it so Peter could think she was dead as well?

"You stole from me, Addie. You lied to me. You caused the death of my son and you dare speak to me of compassion? I should kill you right here and find the boy's body myself, if you're even telling the truth."

Addie stopped her stumbling forward and turned to face him. "Fine, Peter. Kill me."

Noah was so shocked he didn't breathe, and apparently the words shocked Peter as well since he didn't say anything or raise his weapon.

"Do you think I won't?"

"I know you're capable," Addie said. "You killed my sister. She wouldn't run, I realize now. That's why you killed her. I don't know how many other people you've killed, and you've made me into a killer as well. I've been running from you for nearly a year and now here we are and what's the *point*? I'll never have a normal life. You'll always be a black cloud over it, so kill me."

"You will not dictate when or how I kill you."

"I guess we'll see."

Peter raised his hand, presumably to hit Addie, and Noah didn't think, didn't plan, he barely even aimed. He simply raised his gun and shot.

Peter howled in pain, but didn't go down. *Damn it.* His men were already heading toward Noah, so he had to run, rifle in hand.

They were on horseback, so Noah zigzagged through trees, then pivoted suddenly and cut back in the opposite direction. He heard them swear.

"Get off your horse and run!" one of the men yelled at the other.

Noah tried to use the head start to his advantage, but when he circled back neither Addie nor Peter were to be seen. He tried to search the area for tracks, make sense of any of them, but there was a man coming for him and…

A gunshot rang out and Noah dove to the ground. The tree next to him exploded and Noah could only army-crawl through the snow trying to find a cluster of evergreens he could hide from the moonlight in.

"I can't see a damn thing!" one of the men yelled. "Get over here with the light."

Noah heard the horse hooves even over the heavy beating of his heart. He had to get to Addie before these men caught him, but where on earth had she and Peter disappeared to?

Another gunshot, this one even closer, the beating of horse hooves and the shining light of whatever high-powered flashlight they had flashing across him.

But that would give him everything he needed. He zigzagged through trees for a few more minutes before finding a large trunk to settle behind. He pulled the rifle off his back, watched the light move, and then shot.

When the light shook and fell, Noah knew he'd hit his target. But that was only one of the men. He needed to find the one who'd been on the horse. Noah searched the woods for signs of another flashlight beam, but found nothing.

Then, faintly, he heard grunts and followed the sound, finding Ty grappling on the ground with someone next to a prancing horse.

When the man who was decidedly not Ty pulled out a knife that glinted in the moonlight, Noah saw red. He lunged at the man on top of his brother, rolling him onto his stomach and shoving his knee into the man's back as he pulled his arms back. The man screamed in pain, as Noah wasn't very gentle or worried about the natural ways a man's arm should go. The guy's entire body went limp.

Noah didn't believe it at first, but as he eased off the man he didn't move. He glanced over at Ty, who was struggling to get into a sitting position.

"Stabbed me right in the arm," Ty rasped, and Noah winced as Ty easily pulled a large, daggerlike knife out of where it had been lodged in his biceps.

Noah got to his feet, aches and pains and injuries nothing but a dull ache as fear overtook his body. "He's got Addie."

"Go. I'll bandage myself up and get to you soon as I can."

Noah nodded. "You die, you'll be sorry."

Ty smiled thinly in the moonlight. "I've been through a lot worse. This'll be the last thing that does me in. Now go."

So Noah did.

Chapter Nineteen

Peter pushed her until she fell. Again and again and again. She would lie there in the freezing cold until he kicked her, demanding she get to her feet.

"Get up," Peter demanded, kicking her. She wanted to kick him back. Fight him with everything she had, with everything she was, but *time* was the most important thing. Not revenge. Not yet.

"What for?" Maybe she was going a little over the top, but the more Peter believed she wanted to die, the more her lie that Seth was dead held weight. What was there to live for if Seth was dead?

He kicked her harder, enough she cried out. "Get up and show me his body and then maybe I'll put you out of your misery."

"You don't need me to find him."

When he kicked her again, Addie got to her feet. She didn't have to fake her shivering or her exhaustion. She didn't have to fake her fear or her sadness, because she had no idea who'd fired that shot at Peter. She had no idea if Vanessa had gotten Seth to safety.

She knew nothing. So all she could do was move

forward with the determination this would end. Seth would be safe and this would be *over*, once and for all.

Addie had lost track of where she was in the dark forest, but the longer she and Peter walked in circles, the longer Vanessa had to get safe.

When a gunshot echoed from far away, Addie jerked in its direction. Between the moon and Peter's flashlight, his face was a ghostly silver white as he smiled.

"I don't suppose you think whoever failed at saving you just got shot by one of my men."

"Or whoever shot at you shot at them."

He gave her another hard shove so she fell in yet another icy pile of snow. His gun flashed. "Maybe I will just kill you, worthless as you are."

Addie hesitated a moment, not sure if she should goad him into continuing to believe she had a death wish when she most certainly did not. She couldn't find words as Peter slowly pressed the barrel of the gun to her temple.

Addie swallowed, trying to rein in the shaking of her body. "I'll beg," she offered, her voice a raspy whisper. "I'll get on my knees and beg you to put a bullet through my head." Because it would add time. Everything that added time had to be good.

And if he took her up on it, well...

Peter leaned in close, his lips touching her ear as he spoke. She shuddered in disgust as he whispered. "I want you to *suffer*, Addie. I couldn't take time with your sister, but I'll take my time with you. Now, admit you're lying or show me the boy's body in the next ten minutes, or I'll start breaking fingers for every extra minute I'm out here in this godforsaken wasteland."

Her patience was fraying and she opened her mouth to tell him to go jump off a cliff, but managed to swallow the words down before she really did get herself killed. If only because he'd mentioned her sister. Seth's mother, who'd died for no other reason than she'd fallen for the wrong kind of man.

Addie turned away from Peter, trying to study her surroundings, trying to figure out where she needed to go. If she led him to the scene she and Vanessa had created, there'd be no body, but maybe she could convince Peter bears or wolves or some Wild West–sounding animal got there first.

She looked up at the moon and tried to use it as a guide. Where had it been when they'd gotten on Annabelle? Could you navigate via the moon? Someone probably could, but she wasn't so certain *she* could.

Still, she moved. Because it ate up time. Time was the important thing right now. Not her life. Not the moon. Not Noah or the future. Just time.

"Stop," Peter hissed, yanking her by Noah's coat. Peter spanned the flashlight over the trees around them in a circle.

"What is it? Do you think it's a bear?"

He shoved her to the ground and she landed hard on her hands.

"It's not a bear, you idiot."

"Wolf?" she asked weakly.

He shone the light directly in her eyes and she winced away.

"Are there wolves?" Peter demanded.

"Yes. Yes. They're nocturnal. Wolves are. A-and here." She thought, maybe. Noah had definitely men-

tioned coyotes, but wolves sounded a lot more terrifying, and what did it matter if she was wrong? She
wanted Peter to be scared. That was all that mattered.

Again Peter slowly moved the beam of light around
in a circle. Addie stayed where she was in the snow
praying there was no wolf or bear or anything. Just
Noah. She prayed and prayed for Noah.

Peter raised his gun and shot. Addie screamed and
covered her ears as he turned in a slow circle, pulling
the trigger every few seconds.

"What kind of coward hides in the shadows?" Peter
demanded. "A man shows his face when he's ready to
fight."

"A man doesn't chase an innocent woman and her
child across the country, terrorize her and cause the
death of his men because of his own stupidity."

Noah. It was Noah's voice in the woods. Peter shot
toward the voice, and Addie swallowed back a gasp.
Her ears rang with the sound of all the gunshots and
she wanted to go running for him. Save him. Hold him.

"*Her* child? Is that what she told you?" Peter
laughed. Uproariously. "That boy is *mine*. She has no
claim on him."

Silence stretched in the freezing dark, and Addie
wanted to cry, but she couldn't allow herself. It didn't
matter. If Noah was angry or hurt, or if he believed
Peter at all. Nothing in the here and now mattered
except Seth's safety, and Noah's getting out of here
alive. He shouldn't die for the problems she'd brought
to his door.

So if he was hurt that she'd lied about being Seth's
mother, it didn't matter. Couldn't.

"What a little liar you are," Peter said cheerfully. "Your big strong man thought you were a doting mother? How adorable."

"I am his aunt," Addie returned. "And his protector."

"If he's dead, you failed."

"I suppose I did fail, but better him dead than with you where you'd only warp and twist him into a sad, pathetic excuse for a human being. Better him gone for good than turn out to be anything like you."

Without warning, Peter snatched an arm out and curled his hand around her throat. The flashlight thumped to the ground, bouncing light against the snow. Addie tried to fight him, kick at him, but he'd holstered his gun and added his other hand around her throat. He was too strong or she was too cold.

"I'm going to choke her to death," Peter called out. "Are you going to just stand there and watch?"

There were only the gurgling sounds coming from her own throat as she clawed at his hands. He'd wanted her to suffer, but now he wanted Noah to suffer by watching him kill her. What was Noah doing? Why wasn't he stepping in to save her?

She began to see spots, everything in her body screaming in agony. She considered how much of a chance she had at running if she stabbed Peter. Panic rose like bile in her throat and she no longer cared what the consequences were. If she failed, she failed, but at least she'd tried not to die.

She kept clawing at him with one hand, but with the other she reached behind her and pulled the knife in her pants out of its sheath. Peter was too busy searching the dark for Noah, so she swung the blade as hard as she could. It hit Peter's side with a sickening squelch and for a moment she could pull in a gasping breath as his hands eased around her throat.

But then she saw Peter's eyes widen, then narrow, and everything inside her sank. The squeezing returned as his lip curled into a sneer.

She hadn't gotten the blade far enough inside him to cause any kind of damage. And now, since Noah was apparently not coming to save her, she was dead.

As long as Seth's safe. As long as Seth's safe. She let her mind chant it as her vision dimmed again.

"You stupid girl. You think that little knife would—" But Peter never finished his sentence, because the sound of a gun going off seemed simultaneous to him falling to the ground.

FOR A SECOND or two, Noah could only stand where he'd positioned himself behind a tree, rifle still up. But Addie was standing there, next to Peter's unmoving body. Then she collapsed onto her knees, making terrible gasping noises, but gasping noises were alive noises.

Noah's whole body shook as he rushed forward. Peter's body didn't so much as move. Noah didn't bother to look where his bullet had hit. He gathered Addie up in his arms and began to carry her away. He wanted her far away from that man, the ugliness, the violence.

He carried her through the trees, struggling against the exhaustion, his body's own injuries, the cold. But still he moved forward, back toward where he'd left Ty. But his legs only kept him upright for so long.

"I can walk. I can walk," she murmured against his

neck as he leaned against a tree, trying to catch his breath. "We can walk, right? If you got away from the other guys, they're... Do you think they're all dead?"

"I don't know about dead, but you're right, we can walk." He set her down carefully, still leaning against the tree, trying to catch his breath and wrap his mind around all of it.

"Seth's alive, isn't he?" Because that was the most important thing, what this had all been for.

"I think so. I told Vanessa to go with him. We were trying..." She choked on a sob, and it hurt to look at her, even in the shadowy light of night. She was pale and bloodied and dripping wet.

"We need to move. Make sure they're safe. I have to find Ty, and then..." He looked around the forest, the starry moonlit sky above. "We'll get to Seth," he promised, holding out his hand for her to take. But when she slipped her hand into his, he had to pull her close again and hold her tight against him for a minute. Just a minute.

"What's a little hypothermia, right?" she asked, her arms around him nearly as tight as his were around her.

He managed a chuckle against her hair, holding her close to assure himself she was alive and well. This was over. *Over.* "We'll survive it, I think. Let's find Ty. He earned himself a little stab wound in the arm."

"So tetanus shots for everyone."

"All these near-death experiences turned you into quite the comedian."

"Or I've just gone insane." She sighed gustily into his neck. "Noah."

She didn't say anything more, so he held her to

him, trying to will the cold away. "You're safe now. It's all over."

She sighed heavily. "Not all. Noah, Peter wasn't lying. Seth isn't mine."

"Maybe if you hadn't just almost died I'd care a little bit more about that." But mostly, Noah found he didn't care. Maybe before this had all gone down he would have mustered some righteous indignation, some *hurt*, but after seeing what Peter could do, there was no question everything Addie had done had been done to protect Seth from that monster.

He couldn't hold that against her.

She pulled back, looked up at him, and he couldn't read her expression in the shadows. "I lied to you."

"Yeah. Yeah, well. Maybe Seth isn't your biological son, but he's in your care. He's your blood. To him, and to you I imagine, you're mother and child. A lie to keep Seth safe doesn't hurt me, and I know this whole time all you've been trying to do is keep Seth safe. I won't hold that against you or fault you for that, and no one can make me. Even you."

She expelled a breath. "Noah, I want to go home. I want Seth and I want to go home."

"Then that's what we'll do. Because this is over. You're safe, and once we know Seth's safe, that's all that will matter." Ever.

Chapter Twenty

The next few days were nothing but a blur. A hospital stay for her due to hypothermia and pneumonia, a hospital stay for Noah and Ty for their respective wounds. Vanessa and Seth were relatively unharmed, and to Addie, that was all that mattered.

The police and the FBI were a constant presence, talks of being a witness and trials. If charges would be pressed against her or Noah for killing men. Addie was almost grateful for being sick and not quite with it.

She was continually grateful for Laurel's presence and help. For Vanessa's bringing Seth to visit whenever the nurses would let her. Carsons and Delaneys working together to help someone who didn't really belong.

Bent is your home. Noah's voice echoed in her head. Bent was her home. But what did that mean? The Carson Ranch? This town? He'd said he loved her once, and she hadn't had the opportunity to say it back.

Addie sat in the passenger seat of Laurel's car, Seth's car seat fastened in the back. Over three months ago, she'd made this exact trek. She hadn't had a clue what would befall her back then.

She didn't have a clue what would befall her now.

Noah had been released this morning, and he hadn't come to see her.

"Maybe he doesn't want…" Addie cleared her throat as Laurel turned the car onto the gravel road that led up to the Carson Ranch. "He might not want me here. I did lie to him." He'd said it didn't matter, but that was in the aftermath of hell. Now it might matter.

"He wants you here," Laurel replied. "I am under strict orders."

Addie slid Laurel a look. "From who?"

Laurel smiled. "Too many Carsons to count."

"I don't want to… I brought all these terrible things on him, and he didn't even come see me in the hospital. Why would he want me here?"

"I think that's something you'll have to ask the man yourself. I also think you already know the answer to that, so you might not want to insult him and ask him that in quite those words."

"He could've died. A million times."

"So could you. And Seth. But somehow, you all fought evil together and won. I'd pat myself on the back, not worry about if Noah is overly offended by the sacrifices he willingly made." Laurel frowned. "I am sorry we didn't—couldn't—do more. The police, me personally."

"Peter learned how to outmaneuver the police from birth, I think. I don't blame you, Laurel. We all did everything we could, and like you said, we all fought evil together and won."

"I suppose." Laurel smiled thinly. "And when you fight evil and win, then you face the rest of your life."

Addie blew out a breath and watched the house get

closer and closer to view. "It feels like I've been running forever," she murmured, more to herself than to Laurel.

But Laurel responded anyway. "And now it's time to stop. There isn't anything or anyone to run from anymore, and if there ever is again, you have a whole town—Carsons *and* Delaneys—at your side." She stopped the car in front of the house.

Much like that first day all those months ago, Grady stepped out, his smile all for Laurel. Addie stayed in her seat, waiting for some sign, some *hint* that Noah actually wanted her here. She might have believed it in the snow and the woods at night, but in the light of hospital days and FBI questions, all her fears and worries repopulated and grew.

He'd kept his distance. He was spending his days talking to FBI agents because of her. Maybe it'd had to be done, but that didn't make it any less her fault. She'd lied to him. Maybe once he really thought about it, he'd realized he didn't love a liar.

Laurel had gotten out and was pulling Seth out of his car seat. Grady was unlatching the car seat from Laurel's car. And still Addie sat, staring at the house, wondering what a future of freedom really looked like.

Freedom. No longer a slave to whether or not Peter would find her. She was *free*. Sitting in front of the Carson ranch house, it was the first time that fact truly struck her.

She stepped out of the car. Laurel handed Seth to her and he wiggled and squirmed, pointing at the house, then clapping delightedly. "No!"

"Yes, we're home with Noah, aren't we?" Because

she was free now. Free to take what she wanted, have it, nurture it. Free to do what was best for Seth's well-being, not just his safety. Free to build a life.

A real life.

If Noah was mad at her for bringing Peter to his doorstep, mad at her for lying about Seth not being her biological child, well, she'd find a way to make up for it. She'd find a way to make his words true.

Bent is your home.

I love you.

Grady took the car seat to the front door and Laurel placed the bag she'd brought to the hospital with some of Addie's things next to it.

"We're going to head out," Grady said.

"You aren't coming in?"

"Uh, no. You enjoy your homecoming."

"My…" She glanced at the door. *Homecoming.*

"Call if you need anything, or if the FBI get too obnoxious," Laurel offered, walking back to her car hand in hand with Grady.

Then it was just her and Seth, standing on the porch of the Carson Ranch, alone. It felt like a new start somehow.

And it was. A new start. Freedom. A life to build. But she had to take that step forward. She had to let go of the fear…not just of what her life had been, but of what she'd allowed herself to be. A victim of fear and someone else's power.

Never again.

She took a deep breath, steeling herself to barge in and demand Noah have a heart-to-heart conversation with her. No grunts. No silences. No *I love yous* and then disappearances. They weren't on the run anymore and he couldn't—

The door swung open.

"Well, are you going to come in or are you just planning on standing out in the cold all day?" Noah asked gruffly.

She blinked up at his tall, broad form filling up the doorframe. "I thought I'd stare at the door for a bit longer."

"I see you're still being funny."

"No!" Seth lunged for Noah and Noah caught him easily.

"There's a boy," Noah murmured, the smile evident even beneath the beard. His gaze moved up to Addie, that smile still in place as he held Seth and Seth immediately grabbed for his hat hanging off the hook next to them.

"Come inside, Addie."

Right. Come inside. Conversation. She'd tell him what she wanted. What she needed, and…and…

She stepped inside and Noah closed the door behind her.

"How are you feeling?"

"How am I feeling?" she repeated, staring at him, something like anger simmering inside her. She didn't know why, and it was probably unearned anger, but it was there nonetheless. "That's all you have to say to me?"

"No."

She frowned at him. "You don't make any sense."

"You were just released from the hospital," he said, as if that explained anything.

"So were you!"

"I wasn't sick, though."

"Oh, no, just a gunshot wound."

It was his turn to frown. "Why are we fighting exactly?"

Addie turned away from him. She didn't know why she was arguing or what she felt or…

She stopped abruptly in the middle of the living room when she saw a sign hanging from the exposed beams of the kitchen ceiling. Hand-painted and not quite neat, two simple words were written across the paper.

Welcome Home.

He'd made her a sign. Hung it up. Home. *Home.* She turned back to face him, and all the tears she'd been fighting so hard for the past few days let loose in a torrent of relief.

"But… I lied to you. I made your life a living hell for days, and through the beginning and the end I lied to you about Seth. You've had time to think about that now. Really think about it. You have to be sure—"

"I can't say I *like* being lied to, but I understand it. You were protecting Seth, and there's nothing about *that* I don't understand. But…"

Oh, God, there was a but. She nearly sank to her knees.

"We have to promise each other, both of us, no more lies. Even righteous ones. Because the only way we fought Peter was together. The only way we survived was together. There can't be any more lies or doing things on our own. We're in this together. Partners."

"Partners," she repeated, Seth still happily playing with the cowboy hat as Noah held him on his hip.

"No lies. No keeping things from each other. We work together. Always. I promise you that, if you can promise me the same."

Addie swallowed, looking at this good man in front of her, holding a boy who wasn't biologically her son but was *hers* nonetheless. "I promise you that, Noah. With all of my heart I promise you that." She glanced up at the sign he'd made, this stoic, uncelebratory man. "I do want this to be my home," she whispered.

"Then it's yours," Noah returned, reaching out and wiping some of the tears from her cheeks.

"I love you, Noah."

There was *no* doubt under all that hair and Carson cowboy gruffness, Noah smiled, and when his mouth met hers, Addie knew she'd somehow found what she'd always been looking for, even in those days of running away.

Home. Love. A place to belong. A place to raise Seth, and a man who'd be the best role model for him.

"I hear there's some curse about Carsons and Delaneys," she murmured against his mouth.

"I don't believe in curses, Addie. I believe in us. Hell, we defeated the mob. What's a curse?"

"I'd say neither has anything on love."

"Or coming home. Where you belong."

Yes, Addie Foster belonged in Bent, Wyoming, on the Carson Ranch, with Noah Carson at her side, to love and be loved in return for as long as she breathed.

And nothing would ever change that.

* * * * *

COMING SOON!

We really hope you enjoyed reading this book. If you're looking for more romance, be sure to head to the shops when new books are available on

Thursday 15th November